Charlie Owen enjoyed a thirty-year career in the police service, serving with two forces in the Home Counties and London, reaching the rank of Inspector. His novels, *Horse's Arse* and *Foxtrot Oxcar* were widely acclaimed and the film rights have been sold.

Praise for Charlie Owen:

'It's like *Life on Mars* without the time travelling' *Zoo* magazine

'Charlie Owen is a talent. This is the first book since *Layer Cake* to have an authentic voice that exposes the dark and eccentric world of English street crime' Guy Ritchie

'Will have you gripped from page one. The characters, the plotlines and the dialogue are so vivid' *Daily Record*

'Charlie Owen has a talent for humorously exposing the dark world of British street crime' *Leicester Mercury*

'If you love dinosaur DCI Gene Hunt in TV hit *Life on Mars*, you'll find this violent, yet hilarious thriller a delight' *Peterborough Evening Telegraph*

D1352990

# BRAVO
# JUBILEE
# CHARLIE
# OWEN

headline

First published in 2008 by
HEADLINE PUBLISHING GROUP

First published in paperback in 2009 by
HEADLINE PUBLISHING GROUP

6

Cataloguing in Publication Data is available from the British Library

ISBN 978 0 7553 4568 7

Typeset in AGaramond by Avon DataSet Ltd,
Bidford on Avon, Warwickshire

Printed and bound by CPI Group (UK) Ltd, Croydon, CR0 4YY

Headline's policy is to use papers that are natural, renewable and
recyclable products and made from wood grown in sustainable forests.
The logging and manufacturing processes are expected to conform to
the environmental regulations of the country of origin.

HEADLINE PUBLISHING GROUP
An Hachette Livre UK Company
338 Euston Road
London NW1 3BH

www.headline.co.uk
www.hachettelivre.co.uk

For Mum and Dad – with love.

# Acknowledgements

After two and a half years as a police pensioner, I was worried that my memories of my career would fade and be lost, and I would start to smell of piss. At least in the case of my memory, the reverse has been true. The events of thirty years ago are in fact as clear today as they were then – the colours as vivid, the smells as obnoxious, the sounds as clear, and the old men I know today still the vibrant young bucks I knew then.

I'm beginning to forget some things – most often the names of my children and I'm reduced to addressing them as, 'You, that one, the small noisy one,' or, 'You know, your brother,' and I apologise profusely to them, but fortunately I never forget a face.

As ever, I am extremely grateful to so many of my former colleagues who never fail to regale me with long-forgotten stories and anecdotes whenever we meet or talk. Because I can't rely on my memory as much as I used to, I now take notes but they don't seem to mind and I hope they enjoy seeing our stories appear in one form or another in the books.

There is no doubt that the passing of the years puts a rose-tinted perspective on the past. My second book, *Foxtrot Oscar*, was set in the summer of 1976 which I have always remembered as the hottest summer of my life to date. In fact the real heat wave in June that year lasted a mere fourteen days. The rest of the summer was dry, but the ninety-plus degree heat lasted just two weeks. Yet it has passed into folklore as something extraordinary.

This book is set during 1977 and includes the period of the Queen's Silver Jubilee. Again my memories of Jubilee night itself are probably rose-tinted and certainly vague. I know I spent the night going from one street party to another and there was little trouble, but then again, I was absolutely trashed by the time I booked off duty.

My thanks are due specifically to Trish Fleming who transferred my handwritten manuscript into a word document, Paul Dockley for his insight into Operation Julie, Chris Taylor for the chemistry lessons, and Jim Gall, Ken Price, John Bateman, John Sutch, Martin Kosmalski, Rick Moulder and Ken Stewart for an endless supply of outrageous anecdotes.

Lastly, I must again thank my patient editor Martin Fletcher for his support and encouragement during the writing of this book over what was a difficult period. The more I see of Martin, the more I'm convinced we encountered each other during my service. You weren't at Trafalgar Square on 31 March 1990, were you, Martin? Under the scaffolding by the South African Embassy? I'm sure I remember you there! (Martin's note – I definitely wasn't there; I was on another demo elsewhere.)

# Chapter One

## Spring 1977

PC Henry 'H' Walsh could smell the blood before he got to the front door of the dimly lit maisonette. As he pushed gingerly at the slightly open door and put his head into the hallway he detected the telltale metallic smell of the abattoir. His heart pumping and with a lump of fear in his throat, he stepped back to the handrail along the walkway and called down to his colleague waiting alongside the area car, call sign Bravo Two Yankee One.

'Don't look good, Jim. Keep an eye on that bastard.'

PC Jim Stewart didn't reply, but glanced down at the man spread-eagled at his feet, ground his boot harder into the side of the man's neck and twisted the wrist he held firmly in his right hand.

'What you been up to then?' he growled.

The man kept his eyes shut and remained quiet though he grimaced in pain.

'I'm talking to you, you little shit,' continued Jim, grinding and twisting harder.

'Fuck you,' gasped the man, briefly opening his eyes which with considerable effort he rolled in their sockets to flash a look of pure hatred at Jim.

He had fallen foul of H and Jim, otherwise known as the Grim Brothers, a few minutes earlier and quickly became a recipient of the violence for which they were notorious.

The Brothers were the original odd couple. On paper they had nothing in common. H, a public schoolboy and the son of a naval officer – albeit with a punch like a sledgehammer – Jim a former paratrooper who had faced shots fired in anger whilst in Ulster; yet they had gelled from their first meeting. They were the coppers that Handstead New Town just north of Manchester deserved. The Brothers possessed almost telepathic abilities, with each able to recognise when the other was about to get their revenge in first and drop a scumbag. Violence was their calling card and it was rare for them to take prisoners who didn't get a good hammering to be going on with. Where they failed, however, was that they never had a plan B. They approached everything with fists and boots flying, regularly inflaming peaceful situations. Their colleagues at Handstead – the arsehole of the world that they called Horse's Arse – dreaded their arrival at incidents they had peacefully under control, but welcomed them with open arms when the wheels had come off. The Brothers were isolated from the others by their violence, but they were that way because it was the only way to survive in Handstead. Away from work they were the complete opposite. They were, by and large, honest, hard-working coppers with noses for the wrong'uns. In common with their eclectic colleagues, they had worked out that to keep their heads above water in Handstead, they needed to at least match the local villains in terms of mindless hooliganism and had quickly gained reputations with them as a pair of hard-boiled bastards – which pleased them no end. Nothing pleased a busy street copper more than to see his name scrawled on walls followed by comments about his parentage, and the hooligans of Handstead had used many gallons of paint besmirching the names of H and Jim.

'Hard man, are you?' growled Jim in his broad Geordie accent, applying even more pressure.

From the balcony above the Bishops Gate parade of shops, H took a deep breath to compose himself before he went into the house. Around him the darkened Bishops Gate estate was silent in the warm spring night, the only sounds being an insistent dog barking, a plane passing far above him and, downstairs, the frenzied click-clicking of mah-jong tiles and raised, excited Chinese voices from the now closed Chinese restaurant.

It was just after 1 a.m. and the Brothers had been driving along the service road at the back of the shops, lights off, returning to check their cotton traps across the numerous yards at the rear of the shops. Like generations of night duty coppers before them, earlier in the evening they had stretched lengths of dark cotton across the yard entrances at ankle height and had returned to see if any had been broken to signal an intrusion into a yard. As they cruised quietly into the service road with the shops and yards, and the maisonettes to the left, Jim had suddenly hissed, 'Look at this one, H,' and pointed urgently up to the maisonettes. A man was sprinting along the first-floor walkway, clearly visible in the orange bulkhead lights, away from an open, illuminated door. He flew down a set of metal steps, two or three at a time, the noise of his footsteps echoing in the dark, out into the service road and into the path of the unlit Yankee One. He went to dodge past the nearside of the vehicle but was brought to a dead stop by Jim who threw the door open into him, sending him crashing into a pile of rubbish bags.

He was still groggy when the Brothers pulled him

roughly on to his front and Jim stood on his head. It was a surprisingly warm night for early spring, and the Brothers were working in shirt sleeves, but not warm enough to account for the sweaty state of the man they had just flattened. His grey T-shirt was sodden and his shoulder-length dark hair was plastered to his pale, gaunt face. Sweat ran down his clearly broken nose and mingled eagerly with the blood streaming from it.

'What have you been up to and where are you off to in such a hurry?' asked Jim, giving his arm a good twist. There was no reply, only the sound of radio traffic and static from inside Yankee One.

'Hang on to him, Jim, I'll go and have a look round,' said H before returning to Yankee One to get his Maglite torch, switch off the engine and toss the keys to Jim. He had then jogged up the stairs from where the man had come and walked slowly back along the first-floor walkway towards the still open door.

Heart pumping, he pushed the door fully open and stepped into the dingy entrance, lit by a naked sixty-watt bulb. The entrance contained only a pair of bicycles, one a child's, and to the left a flight of stairs led to the living area.

'Hello, anyone here?' called H, his nostrils twitching as the acrid, cloying smell of blood enveloped him. The house was uncomfortably hot. H walked to the foot of the stairs and glanced up to the landing which was similarly lit by a naked bulb. He began to climb the threadbare, garishly carpeted stairs. A Chinese restaurant calendar was tacked to the wall and he noted absently that yesterday's date had been circled and clearly a child had scrawled, 'My birthday!!' At the top of the stairs, H again paused and called out, 'Hello, anyone there?' The awful smell was stronger than ever. Directly ahead of him, in darkness, was obviously a bathroom and toilet. Off the landing were two further doors, probably bedrooms but both doors were shut. An overflowing laundry basket stood just outside the bathroom. H quickly glanced into the bathroom to confirm it was empty before he knocked quietly at the first of the doors. As he waited for a response that he knew he would never get, the click-clicking of the mah-jong tiles and the excited voices downstairs increased in intensity briefly. Then silence again.

Steeling himself, H opened the door slowly and peered into the darkened room. The smell of blood was overpowering, threatening to wash over and drown him. For a moment he felt like turning and fleeing but again he fought against those demons. Using his Maglite he quickly located a light switch on the wall to his left.

A scene of horrific butchery lay in front of him. The young Chinese woman on the double bed over on the right of the room lay on her back amongst a heap of stained bedding and pillows, her mouth open, blood pouring from multiple wounds to her torso, across her windpipe and both eye sockets. Barely able to comprehend what he was seeing and with his heart racing, H walked over to the bed and looked closely at her. The deep wound to the throat would probably have been enough to kill her, but she had clearly been stabbed dozens of times around the chest and abdomen, and several times in the face, but the wounds that caused him to gasp out loud and stagger backwards were the ones to the eyes. Both eyes had been brutally pierced and the dark bloody sockets stared up at H.

'Sweet Jesus,' he stammered, staggering away from the bed and leaning against the wall. Downstairs the click-clicking of the mah-jong tiles continued. H gave himself a minute to control his breathing and regain some composure before he left the room. After a final look at the staring, bloody eyes and the blood splatters up the wall, he stood breathing heavily at the top of the stairs, eyes closed. The child's bicycle, the child's writing on the calendar – 'My birthday'. Oh no, please God, no, H prayed.

The smell of the blood no longer registered as H walked leaden-footed to the second closed door and opened it without knocking. The door opened almost immediately on to a child's bed. To his joy and relief, there was no sign of the child, although the bed had obviously been slept in. Reaching round the door, H found the light switch and illuminated the room. It was little more than a box room. It contained just the bed and on the walls a David Cassidy poster and an identical calendar to the one on the stairwell. This one, too, had yesterday's date circled and some Chinese lettering alongside it.

H stepped backwards out of the room and was about to switch off the light when he saw the pool creeping slowly from under the bed, spreading inexorably towards him across the pale lino floor, like a growing virus. H gasped out loud. He jumped back out of the room, dropped to his knees and shone his Maglite under the bed. The beam hit the small figure immediately. A little girl of about six, her pyjamas stained red, deep stab and slash wounds clearly visible around her head and torso, her hands cut to shreds as she had tried to fend off the attack. She was lying on her side, her eyes wide open, her vacant pupils bearing witness to her horrific last few moments of life as she sought sanctuary under her bed before she was slaughtered there. Click-click went the mah-jong tiles downstairs.

Barely able to breathe, H fled down the stairs and on to the walkway where he stood, arms braced against the handrail, head bowed, and wept. He wept tears of anguish and rage and horror. A veteran of numerous suicides and road traffic accidents and even a murder, he had been terrified by what he had just seen and now he cried like a small child woken by a bad dream. From the restaurant below he heard raised voices again and mah-jong tiles clicking. It was a sound that would haunt H for the rest of his life.

'H, you OK?' called Jim from the service road.

By way of reply, H raised a hand. Give me a moment.

Puzzled, Jim looked down at the prostrate man. 'You're in deep shit, son, by the looks of things. What you done?'

'Fuck you.'

Jim twisted and ground again and looked in disgust at the telltale tramlines on the emaciated arm he held locked. Probably that fucking heroin that was starting to flood into the town, he mused, before really pushing hard, causing the man to cry out in pain.

H had recovered himself by the time he rejoined Jim but his eyes were still red and watery. Even in the dark Jim could see his colleague was distressed.

'H, what the fuck's happened?'

'Two dead up there, woman and a little girl. Cut to fucking pieces,' said H flatly. He was staring blankly at the man on the ground. 'A little girl,' he repeated, still hearing the mah-jong tiles in his head.

'You cunt,' shouted Jim, twisting the man's arm until he was sure it would break and stamping on his head. From the ground, the man spat blood from his mouth, looked up at the Brothers and smiled, his dilated pupils sparkling.

'Fuck you.'

H moved purposefully towards him, fists clenched, the image of the little girl's terrified face frozen in death etched on his mind.

Jim put a restraining hand against his chest. 'Leave him, H, leave him,' he said quietly. 'He's well fucked. Last thing we need now is to have to explain why he's been hammered to a pulp. Give me a hand to roll him over and let's get him searched. You want to call this in?'

H looked up at his mate, his eyes beginning to fill again.

'Yeah, OK,' he said eventually. 'There's a little girl up there, Jim.'

'I know,' replied Jim, himself the father of two young daughters and keenly aware of how H doted on his own infant child. He was also aware that for the last year H had been haunted by a cot death he had gone to alone, involving a child the same age as his own. Jim was worried that this incident was one too many for H; he seemed very close to losing the plot. No matter how hard-boiled coppers thought they were, anything involving children had the potential to strip the armour away and render them as vulnerable and helpless as everyone else.

'Get yourself sorted out, H,' he continued. 'Take

some deep breaths and take your time, have a walk along the back of the shops and check the cottons while you're at it.'

H nodded and stumbled away along the dark service road, shining his Maglite into the deserted shop backyards, seeing nothing but the dead child's face, still hearing the mah-jong tiles and the raised, excited Chinese voices. He returned to Jim and the man on the ground, dropped into the passenger seat of Yankee One and picked up the microphone. He took some more deep breaths as he waited for other main set radio traffic to clear before he transmitted.

'Delta Hotel, this is Bravo Two Yankee One, active message.' An active message was one down from a 10/1 call for urgent assistance and had a similar effect. Other vehicles' crews would stay off air while the message was transmitted. An active message from a Handstead crew, particularly Yankee One, the busiest area car in the county, usually heralded problems.

The main Force control room operator instructed Yankee One to go with their message.

'Delta Hotel, we're at the rear of the parade of shops in Bishops Gate, Hotel Alpha. We have found a woman and young child dead in a house above the shops. We need CID and Scenes of Crime here on the hurry up and a supervisory officer. We have a male detained. This is a major crime scene and we'll need extra resources down here to manage it, please. Show one arrested for murder and en route to Hotel Alpha once we've got some help here.'

There was a long, stunned silence, with only static breaking through, as the control room staff and other crews on the same channel digested what they had heard.

'Understood, Yankee One,' the operator finally said. Behind her in the large open-plan control room her inspector and sergeant began making urgent phone calls to get a major investigation under way. 'Any other Hotel Alpha units can assist Yankee One at the rear of the Bishops Gate shops, please?'

The main set radio exploded in a cacophony of noise as the world and his wife offered to make their way; even two traffic units volunteered to leave the deserted motorway they were aimlessly driving north and south along. The operator asked for some radio discipline and eventually dispatched Bravo Two One and Bravo Two Two to the scene, ruining the traffic officers' night by bringing them into Horse's Arse to cover the ground while the local units did some real police work.

As the main channel went into meltdown, H climbed out of Yankee One and rejoined Jim who was still busy trying to dislocate the man's arm.

'All right if I have him, Jim?'

'All yours, H. Just keeping him warm for you.'

H bent down into the face of the grimacing junkie. 'You are under arrest on suspicion of murder, you cunt. You don't have to say anything unless you wish to do so but whatever you do say will be rolled up and stuffed up your arse,' he hissed.

The man opened his eyes and H saw the evil and danger in his glistening, madly dilated pupils.

'Fuck the pair of you,' he screamed. 'You'll fucking regret this, I promise,' and then he spat a large bloody glob of phlegm on to H's shirt. In a flash H launched a sledgehammer punch into the man's jaw, which collapsed him back on to the ground unconscious.

'Shot,' enthused Jim and released the arm, which dropped limply alongside its owner. 'Come on, H, let's get him searched, cuffed and ready to go.'

The Brothers rolled him on to his back and immediately noticed the handle of a large knife sticking out of the top of his grubby trousers. They glanced at each other before Jim eased it out of its hiding place with a biro and on to the ground. The Brothers looked down at a nine-inch bloodstained Bowie hunting knife. Bloodstained didn't really do it justice; it was covered along its length, handle and scabbard with fresh, dark blood.

Neither spoke for a moment. H had seen the effect that knife had had on two human beings and was desperately trying not to visualise the blade plunging into an eye socket or slashing a young child to ribbons.

'Jesus Christ,' he said quietly, hanging his head, and Jim put a comforting hand on his shoulder.

'Come on, mate, we've got work to do. Pat him down, turn the cunt over and cuff him. I've got a couple of evidence bags in the boot, I'm sure one of them's big enough for this.' He left H to finish the search and returned with a large clear plastic bag a few moments later.

The prisoner was now on his front, hands firmly handcuffed behind his back. The cuffs had been ratcheted tight, the gleaming steel teeth digging deep into the flesh around his wrists, the hands already turning blue.

'Those on tight enough?' he asked.

'Probably not,' replied H, kneeling down and forcing them an extra notch tighter with great difficulty. The unconscious man was beginning to come round and once he had, he began to scream from the pain in his wrists.

'You fucking bastards, loosen them off, they're fucking agony.'

'Comes with the territory, arsehole,' said Jim simply. He and H hauled him to his feet and frogmarched him to Yankee One. Jim opened one of the back doors, placed a hand behind the man's head and said, 'Mind your head,' before slamming him hard into the door frame. The man collapsed against the side of the vehicle, blood streaming from a gash across his forehead. The Brothers again pulled him to his feet and manhandled him into the footwell behind the two front seats. He was trussed like a pig and going nowhere. H remained by the door while Jim returned to the Bowie knife which he carefully placed into the evidence bag and then into the front passenger document pouch.

He and H looked at each other silently and breathed deeply.

'Fucking great result, H,' Jim said finally. 'One in for a double murder.'

'There's a little girl up there, mate. I can't get excited about this, sorry.'

'I know, I know, that's not what I meant. Fucking horrific job but we've cleared it up straight away. There's not going to be weeks of investigations and inquiries, or appeals for witnesses or those fucking stupid photo fit pictures that could be anyone. Mate, we've got the cunt that did it – you and me. This was always going to happen – I'm a firm believer in fate. That woman and little girl were due today, that was their deal, but the result is that we got the bastard as he left. H, you've got to find the positives in this mess, otherwise you're going to lose it.'

H nodded silently. He knew Jim was right and knew

he had seen sights in Ulster that would chill the blood. He was dead right about seeking some good from the bloodbath he had seen.

'I know, Jim, I just need to get my head round it. I'll be fine once we've got this cunt away from here and in a cell.'

They waited in silence for a couple of minutes before the two local beat vehicles, Bravo Two One and Two Two careered into the service road behind them, blue lights spinning, engines raced to breaking point. Two One was crewed by PCs Sean 'Psycho' Pearce and Alan 'Pizza' Petty, while Two Two contained the Scottish duo of Ally Stewart and Andy 'The Mong Fucker' Malcolm. The four of them hurried to Yankee One and looked at the pale faces of the Brothers and the bloodied body in the back of the area car.

'Fucking hell, boys, you OK?' asked Psycho. 'What the fuck have you got here?'

'That house up there,' said H, indicating the still open and illuminated door up on the first floor. 'There's a Chinese woman dead on a bed and a little girl in the room next to it. It's a fucking mess, blood and shit everywhere. We need to lock down the scene and wait for CID and Scenes of Crime.'

'No one else in the house?' asked Pizza, glancing up at the lit doorway.

'No, but I've got a horrible feeling the rest of the

family are in the restaurant downstairs. Someone's going to have to deal with them quickly.'

'I'll do it,' said Pizza, keen not to have to witness the carnage in the house. He was still coming to terms with the demons that plagued him nightly. Fifteen months earlier he had stood alongside a colleague, Dave 'Bovril' Baines, as he was shot and killed in a dingy flat on the Grant Flowers estate by a female member of the local gang, the Park Royal mafia. She had then blown her own brains out and Pizza was still having nightmares about it. To his colleagues, however, he was something special because he had survived an event most of them would never have to experience. He had survived the ultimate test and no one had ever questioned whether he could have done more, or indeed anything, to save his colleague. He had simply survived, which was enough for them. In fact, he had been directly responsible for bringing about the downfall of the Park Royal mafia. Earlier on the day of Bovril's murder he had recovered a bag of bloodstained clothing from garages underneath the Grant Flowers flats. That clothing was subsequently linked to fifteen of the mafia, confirming their involvement in a vicious attack on a pub landlord. Pizza had given evidence at Manchester Crown Court that condemned the mafia to long gaol sentences, including one for attempted murder. He was something of a star amongst his peers as a consequence, and also for his undoubted expertise in pulling off outrageous stunts on prisoners held in the cells at Horse's Arse. Overnight drunks regularly left custody with their heads half shaved, heels removed from a shoe, clothing changed, one sideburn removed, half a moustache shaved or sporting red marker pen slogans on their foreheads. His skill in shaving heads had led to any bad haircut being known around the nick as a 'Middleton' in tribute to the shaving he had given to the appalling son of Chief Superintendent 'Mengele' Middleton of neighbouring C Division. Now, though, he tried to avoid the blood and gore that Handstead generated; even dealing with the family of a murdered woman and child was preferable.

He walked round to the front of the shops, peered through the misted window of the Chinese restaurant and then knocked loudly on it, causing the click-clicking of the mah-jong tiles to cease.

The group of PCs at the rear of the shops were soon joined by Sergeant Andy Collins and two night duty CID officers, DCs Bob Clarke and John Hockley.

'You two OK?' asked Collins of the Brothers.

'Fine,' replied Jim. 'Captured this bastard running away as we came round the back.'

Collins and the detectives peered into the rear of Yankee One for a sight of the double murderer.

'Fuck me, it's Eddie Cheatle,' exclaimed Bob Clarke.

'You know him?' asked Collins.

'Oh yes, very well. John and I bagged him two or three months ago for a couple of burglaries on the Grove estate. Nasty little junkie; always pumping his arms full of shit so he screws houses to support his habit. One of the new Park Royal mafia, such as they are now. How'd he kill them?'

'This,' replied Jim simply, lifting the evidence bag and showing the group the enormous, bloody Bowie knife. John Hockley whistled.

'Fuck me,' he said quietly. 'Where are the bodies, boys?'

'Up there,' said H, pointing again to the open door on the balcony. 'Woman on a bed in the first room at the top of the stairs, little girl under the bed in the next room.'

'Under the bed?'

'Yeah. Looks like she crawled under there when he was busy next door with the woman. Bastard slashed her to pieces under the bed. There's fucking blood everywhere.'

'Next of kin about?'

'Not in the house but the rest of the family are probably in the Chinese restaurant downstairs. Pizza's gone round to try and find them.'

'Excellent. Andy, we'll need to put one of your guys on the door to secure the place and a couple of others to start knocking on doors. We've got Scenes of Crime on the way and Control are turning the DCI and DI out of bed. We'll get the Patrol Group here later today for the searches and house-to-house, OK?'

Collins nodded his understanding and dispatched Psycho to guard the front door while Ally and Malcy began knocking on doors in an attempt to find witnesses.

'Take this bastard back to Horse's Arse,' said Collins, turning back to the Brothers. 'Make sure Sergeant Jones gets all his clothing off him and gets a doctor to see him, OK?'

The Brothers nodded.

'Sure those cuffs are tight enough?' continued Collins. Without waiting for an answer he reached down to the prisoner and with one enormous, ham-like hand crunched both cuffs tighter another two notches, causing the glistening, gory steel teeth to dig even deeper into the wrist flesh. As Cheatle screamed louder, Collins slammed the back door shut. He smiled at the pale, grim-faced Brothers.

'Good job, boys, I'm proud of you. Off you go.'

The Brothers nodded again with the briefest of smiles, got back into Yankee One and drove slowly away from the source of another dream that would haunt H. Jim had assumed driving duties and H laid his head back against the headrest and closed his eyes, the better to ignore the screaming from the footwell behind him. It was a mistake. With nothing else to concentrate on, his mind filled with an image of the little girl and his head with the click, click, click of mah-jong tiles.

# Chapter Two

PC Bob 'Ooh Yah' Young and his partner Alfie had been parked up on the hard shoulder of the motorway for the last hour and a half and Alfie was getting very restless.

'Calm down, you big smelly bastard,' said Young as he absent-mindedly twiddled and twirled at his pride and joy handlebar moustache which he kept trimmed well below Force guidelines. It was very much in keeping with his vision of himself as a porn star. Coupled with his tinted aviator-style spectacles, the skinny little dog cop revelled in his full nickname of 'Ooh Yah Pumpen Harder', but sadly the reality was that his love life was as empty as his bank account. Married to a dour, drab school teacher who hated him, Young's only real friend was the repulsive Alfie who, Young noted sourly, had his knob out again, with a huge

23

dewdrop making its steady, elasticated way down to the cloth seat covers. Their vehicle stank exclusively of Alfie whose personal hygiene and habits left a great deal to be desired.

'Fucking hell, Alfie,' shouted Young, getting quickly out of the vehicle and jogging round to the passenger side. 'Get the fuck out and stretch your legs, go and have a piss or something.'

Young pulled the door open and stood to one side as the shaggy-haired devil child bounded out, briefly fixed Young with his beady copper eyes and bared his teeth at him.

'Behave yourself,' shouted Young as he watched the enormous dog clear the open-slatted wooden fence alongside the hard shoulder and disappear at a gallop into the darkened parkland. Resting his forearms on the fence and shaking his head, Young prayed that Alfie didn't come across any wildlife, but with a bit of luck perhaps a gypsy out poaching. Previously Alfie had returned from a similar comfort break with a small muntjac deer clamped between his jaws which Young had only retrieved after a fearful fight.

Young and Alfie were an extraordinary double act who were rarely seen one without the other. Indeed, Alfie had been granted social membership of Young's cricket club where Young turned out as regularly as he could as an enthusiastic member of the second eleven.

During matches, Alfie would be tethered to a tree at the far end of the ground out of harm's way until at close of play he would accompany Young into the clubhouse where the bar manager kept him topped up with the slops from the drip trays.

Young and Alfie never queued for long, space always being made for the small bison with mean little eyes that began to roll in their sockets when he got pissed. He had been suspended for a fortnight by the Social Committee after he'd got on to his hind legs and attempted to savage a barman who'd declined to serve him. There were club members prepared to swear they'd heard Alfie mutter aggressively, 'You looking at my bird?' as he and Young propped up the bar, brothers in arms drowning their sorrows, unloved by any but the other. Though they would never dare mention it, some of the members harboured serious concerns about the nature of their relationship. It was not unusual to find Young asleep in a chair after a heavy session, with Alfie on his lap, knob out as usual, similarly hammered, almost completely obscuring Young and both snoring loudly. But the club members had a soft spot for the monster, especially after he'd disembowelled the irritating poodle that belonged to their effeminate scorer. The poodle's demise had taken place between innings one beautiful afternoon, on about a good length on the pitch. Thereafter club bowlers, instead of being encouraged to bowl line and length, were always entreated to give a batsman an 'Alfie'.

Young turned back to the mayhem on the motorway that had caused him and Alfie to get stuck. They had been making their way north to Handstead in case they could help out at the scene of the double murder when the traffic ahead of them had ground to a halt. Young had driven Delta One slowly along the hard shoulder until they found the cause of the delay. Stationary across both lanes of the motorway was a white Datsun 100A Cherry, complete with the obligatory orange petrol stain around the filler cap. Its hysterical female driver was running about like a Christmas Eve turkey, occasionally pointing at the elderly man jammed beneath the rear wheels. A quick check by Young confirmed the unfortunate man was as dead as a doornail. He had been badly carved up by the car. Young called for the cavalry, and the grumpy Black Rats who'd been very reluctantly patrolling Handstead raced to the scene of the fatal road traffic accident where they could close the road for hours and irritate the fuck out of everyone.

Eighty-year-old Stanley Murray was a classic example of the National Health Service's neglect of the elderly and mentally ill. He was supposed to be safely tucked up in Handstead Hospital's psychiatric wing, known locally as Fuckwit Farm, but had been allowed to stroll out of his secure ward ten hours earlier, wearing only his thin dressing gown. His absence from the ward had not been noticed, and the sad, deranged old man had wandered the two miles from the hospital and down the exit ramp on to the motorway and into the path of Doreen Knight's Datsun. She had been busy trying to find something decent on the car radio when at the last second she had seen Stanley standing in the middle of the road with his dressing gown pulled apart, having a piss. She hit him full on at eighty miles an hour and felt and saw the car jump as he disappeared under the front wheels and then jam against the rear ones, where he stayed, being torn along the tarmac for a further fifty yards. Stanley died instantly but messily, as he probably would have had he remained on his ward, and Doreen went to pieces as badly as he had done under her car.

The Black Rats worked at their usual snail's pace and even at this late hour had created a five-mile tailback northbound and a couple of miles southbound, with ghoulish passers-by slowing to enjoy someone else's misfortune.

'Can't we start moving this lot down the hard shoulder?' complained Young to one of the traffic cops.

'Not a chance,' replied the Black Rat. 'Still waiting for a Deeper Accident Investigation officer.'

'Fucking hell, what's to investigate? I've got cataracts and I can see what happened here. What the fuck is a DAI going to give you?' exploded Young.

Shaking his head at the dog cop's ignorance of all things traffic, the Rat turned on his heel to join the other kiddy fiddlers standing around the Datsun in their high-visibility jackets, discussing ways to keep the road closed until Christmas. So Young, a furious Scenes of Crime officer from the other side of the county who had a backlog of jobs that would make the Grim Reaper wilt, and two pale-faced undertakers twiddled their thumbs and waited. And waited. They waited until just after 5 a.m. when the traffic officers, living proof that arseholes could grow teeth, declared themselves satisfied that Doreen Knight was not a contract killer and gingerly pulled the Datsun clear of Stanley Murray's battered body.

'About fucking time,' yelled Young from the adjacent field where he had been desperately looking for Alfie who had not been seen since he left Delta One. 'There you are, I told you, he's dead.'

Doreen Knight was now being led tearfully to one of the traffic cars parked on the hard shoulder.

'You cunt,' Young bellowed in frustration into the dark field, causing Doreen to break down completely at what she believed had been directed at her.

'It was an accident, I didn't see him,' she wailed as she was ushered into the back of a Range Rover.

Young was starting to get worried by Alfie's absence. Fuck only knows what he's doing, he fumed. He glanced back at the Black Rats gathered around Stanley's corpse while the simmering SOCO took his flashlight shots. Then the SOCO departed but the two undertakers were still not allowed near.

'Now what?' Young muttered. 'Now what?' he repeated more loudly after climbing back over the fence and joining the group.

'There's bits missing,' replied one of the traffic cops who couldn't wait to get home to bore his wife shitless with more tales of gore and disaster.

'What bits?' asked Young, looking down at Stanley who remained face down on the road, his dressing gown torn to shreds and his scrawny old arse resembling an elephant's knees.

'Left arm's gone for a start,' began the gore fanatic. 'Right ear, couple of toes off the left—'

'All right, all right. Fucking hell, you're not seriously going to start looking for them now, are you?'

'We can hardly piss off without finding the big bits, can we? Look great later this morning, wouldn't it, some punter breaks down and finds a fucking arm by the road? Have a look for us, would you? Sooner we find something, sooner we can all go.'

Sighing heavily, Young trudged back to Delta One where he hauled out his thousand candle-strength lamp which he kept charged into the cigarette lighter. He climbed back over the fence into the parkland, lit up the treeline over a hundred yards away and began to sweep the beam across the rolling grassland. Almost immediately he saw the evil glint of Alfie's eyes, sunk deep down in a large tuft of grass.

'Alfie,' he bellowed. 'Get the fuck over here. NOW.'

Very, very slowly, the eyes rose up in the dark like a pair of alien spacecraft and began to advance towards Young. In the powerful light Young could see Alfie was hunched down in his attack posture and, as he got closer, he could see he was carrying something in his huge slobbering jaws.

'What the fuck have you got there? Put it down and come here.'

The two glowing eyes dropped down as Alfie went to ground again.

'Right, that's fucking it,' bellowed Young, striding purposefully towards Alfie. 'I'm going to kick the shit out of you. What the fuck do you have?'

As he got to within ten feet of the dog, he stopped still in his tracks.

'Oh fuck,' he said quietly, looking anxiously over his shoulder towards the searchers on the motorway. 'Fucking hell, Alfie, where did you get that?' he asked more reasonably.

Now clearly visible in the brilliant lamplight was Stanley Murray's missing left arm, firmly clamped between Alfie's teeth and showing evidence of his attempts at a midnight snack.

'Put it down, for Christ's sake,' hissed Young, moving closer. Alfie growled menacingly and shuffled backwards on his haunches.

Young was in no mood for a deep and meaningful discussion with his partner.

'Leave,' he bellowed, stepping forward and lamping Alfie over the top of the head with a large stick he'd concealed behind his back. Alfie roared and leapt away, dropping Stanley's arm before he hunkered down in an adjacent clump of grass and sulked. Young shone his lamp along the length of the battered arm.

'Look at the state of it,' he yelled at Alfie who glared back at him. 'Where'd you find it?' Young picked up the arm by the hand. 'Come,' he commanded, and walked back towards the motorway, followed by Alfie in his stalking position, just waiting for an opportunity to grab his prize back.

'Don't even think about it, shithead,' called Young over his shoulder.

When they got back to the fence, Young dropped the arm into the grass and snapped the chain lead on to Alfie's check chain collar before helping him vault the fence and locking him securely away in his cage in the back of Delta One. Alfie knew he was in the shit because he was in his cage as opposed to the front seat where he was normally allowed to patrol. As he howled and protested, Young strolled nonchalantly back to where he had dropped the missing arm. The traffic cops were all busy searching the central reservation and not paying him any attention. Young was now standing not far from the Range Rover where Doreen Knight sat sobbing quietly. It was just too good an opportunity. He tapped on the window to her left. Turning, she was greeted by the sight of Stanley Morgan's hand slowly waving across the glass in a wide streak of blood. She began to screech at the top of her voice and attempt to escape from the car.

'Look what I found,' Young announced happily to the traffic cops who had come over to see what Doreen was screaming about now. Triumphantly he held aloft the missing arm. 'We can all go home now.'

'Where was it?' asked one of the Rats.

'Just behind the Range Rover.'

'Was it fuck,' exclaimed the driver of the vehicle as the other traffic cops looked accusingly at him.

'It was,' insisted Young. 'Just in the grass. You probably missed it in the dark,' he continued reasonably.

'Did I fuck miss it,' said the traffic cop. 'I checked, there was fuck all anywhere near the motor. Honestly, guys, I checked. There was nothing.'

Young had deposited the arm on the road and the

traffic cops gathered round to offer their professional opinions.

'Definitely his, I suppose?' offered the gore merchant.

'How many fucking left arms do you suppose might be lying about?' asked the DAI who was not happy at being called out for a no-brainer like this. The other cop coloured up but didn't reply.

'It's a right mess,' continued the DAI, squatting down to view it more closely under the light of Young's lamp. 'What the fuck are those? Look like teeth marks.' He was poking the arm now with his finger and the signs of its encounter with Alfie were clearly visible. 'And that looks like slobber.' The DAI looked up suspiciously at Young who was doing his best to look nonchalant.

'Foxes maybe?' chimed in the dim gore merchant.

The DAI glanced at the other traffic cops who all hung their heads in shame at his stupidity, their body language distancing themselves from him.

'Where did you say you found it?' asked the DAI. He looked up to where Young had been standing but there was now a gap there. 'Where'd you find it?' he shouted as Delta One roared into life.

'Can't stop, got a job,' called Young, snapping up an Advanced Driver salute. Alfie was bellowing in frustration in the back, causing the van to rock violently. The DAI motioned to try and stop Young but wisely moved to one side as he roared past.

'Hedgehogs or badgers perhaps?' offered the brain donor in the white-topped cap, looking down at the battered arm.

# Chapter Three

Handstead New Town, situated fifteen miles north of Manchester, was a simmering pile of contradictions and paradoxes. A settlement had stood at its site since the Bronze Ages and had merited a mention in the Domesday Book, and its rolling parklands had attracted the attention of the Tudor monarchs who had built a superb country manor outside the town. The place simply oozed character and history. It had remained untouched by the Industrial Revolution – not for old Handstead the pits and slag heaps or bellowing chimneys that blighted most of the north. It remained a silent and untouched oasis. Then in the late 1950s the malignant eye of Manchester City Council fell on the area. Aided and abetted by cretinous town planners, Handstead became a dumping ground for all of Manchester's undesirables who were housed in looming tower blocks and soulless estates that sprang up around the new town like poisonous mushrooms in a woodland glade. Employment came to the area in the 1960s with the arrival of the burgeoning petro-chemical industry which saw a ready supply of labour on its doorstep. For a brief period the new town prospered as the old one disappeared under the concrete spread, like a car being sucked into a swamp. Unable to stop themselves, though, the locals once too often bit the hand that fed them with a series of unwarranted wildcat strikes and lengthy industrial disputes. The petro-chemical boys simply pulled down the shutters and disappeared across the North Sea where their petro-dollars were more appreciated.

Handstead died on its feet overnight. Soon it was a depressing wilderness of windswept, shuttered, graffiti-scarred shopping precincts, haunted by groups of feral, disaffected, unemployable locals whose sole source of income other than state benefits was crime. The proportion of criminals living and operating around Handstead was probably greater than anywhere else in the north of the country. Handstead villains preyed on each other for the most part but they were not averse to travelling to find plunder and soon the town had the unwanted reputation as being the arsehole of the world. Indeed, if the world had an arsehole, then the new town would be its piles.

What a shithole like Handstead needed from the county's police was a firm hand and a clear idea of what they were looking to achieve there – like keeping the lid on. What it got was a depressing nick that functioned as a sort of Devil's Island penal colony. Handstead was where police officers ended up if they had really fucked up somewhere else – or were stunningly unlucky when postings were being dished out on appointment. It was on a par with being born with an eye in the middle of your forehead and ginger hair. Handstead teemed with an extraordinary collection of misfits, alcoholics, psychopaths, sociopaths, delinquents, sexual deviants, criminal masterminds and violent renegades. The local residents were a similarly unsavoury bunch and the two opposing sides fought a constant battle to hold sway in the town.

Of all the estates in the town, the septic boil, the anal wart, the blocked anal gland, was the Park Royal. Its elegant name was a classic misnomer – the Park Royal was a cesspit that the local police only ventured on to in vehicles and always paired up. It was hard to pinpoint when or why the antagonism had developed; it had just always been there, the inevitable consequence of having all the wrong sort of people in the wrong place at the wrong time. Or at the right time, depending on your point of view, because some of the cops, like the Brothers, once they had settled in, loved it there.

Anything went – there were no rules. What went on in Handstead in policing terms was unique by any standards. Strokes were pulled, corners cut and deals struck that would never have happened elsewhere because other parties would never have tolerated it. But Handstead was a one-off, where for a few years the law of the jungle prevailed.

By 1977 the town was in a real mess. Violent and lawless things had come to boiling point the previous year with the murder of one of the local cops by a member of the Park Royal mafia. A number of associated but unexplained deaths of mafia members had lanced the boil somewhat, but the end of the mafia as a serious entity had come about the previous summer. Sercan Ozdemir, an ambitious Turkish career criminal, had identified the mafia as a ready source of muscle as it recovered from the loss of its original hierarchy. What he could not have known was that the local Detective Chief Inspector, Dan Harrison, had infiltrated the new mafia and knew exactly what he was up to. On Ozdemir's behalf Harrison had facilitated an armed raid by the mafia at a gunsmiths that left three of the mafia shot dead by waiting police officers and Ozdemir's balls in Harrison's firm grasp. Since the shootings, the town had been very firmly under the control of the local police who currently had the leadership they had been crying out for. DCI Harrison, an unscrupulous but dedicated and determined detective, was aided and abetted every step of the way by his uniform counterpart, Chief Inspector Pete Stephenson, whose penchant for leading from the front had included being amongst the team who had shot the mafia. They were both born to police Handstead and were in their element there.

Sercan Ozdemir was getting seriously pissed off. Since his team of wannabe criminal masterminds had been wasted in the Tamworth gun shop, DCI Harrison had been tugging his chain at every opportunity. Ozdemir knew he had a few loose ends and wrinkles to iron out before he could relax, but locating them was proving extremely difficult. As he saw it, the big itch in the small of his back was the sole survivor of the Tamworth massacre, Brian Jones, the getaway driver and Handstead CID's informant. The other potential problem was Simon Edwardes, a bent solicitor who represented a lot of the Park Royal mafia and supplemented his income by working for DCI Harrison.

In the run-up to the massacre, Edwardes had been instructed by Sercan Ozdemir to take a message into Strangeways Prison that ultimately led to the death of a mafia leader. Edwardes had been persuaded by DCI Harrison to upgrade the original message and as far as the Turkish murderers in the prison were aware, Ozdemir had ordered the hit. Ozdemir harboured serious misgivings about Edwardes' loyalty and had begun to explore ways to test him. The scale of his betrayal to Harrison rankled more than the potential threat to his life from his crime family should they ever find out about his bit of freelancing. An arrogant man, Ozdemir could not see past the fact that he had lost face with his immediate associates and what remained of the Park Royal mafia. A serious career criminal would have put it down to experience and moved on. But not Ozdemir, who now vowed to find and kill Jones and find out about Edwardes before he did anything else. But where the fuck was Jones? He had not been seen since the hot June morning in 1976 when he gunned a rented Rover away from the front of the gun shop. In the immediate aftermath of the massacre, DCI Harrison had visited Ozdemir and let him know that he knew everything and then he removed Brian Jones from circulation.

DCI Harrison couldn't have been happier if Raquel Welch had jammed her bearded clam on to his face holding a glass of his favourite Bushmills. He had Ozdemir where he wanted him, which was on a very short leash. But ever the devious bastard, Harrison was not content simply to control and reduce crime on his division by keeping his foot in the back of Ozdemir's neck. He was planning to use his advantage one day to remove Ozdemir from the equation altogether.

# Chapter Four

June 1976

The Rover that Handstead CID had thoughtfully hired to enable Brian Jones to take the mafia team to their deaths at the Tamworth gun shop had been raced close to destruction. As the windows of the shop disintegrated under the lead storm unleashed on the unfortunate trio of robbers inside, Jones had screeched away with little thought for his accomplices. To be fair to him, it was obvious to any rational observer that little could have survived the fusillade. As he raced the car back to the Handstead railway sidings for the prearranged meeting with his CID handlers, Jones alternated between bouts of screaming abuse about the ambush and rib-cracking sobs of fright and relief at his escape. It had dawned on him, too late, that he had been used by the CID as a

Judas sheep, obligingly leading his three accomplices to their slaughter. He tried to console himself with the thought that he had tried to persuade two of them to pull the plug on the job, and the third, Pat Allen, was a cunt and no loss at all. But his thirty-watt light bulb brain had also worked out that as the sole survivor he was also the obvious grass, not only to his mafia leaders, Briggs and Travers, but to Sercan Ozdemir who had set the whole thing up. With his thumping heart in his throat and his head still ringing from the gunfire, he raced to his meeting with his only salvation – the bastards from CID.

During the ten-minute journey he constantly checked his rear-view mirror in case the police were following him away but to his immense relief the quiet country road behind him appeared deserted. DCs Bob Clarke and John Benson were waiting in the shade at the very back of the sidings as the Rover careered into the yard. There was a pause before Jones spotted the detectives leaning against their unmarked Ford Escort and he raced over to them, skidding the vehicle to a halt in a choking cloud of hot dust. Switching off, he climbed out of the car, slammed the door and stood staring at Clarke and Benson who had not moved. The only sound was the ticking and banging from the white-hot engine of the car.

'You bastards,' hissed Jones eventually. 'You fucking

bastards. They've all been fucking shot and you knew it was coming.'

'So we heard,' replied Benson nonchalantly, standing away from the Ford Escort. 'Sounds like a right bloodbath, from what I hear.'

'Fucking hell,' shouted Jones. 'The place fucking disintegrated, fucking bullets everywhere. I was lucky to get away.'

'Hope you haven't damaged the motor,' said Clarke who had grown quite fond of the hired car. 'We've got to get it back later.'

'Damaged the fucking car?' shouted Jones incredulously. 'Damaged the fucking car, are you joking? Fuck the car, what the fuck's going to happen to me now? I'm on offer, you pair of bastards.'

In his rage Jones had failed to notice that John Benson had kept moving closer to him, and by way of a reply he now landed a swinging right-hander to the side of his head. Jones collapsed in a heap in the dust and lay quietly before he rolled on to an elbow and looked up at the source of all his current problems.

'You bastards,' he said bitterly, rubbing his throbbing and rapidly bruising temple. 'You've sold me right down the river, haven't you? What the fuck happens to me now? It's not going to take Briggs and Travers long to work out what happened, or Mr Ozdemir, and then what? I'm fucked, aren't I? And you don't give a shit.'

'Listen, Brian,' began Bob Clarke soothingly. 'What's done is done, but we're not ungrateful. First thing, though, is you've got to vanish from town fucking quickly. As you say, if Briggs and Travers don't come looking for you, Ozdemir will and he'll find you and it won't be pleasant, trust me. Got any ideas where you can go?'

'Have I got any ideas?' screeched Jones. 'Fucking hell, you're supposed to be looking after me. I fed you everything on this job, absolutely fucking everything, and you're asking me for ideas?'

'Listen, you little prick,' said John Benson. 'You're starting to seriously piss me off. What we mean is, have you got any retard family or relatives you can go to?'

'Couple of uncles in Handstead and my sister lives in Manchester with her old man.'

'Brilliant, no one's going to think of checking with them – you thick twat,' snapped Benson. 'You're going to have to put some miles between yourself and Handstead: the further the better.'

'Fucking hell, like where? All my family are up here.'

'Got any contacts down south?'

'South?'

'Yeah, south. Birmingham, London maybe? Somewhere like that.'

'Fuck all in Birmingham.'

'London then?'

'I did a bit of time with a bloke from London. We got on OK. Kept in touch when we got out but I haven't spoken to him in a while.'

'Still got an address for him?'

'Probably. At home somewhere. Why?'

'Because that's where you're off to on your holidays, son. We'll run you home, get a bag packed and get you on a train south. Up to you if you keep in touch with us, but my advice would be it'd be a good idea if we knew where you were.'

'Hold on just a fucking minute, I'm not going to London. Fuck that.'

'Brian, you want to keep breathing and claiming your benefits, you'll be on the next fast train to London. There's fuck all for you here now. We'll not be holding your hand anymore so you've really only got one option. Get the train, son. Be sensible.'

'Fucking hell, I've never been to London before, I don't know anyone down there. What the fuck am I supposed to do down there? Can't even get a decent pint.'

'What you do, Brian, is get to stay alive. You've no future here now. Everyone will know you're the grass that put the others away and got them wasted. You stay, you die. Give you a lift somewhere?'

'You cunts,' shouted Jones, but allowed Clarke to put a hand on his shoulder and lead him towards the CID car. 'You fucking bastards,' he continued, tears streaming down his face as he slid across the hot plastic back seat and swept empty polystyrene cups and cigarette packets on to the floor. 'You've fucking set me up and now I'm fucked. Why the fuck should I have to go to London?'

'Because you're a nasty little grass, Brian. No one likes a grass. We're doing you a favour and don't you forget it,' snarled Benson through the open window before he turned to Clarke. 'You want to take that Rover back to Harrison's mate, Bob? I'll run shit-for-brains home, get him packed and then take him down to Piccadilly to get a train, OK?'

Clarke replied quietly. 'Fine, John. Thanks. Listen, make sure we have the address he's going to. Could come in very useful and I'm sure Harrison will want it.'

'No worries. Go on, get off with you. You're dying to drive it, you big tart.'

Smiling, Clarke slipped into the Rover and started it up. Benson returned to the Escort, crushed himself into the driver's seat and was about to drive away when he heard Clarke shouting.

'What's up?' he called.

'You little prick,' yelled Clarke. 'There's a fucking petrol shortage and you've done half a tank of fucking petrol. What the fuck have you been doing?'

'What have I been doing, what have I been doing?'

repeated Jones to himself in despair as Benson drove him slowly out of the sidings.

An hour and a half later, Benson slammed the door to the carriage shut as the London train pulled sedately out of Manchester Piccadilly station with a very surly Brian Jones glaring at him through the open window.

'Keep in touch, Brian,' mocked Benson. 'Send us a postcard and mind yourself down there.'

'Go fuck yourself, you big homo,' shouted Jones, then quickly disappeared into the carriage when he saw the big detective begin to run alongside the train and attempt to open the door to get at him.

Benson watched the train disappear from view with a wide smile on his broad, pockmarked face. First stop was Stockport but he was confident Jones would travel all the way to London to escape the rage of Briggs and Travers and the sinister Sercan Ozdemir. All the way, in fact, to Seven Sisters Road, London N7, he mused, looking at the letter he had pulled out of the inner pocket of his suit jacket.

He returned to the unmarked Escort parked on double yellow lines outside the station, threatened to decapitate the traffic warden about to issue it with a ticket, and then drove north to collect Clarke from the car hire garage.

\*

Of the three potential threats to Brian Jones's health, now only one actually drew breath – Sercan Ozdemir. As soon as news of the debacle at Tamworth was relayed to him, Ozdemir had identified the two major dangers to his continued criminal enterprises: Hugh Briggs and Andy Travers, the brain-donor leaders of the Park Royal mafia. They were quickly located holding court in the Park Royal pub and brought to Ozdemir's business premises where the full scale of the fiasco revealed itself. Brian Jones was quickly identified as the fly in the ointment but Ozdemir needed Briggs and Travers out of the way before they got their inevitable visits from the police. Indeed, they had only been gone ten minutes before DCI Harrison arrived to gloat and let Ozdemir know that he had his balls in his hot, sweaty hands.

Racing down the M6 towards the pig farm owned by Ozdemir's aunt, Hugh Briggs and Andy Travers had tried to make small talk with the two huge, silent Turkish goons they were wedged between in the back of the Mercedes with the blacked-out windows.

'Where we going, fellas? Is it far?' asked Briggs.

'Not far, no problems, quiet now.'

'Where we going?' asked Travers as the Mercedes came off the motorway and turned into the quiet, hot countryside.

'Not far, no problems, quiet now.'

Briggs looked at the two monosyllabic monsters who

stared straight ahead and felt a deep twinge of unease in his rolling stomach.

'We going somewhere safe?'

'No problems, safe soon.'

'Fucking hell, don't say much, do you?'

'No problems, safe soon,' repeated the goon, but he looked at Briggs this time and flashed a gold tooth at him.

'You keep saying that. Where the fuck are we going?' The apparently endless countryside held huge terrors for Briggs who had been born and bred on the Park Royal estate and viewed trees as something to be uprooted and used as a weapon. Even in broad daylight, the countryside's unbroken horizon and absence of human life made him feel uneasy.

The one-way conversation in the car petered out altogether as the driver slipped in a cassette of traditional Turkish music and accompanied the mournful wailing with his own tuneless moaning.

Twenty minutes later, the Mercedes turned left on to a rutted, unnamed lane and after a couple of hundred yards of bumping and jolting turned into the still and deserted yard of an isolated farm. As the engine died, Briggs and Travers looked nervously at each other. Neither of the goons made any movement to leave the car.

'We getting out here?' asked Travers nervously.

'Safe soon,' replied the man to his left. He then spoke rapidly to the driver who nodded and got out of the car.

The now very worried Park Royal mafia leaders glanced uneasily out of the car and over the two hundred acres of Carlton Water Farm. On either side of the dusty yard, fields stretched as far as the eye could see, dotted throughout with corrugated pig sheds and thousands of pigs of every shape and size.

Aunt Selina Ozdemir had farmed pigs at Carlton Water since the late 1950s, breeding thousands of pigs for slaughter elsewhere every year. The farm was a perfect front for the Ozdemir crime family to launder their dirty money through pig products, but it had another darker and sinister role in the Ozdemir crime empire.

Ten years earlier, Aunt Selina had imported five pure Russian wild boar, ostensibly for a breeding programme associated with a hunting business that she trumpeted as an alternative to the more traditional fox hunting and deer stalking. The wild boar hunting idea had quietly withered on the vine without any inquiry from the local authority who had allowed the import, but the unique breeding programme had continued quietly in isolated sheds in fields furthest away from the only road on to the farm. By the early 1970s, Aunt Selina was the proud owner of a herd of thirty superb, jet-black Russian wild boars.

The sexes were kept separate, only brought together to breed, and never handled by their human keepers. The mature male boars all weighed in at around four hundred pounds, their short, small-boned bodies rippling with muscle and scarred from the continual fighting for supremacy with their razor sharp tusks and canine teeth. From birth they ate only from human clothing filled with their swill. Every day a bizarre, scarecrow-like object would be tossed into their pen to be torn to pieces by the vicious, squealing animals. The training was deliberate as Aunt Selina's farm was now regularly used to dispose of the bodies of anyone unfortunate enough to fall foul of the family. She preferred to feed these unfortunates to her boars alive as the animals had poor eyesight and relied instead on their keen hearing and smell. The more panicked and terrified their meals were, the better, as far as she was concerned. Her victims generally had their Achilles tendons cut with a machete before being thrown screaming and bleeding into the pen where they would be efficiently disposed of by the boars. The animals performed less efficiently with compliant dead bodies, leaving large chunks, particularly heads, which had to be burnt and crushed. Generally, all that remained of a live one that fought to the end was their fillings, to be found in the boars' stools.

Briggs and Travers watched as the driver walked over

to the main farm building on the left of the yard and knocked on the door. It was answered by an elderly, olive-skinned woman in a pair of filthy dungarees. A heated and unintelligible exchange ensued before the driver returned to the car and the woman shuffled over to the barn directly in front of them. The men in the car sat in silence, watching as the old woman pulled the huge doors open with difficulty. Then the driver started the car again and they drove slowly past the scowling old witch, leathery face set in a sneer and veiny, liver-spotted hands on her hips, into the cool gloom of the enormous barn. The engine died and Briggs and Travers shifted uncomfortably as the barn doors closed behind them and the scorching sunlight disappeared. The barn was still well lit by the light streaming in through lantern windows in the ceiling, the beams filled with swirling dust and pollen.

'Out now, no more,' barked one of the minders before he and his colleague exited the car quickly, leaving Briggs and Travers looking faintly ridiculous squeezed into the centre of the seat. As they left the car by their respective doors they were both met with the barrel of a .45 Magnum stuffed under their noses. Pale, wide-eyed and terrified, they automatically raised their hands and stepped backwards.

'Wh-what the fuck are you doing?' stammered Briggs, his throat dry and tightening quickly.

The old woman walked up to the car and babbled at the two minders, indicating a wooden pen to her left with a nod of her wizened old head which would not have looked out of place on a stake outside a headhunter's hut.

'Move now,' shouted the larger of the two goons, gesturing to Briggs with his gun to move round the car and join Travers. Slowly, Briggs moved, never taking his eyes off the gun held just a few inches from his deathly pale, sweaty and trembling face.

'Mr Ozdemir said we'd be OK. What the fuck is this all about?' shouted Briggs.

'Quiet now, move quickly,' bellowed the larger minder again and they guided the shaking Briggs and Travers through a wicket gate held open by the shrunken skull on legs and into the filthy, straw-covered pen.

The smell was indescribable, the floor covered in about six inches of what appeared to be, and smelt like, shit and straw. Both Briggs and Travers gagged and raised their hands to their faces. Then they heard squealing and scratching and turned to the rear of the pen where they saw a grubby, stainless-steel trap door in the wall. From behind it came the blood-chilling, high-pitched squealing and grunting and frenzied clawing and scratching as the half-starved, ferocious boars fought to get at the meals they could hear and smell on the other side.

'What the fucking hell . . .' gasped Travers, grabbing at Briggs's arm for support.

'Oh no, no,' screamed Briggs, turning to look at the goons and the witch who had closed the gate and stood looking coldly at them. The old woman then shouted something at the two minders. They stepped up to the gate and without a word or a flicker in their stony expressions, shot Briggs and Travers in the stomach.

As the barn exploded with the sound of the gunshots, the screeching from behind the trap door intensified, and increased again when the frenzied beasts heard Briggs' and Travers' screams of agony and smelt their blood. The witch moved to the trap door and pressed a small wooden lever. The steel door sprang smoothly up and six red-eyed Russian boars exploded out of their confined space and fell on the writhing Briggs and Travers.

Briggs was disembowelled by the first thrust of the upper tusks of a large boar. His intestines spilt out on to the animal's head and were then ripped from his stomach by violent, wrenching head-thrashing by two of the blood-crazed boars. A third animal bit into the side of his face, removing his lower jaw and side of his neck, and as he bled quickly to death he watched two of the boars fighting over his liver. The much feared and hated Andy Travers fared no better. He managed to get to his feet in a desperate bid to escape before he was viciously bitten in the crotch, his genitals being torn away with his trousers before a tusk severed an artery in his groin and he was ripped to pieces. It was all over in twenty minutes. Other than a few pieces of clothing which would be recovered and destroyed later, nothing remained of the former rulers of the Park Royal mafia.

As the sated boars snuffled about in the shit looking for titbits or lay about digesting their welcome but reluctant meals, Sercan Ozdemir got a call from Aunt Selina telling him that his immediate problems had gone away. He allowed himself the briefest of smiles and sat back in his office chair. Now he had to find Brian Jones and get to grips with that fat, bent solicitor, Simon Edwardes. God help the pair of them when I find them, he mused grimly.

# Chapter Five

Spring 1977

'Listen up, you lot,' shouted Sergeant Andy Collins above the din coming from the group seated in battered, plastic orange chairs in front of his lectern. Loudest of all were Ally and Ray 'Piggy' Malone, arguing as usual about everything.

'You're a fat bastard, Piggy,' growled Ally in his broad Glaswegian accent. 'How much do you eat a day anyway?'

'It's my metabolism,' grumbled Piggy.

'The metabolism of a T-rex couldn't cope with what you stuff down your neck. Come on, tell me what you've eaten today, come on.'

'What, since this evening?'

'Of course since this evening, you've been in bed all day, haven't you?'

'Yeah, but I had a full cooked breakfast when I got in to help me get off to sleep.'

'A full cooked breakfast?' shouted Ally. 'Before you went to bed? How the fuck can you sleep after that? What did that consist of?'

'You know, the usual. Bacon, sausage, fried eggs, mushrooms, fried slice, beans, black pudding, bread and butter. Just a little something to get me off to sleep.'

'Fuck me,' said Ally. 'What about when you got out of bed?'

'Well, I was up about lunchtime for a bowl of cereal and then went back to bed until about six.'

'And ate what?'

'Well, my tea of course.'

'Which was?'

'Burgers, chips, beans, bread and butter, suet pudding and custard.'

'Fucking hell, Piggy, I know what the problem is, why you're such a fat bastard – you've only got one arse,' shouted Ally triumphantly.

'OK, guys, listen up. Just a few items for you before you get out amongst them,' shouted Sergeant Andy Collins again.

The group settled and listened intently as Collins assigned them to their beats for the night.

'Thank fuck for that,' shouted Ally as he was paired

up with Malcy rather than Piggy who once again got lumbered with the dirty van.

'Wind it in, Ally, officer on parade,' hissed Collins, glaring at him.

Ally blushed at the reprimand but kept quiet – Collins was not the sort of supervisor to start taking liberties with.

'Got another warning from Division here, guys,' continued Collins, reading from a memo signed by the divisional commander, Chief Superintendent 'The Fist' Findlay. 'There's a fucking horrible complaint come in from some poncy solicitor alleging abduction from outside the railway station by uniformed police officers. He claims that he remembers arriving back pissed at Handstead from a do in Manchester and talking to a couple of uniformed officers outside in the street and the next thing he remembers is waking up in a bus shelter in Aberdeen.'

The group began to howl with laughter. Collins frowned and pointed a threatening finger at them.

'I've fucking told you about this before. Leave the drunks alone. If I find out any of you were responsible for this one, you're going to be in deep shit. Anyway, matey boy wakes up in a bus shelter suffering from hypothermia, manages to hitch a lift to the local cop shop where they let him make a phone call. Turns out his missus has already reported him missing. Listen, boys, this has got to stop, now. Losing your jobs for a bit of sport with some pisshead is bollocks. Finish.'

He looked at the smirking group and shook his head mournfully. Not averse to the odd stunt himself as a PC, this lot never failed to surprise him at the lengths they were prepared to go to. What he did not know was that the unfortunate solicitor had been a victim of an ongoing station competition between the uniform groups. They were all committed to getting drunks as far out of town as possible, and the trip had to be supported by photographic evidence. There was a photo doing the rounds of the nick showing the unconscious solicitor and his two grinning escorts (Ally and Malcy) standing by a 'Welcome to the Granite City' street sign. Getting one out as far as Aberdeen and into the land of the hairy backs was the record so far and had prompted others to bigger and better efforts. Officers from F Relief had recently been turned away from Manchester airport by security officers who had become suspicious of the two cops in a car with an unconscious man on the back seat, claiming they needed to get out on to the runway.

'That's all I've got for you for now, unless Mr Greaves has anything to add. Guv?' Collins turned behind him to where the Relief's Inspector Geoff Greaves was sitting. He was unshaven and singing quietly to himself, wearing uniform shirt and tie and his dress tunic, and a pair of blue check pyjama bottoms. He glanced up as Collins addressed him, smiled and looked away.

'Nothing from Mr Greaves then,' continued the ever loyal Collins without batting an eyelid. 'Off you go, boys. Be careful and do it to them first.'

'Praise the Lord,' bellowed the religious maniac Psycho, getting to his feet and leading the exodus to the front office to collect radios and car keys.

There was actually nothing wrong with Greaves, but Collins was amongst the majority who knew no better. A career detective who'd taken one bung too many, Greaves had been returned to a uniform post at Handstead as a punishment and had embarked on a campaign to get himself pensioned off with an ill health pension as a basket case. Very few were in on the secret and as far as his Relief was aware, he was off with the fairies with a bunch of daffodils in his hand. The real power on the Relief lay with Sergeant Collins who would not hear a word against Greaves. He was very old school when it came to his inspector. As the sound of Psycho roaring 'Onward Christian Soldiers' echoed away up the corridor, Collins turned back to Greaves.

'Coming out for a ride tonight, guv?' he asked.

'Nah, probably stay in and do a bit of paperwork, Andy,' he replied, looking mournfully up at the huge sergeant. There was nothing he'd like to have done more than tell him what he was up to, but the fewer that knew the better. One day he'd tell him and thank him for his loyalty. 'Yeah, got loads of paperwork to get out of the way.'

'No problem, guv. You give me a shout if you need anything, OK?'

Greaves didn't reply so Collins left him to his quiet singing and wandered up to the cell block to check in with his colleague, Sergeant Jones.

Jones was a different kettle of fish altogether. He, too, was serving a sentence at Handstead having been caught knobbing the wife of one of his PCs at a rural nick, but despite his initial fears about being there he was adapting quite well. He was currently involved in what he believed was an exclusive and secret relationship with Belinda 'The Blood Blister' Wheeler, the relief's only WPC, who had in fact shared the secret with Psycho who also pumped her up from time to time. Jones was in an appalling mood as he could hear Psycho telling someone very loudly that he'd given the Blister a dry-arse fuck that afternoon and pulled out her pink glove.

'Got many in?' inquired Collins.

'Fucking heaving,' snapped Jones, glaring towards the sound of raucous laughter as Psycho continued to regale his audience about what he had allegedly done to the Blister. 'Immigration brought a load of cleaners in.'

Collins glanced up at the custody board which was

packed with names scrawled in white chalk. Reading them, he smiled.

'Been down and visited them yet?'

'Not had a fucking chance. Fucking late turn bailed out the moment I walked in, no fucking handover, nothing.'

'Have a look at the names,' pressed Collins.

Wearily, Jones looked up and began to read.

'Izzi Akrim, immigration offences, Akkepa Mateef Inajar, immigration offences, Ahmet Himinagaybar, immigration offences,' he droned.

'Fucking hell, Keith,' said Collins. 'Look at the names, they're made up, you twat. There's no one in the cells. Late turn have had you over.' As Jones began to read the names out to himself again, Collins laughed and made his way out to the front office where the appalling Psycho still held court.

'Still here, Psycho? Time you were out on the ground.'

'On my way, Sarge.'

PC Sean 'Psycho' Pearce was very confused. He'd always been a little that way, but his condition had worsened over the last year since he had embraced religion in an attempt to wheedle his way into the knickers of one of the station beauties, Anne Butler. She was a member of the Christian Police Association and Psycho had decided that membership of the CPA was the way in. But so far he had failed miserably, with Anne already smitten with a PC from a neighbouring division. Psycho had thereafter experimented with the Catholic Police Guild which had swiftly had him excommunicated on the instructions of the Deputy Chief Constable, and Islam which he had quite enjoyed as he had insisted on being allowed to pray six times a day, wherever he was. It had led to some bizarre incidents, but the huge lunatic was indulged by his colleagues who waited eagerly for his next religious outburst. He had continued to scare the living daylights out of Sergeant Mick Jones with his loud outbursts whenever Jones took the group musters, and during the long hot summer of 1976 had taken to wearing leather 'Jesus' sandals at work, because 'If they were good enough for him, they're good enough for me.' He had still been able to give the local hooligans a good kicking from time to time and it had become usual for the police doctors examining Psycho's unfortunate prisoners to note that they displayed what appeared to be wounds in the shape of buckles and deep lacerations apparently caused by cutlasses but in fact a legacy of his dreadful gnarled toenails. He had also continued to shag Dawn Masters, the buxom personal assistant to Superintendent Grainger in Complaints and Discipline, until she had gone up to university. With her departure, he had slipped into a bit of a depression. Giving the

Blister a good rear-ending from time to time was no real substitute so he had begun to peruse the lonely hearts columns of the *Handstead Advertiser*. Consequently, he had humped some real heifers and become something of an authority on the wording and hidden messages contained in the adverts.

'What about this one?' asked Andy 'The Mong Fucker' Malcolm, reading from the paper as they waited in the muster room for the late turn crews to hand over the vehicle keys.

' "Adventurous, thirty something and headstrong woman seeks man for adventure and maybe more." She sounds OK.'

'Nah,' replied Psycho despondently. 'She'll be forty-five easily, argumentative and likes it up the arse.'

'And the downside is?' asked Malcy, genuinely surprised at Psycho's dismissal of such a likely candidate.

He didn't reply but remained staring into the distance, swinging an incense orb from side to side.

'OK, what about this one?' continued Malcy, going back to the lonely hearts column. ' "Fun, curvy, new age single mother seeks knight in shining armour to sweep her off her feet." '

'Fucking hell, Malcy, she's an annoying fat bitch with a smelly fanny whose husband traded her in for a new bird with a fangita like a mouse's ear,' explained Psycho patiently. 'No, Malcy, there's only one woman for me.'

65

'She's way out of your league, Psycho,' replied Malcy. 'Hold up, this isn't a message for you, is it?'

'Where?'

'Here in the column – "Sir Richard, you bastard, you nicked my purse when you left the other morning. When I find you, you're dead. Cupcake." That for you?'

'Is it bollocks.'

'Listen, mate, time to move on,' said Malcy, rolling the paper up and tossing it on to the seat behind him. 'Plenty more fish in the sea.'

'I know, I know, but there's something about her. I can't shake it off, Malcy.'

'Fuck's sake, Psycho, get a grip, will you? I'm starting to well up here,' growled Malcy in his broad Glaswegian accent and shifting uncomfortably in his seat as the beast got more maudlin.

Psycho shrugged and sat back in his chair. 'This lonely hearts business attracts some real weirdoes, you know,' he said quietly, looking up at the ceiling and failing to see the obvious implications of his comment.

Malcy stared open-mouthed at the unshaven hypocrite.

'Weirdoes?' he eventually asked.

'Really weird,' emphasised Psycho, reaching inside his tunic pocket and pulling out a couple of grubby envelopes. He unfolded one of the letters inside and began to read aloud.

66

'"Dear Sir Galahad" – that's me, by the way,' he explained. '"Thanks for your reply to my ad. Just a few questions before I give you my contact details. Have you got your own teeth? Can you juggle soot? Are you a homo?" Fuck me, Malcy, look who's asking.' He handed Malcy a colour passport photograph.

'Holy shit,' gasped Malcy, suspecting that the light-fingered Sir Richard and Sir Galahad were probably one and the same. 'It looks like Myra Hindley on speed. You're not going to shag this horror, are you?'

'Mind your filthy heathen mouth,' snapped Psycho, crossing himself. 'Haven't made my mind up yet. I've shagged worse.' He reached over and retrieved the photo and then replaced the letter in his tunic. He opened the other letter and read it, shaking his head.

'How about this one, Malcy?' he said eventually. 'Some French bird, I think. Fuck knows why she advertises in the *Advertiser*; Christ knows where she learnt her English. Listen to this lot: "I have myself two years ago deal has this individual in front of my house. I had succeeded in taking some elements of his identity, when it presented against a passport to me. Without being able at that time to collect information on his identity, I thought it Irish, can be English or American, within sight of his accent, this person claims to name Greta Garbo, alias Greta Garbo, one metre seventy-five to one metre eighty, standard Indo-European, russet red hair, maroon eyes, it was equipped with a behaviour beige, impermeable trousers of beige colour and claimed herself a friend, in business with my establishment. I remain has your provision for all questions." It gets fucking worse,' sighed Psycho, folding the letter in half and tucking it away with the other.

Malcy puffed out his cheeks but said nothing. While he thought he might have problems, they were clearly nothing compared to Psycho's chaotic love life.

'You know, I've been thinking about it for ages,' continued Psycho, 'and it still beats the shit out of me. There's an inherent design fault with women, but we still keep going back for more, don't we? What the fuck is the matter with us?'

'Design fault, what are you on about?'

'A serious design fault – who the fuck thought it was a good idea to put the shithouse next door to the snack bar?'

While Malcy digested this insight, Sergeant Collins strode into the muster room with a huge pile of paperwork under one of his enormous hairy arms.

'You still here, Psycho? Why aren't you two out on the ground?' he asked threateningly.

'Waiting for the late turn crew to get the motor back, Sarge,' replied Malcy, getting to his feet.

'Don't hang about in here. If you haven't got a motor, get your big hats on and get moving. If you're still here when I get back from the crapper, you'll be sorting this fucking paperwork out for me,' said Collins, bustling back out into the corridor, cigarette clamped firmly between his teeth.

'We're gone, Sarge, we're gone,' replied Malcy urgently. He tapped Psycho on the shoulder. 'Come on, let's get the fuck out of here.'

In the rear yard of the station, Pizza settled himself into the driver's seat of Bravo Two Two, ran his hands round the hard plastic steering wheel and got his brain in gear for another eight-hour shift. He glanced over at his operator. He could have been looking in a mirror and he groaned inwardly.

PC John Jackson was nineteen years old, terrified and covered in spots. Pizza saw himself eighteen months ago. Such had been Pizza's development, both as a man and as a copper, since the murder of Bovril the previous summer that he was now being used to tutor some of the young cannon fodder being churned out of the training school and marked up for active service at Horse's Arse. Ten weeks to make or break the next generation of street coppers under the wing of a twenty-year-old, still to complete his own probationary period, didn't sound like much of a deal. But Pizza was different.

Like Jackson, Pizza's first few months in the Job had been a hazy nightmare. Ignored and ridiculed by his peers as he underwent an unofficial rite of passage endured by all coppers until they were accepted, Pizza's life had been changed and shaped beyond recognition the day Bovril had bled to death in his arms at the Grant Flowers flats. Not only had he survived the shooting, but his evidence had secured lengthy gaol sentences for the hardcore Park Royal mafia.

His professional status secure, his personal life had also blossomed with his relationship with Lisa, a friend of Bovril's. Under her tutelage, the shy, gauche virgin had been transformed into a confident and accomplished young man. Pizza was not, however, aware of the true nature of her relationship with Bovril, or that the young boy he was now helping to raise was Bovril's. The child's father was of no consequence to him. He innocently assumed that the father was probably Lisa's former live-in boyfriend who had abandoned her when he discovered she was pregnant. He was simply madly in love with his first real girlfriend, certainly his first lover, and everything that she brought with her, which included an infant son now. He regarded the child as his own, doting on the small boy, and even went so far as to exercise parental rights by insisting that the boy was named David after his dead friend. Unsurprisingly, Lisa had not argued about the choice of name and the three of them had quickly settled into the routine of a happy family unit. But despite her happiness, Lisa harboured worries about what and when, if ever, she should tell Pizza.

'You ready then?' he inquired of Jackson who was awkwardly trying to get his twisted seatbelt clipped in. 'Don't put that fucking thing on, you may need to bail out in a hurry. You don't want to be fucking about with a seatbelt if you've got villains to get after.'

'But at training school they said—'

'Fuck training school, John,' interrupted Pizza with all the aplomb and panache of a thirty-year veteran. 'Forget most of what you learnt there. The definitions will come in handy, but all that role play and those real-life scenarios? Complete bollocks taught to you by geldings who haven't done any real police work for years. Forget the fucking lot, mate. You'll pick up what you need to know over the next few weeks, OK?'

Jackson nodded, chewing his bottom lip nervously, and stuffed the useless seat belt down the side of his seat.

'Know how to use the radio yet?'

'No, sorry.'

'Not your fault. Know your phonetic code?'

'Yeah, sort of. Alpha, Bravo, Charlie and all that.'

'Want to book us on?'

Jackson's eyes widened with a mixture of fear and longing.

'Well, yes,' he began nervously. 'What do I say?'

'Our call sign is Bravo Two Two. All you have to say

is Delta Hotel, this is Bravo Two Two, show us on watch please. OK?'

Jackson repeated the mantra and then looked hopefully at Pizza.

'Pick up the handset, John,' said Pizza patiently. 'When there's a gap in the traffic, you talk.'

Jackson nodded again and stared intently at the blinking green 'air busy' light on the metal main set box as though waiting for a magic signal that it was his turn. Pizza found himself staring at it too, just as he had done as a brand new, shiny probationer.

'Go on, quickly,' he urged when there was a brief lull.

'Delta Hotel, Bravo,' shouted Jackson before Pizza thumped him on the arm.

'Press the fucking button to transmit. Fuck's sake.' He sighed, leaning back in his seat.

'Sorry.' Jackson grimaced, looking shamefaced, and leant even closer to the main set, determined not to miss his chance, rocking gently as he concentrated.

It was 10.20 p.m. and night duty crews across the vast east of the county were booking on en masse; it was pot luck as to when you got in.

'Now,' bellowed Pizza.

'Delta Hotel, fuck,' screamed Jackson as his brain and mouth stopped communicating.

'Fucking hell, John,' snapped an irritated Pizza. 'Fucking sort it out, will you? Get us booked on.'

He fired up Two Two and manoeuvred out of the parking bay as Jackson continued to peer intently at the squawking, crackling, blinking radio.

'Delta Hotel, Bravo, fuck, shit, sorry,' bellowed Jackson again as they left the rear yard and headed out for eight hours in Horse's Arse.

Shaking his head ruefully, Pizza mused that it would probably take them most of the fucking shift to get booked on at this rate.

It was another warm spring evening as Pizza took Two Two out into the early-evening traffic to give Jackson an overview of the shithole he had been condemned to work in. As Pizza drove, listening without hearing to the incessant chatter on the main set radio, he glanced occasionally over at Jackson who wore an expression of permanent apprehension.

Jackson sat silently as Pizza pointed out troublesome estates, particular houses, roads, the odd individual they passed, but he was already beginning to despair that he would ever get to grips with the world he had entered. Yet here was Pizza, not yet out of his own two-year probationary period, prattling away with the panache and confidence of a hugely experienced veteran. Having spent his brief career to date rummaging about in the world's lower intestines, he had already logged away experiences that would have taken years to accumulate elsewhere.

Pizza had also acquired the skill of completely tuning out all radio transmissions until his ear picked out his call sign or references to his division or town, or the urgent tone of voice as a cop somewhere else put up a chase or a suspect disturbed or a call for urgent assistance. The rest of the time, the radio transmissions were little more than white noise. The really experienced street cops could recline their seats in their cars, pull down their caps over their eyes and drop into a deep sleep, and still register their own call signs in time to answer. Pizza had yet to master the skill of sleeping in his patrol car, but the truth was that he was far too switched on and buzzing to waste time sleeping. Despite everything that had happened to him, he knew he had found his vocation in life. His few remaining friends outside the Job often regarded him with puzzlement when he occasionally gave them an insight into his new life.

'What the hell is the attraction in being out in the freezing cold at three in the morning? What the fuck is that all about?'

'Because that's when it's happening,' Pizza would try to explain. 'It's just you and them and the dark. Everything's so intense, you can hear everything, see for miles, smell things that no one else can. You can walk round a corner and smell the cigarette that someone was smoking ten minutes earlier. You can see their footprints disappearing in the frost or damp. Just stand still and listen outside a house – you can hear someone turning over in bed. You're so alive. The darkest hours are just before dawn breaks so if you're going to nick the milk and papers off someone's doorstep, that's the time to do it.'

'What the fuck are you on about?'

'I think it was Napoleon who said that the bravest acts are the ones done in the early hours, when generally you're at your lowest ebb, and he was right. When you walk, alone, into a dark and apparently deserted car park at three in the morning, I swear you can hear the place breathing. If you stand still and listen, I swear you can hear it breathe.'

They didn't understand – why should they? Only other street coppers would ever understand what it meant to be out and about when the rest of the world, other than the bad guys, were fast asleep.

'Listen up, answer it,' said Pizza urgently, gesturing towards the flashing radio light.

'What?' said Jackson, mouth open.

'They're calling us, Bravo Two Two. Come on, answer the fucking thing, will you?'

Jackson grabbed the handset and quickly gave their call sign.

'Bravo Two Two, call to the rear of Handstead railway station, no better location I'm afraid, report of a large black vehicle with blacked-out windows considered suspicious. Anonymous caller said the vehicle's been parked up for the last ten minutes with the engine running,' said the control room operator.

'Fucking say something,' shouted Pizza after a lengthy pause.

'What do I say?' spluttered Jackson desperately.

'Tell them, all received, en route,' sighed Pizza, convinced he'd never been this fucking useless when he started – which in fact he had.

Jackson passed the message as instructed and sat back forlornly in his seat, glancing shamefaced towards Pizza.

'Sorry,' he said quietly. 'I can't get to grips with any of this yet.'

Pizza smiled at him, recognising the same anxieties and worries he himself had experienced during his first traumatic months on the street.

'Relax,' he replied softly. 'It'll come, I promise, but if you don't do anything else, just listen to the radio, OK?'

'I can't understand a fucking word they're saying. They might as well be speaking Flemish.'

'I know, but in time you'll get it. Soon you'll be able to pick your call sign out of hours of crap, trust me. Just listen, it'll come.'

Reassured by his young tutor's words, Jackson smiled thinly, silently thanking Pizza for his kindness, the only sample he had experienced as he underwent the unofficial rite of passage before he would be accepted as one of the group. Right now, as Pizza had endured before him, he was a non-person, ignored, humiliated and rejected until he could be tested and either found wanting and disposed of, or hopefully show his mettle and be accepted as one of the group.

# Chapter Six

Back in the report writing room at Handstead, the Brothers were busy meticulously logging all the personal effects they had removed from the bruised and battered Eddie Cheatle. He had been stripped naked, all his clothing tagged and bagged by the night duty divisional SOCO who was wishing he'd copped for the fatal on the motorway, which would be a lot simpler – couple of snaps and away. Cheatle now sat in a cell wearing a white paper suit, nursing his torn, bleeding wrists, screaming vengeance on the Brothers at the top of his voice. While the SOCO busied himself with the clothing and shoes, the Brothers got on with carefully recording everything else, including the gruesome, bloody Bowie hunting knife. They were working in silence at a desk when Jim suddenly said, 'Have a look at this, H.'

H looked up from his writing to see a small perforated strip of three small squares of what appeared to be blotting paper. He pulled a face.

'Fuck knows,' he replied, flipping the paper over with his biro to reveal three bright Mickey Mouse faces on the other side. 'Never seen anything like it.'

'I have,' said Jim. 'Turn on, tune in and drop out?'

'LSD?'

'Yeah, serious psychedelic shit. Love, peace and inner awareness or some such bollocks. Very big with the flower power arseholes.'

'And now it's turned up in Cheatle's pocket. Nice one. Where was it?'

'In a matchbox, stuck to the underside of the top.'

'Thought Cheatle was a heroin addict.'

'Sure he is, his arms are jabbed to fuck, but I guess he'll give anything a go. This stuff's a load cheaper as well – only about fifty pence a blot and gives them a serious trip apparently.'

'Must be fucking mental. Better let CID know, they'll need that for interview.'

'Already in my notes, big fella. How you getting on with the labels?'

'Getting there, Jim, getting there,' replied H wearily.

As the Brothers continued their labours into the small hours of the night shift, three miles away Sercan

Ozdemir, sitting alone in his darkened office, considered his latest significant career decision. He was working his way steadily through a large bottle of real imported Turkish raki as he pondered.

For almost a year he had kept his head down, waiting for DCI Harrison to make his move and lock him up. But he had not come for him yet. Ozdemir was beginning to feel bold and confident again, beginning to look around for another opportunity to go solo, but closer to home this time. After the disaster at the Tamworth gun shop, his contacts in Amsterdam and Burma had made themselves scarce. The opportunity to import high-quality heroin direct from the source in the Triangle was gone, but he recognised that illicit drugs remained the golden goose. He had turned his eyes west across the Atlantic to the United States and particularly to the West Coast around San Francisco where flower power, free love and routine manufacture and use of narcotics had continued to flourish beyond the 1960s. Cursory inquiries in the criminal fraternity soon identified Bob Lauren and his cult-like group, the Ministry for Spiritual Freedom, as the people to talk to. So, early in 1977, Ozdemir flew unaccompanied to San Francisco where he eventually met with Lauren and his people. The trip was not noted by any law enforcement agency on either side of the ocean and on his return to Handstead, Ozdemir had in place a guaranteed supply of what he needed – but only after he had made certain arrangements at home. Which was how two men, from completely opposite ends of the spectrum, fell into Ozdemir's clutches, apparently handing him what appeared to be the answers to all his prayers.

Rod Allan was an obnoxious, pompous old twat of a man responsible for managing the maintenance and upkeep of Handstead police station. Building Manager was the title most people would apply to the role, but Allan had reinvented the position and now had a large sign on his office door in the basement that described him as the Senior Building Operations Manager. He was a shameless self-publicist, and over the nine years he had been with the Force he had convinced the other building managers that he was the man to speak for them all. It hadn't taken too much persuasion. The truth was that most of the other bog washers couldn't give a fuck who said what to who, and by the time they realised that Allan was dealing and negotiating, making and breaking their careers, it was too late. The megalomaniac had gone so far as to create an association for the building managers which he had graciously agreed to run for life and thoughtfully named it the Association of Cleansing, Resupply and Procurement Practitioners. Someone had pointed out that ACRAPP was probably not the wisest acronym but, ever the stubborn mule, Allan had refused to show weakness to his members and change it.

ACRAPP met monthly at Handstead police station to discuss best practice and innovations in toilet cleansing and it was not unusual to hear tannoy messages such as, 'Rod Allan, there's ACRAPP in the front office for you,' as association members arrived. Allan was the toilet godfather. Membership of ACRAPP wasn't compulsory, but if you weren't a member you weren't part of the in crowd and wouldn't be kept up to date with sanitary ware upgrades and gratis cleaning products. The other building managers now found themselves dependent on their continued membership of Allan's club and had to show unswerving loyalty to the stool meister. So the meek and compliant members regularly presented themselves at Handstead for what were billed as meetings but were in fact little more than updates on the great man himself.

Allan also prided himself on being a bit of a ladies' man, regularly regaling the male members of his association with tales of his legendary sexual prowess with unfortunate female cleaners. They were regarded as mere chattels and he had a reputation with them as having a 'wandering hands' problem. His self-elevation to sexual god was all the more hilarious considering his physical appearance. He was in his early fifties, short and podgy, with thin, wispy, receding fair hair combed over from behind his left ear in a fashion Bobby Charlton would have approved of. Allan was a heavy drinker and his jowly face was permanently puce red with livid red streaks on both sides of his bulbous nose, but the thing that made most of his female victims shudder were his hands. He had long, almost feminine fingers, deathly white and cold as his poor circulation failed to cope with the journey, and manicured nails that were always buffed to a shine. As the dreadful Poisonous Pat, one of his band of psychotic cleaners, aptly put it, 'The old cunt's got hands like a fucking undertaker.' The truth behind Allan's claims to be a formidable shagger was that he was in fact as limp as cooked spaghetti. Impotent for the last decade because of his drinking, he hid behind his created image while his long-suffering wife had herself pumped up every Wednesday and Friday afternoon by her driving instructor. She'd been taking driving lessons for seven years and had failed nine tests but Allan still hadn't cottoned on. He regularly belittled her driving skills in company, while she would smile gamely and promise to keep taking her lessons and emptying her instructor's tanks.

To aid and abet his rise to power, Allan had enrolled the intellectually challenged Joe Aldrin, the building manager at neighbouring C Division, as his deputy. It was an inspired choice as Aldrin had the panache and imagination of a bedside table. An ingratiating, fat sycophant, he simply agreed with everything Allan said, acting as his chief whip and enforcer to deal with anyone who looked as if they were thinking about stepping out of line. He was a portly five foot eight, in his early thirties, with shoulder-length, lank blond hair that hung like a pair of cheap curtains over his face. His constantly open mouth gave him a look of permanent astonishment or, as many a Handstead cop had observed, as if Allan was doing him up the arse again without the aid of a lubricant. He had recently grown a small goatee beard to make himself more attractive to the cleaners he supervised and begun smoking small cigars to give himself an air of mystery, but they had been abandoned after Poisonous Pat had described the sight of him smoking as 'looking like Lassie curling one off'. It was the first time in his life that Aldrin had ever nearly been in charge of anything more difficult than a shopping trolley, and he revelled in what he saw as the reflected power and glory of the great man. Utterly loyal and devoted, he was unctuous in the extreme and Sergeant Collins, a bit of a classic film buff, had spotted a resemblance to the actor Peter Lorre. Aldrin was usually greeted by cops with the phrase, 'Stop it, master, you're hurting me,' and rolling their eyes about until they cried with laughter. Allan and Aldrin were a loathsome and quite dangerous pair, who terrorised the reluctant members of ACRAPP, running it like a fiefdom with the red-faced Allan on the throne, so to speak.

But Allan's Achilles heel was his impotence which had become quite an issue to him. Convinced it was something that just needed the right remedy, he had decided that prostitutes were the answer. Aldrin had been dispatched to make inquiries and one day returned to Allan's office with a stupid grin on his thick lips and his close-set eyes sparkling with joy. He had located a brothel in nearby Birchwood Avenue and hurried back to tell the great man.

'Took your time, didn't you?' snapped Allan irritably and unconsciously squeezing his lifeless cock under his desk. 'Where is it?'

'Birchwood Avenue, upstairs above the bookies.'

'How many girls they got working there?'

'Four when I was there, including a couple of right young ones,' he leered.

Allan was horrified. The thought of his idiot deputy being able to winch one up and poking one of his toms was awful.

'You better not have shagged them, Joe,' he warned. 'No way I'm following you in. They've got to be exclusive.'

Even Aldrin understood the word exclusive.

'Exclusive? But they're prostitutes, Rod. Fuck knows how many they get through in a day.'

'Did you shag any of them? No way am I catching any of your diseases.'

'No,' insisted Aldrin, sounding a little aggrieved but not wishing to make a scene. 'They were all busy but I saw the two young ones taking punters off when I was in the main room.'

'Fucking hope so, son, I fucking hope so for your sake. I'll ask when I get there, you know. Got the number for me? Good. Go on, you can fuck off now, I'm busy. Of course, none of this would be necessary if my bitch of a wife put out occasionally,' he lied.

After Aldrin had slithered out of his office and back under his stone, Allan busied himself preparing for a visit to the brothel which he was quite convinced would cure his limp dick.

The following day, as he walked briskly down the front steps of the nick at lunchtime, his purposeful progress was watched with interest by a man on a bench on the other side of the road. The man nodded to himself, stubbed out his cigarette and began to follow Allan on the adjacent pavement, mingling with the bustling lunchtime crowds. Allan was totally focused on his mission to put some lead in his pencil and noticed nothing. He'd phoned the previous afternoon from a phone box in Bolton Road East near the nick and made an appointment.

'I'm going to need a couple of girls,' he'd announced

to the bored grandmother who answered. 'And they'd better be clean.'

As if clean makes any difference to you, you sleazy old bastard, thought grandma, glancing at the wall clock to ensure she wasn't running late for her shift at another premises where she answered dirty phone calls and posted 'soiled' knickers to sad perverts with money to burn.

'Of course, sir, all our girls are regularly checked for hygiene and I can assure you they're all in perfect condition. What name shall I make the booking in?'

The question floored him. Flustered, he eventually blurted, 'Joe Aldrin, just put Joe Aldrin.'

'Very good, Mr Aldrin, two of our finest younger girls will be ready and waiting for you at one p.m. tomorrow. The charge will be twenty pounds, that's twenty pounds cash, I'm afraid. We don't accept personal cheques for obvious reasons, as I'm sure you'll understand.'

'Of course I understand,' snapped Allan, slamming the phone down and hurrying back to the nick, kneading at his crutch like a demented baker.

'Cassie,' yelled grandma into the corridor behind her as she made a note on her pad. An emaciated eighteen-year-old scaghead who looked at least twenty years older put her head round the door, a cigarette hanging from her pinched lips, her poorly applied mascara making her look like Alice Cooper's sister.

'What?' she asked, scratching her scrawny arse.

'You and Maxine up for a double header tomorrow lunchtime? Got a punter reckons he's up for it, sounded like a first-timer.'

'Put us down, Marge.'

'Make sure you've scrubbed up, darling, plenty of vaggie fresh. The sicko was insistent you're clean and likes them young, OK?'

'Schoolgirls it is then. Thanks, Marge,' said the junkie, disappearing back into the large flat to score another bag of gear from one of the two minders before she dealt with her sixth customer that day. She was injecting directly under her toenails to avoid the telltale tramlines along her arms but had recently scared off one punter with a toe fetish who had started to lick her filthy abscessed feet. Now she always wore knee-high boots which helped hide the ravages to her feet and calves. She and Maxine regularly performed double headers and this one promised to be no different.

The man following Allan was one of Ozdemir's goons. For the past eight months, Ozdemir had had teams watching Handstead nick, clocking the movements of pedestrians and vehicles in a desperate effort to find Brian Jones. He knew that the only way he was going to lay hands on him was to have a pair of eyes and ears inside the nick and he was determined to find a chink in

DCI Harrison's apparently impenetrable armour. His teams had followed off numerous unmarked and private vehicles and Ozdemir now had a comprehensive list of all CID cars, which could well prove useful in the future as they were rarely changed. Officers stationed at Handstead were more careful in their own vehicles, adopting counter-surveillance techniques to throw off unwelcome followers, but Ozdemir now knew where a uniformed sergeant and a senior traffic warden lived. Something for the future maybe, but absolutely no use to him in his current quest. All the foot follows away from the nick had proved fruitless – none of the nick's residents appeared to walk to work – and to date all the pedestrians tailed off had returned with bags of shopping. No doubt this one would be the same, sighed Mustapha Tungay. He glanced over at his colleague sitting nearby in an inconspicuous BMW, ready to go after any unknown vehicles. His mate briefly nodded as Tungay set off after Allan.

Twenty minutes later Tungay was in a phone box in Birchwood Avenue, sweat pouring off him in the greenhouse-like interior that also appeared to double as a public urinal. Wrinkling his nose against the acrid stench, Tungay pushed a 10p piece into the box with shaking, sweaty fingers, dialled and waited. A minute later, Ozdemir got abruptly to his feet behind his desk and smiled broadly as he listened.

'Who is he?' he eventually asked.

'Called himself Joe Aldrin when he made the appointment. Marge says she called to him by that name when he arrived but he looked puzzled for a moment – obviously not his real name.'

'He ever been there before?'

'They've never seen him before.'

'I need to know who he is. Is he still there?'

'Yes, he's with Cassie and Maxine for another twenty minutes.'

'You've done well, Mustapha. Dip him, find out who he is and get back to me,' commanded Ozdemir, dropping the phone back on to its cradle and slumping back into his leather chair. He leant back as far as the chair would allow and smiled up at the ceiling. He had hit pay dirt – someone who worked at Handstead police station was getting it on with two of his toms in one of the crime family's brothels and he now had a foot in Harrison's front door. Whoever the punter was, he was going to be Ozdemir's way in. Brian Jones was getting closer by the minute.

# Chapter Seven

June 1976

While Ozdemir had fretted about how to find Brian Jones, DCI Harrison had been just as keen to lay his hands on Baker and Travers, the gormless leaders of the Park Royal mafia. Blissfully unaware that they were now making their way through the intestines of a herd of wild boar, he had led raids first on their flats on the estate, and then on all family members and known associates' addresses. It was classic method index stuff – round up all the usual suspects and nine times out of ten you came up with the goodies. But not this time. Accompanied by Unit Three of the Patrol Group, Harrison had rampaged across the Park Royal estate and then the town, but had not got a sniff of the missing pair. First stop had been their flat where the front door had been taken off its hinges without much ceremony. Needless to say, the flat was empty but did reveal plenty of evidence confirming their involvement in the ill-fated raid on the gun shop, but nothing as to their current whereabouts. Next stop was the home address of Travers' parents. Once their front door lay in several pieces in the hallway, Harrison had run upstairs while the Patrol Group boys secured and searched downstairs. He burst into a bedroom where he encountered an irate Mr and Mrs Travers, themselves career criminals with records to be proud of in Handstead. As expected, they denied all knowledge of their son's whereabouts.

'You're both nicked anyway,' announced Harrison. 'Get some fucking clothes on.'

'Nicked, what the fuck for?' screamed Mrs Travers.

'I'll think of something, don't you worry,' said Harrison, discreetly dropping one of the shotgun cartridges he had recovered from their son's flat on to the floor alongside the bed. 'What's that then?' He pointed to the floor.

'What's what?'

'Down here by the bed.'

'What the fuck are you on about?' yelled Mr Travers, rolling out of bed in his grubby Y-fronts to see what Harrison was pointing at.

'Looks like a shotgun cartridge to me,' said Harrison

breezily. 'You got a licence to hold ammo?'

'You cunt,' screamed Mrs Travers, still in bed. 'You fucking planted that, we know fuck all about any shotgun ammo.'

'Of course you don't, but you're both nicked. Get some clothes on.'

Accepting that the occasional fitting up came with the territory, but still deeply unhappy that it was their turn, Mr and Mrs Travers began to dress themselves slowly, cursing Harrison to the heavens. He leant happily against the door frame waiting for them, having made a great show of recovering the planted shotgun cartridge and placing it in an evidence bag.

'Still getting down the gym then, Alistair?' he inquired conversationally, eyeing Mr Travers' enormous gut hanging over the front of his trousers.

'When I can, when bastards like you aren't giving me a hard time.'

'That'll be the gym with the chocolate machine, will it?'

'Fuck off, you bastard,' roared Travers as he registered the barb.

Harrison was nearly flattened as the door behind him burst open and the four Patrol Group officers who had been downstairs careered in and slammed the door behind them. They stood red-faced and panting, staring at Harrison and Mr and Mrs Travers.

'What the fuck is going on? Why aren't you downstairs?' asked Harrison eventually.

'Sorry, guv,' one of them replied. 'Fucking huge dog downstairs, chased us up here.'

The Traverses exploded in mocking laughter.

'You wankers,' roared Mrs Travers. 'Adolf too much for you, was he?'

'Adolf?' queried Harrison, looking at the officers.

'An enormous Dobermann, guv, size of a fucking horse,' panted the Patrol Group officer.

As proof of what they had encountered, the bedroom door was hit by what sounded like an enraged tiger which then began to attempt to dig its way through the wooden panels. The frenzied clawing was accompanied by blood-curdling snarling and further attempts to take the door off its hinges.

'Go on, Adolf, do the bastards,' encouraged Mr Travers loudly as he sat on the bed pulling on his trainers.

'Fucking hell,' exclaimed Harrison, very gingerly opening the door a crack to peer outside. He was met by a pair of manic, bloodshot eyes set on a collection of teeth the size of a bear trap.

'Fucking hell,' he repeated more loudly, slamming the door shut and keeping his own weight against it.

'What you going to do now, you bent bastard?' laughed Mrs Travers, tucking what looked like empty leather tobacco pouches into her grubby vest.

Grimacing at the sight of her breasts, Harrison quickly weighed up his options which were, at best, limited.

'We need a dog handler here,' he finally announced.

'Alfie's on duty,' announced one of the Patrol Group. 'Get him over to kill that thing?'

It was significant that whenever Ooh Yah booked Delta One on, other listening officers immediately clocked the fact that Alfie was out and about. Not his handler and Alfie, just Alfie, he was that well regarded. Young was seen as merely an extension of his fearsome dog, a bit of a makeweight.

'No, we can't do that, but the handlers know how to deal with mad dogs, don't they? They've got those lasso things to take them out. Who's got a radio with them?'

One of the Patrol Group guys pulled a hand-held Channel 1 VHF set out of his pocket and handed it to Harrison. He switched it on and immediately got heavy radio traffic as the triple shooting at Tamworth still dominated events. As soon as there was a lull, Harrison dived in.

'Delta Hotel, this is Bravo Hotel Alpha Three, active message,' he transmitted. As usual, the active message tag cleared everything away.

'Go with your message, sir,' said the main Force control room operator, recognising the call sign of the Handstead DCI.

'I'm at nineteen Broadwater Gardens on the Park

Royal estate and I need the assistance of a dog handler to remove a dangerous dog from the property. This is connected with the Tamworth incident and is very urgent.'

Before the operator could acknowledge his message, Bob Young in Delta One was transmitting.

'Delta Hotel from Delta One, I'm five minutes away, show me en route please.' In the background, quite clearly, could be heard the sound of Alfie going berserk as the twos and blues went on.

'Thank you, Delta One. Hotel Alpha Three, you've got Delta One on his way, ETA is five minutes. Do you need anything else at your location?' asked the control room operator.

'Negative, thank you, Delta Hotel – your air now, Hotel Alpha Three out,' replied Harrison, switching off and turning to smile at the Traverses who were no longer looking so pleased with themselves. 'We'll be on our way soon enough. You two better get finished.'

Young was on scene within a couple of minutes and ran into the downstairs hallway. The noise inside the house, clearly audible outside, gave him a rough idea of what to expect. He cautiously climbed the threadbare stairs armed with his dog-catching kit, but he had a change of heart when he clapped eyes on the berserk Dobermann. It was huge, the largest he had ever seen.

'Fucking hell,' he muttered, retreating a couple of steps to think this through. He was going to struggle to get this bastard down himself. He could bring Alfie in to bite its head off but last time he'd pulled that stunt he'd ended up writing reports for two months. He decided it would take two handlers to take this brute on and returned to Delta One. He got on air and had talk-through with his mate Jack Gall in Delta Six in the north of the county, told him what he had and called him down to Handstead.

Even with all his music playing, Gall would be at least another fifteen minutes. Young accepted reluctantly that he would have to at least get his rope on the raging Dobermann and keep it subdued until Gall arrived to help him remove it. He returned to the foot of the stairs and bellowed towards the bedroom where Harrison and the Patrol Group officers remained marooned.

'Guv, you all right in there?'

'Are we fuck all right, it's nearly through the door. Get the fucking thing tied up or something, will you,' shouted Harrison, barely audible above the commotion in the hallway.

'Fucking brilliant, why didn't I think of that? Of course, do something, that's why he's a DCI,' muttered Young bitterly.

Suddenly things went quiet. Young looked up to the landing.

'Oh fuck,' he said as the glistening, muscle-rippling, drooling Dobermann eyed him and bared its huge teeth. The beast then launched itself at Young from the top of the stairs. More in panicked reaction than as the result of any training, Young held his dog-restraining kit out in front of himself, loop open, his face frozen in terror and a scream forming in his throat. The Dobermann's huge head popped neatly through the loop and as its momentum carried it past Young, the loop tightened round its bulging neck. The animal landed with an enormous crash on the bare lino floor and for a split second lay stunned. It was the opportunity Young needed. Recovering his composure quickly, he grabbed the aluminium pole and pulled the noose tight.

'One hundred and eighty,' chanted Young happily. But then things went pear-shaped.

The Dobermann quickly recovered from its fall, saw its intended prey again and went for it in a flurry of gnashing teeth and scrabbling claws. Young was soon fighting for his life as the dog leapt madly in the noose, trying to get at Young who resembled a demented fly fisherman trying to land a very big fish. Harrison and the Patrol Group officers remained where they were, leaving Young to get on with it. His shouts for help were drowned out by the raging monster and the sound of ornaments and pictures crashing off the walls and mantelpiece as Young was forced down the hallway and into the living room. It was all Young could do to hang on to the pole. He was still fighting like this when Jack Gall arrived in the hallway.

'Whoah. Fucking hell, Ooh Yah,' called Gall cheerfully from the door to the living room. 'Need a hand?'

'What's it fucking look like?' screamed the exhausted Young, his face bright red from the strain, sweat pouring down his face and his specs steaming up badly. 'Get your kit and get it over this fucker's head, quickly.'

Gall hurried away and was back in a minute. Cautiously he approached the struggle, his loop opened wide, and as he got near to the Dobermann he slipped the loop over its head and pulled the rope tight. The animal's eyes bulged and its tongue fell out of the side of its mouth, but it continued to leap about, desperate to kill either one of them, or preferably both. Young and Gall were both now thrashing about like novice anglers and the dog was leaping above shoulder height when it suddenly made an awful grating noise deep in its throat, its eyes rolled over in their sockets and its enormous tongue fell limply to one side. It crashed to the living-room floor at the end of the two ropes and lay still. Panting, Young and Gall approached it slowly and pushed it gingerly with their feet. It didn't move.

'Fucking hell, Ooh Yah, you've killed it,' announced Gall.

'What d'you mean, I've killed it? You were here as well.'

'Could have had a heart attack, I suppose.'

'Bollocks, we've strangled the fucking thing. How the fuck are we going to square this one up?'

'Fucking hell, I'm off,' said Gall, stooping to release his rope with some difficulty.

'You're a fucking mate,' called Young as Gall bid him farewell and buggered off as quickly as he could.

Young polished his glasses and had another look at the dead Dobermann and then walked upstairs to the bedroom where Harrison and his team remained barricaded.

'You can come out now, guv,' he called.

'All clear?' asked Harrison, opening the door an inch and peering out.

'Yeah. I need a word, though, guv,' replied Young.

'You four keep an eye on these two,' said Harrison as he shut the bedroom door behind him and joined Young on the landing.

'Where's the dog?' he asked, looking nervously around him and down the stairs.

'Down here,' replied Young, leading the way down to the living room.

'Oh fuck, what happened?' asked Harrison as he clapped eyes on the obviously strangled Dobermann.

'We strangled it by accident. What the fuck are we going to do?'

'Strangled it by accident?' repeated the incredulous Harrison, staring closely at the throttled animal

'Bloody thing was going berserk, boss,' apologised Young. 'It was bouncing about like a mad bastard.'

'Yeah, it was a handful all right,' agreed the DCI, stepping back and stroking his chin thoughtfully as he sought a way out of the mess. 'Got it,' he finally exclaimed triumphantly. 'It escaped, got out of the house and had an accident. Get it out into the road quickly and run over it, make it look good.'

'Run it over? In the van?'

'Yeah, run it over. Got any better ideas?'

'No, suppose not. I'll run it over then. Give us a hand, will you?'

'Will I fuck. I'm going back upstairs to tell the Traverses that not so little Adolf has gone to the big mad dogs' pearly gates. Come on, get a move on, you haven't got much time.'

Shaking his head bitterly, Young freed his rope from the animal's neck and then quickly dragged the corpse across the living-room floor, down the hallway and out on to the front step. As luck would have it, most of the neighbours had gone back to bed after the initial chaos of the early-morning visit – it was a routine event on the Park Royal estate – and Young was able to haul the dog down the garden path and out on to the deserted road. Hoping against hope that there might be some early-morning traffic around to do the deed for him, he looked up and down the street but was disappointed. Sighing deeply, he retrieved his kit from the house, loaded it up and got back into Delta One. Alfie was strangely quiet in his cage in the back, but in his rear-view mirror Young could see his partner watching him intently. Ahead of them in the road lay Adolf.

'Sorry, Alfie, it was an accident,' said Young apologetically. 'We didn't mean to kill him.'

Alfie growled by way of reply and began moving restlessly in his cramped cage.

'Let's get this over with, big man, and I'll get you out for a run,' continued Young, switching on and revving the engine. He put Delta One into gear and quickly powered the van towards Adolf, aiming his nearside wheels for the dog's head. The van jumped slightly and there was a sickening crunch as Adolf disappeared under the van before reappearing in a crumpled heap at the side of the road. Young looked guiltily in his side mirrors; in death Adolf appeared to have been reduced in size by half. Alfie was staring at him again.

'It was a fucking accident,' shouted Young, heading Delta One towards one of Alfie's favourite exercise spots.

\*

Back at the house, Harrison bowled back into the bedroom where Mr and Mrs Travers were arguing furiously with the Patrol Group officers.

'Bad news, I'm afraid,' he announced.

'What?' grumbled Mrs Travers.

'The dog escaped.'

'I'll bet one of you bastards let him out,' she answered. 'He'll be back soon enough, he always comes back.'

'Hmm, there's another problem,' said Harrison.

'What's that then, bitten one of you arseholes, has he?'

'No, he's had an accident.'

'What sort of accident?'

'He was hit by a car, hit and run. He's dead, I'm afraid.'

The news stunned the Traverses who stood open-mouthed, staring at Harrison. Then Mrs Travers began to sob and wail at the top of her voice.

'Adolf, no, not Adolf, not Adolf.'

The Patrol Group officers, who until very recently had been threatening to punch her lights out, looked at their feet and shuffled about awkwardly. Then Mr Travers joined his wife in an outpouring of uncontainable grief. All their fight was gone and they were now like pliable putty in Harrison's hands.

'Come on,' he said gently. 'Let's get you down to the

nick and get it over with. At least on the plus side you don't have to worry about Adolf being destroyed because a court considers him dangerous and a menace to the community. See it as him going out on a high, doing what he liked best, being fucking unpleasant.'

They seemed to agree with him and got meekly to their feet before being led out of the house and put into the back of separate unmarked CID cars. As they pulled away, Mrs Travers caught sight of the mangled Adolf by the side of the road and the street echoed to her anguished screams.

'Oh Adolf, no, oh Adolf.'

Had Mr and Mrs Travers but known it, the scale of their loss over the last twenty-four hours was, of course, much worse. Their devil child, Andy, a once feared hard man and leader of the Park Royal mafia, was dead as well, and at that precise moment parts of him were being squeezed with a great deal of effort and noise out of the rear end of a very contented Russian wild boar.

# Chapter Eight

Inspector Hilary Bott was feeling very pleased with herself. Desperate to endear herself to her boss, the enormous and misogynist Chief Inspector Pete Stephenson, she had spent considerable time and effort looking for an initiative that would improve both the service the station provided to the simmering hordes of Handstead and the image of the officers stationed there. In his own mind, Stephenson had already decided on the best solution: they couldn't really shoot enough of the inhabitants, especially members of the Park Royal mafia, but the survivors of the cull could perhaps be used in place of unfortunate rabbits and beagles currently languishing in vivisection laboratories around the country. He kept such thoughts to himself, though, allowing the stammering Inspector Bott to ponder on the way forward. To date, every one of the fourteen plans she'd presented to him had been filed in the wastepaper basket by his desk. This time, though, she'd come up with a real humdinger.

She knocked timidly on his closed office door as she'd been very clearly instructed and waited for his summons. After five minutes of repeated knocking she eventually heard him bellow, 'Yes,' and popped her head round the door. As her pasty face and home haircut hove into view, Stephenson groaned loudly and rolled his eyes.

'Hilary, what do you want now?' he asked impatiently.

She was always apprehensive about entering his office since he had warned her that he was a prolific wanker and needed to relieve himself regularly throughout the day. As always, she glanced down to the floor to ensure that his trousers weren't round his ankles.

'Got a minute, sir?' she asked, relieved to see that she had apparently called either pre- or post-wank.

'For what? I'm due one pretty soon,' lied Stephenson who was well aware that his fictional habit had her as twitchy as a Korean dog owner.

'I've been looking at the crime figures for the last six months,' she stuttered, coming into the office but leaving the door open in case he suddenly decided to pull himself to shore. 'There's definitely a pattern emerging.'

'Enlighten me,' said Stephenson, opening and closing the drawers on either side of the desk for the items he needed to get rid of her.

'Well, there's a clear link to alcohol. All our serious assaults and robberies are committed either at or within half a mile of eleven licensed premises. We need to target those pubs and clubs.'

'How, why?'

Her stammer got worse as she was put under scrutiny. 'If we direct our resources at the top five pubs and clubs I've identified, I think we'll dramatically reduce crime and reassure our community.'

'Reassure the community? Are you serious, Hilary? The scumbags are robbing and battering each other, they're doing us all a big favour. The shame is they're not killing each other more often. Filling the fridges at the morgue might reassure the rest of us.'

She pressed on, ignoring the clearly homicidal tendencies of her Chief Inspector, and promised herself that she would bring his views to the attention of her mentor, Chief Constable Daniells. Unknown to her, that would prove to be a waste of time; events of the last twelve months had persuaded Daniells that Handstead was the ideal place to locate an army live firing range.

'I've drawn up some proposals and tactics,' she said, handing a manila file to Stephenson who began to leaf disinterestedly through it. He was about to stop and drop the entire file into his bin when his eyes alighted on tactic number seven in her cunning plan. His mouth dropped open and he read it twice. Then he looked up at Bott.

'Are you fucking mad?' he asked slowly.

'Why do you ask?'

Stephenson began to read out loud to her. '"Officers will distribute lollipops and chocolate bars to people leaving licensed premises as evidence suggests this has a calming effect on people." We're going to give them sweeties? Laced with arsenic, I hope you mean.'

'Well, no, of course not laced with arsenic.'

'You propose to get my officers to give the pissed-up, off their faces on drugs and glue scumbags and shitheads lollipops and chocolate because it'll send them home in a good mood?'

'A study in the United States showed a connection between this sort of initiative and a reduction in alcohol-related crime.'

'Have you completely taken leave of your senses?' shouted Stephenson, his red face becoming a deeper hue. 'What these fuckers know and understand is a crack round the chops with a heavy stick. Give them a lollipop and they're likely to try and stick it up your arse.'

Stephenson had found what he had been looking for

in his desk drawers and placed a box of tissues on the desk top.

'This is very controversial, Hilary,' he continued. 'All a little too New Age, don't you think?'

'Well, I don't think so,' she began hesitantly before stopping as she saw Stephenson start to snap on a pair of bright yellow washing-up gloves.

'Oh my God, what are you doing?' she gasped.

'Go on, go on, you were saying?' replied Stephenson, cracking his large walnut-sized knuckles loudly.

'Got to go, can't stop,' shrieked Bott, fleeing from Stephenson's office and back to her own, which she locked securely.

Chuckling to himself, Stephenson got to his feet and kicked the door shut, peeled the gloves off and threw them and the box of tissues back into a drawer. He glanced again at Bott's file before he snapped it shut and dropped it into the bin.

'The woman's fucking mental,' he muttered to himself before he picked up the phone and dialled his contact in the Personnel Department to see if any chief inspector vacancies had come up elsewhere in the county.

That phone call, like the dozens of others he had made over the last eight months, proved fruitless. There was no way he was just going to be allowed to walk out of Handstead because he'd served his time and proved his worth. Handstead was, and would continue to be, a punishment posting at every rank, and the best Stephenson could hope for was that a uniform chief inspector somewhere else in the county got themselves into some serious shit.

Sighing deeply, he glanced around his office, which despite all his efforts was still deeply impersonal. The desk was battered and scarred, having served time all round the county, his chair was threadbare and on the verge of collapse, and the bookcase in the far corner was missing a shelf. He'd put up a few of his course photographs and replaced the ubiquitous Police Federation calendar with his own Aberdeen Football Club one, but even the framed photograph of his wife and son on his desk failed to eradicate the impression that he only ever planned to camp there temporarily. As soon as his turn in the barrel was over, he was gone.

His deliberations were interrupted by a loud knock on the door, followed by DCI Harrison sticking his head into the office.

'All right, Pete?' he asked, smiling broadly. 'You been upsetting Colonel Klebb?'

'Why, what's she said?'

'Nothing, but she's barricaded herself in her office again. What have you said this time?'

'Just the usual, Dan – let her think I was about to bash one off. The bloody woman's driving me potty.

She's come up with a plan to give the drunken scrotes sweets and chocolates to send them home happy. She's fucking deranged, I swear it.'

'Laced with rat poison, I hope?'

'I suggested the same, but no such luck. Fancy a snifter?'

'Yeah, go on,' replied Harrison, shutting the door and slumping down into the dilapidated armchair in front of the desk. Stephenson opened his large bottom drawer and placed a bottle of Laphroaig and two crystal tumblers on the desk. Harrison was a Bushmills man himself but appreciated a good single malt and had been overjoyed to discover that Stephenson took his drinking as seriously as he did, insisting on cut-glass crystal tumblers. Stephenson poured them both a large one and the two men sat in silence as they sniffed and sipped at their drinks.

'Ever see this stuff before?' Harrison eventually asked, tossing a small clear plastic envelope on to Stephenson's desk.

He picked it up and peered closely at the small squares of paper with the pictures of Mickey Mouse.

'LSD?' he asked, holding the envelope up to the light.

'Bang on. Third lot we've turned up this month.'

'Where'd it come from?'

'The arsehole that topped the Chinese woman and

her kid had it on him. Your guys found it hidden in a matchbox.'

'Interesting. Third recovery this month?'

'Yeah. I've got a horrible feeling this is just the start. Fuck knows where it's coming from. It's so bloody cheap, the junkies are dropping their heroin and coke habits for this instead. It's only about fifty pence a tab and the high they get is something else apparently.'

'Anything I can do to help?'

'Ask the uniforms to bear it in mind when they search people – these blotters are so easy to hide.'

'Yeah, no worries. Let me know if there's anything else you need. Want another?' Stephenson asked, indicating Harrison's empty glass.

'Nah, that'll do me, Pete,' replied Harrison, getting to his feet. 'Just get your guys switched on to what's about to rear its ugly head around here. If I get any more information, I'll let you know, OK?'

After Harrison had left his office, Pete Stephenson sat back in his chair, folded his arms and stared at the ceiling as he contemplated his future at Handstead. So much of the future was in the hands of DCI Dan Harrison, he mused. The reality of life at Handstead was that it was a force in its own right, left very much to its own devices by both Division and Force Headquarters. B Division's ineffectual Chief Superintendent Phillip

'The Fist' Findlay owed his rank to the Freemasons and rarely ventured into the Handstead war zone, preferring to police it by memo, bombarding Harrison and Stephenson with all manner of instructions and initiatives which they largely ignored. There was no complaint from Findlay; if it ever came to it, he could produce reams of paper to prove that all his good work had been stymied by the two hooligans at Handstead. Chief Constable Daniells took more interest in the town, fearing that media interest in its unique problems could prove troublesome. His early plans to move Inspector Hilary Bott there to support Stephenson's perma-tanned predecessor Pat Gillard had proved disastrous, as had the promotion in the field of his staff officer, Kevin Curtis. Both had suffered nervous breakdowns at the hands of the uniform officers. Bott had only recently gone back to work with a stammer and Curtis was currently receiving gentle therapy at the convalescent home and tuition in basket weaving. Grudgingly, Chief Daniells had accepted that the current DCI and uniform Chief Inspector were probably just what the town needed.

He was right. Harrison had taken an immediate shine to Stephenson, who had a similar outlook on effective policing styles. Neither had any time for public meetings or consultations, seeing themselves as the people who knew what the problems were and had the answers – and they were getting results. Street robberies and domestic burglaries were down sixty per cent over the year as a direct consequence of targeting six local scumbags in an intense operation, at the end of which they had been soundly fitted up and taken out of circulation for six months. Anyone who believed that the ends never justified the means would have met vociferous condemnation as an open-toed sandal-wearing pinko leftie bed-wetter from the majority of Handstead residents who had endured years of hell from just six criminals. Capital punishment could have been quietly introduced in Horse's Arse and the world would have been none the wiser. The ends always justified the means there. Chief Daniells knew it and preferred to look the other way most of the time. Harrison and Stephenson were the perfect partners. One a scheming and streetwise career detective, the other a fearless, focused and driven arse-kicker. Between them they had the young scumbags of Handstead on the back foot, but Sercan Ozdemir was a different proposition and would require careful handling.

Stephenson leant forward on to his desk and reread the memo in front of him. It was from the loathed Superintendent Grainger at Complaints and Discipline, detailing yet another complaint against Psycho and announcing Grainger's intention to visit Handstead once Psycho was back on a day shift, to serve him with another Regulation 9 Discipline notice. Psycho could wallpaper his squalid flat with the notices he had received over the years – most of them served on him by Grainger.

Grainger had been beside himself when the complaint had arrived in his office, quickly summoning his sidekick, the effeminate confirmed bachelor Detective Inspector Paul Chislehurst. Grainger was still suffering sleepless nights from his last humiliating encounter with Psycho when he had claimed to be a persecuted homosexual Christian and goaded him into a homophobic outburst that had totally alienated Chislehurst. That particular complaint investigation had withered on the vine, leaving Grainger grinding his teeth in frustration as Psycho escaped his clutches yet again. But he knew that Psycho never behaved himself for long and it would only be a matter of time before he would get another chance to rid the Force of the mad monster. And so it proved.

'He's fucking back in our sights, Paul,' Grainger had yelled, spittle spraying from his mouth, eyes bulging oddly as Chislehurst wandered into his office.

'Who?'

'That mad bastard Pearce.'

Chislehurst stared suspiciously at his boss whom he loathed for numerous reasons, not least because of his rabid homophobia, but mostly because he was the chief lizard and cocksucker and not him. Chislehurst felt badly let down by his uncle, the Deputy Chief Constable, who had failed miserably to further his nephew's career by moving Grainger out after his repeated failures to bag Psycho. What Uncle Chislehurst could not know was that Chief Daniells had no intention of moving either of them out of Complaints and Discipline, preferring to keep them where they could be the least trouble to operational street cops who regularly ran rings round them and their hopeless investigations.

'What's he done now?' asked Chislehurst, who still harboured hopes that the beast might really be that way inclined and might be persuaded to slip him a crippler one day.

'Only fucking indecently assaulted an old age pensioner,' laughed Grainger hysterically, throwing him a thin manila folder.

Chislehurst pulled out a witness statement and began to read.

On the face of it, Psycho was indeed in deep shit again, as the 78-year-old widow, Mrs Agnes Myers, with her sore arse was prepared to testify. Agnes was not one of Psycho's lonely hearts conquests. She had been wandering aimlessly around a discount supermarket on the edge of town, comparing the price of cat food and keeping out of the rain, when Psycho had walked in, off duty, to pick up some cheap booze. He had brushed past the lonely Agnes who glanced up at the large man with the brutal, unshaven face highlighted by a large port wine stain, and saw the opportunity for a chat.

'Young man,' she called, tugging at Psycho's coat sleeve. 'Would you mind getting something for me?'

Psycho turned to look at the tiny coffin dodger with her wispy blue-rinsed hair, make-up a couple of inches thick and teeth that resembled small pieces of corn on the cob.

'Yeah, of course, dear. What do you need?' he replied pleasantly.

'I can't reach those boxes on the top shelf,' she said, pointing a gnarled, liver-spotted old hand towards the top shelf of the display they were standing next to. Psycho looked up and frowned.

'You sure? Pork scratchings?'

'Oh dear, is that what they are? My eyes aren't what they used to be.'

Psycho smiled and shook his head sadly before he walked on in search of cheap Scotch. But his encounter with Agnes was not yet over. She collared him in a further three aisles, with dubious requests for out-of-reach items. These requests were all dealt with politely, but by the time she tugged at his sleeve a fourth time in the bread aisle, he had had enough. He couldn't find the booze anywhere.

'Young man,' she'd whined loudly, 'would you mind helping me get one of those loaves off the top shelf. I'm afraid I can't reach.'

'My pleasure, grandma,' snapped Psycho.

He reached down to the beaming and adoring Agnes, took hold of her scrawny, bony waist, gripped her garish, green polyester dress, and inadvertently her huge cotton knickers. Lifting her into the air by her knickers, Psycho gave Agnes a huge wedgie as her knickers disappeared up her ancient baggy arse, causing her to gasp out loud. With one swift movement, Psycho deposited Agnes on the top shelf amongst the bags of bread, scrabbling desperately at her nether regions as she tried to extract her underwear from somewhere near her lower colon and screeching loudly. A crowd soon gathered to watch the circus spectacle of an elderly woman on the top shelf of a supermarket display trying to rip her knickers off. Psycho quickly disappeared and left the shop, but not before he'd been seen and recognised by the manager.

The shop tannoy called the store maintenance man to the bread aisle with a ladder. The manager watched as the mocking crowd, typically of Handstead residents, encouraged Agnes to jump before booing loudly as she theatrically sniffed her fingers, having successfully removed her underwear from her throbbing crack. She was brought down and taken to the manager's office to recover and explain her ascent to the top shelf, during which Psycho's role was fully established. Agnes was given a lift home to her sheltered housing project where the resident care worker later took her to Handstead nick to register her complaint against Psycho.

Having digested the contents of Grainger's rambling memo, Stephenson picked up his desk phone and dialled the front office to check when Psycho's group would next be working a day or late shift. He immediately regretted doing so as the call was diverted to the main switchboard where it was answered by the new station telephonist, Roy Hastings.

Until recently, switchboard duties had fallen to the front office PCs or the station sergeant, but for the last month the nick had had a dedicated civilian switchboard operator. However, fifty-year-old Roy Hastings was not fitting in. He was severely disabled and wore callipers on both legs, using two aluminium sticks to hobble slowly about, which the cops at Horse's Arse in their usual unsympathetic style had seized on as an opportunity to rip the piss out of him. It was generally light-hearted, typical cop piss-taking, but unfortunately Hastings was a humourless, embittered and belligerent individual who bridled at every joke and in his first month had made five complaints against officers. Needless to say, Psycho had been one of the officers reprimanded and he now loathed Hastings. Hastings' other unpleasant characteristic was his appalling body odour. Psycho's take on that was that it was probably a good thing as blind people could hate him as well. Psycho blamed Hastings for the demise of his relationship with Superintendent Grainger's PA, Dawn Masters, as Hastings had refused to pass on any of the numerous messages she had left for him.

'I'm not your bloody secretary,' he had snapped when Psycho had confronted him about a message he knew Dawn had left.

Thereafter, Psycho had conducted full-on guerrilla operations against him, removing the rubber bung from the end of one of his sticks, causing him to go arse over tit on the lino corridor, and hiding his invalid carriage behind the station car park.

'Ah, Mr Stephenson, I was just about to ring you,' began Hastings.

'Oh God, what is it now, Roy?' groaned Stephenson, throwing his head back in despair.

'They've stolen my bloody sticks again.'

'I'll be right down,' said Stephenson, slamming the phone down and striding out of his office. He trotted downstairs to the main ground-floor corridor where he was horrified to find Hastings pulling himself along the floor on his belly like an alligator as he went in search of his sticks. Worse, he was in full view of the throng in the front office who were watching enthralled as a desperate cripple apparently tried to make good his escape from the nick.

'Jesus Christ, Roy,' bellowed Stephenson, before hauling him up by his sweaty armpits and manhandling him back to his humming switchboard room and dumping him into his equally unfragrant chair. The mob in the front office began to complain loudly to the front-office PC about the assault they had just witnessed on an escaping crippled prisoner.

Stephenson glared down at the perspiring Hastings.

'Stay there, Roy. I'll find the bloody things,' he said before he stormed back out into the front office, wincing as he sniffed at his damp hands.

His first stop was the male officers' toilets where he scrubbed furiously at his hands to remove all traces of pungent Roy and where he noticed the missing sticks propped up in one of the cubicles.

As Stephenson returned the missing sticks to the biggest pain in the arse currently working at the nick after Inspector Hilary Bott, the second fly ended up in Sercan Ozdemir's web.

Guy Mitcheson was a thirty-year-old chemistry graduate from a titled family in the Midlands, with a serious cannabis habit that had precluded him from holding down a job for any period of time since he had graduated from Cambridge with a 2:1 degree. He spent most of his waking hours happily stoned as he experimented with every available type of weed and kept the wolves from his door by dealing what he couldn't smoke himself from his dilapidated, inherited farmhouse just outside Handstead. He lived far enough out of town never to have come into the frame as a dealer, and to date none of his clients had ever felt inclined to give him up to the Old Bill because his stuff was usually top drawer. He was the classic, long-haired, usually unwashed but educated drop-out who if he had only used his innate intelligence and expensive education could have done any job that took his fancy. But he was bone idle, lived alone in abject squalor and in more lucid moments dreamt of becoming a major player in the illegal drugs market. Which is exactly what Sercan Ozdemir came to offer him.

Mitcheson had been frequenting the brothel in Birchwood Avenue for months, popping in to pump up a particular favourite tom whenever he was in town to deal dope. As they lay in their filthy bed sharing one of his superb joints, Mitcheson had given her his full life history, including his current dope-dealing operation and his hopes to move on to something bigger and better by utilising his chemistry degree. The tom, aware that her boss had instructed that all clients were to be dipped and their lives minutely examined, passed this information on and it eventually arrived on Ozdemir's desk. Mitcheson was just what he was looking for and he arranged to have words with him next time he popped into the brothel.

Ozdemir's day just seemed to get better and better. No sooner had he replaced his phone than Mustapha Tungay arrived in his office with a huge grin on his dark, swarthy face, his teeth flashing like halogen headlamps.

'Great news, boss,' he babbled. 'That punter called Joe Aldrin isn't Joe Aldrin.'

'And?' pressed Ozdemir.

'His name's Rod Allan, life President of the Association of Cleansing, Resupply and Procurement Practitioners at Handstead nick.'

'The building manager,' said Ozdemir, getting to his feet in a rare display of emotion. He's the fucking building manager. How did you find out who he was?'

'We had him dipped like you said. He had a driving licence in that name and some business cards with the police station address on them. He's definitely Rod Allan and he works at the nick.'

'With pretty much free access around the nick, I would imagine,' mused Ozdemir. 'I think we've found the key to the lock, Mustapha. I reckon we're in. Is he a regular with the girls? When's he due back?'

'Got an appointment tomorrow lunchtime, two girls, booked in as Joe Aldrin again.'

'Excellent. This time I want him filmed, OK? Put him and his girls into the special room and I want it recorded from start to finish, understood?'

Mustapha nodded.

'I'll get over there after he's arrived and see him once he's done. You don't let him leave or I'll have your hands off, OK?'

Mustapha nodded again and replied, 'It could be ages, boss, he's as limp as a lettuce leaf, just spends his time pulling at himself while the girls entertain themselves.'

'You tell them to get him on the bed with them and give him the works. I don't give a fuck if he never gets a hard-on, but I do want to see the girls giving him the business, OK?'

'Will be done, boss. He's due in at one fifteen tomorrow.'

'I'll be there, Mustapha. Go and tell the girls what I want done, and I want it done properly. Any fuck-ups and I swear I'll be chopping heads off.'

Ozdemir's face was set like stone and Tungay was in no doubt that his boss was deadly serious. Like the other goons in his employ, Tungay knew of Ozdemir's desperate quest to get eyes and ears and preferably some sticky fingers into Handstead nick as he sought the whereabouts of Brian Jones. If nothing else, Rod Allan might at least signal the end of the endless watching and fruitless following of cars and pedestrians coming from the battered and unloved nick.

Ozdemir sat back in his chair and folded his arms behind his head, daring for the first time in almost a year to believe that he might, very soon, know where DCI Harrison had hidden Brian Jones away. At last, he would have an insider able to nose around the nick and come up with the goods – he was confident he'd be able to make Allan an offer he couldn't refuse. Ozdemir resolved that once he had Jones's location, the man's demise would be swift. First a brutal interrogation to establish what he knew and who he'd told it to, followed by a trip to Aunt Selina's pig farm for a bullet to the gut and a gory end at the hands of her evil boars.

While Ozdemir silently celebrated his apparent change of luck, DCI Harrison did what he had done at least twice a week since Brian Jones had been sent south – he made his usual phone call to his old pal, DI Paul Johnson of the Met's famous Flying Squad at New Scotland Yard. Harrison and Johnson had attended a number of national courses together in the past and become close friends, regularly turning to one another for advice, guidance and the odd favour as circumstances dictated.

Brian Jones was unaware that since he had been in London he had been under the watchful eye of Paul

Johnson's A Squad. Without ever telling them why, Johnson had ensured that his team of three detective sergeants and eight detective constables had, whenever time permitted, paid passing attention to Brian Jones's grubby and nondescript flat in Lennox Road, on the Six Acres estate, just off Seven Sisters Road in north London. One of the junior DCs had been assigned to scrutinise the custody records that the Squad had access to, to ensure they knew if Jones ever came to the Met's attention; and though he did not know it, and wouldn't thank them for it, Brian Jones was as safe in London as it was possible to be.

In his office on the fourth floor at the Yard, Paul Johnson smiled broadly as he instantly recognised the gruff voice at the other end of the phone.

'Dan, you northern monkey. How you doing, son?'

'No complaints, Paul,' replied Harrison, grinning as he received the usual barrage of insults from his old pal. 'Just ringing to see how my little package is doing down in the smoke.'

'Same old, same old,' sighed Johnson, signalling to a passing DC to shut his door for him. 'Daft little twat got himself locked up at Islington last week but nothing serious; managed to have a word with the DI over there and it's all gone away.'

'Appreciate it. What'd he do?'

'Got locked up on sus by the uniforms who saw him

hanging about outside a bookie's. Got any plans for him yet?'

'No, still bubbling up here but nothing definite happening. I know my man's still looking hard for him but I'm pretty sure he hasn't a clue he's down on your patch. He's been roughing up all his friends and family round here but they've been as much use as men's tits to him. To be honest with you, Paul, I reckon the biggest problem I've got is that the daft sod gets bored down there and comes home.'

'Well, we're keeping an eye on him best as we can. He's drawing his rock and roll regular as clockwork, hasn't broken a bead of sweat doing any work, and as far as I can tell he spends most days getting pissed in the Hobgoblin on Holloway Road. Couple of my guys saw him getting chucked out of there early one afternoon last month. Looked a right fucking mess apparently. That's the trouble, you see, Dan, you monkeys come down to the smoke and you just can't cope with the bright lights and the noise, especially riddled with rickets.'

Harrison laughed out loud as Johnson delivered his usual northern jibes – he could have been working from a script, but he indulged him, mindful of the fact that Johnson was his only tenuous link to Brian Jones who still represented the biggest thorn in Ozdemir's fat, Turkish arse.

'Keep him locked up safe for me, Paul. I owe you a large one,' interjected Harrison. 'Got any plans to come up my way soon?'

'You're having a fucking laugh, aren't you, Dan? My oxygen supply cuts out at the bottom of the A1, son. You get yourself down here, mate, and we'll take you out and about, get you out for a proper drink.'

'I'll be down soon, Paul. You take care and thanks again.' Harrison hung up and sat back to stare at the ceiling. The impasse couldn't last for ever, he mused, before opening his bottom drawer and reaching for his ever present bottle of Bushmills and a cut-glass crystal tumbler.

# Chapter Nine

'Fuck me, have a look at that,' said Pizza, interrupting Jackson who was telling him about a WPC from Merseyside who'd pulled a train for him and a couple of mates at the Bruche Training School.

'What?'

'Dark vehicle with blacked-out windows,' said Pizza, looking intently into his rear-view mirror and braking Bravo Two Two hard.

Jackson looked over his shoulder. 'It was a hearse, wasn't it?' he asked.

'Exactly, a fucking hearse.'

'Well, maybe someone's died.'

'Fucking hell, John, nobody gets buried at one in the morning. And they don't pick up stiffs in a hearse, they use little Escort vans with no rear windows. What the fuck is a hearse doing out and about?'

'Oh,' was Jackson's simple reply as his education on the street continued apace.

Pizza executed a swift three-point turn and got after the hearse. They were behind it inside a minute and sitting well back.

'Right, we're going to do a moving vehicle check, OK?' said Pizza, continuing the tutorial. 'You stay on this channel and when there's a gap you dive in with Delta Hotel, Bravo Two Two, moving vehicle check in Church End, Handstead. Give the registration number and tell them you're accompanied, OK?'

Jackson began to repeat the instructions but Pizza interrupted him again with a loud shout of, 'He's clocked us, he's off,' and floored Bravo Two Two as the year-old Mercedes hearse suddenly put a hundred feet between them. The clapped-out 1974 Ford Escort was screaming in protest as Pizza went after the hearse in second gear.

'Get on the fucking air, John,' he shouted urgently. 'Just interrupt and tell them you've got a chase.'

Jackson nervously grabbed the main set microphone and began to talk over a transmission.

'Delta Hotel, this is Bravo Two Two, sorry to interrupt but I'm afraid we've got a chase.'

Pizza closed his eyes momentarily. 'You cunt,' he shouted, looking briefly over at Jackson. 'Don't fucking apologise. Get on with it then.'

Across the county, other vehicles operating on Channel One made similar observations about the crew of Bravo Two Two while they waited to hear what they were chasing.

Jackson began to painstakingly repeat what Pizza was bellowing at him as he drove.

'Delta Hotel, Bravo Two Two, we're in pursuit of a black Mercedes hearse, Church End towards Handstead town centre, speed is seventy miles an hour, failing to stop for police, solo driver.'

'Give them the registration number, for fuck's sake,' shouted Pizza as he coaxed the protesting beat vehicle closer to the hearse.

What happened next passed into legend and spawned a new language around the Force.

'Delta Hotel, index of vehicle is, oh fuck, index is . . .' Jackson's brain began to curdle under the pressure and he looked desperately at Pizza. Pizza was concentrating on his driving and did not glance over or help.

'Index is, oh fuck, index is Tango, Teakettle, Barbecue, oh bollocks . . .'

There was a brief silence as Pizza digested what Jackson had just transmitted.

'Tango, Teakettle, Barbecue?' he repeated incredulously and then repeated it again. 'You cunt,' he shouted loudly. 'The whole fucking world's listening. It's Tango, Tango, Bravo – oh fuck it, forget it and tell them he's going for it, Church End junction with Hanson Crescent.'

The hearse continued towards the town centre at a steady sixty mph, with Pizza giving a commentary as best he could while driving.

Amongst many others listening intently around the town was Psycho who had parked up in the town centre behind Radio Rentals for a snooze. He perked up as he heard the chase coming towards him. Realising it was likely to come straight past him, he quickly hurried along the darkened service road that led him back to the lit High Street and waited in the shadows at the side of the showroom, peering intently in the direction the two vehicles should come from. He didn't have long to wait and soon saw the two sets of headlights swing round the roundabout at the far end of the High Street, the blue light on Bravo Two Two reflecting off surrounding shop windows and its clapped-out engine screaming in protest at the stick Pizza was giving it. Neither vehicle was moving particularly fast as chases go and Psycho had plenty of time to make his run. He launched himself out of the shadows and began to run along the pavement towards the headlights. As he got within twenty feet of the hearse, he hurled the heavy, black rubber torch he was carrying directly at its windscreen.

The driver had seen the copper running at him and then throw something towards the vehicle but he was taken by surprise and completely failed to react. He flinched as the torch hit the middle of the windscreen with a loud thump and when he straightened up again he saw Psycho taking avoiding action as the torch whistled back past his head and through one of the huge plate-glass windows in the front of Radio Rentals. Both the hearse and Bravo Two Two slowed as they passed, watching the enormous window disintegrate, large guillotine-like shards of glass smashing into thousands of little pieces on the deserted pavement. It was warning enough for the driver of the hearse and within two hundred yards he was slowing and indicating left. Pizza threw the handset back to Jackson.

'Tell them he's pulling over, Handstead High Street,' he snapped.

A crestfallen Jackson did as he was told and sat chewing his bottom lip in shame as the hearse pulled sedately into the kerb and came to a halt, the huge five-litre engine purring smoothly and pumping a noxious exhaust cloud into the clear night sky. Pizza brought Bravo Two Two to within ten feet of it and then tersely told Jackson to get out and get the keys from of the hearse's ignition. Pizza watched as Jackson did as he was told and the exhaust fumes died away, then he switched off Bravo Two Two and joined Jackson by the side of the hearse. He looked at the driver and smiled.

'Fucking hell, should have guessed, shouldn't I? Hello, Simon. Where'd you get this one from?'

Simon Randall, a spotty bespectacled village idiot from Parsons Green just outside Handstead, squinted back at Pizza and smiled in recognition.

'Hello, Mr Petty. How are you?'

'Very well, Simon. Where the fuck did you get this?'

Randall, although only seventeen and almost brain dead, was an extraordinarily prolific car thief. There was nothing he could not, or would not, nick and his convictions for car theft ran into the tens of dozens. He had nicked his first car aged eleven and had continued to nick them remorselessly ever since. But all he ever did was nick them, drive them and leave them. He'd even been known to return them to where he'd found them. He just loved cars, and despite never having had a lesson or taking a test he was quite a proficient driver. He never gave the Old Bill a hard time by making them chase him and the truth was they all had a bit of a soft spot for him. The fact was that if things were quiet, it was not unusual for Simon to get a visit from Handstead cops at home.

'Hello, Simon, you're nicked.'

'What for?'

'That motor you had away the other night.'

'How the fuck did you know about that?'

'It's what we're paid for, Simon, we know these things. Come and tell us all about it.'

Simon would subsequently put his hands up to a couple of motors and take into consideration a good half-dozen more and the local police would clear up loads of crime they had known nothing about. It was a great arrangement and simple Simon seemed quite happy with it.

'It was outside the crematorium with the engine running,' said Simon happily.

'When was that then?'

'Lunchtime I think.'

Leaving Jackson to guard Simon, Pizza returned to Two Two where the Police National Computer operator confirmed that the hearse had indeed been stolen from outside Handstead Crematorium that afternoon, leaving an irate and tearful funeral party to get taxis home.

'You're a bad lad, Simon,' said Pizza cheerfully as he handcuffed him and helped him into the back of the beat vehicle, joyfully anticipating another shed load of clean-ups.

Having made arrangements with the Brothers in Yankee One to recover the hearse back to the yard at Handstead, Pizza took Simon to the cell area at the nick where he was greeted like a long-lost friend by cops who playfully punched him in the ribs and ruffled his hair. Simon loved cars but he also loved being nicked because the cops provided him with the only affection he had ever known in his short, sad life, which had been spent in a succession of foster homes after his mother had abandoned him aged four when it became apparent that he had a gene or two missing.

Once Sergeant Jones had booked him in, Simon was interviewed by Pizza and Jackson, with Jackson making contemporaneous notes.

'Tell me where you got the hearse from, Simon.'

'I told you, it was outside the crematorium.'

'With the engine running?'

'That's right, engine running. I think they were all inside.'

'What time was this?'

'Lunchtime.'

'Lunchtime yesterday?'

'Yeah.'

'Where have you been in it?'

'Just mooching about, here and there.'

'Where exactly?'

'Well, I did a bit of cabbing in it.'

'Cabbing? You've been cabbing in a hearse? Are you serious?' asked Pizza.

'Just the one fare.'

'You picked up a fare in a stolen hearse?' asked Pizza slowly.

'Just the one.'

'Where from, for fuck's sake?'

'Manchester airport.'

'What time was that?'

'Late afternoon, teatime-ish. I just pulled up on the rank and there was a bloke waiting with his suitcases so I asked him if he needed a cab.'

'In a hearse?'

'Yeah, he didn't seem too bothered.'

'Where did you take him?'

'Just outside Liverpool – he gave me directions.'

'How much did you charge him?'

'A quid.'

'You gave a bloke a cab ride from Manchester airport to Liverpool in a hearse for a quid?'

'Yeah, he seemed fine with it.'

'Didn't he think it was a bit odd, sitting in a hearse and all that?'

'He didn't say anything.'

Pizza shook his head slowly. 'What did you do after you'd dropped him off in Liverpool?'

'Drove about a bit more, put some petrol in and then had a kip in the back earlier this evening.'

'You went to sleep in the back?'

'Yeah, there's a sleeping bag in the back.'

'Sleeping bag?'

'Yeah, a big green plastic thing. Carrying handles on either end, big zip down the side. Big sleeping bag it was.'

Pizza stared open-mouthed at Randall as it dawned on him what he was being told.

'You had a kip in a sleeping bag?' he asked again.

'Yeah, had a couple of hours on it – fucking smelly it was though.'

'It's not a sleeping bag, Simon,' said Pizza flatly.

'No?'

'It's a fucking body bag, you twat. You've been kipping in a body bag. Why would there be a sleeping bag in the hearse, Simon?'

'Hmm, I hadn't really thought about it, Mr Petty,' replied Randall quietly. 'Perhaps you're right. A body bag, you say? That explains the smell then.'

The interview never really recovered after that revelation, though true to form Simon put up another four motors that he'd had away from surrounding divisions. Pizza duly put them on to TIC forms and claimed them as clear-ups for Handstead.

Jackson's balls-up on the radio earlier, however, had generated enormous discussion and debate and within a couple of days had brought about a new phonetic code that was first used on Channel One and then on channels across the county. Aware that Handstead cops referred to their nick as Horse's Arse, other stations were renamed accordingly. Delta Bravo became Dangle Berries, Charlie November was referred to as Clag Nuts, Foxtrot Bravo as Fanny Batter – and so it went on, with each shift at each nick refining and changing the code until complete mayhem reigned. It became a point of principle for crews to use their own codes during chases but the practice was ultimately outlawed at the highest level after a Charlie Division area car crew reported that the driver of a vehicle they were chasing was a BUB C.

'BUB C? What's that one stand for?' queried the main Force control room inspector who was standing behind the operator controlling the chase.

'Er, not really sure, boss,' mumbled the operator unconvincingly.

'Oh, come on,' said the inspector. 'You can tell me.'

'I don't really know,' she insisted.

'Come on, I know you know, I used to be a PC myself once upon a time, you know,' he continued with a condescending smirk.

'Big Ugly Black Cunt,' explained the operator to Inspector Openyami who hailed from a village outside Lagos and was the Force's only West African officer and currently on the accelerated promotion course at Bramshill.

Twenty-four hours later, Chief Daniells himself declared that the practice would stop or cops would find themselves looking for alternative employment. Handstead, however, remained Horse's Arse in everyone's phrasebook.

# Chapter Ten

As he hurried along Bolton Road East towards the Birchwood Avenue brothel for what had become a regular block booking with Cassie and Maxine, Rod Allan was rubbing his hands with glee. He had definitely detected signs of movement in his nether regions earlier that morning and was quietly confident that today would be the day that he finally winched one up and boned the two hookers like they had never been boned before. Ever professional, and never likely to bite the hand that fed them, they had not once remarked on his limp dick and spent his hour-long sessions drinking from each other's withered furry cups while he sat alongside them whispering encouragement and furiously stretching his old chap like an elastic band. Despite that, he was sure they were laughing at him and if there was one thing Allan insisted on, it was being taken seriously and afforded due respect. The two bitches were going to get large portions today, he insisted to himself, punching a fist into the other palm loudly and scaring the shit out of two truanting schoolgirls he was passing.

He bowled into the brothel bang on time as usual, where he was greeted like a long-lost relative by Marge who overstepped the mark as she leant forward to peck him on the cheek, causing him to recoil in horror at her moustache. Mustapha Tungay gave him a curt nod of acknowledgement as Cassie led him by the arm to the special room for a treat they only ever gave to their favourite punters. Glowing with self-satisfied pomposity, the porky idol with feet of clay allowed himself to be hurried off to the room especially prepared for his performance of a lifetime. He was quite pleasantly surprised by the interior of the room.

Cassie kicked the door shut behind her.

'Like it?' she asked as she limped over to the large bed – one of the abscesses on her feet had burst and hurt like fuck.

'Quite an improvement,' remarked Allan who had so far been used to tugging himself to a sweat in a dingy, badly lit and smelly side room. 'Not bad at all.'

The room was decorated with Anaglypta paper covered in pale yellow emulsion and an ancient print of the enigmatic Mona Lisa hung on the far wall, but the eye-catching item in the room was a large, very ornate, gilt-framed mirror.

'Very Louis the Fourteenth,' remarked Allan, desperate to impress the old whore who definitely wouldn't know Louis the Fourteenth from Woolworth's.

'I think it's Georgian actually,' she replied casually, puncturing his enormous but fragile ego. She took off her top, revealing her frayed, grey bra. Allan was about to rebuke her for her insolence when the door opened and Maxine walked in. Behind the two-way mirror, two giggling Turkish minders cupped their mouths and one hit the power switch on the camera sitting on a tripod.

Cassie and Maxine wasted little time in hauling the limp porker on to their bed and pulling his trousers and pants down, with Cassie taking first watch on his reluctant noodle. Maxine hovered around his head, talking dirty to him and rubbing her sagging breasts in his face. Allan closed his eyes in concentration and willed something to happen. But there was no movement even after the girls changed places, and Cassie began to make despairing gestures of defeat towards the large mirror. Whilst their film would not win any awards on the homemade porn circuit, the two Turks behind the mirror knew they had more than enough to slaughter Allan and one went to telephone Ozdemir.

'Get him into the side room. I'll be over in ten minutes,' instructed Ozdemir, before calling to his secretary loudly to get his Merc and driver round to the front.

Ten minutes later, with Cassie and Maxine's jaws beginning to ache and their tempers beginning to fray, the door to the room burst open and the two budding film producers strode purposefully in. As the girls rolled away from him, Allan sat bolt upright, his normally puce face deathly white, eyes like saucers and mouth open like a goldfish.

'What the fuck?' he blustered before the two goons grabbed him by the arms and pulled him off the bed and on to the shabby carpet.

'This is outrageous,' stammered the terrified Allan as he desperately tried to unroll his trousers and pants from around his ankles.

'Shut it, fat limp boy,' snarled one of the Turks. 'Get dressed and be quiet.'

His thumping heart in his throat, Allan got unsteadily to his feet and began to dress himself, casting glances of pure hatred at Cassie and Maxine as they slipped, sniggering, out of the room.

'What's going on here?' he asked quietly as he did up his belt buckle.

'You come with us, fat boy, you see everything soon,' replied one of the heavies, unceremoniously grabbing Allan by the shoulder and frogmarching him out of the room and down the dimly lit corridor. He stopped him outside a closed door at the far end and knocked. A voice replied in a language Allan didn't recognise and the goon reached forward to open the door and pushed Allan into the room.

It was a tiny, windowless box room with a rack of electrical equipment at the far end and a large television screen on the middle shelf. Sitting in front of the screen with his back to Allan was Sercan Ozdemir, busily fast forwarding, rewinding and playing a tape on a Phillips video cassette player. And the film he was watching, in glorious Technicolor, was Allan getting his limp dick blown by two listless, scabby whores. Realising finally the enormous mess he was in, Allan hung his head and felt physically sick. His meaningless, overblown, egotistical world was crashing around his ears as he listened, wincing, to the two whores exhorting him to winch just a little one up for them.

Ozdemir turned towards him, grinning so broadly his face began to ache. He nearly laughed.

'Good afternoon, Mr Allan. It is Mr Allan, isn't it?'

Allan looked at him but said nothing.

'Mr Allan, life President of the Association of Cleansing Resupply and Procurement Practitioners?' continued Ozdemir, reading from the business card one of the girls had lifted from his wallet on a previous visit.

Allan still remained silent.

'Living at number twenty-six, Queens Road,

Handstead,' went on Ozdemir, reading from the driving licence they had also taken.

Realising he was fucked, Allan sighed deeply. 'What of it? What's this all about? What you after, money? If it is, you can forget it, I've got fuck all.'

'Relax, Mr Allan.' Ozdemir got to his feet and motioned Allan to sit in the chair in front of the television where Cassie's head was bobbing like a buoy in a heavy swell. 'I'm not after your money; but I guess you wouldn't want your employers to know about your terrible secret, would you?'

'Of course not. Where's this going?'

'Or Mrs Allan, I presume?'

'This is all her fucking fault,' snapped Allan. 'If she came up with the goods occasionally I wouldn't be looking elsewhere, would I?'

'Even with your limp dick?' asked Ozdemir.

Allan coloured up at the barb but said nothing, trying to look anywhere other than the television where Maxine was shrieking loudly about his balls looking like picked walnuts.

'Dreadful woman,' said Ozdemir, patting him paternally on a knee, 'but a great worker, you know. Probably does ten clients a day, all bareback.'

Allan closed his eyes and groaned inwardly, almost grateful for his impotence, before dropping his head into his hands in utter despair.

'What do you want?' he eventually asked quietly.

'Not money, Mr Allan, oh no. What I want from you, my dear friend, is information.'

Allan looked up. 'Information? What information?'

'Information on someone's whereabouts, Mr Allan.'

'Someone's whereabouts? What are you on about?'

'You're not a stupid man, Mr Allan, or at least I hope you're not, for your sake. You're going to find out where someone is for me. It's that simple.'

'I can't get information like that,' protested Allan. 'Where am I supposed to get stuff like that?'

'As the building manager at Handstead police station, you must have access pretty much anywhere, am I right?'

'Suppose so,' agreed Allan, sitting up straight and looking fearfully at Ozdemir. 'What about it?'

'My dear friend Mr Harrison is keeping me from a very close associate who I need to speak to. Mr Harrison has him at an address unknown to me currently and you're going to get it for me.'

'DCI Harrison?'

'The very same.'

'How do you expect me to get that information from him?'

'Well, he's certainly not going to give it to you even if you ask him nicely, so I suggest you have a good look round his office. He's bound to have a file or something on my associate. Mr Brian Jones.'

'Never heard of him.'

'Of course you haven't, you're a fucking bog washer, you limp-dicked, fat bastard,' shouted Ozdemir into his face.

Allan flinched away from him in fright.

'You're fuck all, Mr Allan, but you're going to do this for me or copies of your film will be posted to every officer at Handstead and of course one to your unfortunate wife. You'll find that information or you're finished. Am I getting through to you?'

Utterly humiliated and broken, Allan nodded silently and hung his head. He was struggling to breathe, such was the lump of apprehension and fear in his throat, but even in this darkest of moments, his rodent-like mind was already seeking out ways to save himself. He'd need to be careful, but he could easily search Harrison's office.

'I'll let you know when I've got it then,' he said, starting to get to his feet. Ozdemir pushed him firmly back on to his chair and leant close to his face. Allan could smell the raki on his breath and the brilliantine in his dark, wavy hair.

'Listen carefully to me, Mr Allan. You've got two days, including the rest of today, to get that information. The day after tomorrow sees your world premiere, understood? Two days. Now fuck off,' snarled Ozdemir, stepping back and motioning to one of the minders to take him away.

As he was unceremoniously bundled out of the front door and on to the pavement, Allan barely glanced at the man who passed him accompanied by two large Turks in dark suits.

The man was Guy Mitcheson who was responding to the very polite and respectful invitation he had received from a respected local businessman and entrepreneur, Sercan Ozdemir. He was somewhat surprised to be meeting him at his favourite brothel but had been assured by his escorts that they were only picking up the great man and would be discussing business elsewhere. It was in fact all part of Ozdemir's plan to let Mitcheson know who he was in the grand scheme of things and this hadn't been wasted on Mitcheson – not that he was unduly worried. He was unemployed and unmarried, his reputation was in the gutter, he existed on state benefits and his cannabis deals and lived rent-free in a farmhouse controlled by his family's management company. The only thing he actually owned himself was his dirty brown Range Rover. He was quietly confident he wasn't going to be blackmailed by the owner of the brothel and was looking forward to whatever developed between them.

He waited with his escorts just inside the front door in silence for a minute until Ozdemir came trotting down the stairs in an expensive petrol-green suit and crisp, plain white double-cuffed shirt with heavy gold cufflinks. His highly polished leather shoes gleamed as brightly as the perfect teeth set in his handsome dark face which was creased in a wide smile. He held out his hand.

'Mr Mitcheson, thank you for coming at such short notice,' he said brightly, his brown eyes assessing the long-haired bag of shit shaking his hand. Ozdemir was a shrewd enough operator and quickly made up his mind about Mitcheson. His handshake was firm enough, and although his eyes showed evidence of his prodigious cannabis use, they were alert and showed intelligence.

'It's my pleasure, Mr Ozdemir,' Mitcheson replied, also assessing the clearly wealthy man in front of him. 'I wasn't doing much and didn't have too many plans for the rest of the day anyway. I understand you'd like to have a chat with me. Your staff didn't elaborate when they picked me up at home I'm afraid.'

'I didn't think it appropriate to divulge too much to them, Mr Mitcheson,' said Ozdemir, determined to hold his own with this bright and articulate university graduate. 'I thought perhaps we could talk over lunch at my office, if you've got time.' He began to guide

Mitcheson back out of the brothel and towards the Mercedes purring at the kerbside where one of the goons stood holding a rear door open.

'As I said, the rest of my day is pretty clear,' said Mitcheson, allowing Ozdemir to guide him to the car. This guy clearly wants to put something my way, he thought to himself as he slid across the smooth leather back seat. Family connections maybe? Can't be the dope-dealing, far too small fry. So what?

As the Merc pulled silently and smoothly away, Ozdemir answered his unspoken questions.

'I understand you deal a bit of cannabis around the town, Mr Mitcheson.'

Mitcheson gave a low laugh. 'You sound like a policeman, Mr Ozdemir. I don't know what you mean, really I don't.'

'Of course not, that was very clumsy of me, please accept my apologies. I'm not interrogating you and I'm certainly not a policeman. You've probably been dealing some of my dope, you know.'

'Your dope?'

'Yes, mine. I import a fair amount which is distributed around the north mainly. Chances are you sell on some of my stuff.'

'Interesting,' said Mitcheson quietly, keen not to give anything away yet.

Ozdemir looked long and hard at him for a moment.

'I'm not looking to give you a hard time or ask you to compromise yourself with a complete stranger. I am aware of your dealing, but that's not really of any interest to me.'

'So why are we sitting in your car?'

'What really interests me is you, Mr Mitcheson.'

'Me?'

'Yes, you. Mr Guy Mitcheson the chemist.'

'The chemist?'

'You've got a degree in chemistry, haven't you?'

'Yes I have, but I've never worked as a chemist. Actually, I've not worked since I left university.'

'That doesn't bother me. What I'm interested in is what you know.'

'What I know?'

'Tell me what you know about LSD,' said Ozdemir, eyeing him carefully.

Mitcheson smiled and relaxed back into the comfy seat. 'Ah yes, lysergic acid diethylamide, the hallucinogenic drug first synthesised by the good Dr Hofmann. The world has so much to thank the Swiss for, don't you think, Mr Ozdemir? Discreet bankers, wonderful chocolate, the Swiss Army knife, E equals MC squared and LSD. Quite a race of inventors, all in all.'

'E equals MC squared?' asked Ozdemir.

'Einstein's most damaging formula', sighed Mitcheson. 'Basically, matter can be turned into energy and energy into matter. It adds up to nuclear fusion and the atomic bomb.'

'Right,' replied Ozdemir, trying to keep up. 'LSD, it's manmade, isn't it?'

'Certainly.'

'Could you make it?' he said, cutting to the chase.

'Anyone with a basic knowledge of chemistry would know the ingredients. The problem is knowing how to combine them – and of course acquiring them in sufficient quantity to make the exercise worthwhile.'

'I can take care of that. What would you need?'

Mitcheson puffed out his cheeks and began to run through a list, using his fingers as counters. 'Hydrazine hydrate, hydrazide, hydrochloric acid, sodium nitrate, sodium bicarbonate—'

'OK, OK,' interrupted Ozdemir. 'You know what you need but can you use it to produce the goods?'

Mitcheson gave a soft laugh. 'Oh yes, Mr Ozdemir. I made a decent batch when I was still at university. I didn't pop any myself but I'm told it hit the mark.'

'OK, you can make it, so here's the proposition I want to put to you, Mr Mitcheson.' Ozdemir turned in his seat and fixed him with his dark eyes. 'I know you live in the middle of nowhere, no neighbours, no disturbances. You're rattling about in a huge farmhouse on your own, loads of room and privacy. You tell me what you need for a major production enterprise and I'll supply it. It costs you nothing to be part of this and I'll give you twenty-five per cent of my net profit.'

Mitcheson had been doing his own calculations.

'Gross profit, Mr Ozdemir, and we've got a deal.'

Ozdemir frowned at him. Once the operation was up and running, he decided that Mitcheson would be due a visit to Aunt Selina's pig farm.

'OK, gross profit, but there's a little more, Mr Mitcheson,' he said finally. 'I don't take kindly to failure or disloyalty. You screw with me and I'll have you chopped into little pieces.' His face was set in a snarl as he spoke and he held Mitcheson's arm tightly. 'Don't fuck with me, Mr Mitcheson.' He leant closer to him. 'You play fair with me, you'll be able to disappear and smoke yourself to death if that's what you want to do. But don't ever make the mistake of thinking you can have me over.'

Now genuinely fearful, Mitcheson stared at him, his mouth open, his throat dry and sticky.

'I wasn't, Mr Ozdemir, I guarantee you,' he choked. 'I want this to work as much as you do. This is the opportunity, the really big one, I've always dreamt about. There's no way I'm going to screw you around.'

Ozdemir's smile returned and he released his vice-like grip and settled back. He opened his window to relieve the heat and tension in the back of the car.

'You let me have a list of what you'll need and I'll get it delivered at night by prior arrangement, OK?'

'Of course. What sort of volume were you thinking of?'

The truth was that Ozdemir hadn't thought that far ahead.

'Big, very big,' he blustered.

'I was thinking of somewhere in the region of eight million doses,' said Mitcheson casually. 'On to blotters probably.'

'Eight million?' echoed Ozdemir, desperate not to show his ignorance or excitement at such a huge figure. 'What would the return be on that?'

'Millions.' Mitcheson laughed. 'Absolutely millions. I'm talking about half the world's LSD market.'

Ozdemir began to laugh with him and the two men shook hands vigorously as the Mercedes turned into the forecourt outside Ozdemir's legitimate haulage business.

Back in his basement office at Handstead nick, Rod Allan sat with his head in his hands, frantically making plans to meet his unwelcome obligation to Sercan Ozdemir. A born survivor, a part of him was already wondering whether there might be any mileage in some sort of future arrangement with the Turk. Allan harboured no feelings of loyalty for the Force that had employed him for the last nine years and had always had one simple agenda: himself. Self-promotion and particularly his reputation, which he fancied was something worth hanging on to, were always top of his list of priorities, and right now he felt his very survival was at stake. His task seemed simple enough. DCI Harrison had the information Ozdemir was after – it was unlikely any of his DSs or DCs would have it. So the place to look for it was his office and Allan resolved to pay it a visit late the following evening when the nick would be at its quietest but his presence there would not be questioned. After all, he ran the place.

# Chapter Eleven

Jackson had had to endure a pretty horrific muster after his phonetic faux pas the night before. He had sat quietly through the abuse and insults, gaining some encouragement from the fact that Pizza had not got involved and had even called for a halt to it eventually.

'Come on, we've all fucked up in the past,' he shouted. 'Enough, give him a break, will you?'

'Not like that, we haven't,' replied Psycho who was dressed in druid headgear in preparation for the summer solstice which wasn't too far away.

'Stones in glasshouses, Psycho,' warned Pizza, but doing it with a smile on his face in case the monster got the hump and went for him with his lethal sandals.

'What the fuck are you on about?' said the clearly irritated Psycho.

'You've obviously forgotten about the resurrection.'

The group exploded in raucous laughter at the mention of it and even Psycho managed a wry smile. A year ago, he'd have chinned Pizza for being a gobby probationer but not now, he was an accepted member of the group. Three weeks earlier he had put the front door in of an old age pensioner's bungalow after concerned neighbours had reported having not seen her for a week. He had found her slumped in a chair in the living room in front of a blaring television, stone cold to the touch and not responding to anything. He had called it in as a sudden death, no suspicious circumstances, and was waiting for the police doctor and undertakers to arrive when the corpse had asked him if he wanted a cup of tea while he waited.

'It was a fucking miracle, praise the Lord,' shouted Psycho, getting to his feet and raising his arms to the heavens. 'Dead as a fucking doornail she was, but He still had work for her here so He brought her back.'

'Of course she was, Psycho, course she was. Just give Jackson a chance, OK? He'll muddle through – he's got to.'

The sneers and laughter faded away and Jackson shot Pizza a look of thanks. Pizza nodded briefly at him. He knew only too well the private hell Jackson was currently in and would do what he could to help him through to the other side.

Sergeant Collins strode to the lectern and looked happily at his band of dubious warriors.

'Evening, boys. Just the one item for you tonight but I suspect it'll keep us going for the shift. As you probably know, while we were in bed today, United beat Leeds in the FA Cup semi-final down at Hillsborough. Apparently it went tits up before, during and after the game and the locals are kicking the Leeds fans on to anything that's leaving town to get them out. Traffic officers have just seen two coaches from the Leeds area with known connections to the Leeds Service Crew coming off the motorway and headed towards us. Put some money on them ending up at the Stonehouse. Soon as we're finished here I want Pizza and his sidekick to have a punt past to see if they've turned up. OK?'

Pizza nodded his understanding. 'Didn't the traffic guys give them a tug then'? he asked.

'What do you think?' spat Collins disdainfully. 'End of shift and got to get back to wash and hoover the car before they hand it over to the night crew; fuck them, I suppose we should be thankful they at least gave us a heads up.'

'All three units of the Patrol Group have been called out for this,' he added, 'so I need a call from you, Pizza, soon as you can, OK? Any sign of the Leeds fans, we'll have a briefing nearby to decide what we do next.'

The group hurried away to get what they would need

for the expected clash with the hooligans who made up the Leeds Service Crew, chatting excitedly.

'Psycho, get that fucking towel off your head, the summer solstice isn't until next month,' shouted Collins as Psycho began to sing 'Onward Christian Soldiers' while playfully thumping Piggy in the back as a warm-up.

As Collins finalised his muster, two battered forty-seat coaches pulled on to the huge forecourt of the Stonehouse pub on the northbound dual carriageway that divided Old and New Handstead. The Stonehouse was an enormous barn of a pub with three public bars all designed for the sole purpose of consuming beer. The bars were absolutely soulless, devoid of any decoration or comfort and bearing the scars of numerous previous blow-ups. The staff worked behind huge chicken-wire screens, taking money and passing pints under the small gap at the bottom, and the doors giving access to the rear of the place were armoured and bolted from the inside during opening hours. Trouble there was frequent and always expected.

It was a well-used venue for coaches of football supporters heading north, just off the main motorway and with loads of parking and the potential for a good ruck. The numerous boarded-up panes of glass in the windows and the cracked panels along the front of the lengthy bar tops were ample proof that this was not a place to bring the wife or girlfriend for a quiet drink. Now the bruised and battered Leeds Service Crew were on site, clambering off their coaches, chanting at the tops of their voices and keen to even things up.

They were a notorious gang of hooligans from the Leeds area who followed their team everywhere in search of a scrap with opposition team fans. The real hardcore members could be identified by two distinctive tattoos: the club crest on their left forearm and a white rose of Yorkshire on the right. Plenty of those emblems were on display as the shaven-headed, denim-clad Neanderthals climbed down the steps of the bus in their twelve-lace Doc Marten boots and headed for the pub.

Losing to Manchester United was bad enough, but the hiding they had received at the hands of the Birmingham police after the game and the abuse from the Red Army really rankled and now the locals were going to get some by way of revenge. Had they but known it, eagerly anticipating such a meeting were a group of hooligans in uniform who relished the thought of being paid to go out fighting without having to give a moment's thought to the repercussions.

Even the normally unshockable bar staff at the Stonehouse were starting to get worried. They reckoned they had seen it all but the arrival of the Leeds Service Crew made them think again. They were simply cavemen. The bar had emptied on their arrival and now the forty-five-strong group were fighting amongst themselves until some locals turned up and the real sport could begin. One of their number lay unconscious at the entrance to the toilets where he had been felled by a flying bottle and another had a deep gash under his left eye where he had been glassed. Despite the blood pouring from the wound, he was now jumping up and down with the others who were chanting 'Super Leeds' incessantly at the tops of their voices. Nervous glances were being exchanged behind the chicken wire but the staff failed to spot the panda car that drove into the car park, slowed and then sped off. Salvation in blue was just around the corner.

'Bravo Two Two, talk-through with Bravo Two,' said Pizza urgently into the main set soon after he had pulled into the layby a little further along the dual carriageway.

Sergeant Collins was waiting for his call and took talk-through immediately.

'Bravo Two, the two coaches are in the car park and I reckon there's forty plus inside and getting at it,' reported Pizza.

'Thank you, Two Two. Delta Hotel from Bravo Two, I need all Hotel Alpha units to rendezvous in five minutes at the Comet Hotel car park. Can you give me an ETA for the patrol group to that location?' transmitted Collins.

'Wait one, Bravo Two,' answered the control room operator. 'All Hotel Alpha units make your way to the Comet Hotel car park and see Bravo Two. Ranger One, Ranger One, your location now please.'

In the lead vehicle of the three liveried Patrol Group vans that were speeding south along the motorway, Sergeant Phil Gilbert struggled to make himself heard above the screaming engine.

'Delta Hotel, we're five minutes away,' he shouted.

'Thank you, Ranger One. What's your strength tonight?'

'Show one PS and eighteen PCs for your log.'

'One and eighteen it is, thank you, Ranger One. Bravo Two, one and eighteen Patrol Group officers should be with you in five minutes.'

'Thank you, Delta Hotel. I'll update you after our briefing. Your air, Bravo Two out.'

As the night duty Horse's Arse officers and the Patrol Group raced towards the Comet Hotel, the main Force control room put into operation a well-oiled plan and began to draft in vehicles from surrounding Division to patrol around the periphery of the town in holding patterns, waiting to be called in to take routine calls or, more likely, provide back-up when the wheels came off at the Stonehouse. The inspector in the air-conditioned operations room was leaping about like a novice hot-coal walker; it was his first experience of a Handstead carve-up.

'Relax, boss,' advised his hugely experienced sergeant as he updated the situation board at the front of the room. 'Happens regular as clockwork there. There's fuck all any of us can do when it goes off, other than make sure we get more bodies in and we've got that covered. If it goes horribly wrong, i.e. we end up with dead bodies, there's a list on your desk of who you need to call.'

'Brilliant,' snapped the inspector. 'How am I supposed to run things from up here?'

'You're not boss, primacy always passes to the guys on the ground. Bravo Two's calling all the shots, it's his arse in a sling.'

'Thank you for that,' muttered the inspector, whose hopes of a glorious rise through the ranks needed a catastrophe at Horse's Arse like a hole in the head.

Officers inside the three Patrol Group vans were donning their NATO helmets as their Class One Advanced drivers raced the vehicles at breakneck speeds towards the rendezvous. Late-night car drivers took sharp intakes of breath as streaks of white and flashing blue lights flew past them. 'Someone's in the shit then,' commented one driver to his passenger. Inside the vans, conversation had to be shouted to be heard above the radio broadcasts which were set at maximum volume to ensure nobody missed a word. The smell of anticipation was overpowering as nineteen burly, fit and extremely aggressive young men prepared themselves mentally for what they had trained so hard for.

The Patrol Group consisted of three units, each with their own area, and they had gained a reputation for gratuitous violence throughout the county in their role as a rapid response force deployed to outbreaks of public disorder. The previous year, in the aftermath of Bovril's murder, they had really earned their spurs on the Park Royal estate where they had locked up and banjo'd anything that moved. The Patrol Group officers had all proved themselves to be switched-on thief-takers and street fighters at various divisions within the Force before applying for two- or three-year attachments to the Group. These attachments were much sought after and, typical of any police squad, allegiances were parochial in the extreme. The three units were permanently at war, constantly trying to outdo each other with more arrests and fights. Injuries were paraded as signs of success and sick leave as a result of injury was virtually unheard of. Indeed, one of the officers hanging on to a strap in Unit One's van had two broken fingers strapped up and two of the officers from Unit Three, the local unit, each had a black eye they could barely see out of. There was absolutely no question of any of them not being on this call-out. Their machismo code of honour forbade such signs of weakness; that was for traffic officers who were often off with bad backs, piles and once, memorably, a swollen ankle from too much energetic gear-changing.

Pizza and John Jackson – he would not be given a nickname until he had been accepted – were first to arrive in the Comet Hotel car park and were pleasantly surprised to see the burger van still there for business. The van had seen better days; the original large painted claim 'Satisfaction Guaranteed' had been replaced by some yob with a spray can to read 'Salmonella Guaranteed'. Obviously not a Handstead yob as salmonella had been spelt correctly. Hungry night-duty officers from around the Division used it regularly despite the dubious hygiene standards of the van and its owner, Greasy Graham – no one knew his surname.

As Pizza pulled up opposite the dilapidated converted Transit van with the tattered blue and white awning, he spotted Greasy idly flipping some rubberised burgers on his hotplate. He paused to stir a large pot of greasy processed fried onions before sneezing loudly over the hotplate.

'We're not having any of those, are we?' queried Jackson, looking very worried.

'Relax, John,' replied Pizza, getting out of the car. 'Most of the germs get killed on the hotplate and the rest are harmless.'

Very reluctantly, Jackson left the vehicle and walked slowly behind Pizza who was sorting through the change in his pocket for a fifty pence piece before he could go through the charade of offering to pay for his poisoned burger. If there were other punters about, the arrangement was that the Old Bill would give Greasy a fifty pence piece or a pound note in payment and he'd give them back the same amount in shrapnel. But if like tonight it was only Old Bill, Pizza would chuck a coin on the counter and Greasy would smile benevolently and tell them it was on the house. Food poisoning cost nothing in Horse's Arse if you knew the right people and wore a blue uniform.

'All right, Greasy?' inquired Pizza, tossing a coin on to the scarred counter. 'Couple of cheeseburgers, please.'

'On the house, officer,' leered Greasy, showing his stained and crooked teeth which always reminded Pizza of a wood devastated by a gale. 'Your money's no good here.'

'Cheers, Greasy,' said Pizza before he saw movement at the back of the van and gasped, 'Oh God, no.' He looked urgently at Jackson. 'I think I heard our call sign, John. Haven't got time for a burger. Sorry, Greasy,' he said hurriedly.

'Wasn't us, Alan,' replied Jackson, causing Pizza to close his eyes in frustration and then glare angrily at him as the person behind Greasy came into view.

It was none other than the man known to all the Handstead cops as 'Claws'. He was the retarded nephew that Greasy occasionally took out in his van to give his sister and brother-in-law a break, and who had one simple task to perform. As he appeared alongside his uncle, the tools of his dreadful trade became immediately apparent – he was prising apart frozen beef burgers with fingernails a Chinese Mandarin would have been proud of, the lengthy nails packed with weeks of dirt and rotting mincemeat from his previous night's work.

'Hello, officers,' he gurned before scratching his nose with one of the encrusted digits and then sweeping his filthy hair aside.

'Jesus Christ,' gasped Jackson, staring open-mouthed at this ghastly spectacle. 'I think it was us they were calling, Alan.'

'Sorry, Greasy, got to go and answer that call,' said Pizza and he and Jackson beat a hasty retreat to their car.

Soon other vehicles began to arrive in the car park.

Sergeant Collins struggled to get his large bulk out of Bravo Two and was heading for Greasy's van when Pizza ran over to him.

'Forget it, Sarge. Claws is in there,' he whispered urgently.

'Oh bollocks,' muttered Collins. 'I'm fucking

starving. I could manage a scabby horse between two pissed mattresses but anything Claws has had in his hands is out. Fuck it.'

The Brothers were standing nearby and had heard the conversation.

'We've got a curry, Sarge, if you fancy a bit,' offered Jim.

'Where's it from?' asked Collins dubiously, painfully aware that like most cops, the Brothers ate as cheaply as possible and that in Handstead you always got what you paid for.

'The Bucket.'

'Fucking hell,' groaned Collins, rolling his eyes in despair. 'What the fuck is the matter with you two? Those bastards will poison you one day.'

The Brothers' curry had been bought from an unlicensed balti restaurant on the Pound Court estate, run from what used to be the front room of a private house, and with hygiene standards that even Greasy and Claws would have found unacceptable. Its nickname, the Bucket of Shit, was well deserved and most meals bought there (admittedly for not very much) usually preceded a bout of uncontrollable diarrhoea or vomiting. The Brothers ate there regularly and appeared to have stomachs of cast iron. So far they had avoided most of the diseases coming out of the restaurant; Psycho's claim that they had probably built up immunity to everything other than the plague was probably not far off the mark.

Jim shrugged and he and H returned to Yankee One to eat their curried rat or whatever it was they put into the curry, before the evening's violence got under way. They always found fighting more enjoyable on a full stomach and usually started every night shift with a visit to the Bucket where they were well known. The only time they had questioned the wisdom of eating there was after Psycho had posed a question for them.

'When did you last attend an Asian sudden death?' he had asked early one morning as they ploughed through a bright pink chicken jalfrezi.

The Brothers looked at one another.

'Never,' replied H eventually.

'Me neither,' said Psycho triumphantly. 'Anyone else here ever been to an Asian sudden death?' he asked.

No one had.

'There you go then,' continued the unshaven philosopher. 'There're only two possibilities, aren't there? Either they curry their dead or the Chinks have discovered they taste like chicken. Those slant-eyed little fuckers will stir fry anything it if stops moving long enough.'

The Brothers were sufficiently concerned to have words with the owner of the Bucket next time they visited him.

'We ever find out you're putting fucking dead bodies in the curry, my little brown friend,' warned Jim, 'you're next into the pot, understood?'

'What you mean dead bodies, sir?' queried the quaking Bangladeshi illegal immigrant. 'What dead bodies you mean, sir?'

'Listen, pal, just keep the family out of the pot and we'll get along fine, all right?' finished Jim. 'We'll have a couple of lamb bhunas to take away.'

'Without ears,' warned H.

As Sergeant Collins grumbled and mooched about disconsolately, the Patrol Group vehicles tore into the car park and stopped alongside the Handstead cars. Gilbert got out and strode over to Collins, offering him a handshake.

'Bravo Two?' he asked.

'That's me, Andy Collins.'

'Phil Gilbert. What's happening?'

'Got the Leeds Service Crew in trashing the Stonehouse so we're going to get them out and lock up as many as we can,' replied Collins simply.

'OK. What's the plan then, Andy?'

Collins the film buff and keen amateur historian had been praying for an evening such as this when he could call on one of his favourite films for tactics.

'Ever watched *Zulu*?'

'*Zulu*, yeah, but what's that got to do with anything?'

'The Zulus used to fight their enemies by taking the shape of a fighting buffalo,' explained Collins who was now surrounded by incredulous Patrol Group boys. 'They would feint to withdraw and bring the main body of the enemy into the chest, then suddenly turn and attack while the two horns of the buffalo on the flanks encircled them and drove them into the chest where they'd be destroyed. That's what we're going to do with the Service Crew. You and your boys are the horns.'

There was a long silence as Gilbert and his boys stared at the huge grey-haired sergeant with a cigarette clamped between his teeth.

'The Zulus got hammered in the film,' offered Gilbert eventually.

'Not a good example of their tactics, you're right,' agreed Collins, 'but they used it plenty of other times successfully.'

'Right,' said Gilbert slowly. 'We're the horns. I take it your guys are the chest, are they?'

'Correct. We'll draw them out, turn on them and then you and your boys take them from the sides and the rear.'

'How are you going to get them out?'

'That's where he comes in,' said Collins, indicating the beaming Psycho who was standing slightly behind him.

Gilbert looked him up and down with scarcely concealed disdain.

'He's got fucking sandals on, for fuck's sake.'

'Don't you worry about that, Phil,' said Collins cheerfully, rubbing his hands together. 'He can fillet a fish with those toenails, trust me.'

Psycho stepped forward in preacher's mode, arms raised to the heavens.

'Dear Lord,' he bellowed, 'grant mercy on these your warriors—'

'Shut the fuck up, Psycho,' interrupted Collins. 'Get in your motor and get over to the Stonehouse. Everyone off to the Stonehouse,' he shouted. 'Park up at the far end furthest from the doors. We'll walk round without them spotting us.'

As the Handstead boys hurried back to their cars and sped away, a bemused Gilbert stood with the Patrol Group, watching the red tail lights disappear.

'They're fucking mental,' he said finally. 'Zulu fighting buffalo, what the fuck is he on about?'

'Seen it used here before, Sarge,' one of the local Group officers offered up. 'Very effective as well.'

Utterly unconvinced, Gilbert returned to his van in time to hear Collins on air letting the expectant control room know that the curtains would be going up in five minutes.

'They're all fucking mental,' he repeated to no one in particular as the three Patrol Group vans sped after the locals.

\*

First again, this time into the Stonehouse car park, Pizza and John Jackson sat in the darkened car listening to the heavy early-evening radio traffic. Most of it concerned the deployment of other vehicles around Handstead in the event of the almost inevitable bedlam at the Stonehouse. Pizza settled back in his seat and closed his eyes with a half-smile on his face while Jackson looked anxiously towards the pub where the noise inside could be plainly heard and then back to the numerous police vehicles sweeping quietly into the car park, lights off, and parking up alongside them.

'What's going to happen, d'you think, Alan? Is there going to be trouble?'

The tone of his voice struck a chord deep inside Pizza and he was transported back a year to the passenger seat of a panda car alongside Bovril as they waited to raid a flat in the Grant Flowers tower block. Trouble had been anticipated that morning too and Pizza could hear his words to Bovril that day as clear as if he was speaking them again. 'What'll it be like when we get in there?' he had asked his new pal, painfully aware that he had never had a fist fight in his young, sheltered life before.

'A fucking bloodbath, in all likelihood, but don't worry, you'll be fine if you stay close to me and don't get separated,' answered Bovril from the grave.

And Pizza had stayed close to him in the mayhem

that followed – so close that he had been standing next to him when Myra Baldwin had shot him in the guts and then blown the back of her own head off. So close. So close. And then he'd held Bovril's head in his lap as he bled out on the floor of that rathole of a flat, his warm blood coursing over his shaking hands as he shouted at him to stay with him – so close.

'A fucking bloodbath, in all likelihood, but don't worry, you'll be fine if you stay close to me and don't get separated,' echoed Pizza quietly without opening his eyes. He was lost again in that life-changing moment, his waking hours still racked with the frustration that he could not hear what Bovril had been trying to say to him in his last moments, and his sleep always disturbed by dreams of Bovril in a crowded room, his lips moving as he again tried to tell him something. He would push through the throng to get alongside Bovril but he always woke up before he got to him. He was getting closer every night, but he had still to hear what his friend needed to tell him.

He had told Lisa about the dream recently after he had woken with a start of frustration in the small hours. She had cradled his head and gently stroked his sweat-drenched hair as he spoke quietly into her stomach.

'I keep dreaming about Bovril, every night.'

'It's only a dream, darling. He's gone, you know that.'

'He's trying to tell me something, but I can never get close enough to hear him. It's doing my head in.'

She didn't reply but lay quietly in the dark looking up at the ceiling as she stroked him, her eyes filling with tears and her throat clamped tight. She had often thought of telling him about the true nature of her relationship with Bovril but he'd never pursued the matter despite knowing that they had been friends. There seemed little point in revealing that the child Pizza now referred to as his son had been fathered by Bovril. There was no need, she reasoned, to jeopardise the happy family unit they had become, with little David the apple of his surrogate father's eye.

'Go to sleep, honey, it's only a bad dream,' she said through her tears as she ran her fingers slowly over his damp shoulders.

Jackson's voice brought Pizza back to his surroundings.

'What should I do?' Jackson asked anxiously.

Pizza sat upright and turned to face him, looking long and hard into his frightened eyes.

'You've never been in a punch-up before, have you?'

'No, never.'

'Listen, John, this is going to kick off big time, trust me. And when it does, there really aren't any rules. Got your stick with you?'

'Yeah, of course,' replied Jackson, patting his

truncheon pocket nervously, relieved to find that he had remembered to slip it in when he dressed for work.

'Get it out now. Chances are you'll forget you've got it when you need it. First one that gets near you, take him out. Don't think about it, just deck him. And then do the one nearest to him. Don't stop hitting them until you're safe, understood?'

'Yeah, but at training school they said you should only hit people as a last resort.'

'And I bet they told you that you should try and calm things first and avoid the head.'

'Yes.'

'Forget it, John, forget it all,' said Pizza in an exasperated tone. 'That's the bollocks that people who've never faced a crowd like this tell you to do from the comfort of a classroom. You can't talk to animals like this lot. You pause to have some kind of meaningful dialogue and you'll wake up in hospital, trust me. They've got one aim – to do you, so you do them first. And don't fuck about looking to crack them across the elbows or arms. Put their fucking lights out with one across the top of the head and a good kick in the nuts to be going on with. Don't fuck about with them, John, or you'll be on the floor quick time.'

'OK.' Jackson eased his stick out of its pocket and clenched it between both hands on his lap.

'Get the strap round your wrist and wrap it tight so

it feels like it's welded to your arm,' continued Pizza. 'They'll try and take it off you and if they do, they'll shove it up your arse.'

'Fucking hell,' murmured the young cop who could feel his legs starting to shake as fear took hold of him. He'd never known fear like it and was beginning to worry that he might not be physically able to get out of the car.

'You'll be fine, John,' Pizza said firmly. 'Stay close to me, always keep me in sight, and whatever you do, don't run away.'

'Run away?'

'Yeah, run away. You might get away unscathed but you can never come back.'

Jackson understood clearly the message Pizza was spelling out. He was beginning to understand the hard-won bonds of trust and camaraderie that bound street cops together. He had listened quietly as the group had reminisced about past battles and wished he could have joined in their banter. God willing, after this, perhaps he could in future. He set his jaw to stop his teeth rattling and closed his eyes as he waited for the word to go. He was determined not to let Pizza down but deeply unsure of how he would react when it kicked off.

Standing by his car, Sergeant Collins spoke quietly to Psycho.

'You ready, Psycho?'

'Ready to go, Sarge,' said Psycho, his face set as he stared at the doors to the pub where the noise was getting louder.

'Got everything you need?'

'Everything.' Psycho coiled his scarf round his neck and checked his tunic.

'In and out, OK, Psycho? Don't fuck about in there. Get it going and get out, we'll be waiting just outside.'

'Yeah, I know,' replied Psycho flatly. 'Get them in place, Sarge,' and with that he began to stride towards the double doors.

The doors slamming open went unnoticed inside the pub. Outside in the car park, the waiting cops heard the din briefly increase then fade as the doors shut behind Psycho. The pub seemed like some nightmarish demon that had swallowed him whole. But he was the only demon on the premises that night, standing in full uniform just inside the doors, waiting for someone to clock him, which they did, gradually.

Outside, Collins and the others heard the clamour die down and then stop altogether.

'Any minute now,' called Collins to the fighting buffalo formation.

Inside, the bullet heads stared aghast at the huge, ugly copper standing by the doors with his hands on his hips, smiling at them. The only sound was the low whirring of the huge, spinning fans that hung from the vaulted ceilings on poles. It didn't seem possible. A lone copper, wearing sandals and a Manchester United scarf and rosette on his tunic.

'Praise the Lord,' bellowed Psycho, raising his arms slowly. 'Bestow thy mercies on the mighty Red Army that they may scatter the heathen hordes arranged before them.'

Danny Braithwaite, the self-styled Commander of the Leeds Service Crew, jumped down from a table and pushed his way through the confused ranks, walking to within a few feet of the big cop. Braithwaite was nearly as tall but nowhere near as broad as Psycho and he completely failed to spot the telltale manic glint in Psycho's eyes. He fancied his chances with the big Jessie in the sandals and decided to give him some verbal first.

'You've got some front coming in here on your own, you Manc cunt.' His sparkling wit prompted howls of laughter from his followers and he turned to grin at them before continuing. 'Why don't you go and get some of your mates to give you a hand?'

'Son, I've unloaded harder turds than you before,' said Psycho cheerfully. 'Forgive him, Lord, for he knows not what he does,' he shouted at the ceiling fan, then lowered his gaze to Braithwaite. 'Repent your sins.'

'Tell you what, copper, how about you make me repeat my sins,' said Braithwaite.

'Repent, you dickhead,' corrected Psycho. 'Repent your sins.'

'Whatever. Why don't you come and make me?'

'Forgive him, Lord, forgive him,' yelled Psycho to the ceiling.

'You're starting to piss me off now, copper,' said Braithwaite, moving closer to Psycho and into his range.

It was a mistake Psycho knew he would make eventually.

'All that religious shit, you're really pissing me off.'

'Unbeliever, infidel,' shrieked Psycho, suddenly changing his religious affiliation, before moving with lightning speed and wrapping his huge arms round Braithwaite, pinioning him. 'God loves a sinner, come back to Him,' he breathed beerily into Braithwaite's face who was struggling desperately to free himself.

In one swift movement and before any of the Service Crew had time to react, Psycho lifted Braithwaite off his feet and up above him – straight into the spinning ceiling fan directly above. Whilst not quite as fast as helicopter blades, the fans still turned at a fair lick. More used to moving clouds of smoke around, they made a good effort to get through the head that had been placed in their path, neatly removing the very top of Braithwaite's head before the next blade round dug into his skull slightly lower down. Then they got stuck and stopped. Braithwaite was dropped unceremoniously on to the floor, blood pouring from the two wounds to his head, and before anyone could move, Psycho had gone, the doors swinging quietly shut.

In the car park, Collins was relieved to see Psycho come racing out of the strangely silent pub with a triumphant smile on his face.

'What the . . .' began Collins, before the silence was broken by a roar from the enraged Leeds fans. 'What the fuck did you do?' he shouted at Psycho. 'I only told you to wind them up and get them out.'

'God moves in mysterious ways,' giggled Psycho, using one of his favourite lines. He got his stick out.

The double doors crashed open against the walls, shattering the glass panes, and the furious mob surged out of the pub like a dam bursting, intent on revenge for their leader who lay unconscious inside, blood seeping from his shaven head which now resembled a neatly topped boiled egg.

'Withdraw,' bellowed Collins in his best Colour Sergeant Bourne voice, jogging backwards with his Handstead team, ensuring that the Service Crew were drawn fully into the rat trap. A second later he stopped and yelled, 'Get the fuckers,' and as one man the Handstead boys stepped forward and began to lay about themselves with their sticks. The odds were not good, they were outnumbered easily two to one, but Collins was banking on his boys taking out at least two yobs each, if not more. If one of the cops went down, they would be in the shit.

In the first few seconds, Collins himself dispatched four would-be assailants, two with perfect head shots with his stick, the others with stinging left-hand jabs. The others were enjoying similar success and the Leeds Service Crew crashed against the thin police line like waves breaking on a promenade. But they just kept coming, despite the battering they were getting. Psycho was swinging a baseball bat in one hand, a blood-stained bardic lamp in the other, and administering the *coup de grâce* with a jab from his toenails as they went down.

'Now, Patrol Group,' roared Collins, satisfied that most of the Service Crew were now outside.

With a loud yell, the Patrol Group boys fell on the throng from both sides. Equipped with hickory pickaxe handles, the visors on their helmets locked down, the Patrol Group began to carve through the opposition. Horrific beatings were being dealt out and the pile of groaning, bleeding bodies was growing. The sound of stick and pickaxe handles on heads rang around the car park.

\*

Rousing himself from the floor of the pub, Danny Braithwaite was surprised to find the bar empty save for the staff looking at him from behind the chicken-wire enclosure. His head felt as if someone had stamped on it.

'Where the fuck is everyone?' he shouted, staggering up to the wire and shaking it wildly.

By way of reply, the bar manager emptied a soda siphon into his face while one of his staff stabbed both Braithwaite's hands with the business end of a corkscrew. Screaming, Braithwaite fell back from the wire and raged at the staff from a safe distance.

'I get back here, you're fucking dead,' he shrieked, his face a red mask from his head wounds, both hands throbbing painfully. His previously white T-shirt was now a fetching pink as he bled all over it.

'Fuck off outside with your pals, arsehole,' shouted the manager. 'Sounds like they need a hand.'

Braithwaite, still groggy from his encounter with the ceiling fan, turned and lurched towards the double doors. He could hear the sound of a major fight outside and he was desperate not to miss out on the opportunity to give a copper a good kicking. He pushed the doors open and came to an abrupt halt, struggling to comprehend what he was seeing. His boys appeared to be getting a good hiding. Surely not.

Sergeant Phil Gilbert was nearest the doors, busily

beating two of the Leeds fans like a pair of bean bags until they seemed to split at the seams and leak all over the place. He heard the doors open with a bang and swiftly turned to protect his back. He saw the shaven-headed yob with blood pouring down his face and stepped quickly towards him. Braithwaite saw him coming but in his befuddled state didn't react.

'Night-night, son, sweet dreams,' called Gilbert before he delivered a perfect backhand shot with his pickaxe handle full into Braithwaite's face, shattering his nose and cracking a cheekbone. He followed it up with a forehand shot across the mouth, shattering his teeth and splitting both lips. Braithwaite flew backwards through the broken doors and crashed unconscious again in his first pool of blood, courtesy of the ceiling fan.

'I've fucking told you, you're barred,' shouted the bar manager from the safety of his enclosure.

John Jackson had found his vocation; he was having a ball. As the Service Crew had surged towards him, everything had gone quiet and he developed a sort of tunnel vision. All he could hear was his own breathing and his thumping heart. As a large, ugly brute raced towards him, Jackson had found himself moving towards the thug, not racing in the opposite direction as he had expected. Then his right arm had snapped out in front of him, his stick connecting perfectly with the yob's head. As the eighteen-stone shitbag began to collapse like a dynamited building, Pizza's coaching course filled his head and he put the man's lights out with a huge kick in the balls. This is fucking great, Jackson exclaimed to himself, desperately looking for his next target which turned out to be one of a group of three going for Pizza. Two beautiful shots to the back of two heads quickly reduced the odds in Pizza's favour.

'Quality, John. Mind your back,' shouted Pizza, stamping on the crotch of the hooligan he had just felled.

Jackson turned and moved slightly to his right to deliver another perfectly timed blow to the jaw of a passing Service Crew member. What a fucking great job, he thought to himself, glancing at his stick. The blood on it had run on to his hand and was beginning to stain his shirt cuff. We get paid to do this?

It was the making of John Jackson; in a few minutes he had discovered that he was born to be a street fighter, he had all the animal instincts and cunning required. He could sense danger approaching and kept moving to deal with it. The others saw it too. The stupid little kid who fucked up on the chase and made himself look a cunt because he didn't know his phonetic code was a natural. He was a whirling dervish and no one could get near him; his work rate was simply phenomenal, his right arm a constant blur as he beat the living shit out of anything not in a uniform.

The sheer scale of the violence took the Leeds Service Crew totally by surprise. There had been no preamble, no negotiation or discussion. They had ventured out into the car park and then had been set upon like a flock of sheep wandering into a den of wolves. Their initial surge had been hammered back and the Patrol Group had shut off their escape route; all that awaited them was a hammering. It was the Handstead way and a lesson that would not be forgotten by the hooligans. News of their annihilation at the hands of the police took several weeks to filter into hooligan circles, but when it did, the damage to the reputation of the Leeds Service Crew would take some time to mend.

Missing out on all the action had been Ooh Yah and Alfie who'd been stuck up in the north of the county on a track away from a domestic burglary, which had come to nothing in an underground car park. Fuming, and leaving the locals to continue their inquiries, Ooh Yah and Alfie had raced south to get a piece of the action.

'Delta Hotel, show Delta One en route to the Stonehouse,' he yelled above the scream of his sirens and Alfie's primeval roaring.

'Everything's in hand there, Delta One,' reported the control operator. 'Continue routine patrol please.'

'Will I bollocks,' snorted Young, throwing the handset into the footwell alongside him. 'Don't you worry, big fella, we'll get you something, I promise,' and he floored the accelerator.

Young was still in Alfie's bad books after the unfortunate death of Adolf the Dobermann and he was desperate to make amends. Since Adolf's demise, they had not had a single job where Alfie had had the chance to chew somebody up. Young had harboured high hopes of a nice burglar after their recent track, but the bastard had got away in a car and Alfie was still sulking. Young was sure he could generate a bit of business for them at the Stonehouse despite the instruction from the control room.

Things were certainly well under control there. Sergeants Collins and Gilbert and their exhausted, perspiring troops stood in a large circle round thirty-three bruised, battered, bloodied and, in some cases, unconscious Leeds Service Crew members. It resembled the field in the aftermath of Waterloo. They were all breathing heavily after their exertions; fighting at full tilt for nearly ten minutes would test the stamina of the fittest man, let alone a fat bastard like Piggy who was breathing through his arse. Whilst not as prolific as the others, Piggy had gone his bit, and now he stood dripping with sweat, bent slightly forward and panting like a dog. They were all soaked, their uniforms glued to their bodies, hair plastered to their heads and faces shiny and red with the sweat of their labours and adrenalin. What a rush, enthused Jackson, looking round for his mentor.

'Alan, that was fucking amazing,' he whispered as he got alongside Pizza. 'What a buzz.'

Pizza looked at him and smiled. 'You enjoyed that, didn't you? Doesn't always work out for us, John, got to be prepared to take a kicking occasionally, but you did well – actually, you did brilliantly.'

Jackson glowed with pride and noticed that the Brothers were looking at him with expressions of grudging respect on their faces. Psycho patted him on the shoulder.

'Praise the Lord, young JJ here is the real deal after all,' he declared, and thereafter for the rest of his service he was known to all simply as JJ.

'Got a few bodies to get back here, Andy,' remarked Gilbert casually. 'We got any vans available?'

'Have we fuck, everything's off the road at Handstead,' grumbled Collins. 'We're going to need a bus. Tell you what, Pizza, you and your boy get out on to the main road and find me a night bus, see if we can get this lot back in on it.'

Pizza and JJ trotted out of the car park and stood by the side of the dual carriageway looking south, hoping that one of the infrequent night buses might happen along.

Their luck was in. Ten minutes later, the Manchester City Centre to Handstead night bus rolled into view, driven by none other than Elijah 'The Alligator' Adams. He was well known to most of the local cops and well liked. The *Empire Windrush* had brought Elijah and his family to the promise of a new and better life in the UK in June 1948. Nearly thirty years later, Elijah had been settled in Handstead for several years and had witnessed despondently the decline of a town he had been proud to call home. He was a dapper little man, always immaculately turned out, scrupulously polite to his fares and enormously popular as a consequence. He had endured his fair share of racist abuse over the years but such was his charm and personality that sometimes people had to be reminded that he was a different colour to the majority. He was a devout Christian and firm believer in right and wrong and the rule of law and order; he always wore a suit, shirt and tie to church on Sunday and expected others to respect him as he respected them. Which didn't always work in Handstead and led to his nickname. He had been working a late shift a couple of years earlier and had stopped at a request stop for two young West Indian guys who had jumped on to his bus and pushed past without paying.

'Hey, guys, you gotta pay, you know, this service ain't free.'

'Go fuck yourself, old man,' laughed one of the two lads. 'You just some Uncle Tom coconut anyways.'

Elijah was minded to hammer the pair of little shits himself, but ever mindful of his position and obligations, he instead used the nearby phone box to call the police. Yankee One had taken the call immediately on hearing the name of the informant and five minutes later the harassed crew were refereeing a verbal bout between Elijah and the lippy teenagers.

'Officers, I'm requesting you to get this black trash off my bus,' said Elijah politely. 'They ain't paid and they got bad mouths.'

'Who you calling black trash, coconut?' yelled one of the boys, trying to push past the two cops to get at him.

'Officers, it's niggers like this fuck it up for everyone else,' continued Elijah as if they weren't there. 'They ain't paid, they's got to go,' he said in his wonderful, lilting Jamaican patois.

'Who you calling niggers, nigger?' screamed the Mancunian youngster. 'You're going to get your scrawny arse kicked, motherfucker.'

'Hold on, hold on,' shouted Yankee One's operator, holding his hands up for quiet. 'Who's making an allegation here?'

'Officer,' said Elijah with dignity, 'I am the allegator here.'

The cops in the car park looked up as the double decker night bus rolled in with Elijah at the wheel, grinning like the Cheshire Cat. He waved at the cops he knew.

'We found the Alligator,' said Pizza, getting off the bus and walking over to the group. 'Says he'll run all this shit back to the nick for us.'

'Good man, Elijah,' shouted Collins, giving Elijah a thumbs-up before he turned to address the heap of groaning football hooligans.

'Right, listen up, you shower of shit,' he began. 'I'm not sure if anyone's mentioned this to you but you're all nicked and you're all going back to Handstead police station on this bus. You will behave in the bus or pay the consequences, believe me. At the police station, you will be charged, remanded in custody and appear in court either tomorrow or the day after, where you will be remanded again until your court dates. And by the way, you don't need to say anything,' he finished by way of caution.

'Fuck you,' slurred one of the bloodied lumps at his feet.

Collins began to batter him about the head and shoulders with his stick, shouting, 'No, no, no, that is not how to address a police sergeant,' until the man lay senseless again. There was no further discussion from any of the others.

The prisoners were either hobbling or being carried on to the bus, with Elijah occasionally calling, 'Fares please,' when Delta One careered into the car park and Ooh Yah leapt out.

'Oh bollocks,' he shouted when he saw it was all over.

'Sorry, Ooh Yah,' called Collins as he frogmarched one up the stairs, 'all done and dusted. What happened to you?'

'I got tucked up with a job up in Hartwell, got here as soon as I could. Nothing left at all?'

'Fuck all, I'm afraid, but you could put the beast on a lead and let him have a nip or two to hurry them on to the bus if you like.'

'Better than nothing, I suppose,' moaned Ooh Yah. 'You might have waited for me.'

He wandered back to Delta One and with great difficulty got the over-excited Alfie on to his lead, before going back to the bus. Alfie was on his back legs lunging desperately at anything that moved, his enormous jaws snapping shut with a loud click, slobber flying about. He managed a couple of nips on cowering Service Crew members and tore the trousers off one of them, but it was just not enough.

And then Ooh Yah's salvation staggered unsteadily into view. Danny Braithwaite kicked open the bar doors, having recovered consciousness a second time. His head resembled a bright red overgrown pumpkin, it was so swollen and distorted from the hammering he had received. His mouth was a bloody puffy slit and a couple of teeth had stuck in dried blood on his chin. Both eyes were closed and blood still oozed from his destroyed nose and his boiled-egg head. Some of the cops in the car park gasped at the dreadful spectacle, but Ooh Yah just yelled, 'Thank fuck for that.'

Alfie had also spotted Braithwaite and was down in his attack posture, waiting for the off.

'You cunts,' yelled Braithwaite through his painful mouth, spitting teeth out into the car park. 'You're all fucking dead.' He began to stagger slowly away from the doors, barely able to see where he was going and only vaguely aware that one of the cops was shouting.

'Police officer, with a dog, stand still or I'll send the dog,' bellowed Young, and then from the bottom of his boots he continued, 'Arthur Scargill, Arthur Scargill.' He reached down to Alfie's chain collar to release the spring catch and hissed into his ear, 'Kill him.'

Braithwaite registered that the shouting had stopped and the next moment nine and a half stone of enraged shaggy black Alsatian hit him hard in the chest. He flew backwards again through the doors to the pub, this time with Alfie attached to his face. He hit the bloodied floor on his back, with Alfie biting the top of his head in a frenzy as he smelt the blood. Screaming as best he could, Braithwaite tried desperately to push off whatever it was that was trying to eat him, but he was no match for Alfie who was exacting revenge for what had happened to Adolf.

From the car park, the cops listened for a few seconds to the noise of a football hooligan being eaten alive, before Collins stepped alongside Young.

'Get him off, Ooh Yah,' he said firmly. 'We don't need any corpses down here. Job done, OK?'

'Yeah, no worries, Sarge,' replied the beaming Young. He knew that Alfie would have forgiven him now and that they'd be friends again. Their relationship since the death of Adolf had been strained, with Alfie keeping his distance. Young was due to play cricket the following afternoon after a few hours' sleep and he would take Alfie along to watch and get pissed together in the clubhouse afterwards.

He hurried into the pub. Braithwaite had managed to get his head out of Alfie's mouth and had crawled under a table, where he had barricaded himself behind a couple of chairs. His head wounds were streaming, the blood running off his chin, and he was starting to go into shock. The staff behind the chicken wire began to applaud as Ooh Yah walked in; they had witnessed a truly primeval display of savagery from Alfie that none of them would ever forget. As Young quickly clipped the lead on to Alfie's collar and pulled him back, he gave an exaggerated bow to the still applauding staff.

'Fucking brilliant that, officer,' called the manager. 'You boys have done a brilliant job. Compliments of the house,' he said as he and one of his staff dumped two crates of bottled lager on the bar top.

Ooh Yah hurried out to let Collins and the others know of their windfall and Collins went back to collect it. The shaking and incoherent Braithwaite was dragged from under the table by two Patrol Group officers and hauled on to the bus where his troops stared in horror at the remains of their feared leader.

'What the fuck happened to him?' whispered one.

'Looks like he's been in a car crash and been through a fucking windscreen.'

Sure now that Alfie was safely locked back in his van, the bar staff helped Collins into the car park with the crates and soon everyone was toasting their success. Young secured a bottle for Alfie which he emptied into his battered steel drinking bowl and put into his cage where it was instantly dispatched.

'Listen up, boys,' announced Collins loudly. 'First up, great job, all of you.' He raised his bottle in salute to them and they responded in kind. 'Let's get this lot locked up and then everyone into the muster room to get our notes done. Phil, can your boys do the escort on the bus, make sure nothing happens to Elijah or his bus?'

'No problem,' said Gilbert, offering Collins a hearty handshake. 'That was quality, Andy, fucking quality. I'd heard you were all mental down here but I didn't really appreciate just how much. See you back at Horse's Arse.'

Leaving his drivers to get their vans back to the nick, Gilbert boarded the bus with the rest of his boys for the trip back to Handstead. The Leeds Service Crew were totally subdued with not even an insult offered during the short ride. Of their total strength in the pub of forty-five, eleven had managed to escape the ambush and slip away into the night. The rest now faced the unique Handstead criminal justice system.

# Chapter Twelve

Shortly after 5 a.m., Pizza drove out of town on his own, leaving JJ swapping war stories with the others in the muster room, and headed for Teakettle Corner. From its elevated position, the strangely named location afforded fabulous views across Handstead towards the distant metropolis of Manchester, and because it didn't lead anywhere in particular, it was generally deserted. At this time of the morning it certainly was.

Pizza switched off the engine, stepped wearily out of the car and sat against the warm bonnet. He sighed deeply and closed his eyes as the cool early-morning breeze wafted around him and slowly dried his still sweaty face. The only sound was the wind in the trees in the small valley below him and the birds. The silence and solitude were the perfect contrast to the evening he had just experienced and Pizza now found himself regularly driving out to Teakettle Corner to put things back in the locker. In common with all the cops at Handstead, he had developed a routine to counteract the lunacy he was now an integral part of; without some sort of antidote there would have been no let-up. He looked over towards the distant tower blocks of Manchester and detected the first flush of sunrise. It quickly spread like a bloodstain across the horizon until he was forced to shield his eyes from the glare. This was the time of day when any cop with an imagination reflected on his lot, the fulfilling and unhinged life he led – the power and the glory, the good and the evil, the bravery and the fear.

The long fingers of light spread across Handstead, bathing its battered, grubby estates and ravaged parks in a soft ethereal glow that seemed totally out of keeping with the town's true nature. Like ancient man after a long, frightening night spent squatting in his cave, Handstead emerged blinking into a fresh new dawn.

The Brothers didn't get finished with their six prisoners until after 7 a.m. Everyone had been allocated at least two prisoners each and once they had been booked in and dumped en masse into the large detention room, all the officers involved in the disturbance had sat down with Collins and Gilbert in the muster room and divvied up who had who after a lengthy discussion about what had happened. The names of each of the prisoners was written on to the whiteboard on the wall at the rear end of the room, an arresting officer's name alongside, with the name of a corroborating officer next to that, and then they wrote their pocket books up. It was how things had to be done and by 6 a.m. all the pocket books had been completed and photocopied ready for the unfortunate early turn CID officers to take over, interview if possible, charge the prisoners and get them to court. It was most unlikely that any interviews would take place.

Jim and H wandered wearily across the rear yard in half blues towards the garages where their cars were parked.

'Quality night, H,' remarked Jim, casually examining his cut and bruised knuckles which had been injured despite wearing his Northern Ireland-issue gloves with iron flats in the padded knuckle area. H had worn an identical pair and had sustained similar damage. He laughed and cast a look at his own, iron-hard fists.

'The best for a while, mate.'

'You get some sleep, son. See you tonight, OK?' said Jim, slapping H on the shoulder as they parted and opened their motors.

They followed each other out of the rear yard and then drove in opposite directions along Bolton Road East, H heading towards the motorway and then north,

Jim towards the village of Bathurst where his wife and daughters waited for him. He was tired and had switched off, which was why he didn't spot the BMW pull out of the youth club car park opposite the nick and start to follow him.

With the window wound down and cool air flowing round his face, Jim began to brighten up and for the first time noticed the BMW in his rear mirror. He frowned and without even thinking began to employ counter-surveillance driving tactics. It was a practice familiar to all the cops at Handstead who had learnt the hard way that the local villains were not averse to following them home. As he increased his speed, the BMW did likewise. At the traffic lights at Liverpool Road, he slowed as he approached the green light before accelerating through the amber as it turned to red. Watching the BMW race through after him, Jim knew he had a tail and began to ponder his options. One was to return to the nick and wait, another was to burn the tail off, but his preferred option was to confront the follower. As he turned off Liverpool Road into a quieter B road, he again slowed to allow the BMW to get closer and finally got a better view of its only occupant, the driver.

In the BMW, Kazim Dimiz cursed his carelessness as he got too close to the cop's car, braking heavily to drop back but fearful he may have been made. The Vauxhall Viva in front of him continued as before, the driver giving no indication that he had spotted him, so Dimiz relaxed and tried to shake his head clear of the fatigue that was threatening to envelop him. He had been plotted up outside Handstead nick without a break for nearly thirty-six hours and he was shattered. He had followed off and lost two cars during the previous evening and opted to follow Jim's Viva for no other reason than he had been playing 'car snooker' with passing vehicles to pass the time and needed to pot a green. The Viva suddenly stopped dead in its tracks and the exhausted Dimiz failed to react quickly enough, nearly rear-ending it, and as he recovered from the near miss he saw the driver of the Viva leave his car and come running towards him. In his panic, Dimiz had stalled the BMW and before he could even reach for the ignition, the big man in the blue police shirt pulled open his door.

'You fancy me or something?' snarled Jim, leaning in close to Dimiz's face. 'You queer or something?' As he spoke, he was aware of a vehicle pulling alongside him. Fearing he was about to fall victim to his tail's back-up, Jim reached in and grabbed the BMW's keys, then turned to face the newcomer with the keys in his clenched fist, the large ignition key protruding from between his fingers.

'Everything OK, officer? You need a hand?' asked the beaming Elijah Adams, who was also on his way home from the nick in his son's car. His three devoted boys had come to collect their father from Handstead after he'd put his signature to a lengthy and largely fabricated witness statement about what he would claim to have seen of the fight outside the Stonehouse.

Before Jim could reply, Kazim Dimiz hissed, 'Why don't you just fuck off, you black cunt.' Before the full stop, the three Adams boys were out of the car and beside the BMW.

'Excuse me, officer,' said the smallest and youngest of the brothers, who stood six feet three and weighed seventeen stone. 'No one speaks to our dad like that.' Politely but very firmly so as to leave no doubt in Jim's mind that he should move, young Adams put a hand on Jim's chest and moved him back from the BMW before reaching in and hauling Dimiz out by his thick black hair. Not a word was spoken as the three enraged boys then proceeded to batter Dimiz to a pulp on the road with their ham-like fists. When he lay senseless, young Adams got to his feet and dusted down his trousers.

'Good morning, officer,' he said, while his elder brothers politely nodded to Jim and got back into their car, Elijah waving merrily out of his window.

The road was quiet and empty, the only sound being the early-morning birds and Dimiz groaning as he came around.

'There's a lesson to be learnt there, pal,' said Jim, squatting down alongside Dimiz whose face was already swelling to twice its normal size, both eyes closing, his front teeth missing and blood coursing from his broken nose and split lips. 'You need to have a good look at who you're calling a black cunt in future, don't you, you horrible bastard. Why were you following me anyway, who you working for?'

'Go fuck yourself,' mumbled Dimiz through swollen and painful lips.

'You just don't learn, do you?' said Jim calmly before planting a peach of a right-hander between his eyes. 'I see you again, arsehole, I'm going to break your legs. You get yourself off home and behave yourself.'

He stood up and stretched before hurling the keys to the BMW as far as he could over the adjacent hedge into a field. Making a quick mental note of the BMW's registration number, he wandered back to his car, got in and drove home by another route, constantly checking his rear-view mirror. Sometimes, he mused, the right things happen to the right people. Usually not – usually all the bad things happened to people who least deserved it, but occasionally, what goes around, comes around. On mornings like this, Jim could almost believe there was a God.

Rod Allan had arrived at work early, before the night duty boys had finished, on the off chance he might get an opportunity to spin DCI Harrison's desk before anyone got in, but the events of the previous evening meant the nick was packed. He sat alone in his office in the basement, stewing with frustration and pulling angrily at his limp dick which had got him into this awful mess. He had a long wait ahead of him.

Pizza and JJ hadn't gone home and at 9 a.m. were waiting in the underground passageway between the nick and the magistrates' court to help the gaolers take all the overnight remand cases across to the court. It was an ideal opportunity for JJ to get some court experience under his belt. It was regarded as good practice for probationers to spend as much time as possible in the box at the magistrates' court rather than waiting for their first exposure in the cauldron of the Crown Court. Every arrest and traffic process that a probationer had gone through would be routinely marked up by their sergeant, 'Guilty plea anticipated, probationer to give evidence.' The magistrates were sympathetic to the practice and regularly listened to nervous probationers stumbling through dull as ditchwater evidence about defective lights and red light offences. It was invaluable experience and this morning JJ was going to be outlining the evidence against the Leeds Service Crew to remand them in custody for seven days.

It was not expected to prove too onerous a task. Having moved the heaving masses of overnight remands

in dribs and drabs down to the court cells, JJ sat
nervously alongside Pizza on a hard wooden bench
behind the court inspector waiting for Court One to go
into session under the stern gaze of the formidable
Colonel Mortimer. Pizza had chosen the court carefully,
well aware that Mortimer was so pro-police and biased
against all defendants that it would not have raised
eyebrows had he appeared on the bench in full uniform
and a helmet. Defence solicitors would try to move
heaven and earth to shift cases from his court, always
unsuccessfully as the court listing office was in cahoots
with Mortimer who had instructed them to list any case
to him involving foreigners, drunkenness, fighting and
especially assaults on police. He enjoyed his reputation
with his fellow magistrates and around the town as a sort
of Judge Jeffries 'hanging judge' who struck fear into the
hearts of Handstead villains. 'Not guilty' verdicts from a
bench presided over by Colonel Mortimer were as rare
as an Amish porn star and remands in custody taken as
a given.

On the stroke of 10 a.m. Colonel Mortimer strode in
with the confident gait of a man with a distinguished
military background, most of which had been spent
with military intelligence torturing confessions out of
perceived enemies of the state. As he took his seat, his
two timid colleagues waited deferentially until he had
adjusted his gown and colostomy bag before taking their

own seats, as interested as the rest of the court in what outrageous abuses he might indulge himself in today.

The first piece of business for the day was the appearance of the Leeds Service Crew prisoners who were brought up the narrow single staircase from the cells for what seemed an eternity until the large dock was packed. They looked horrific – a combination of the lack of any sleep and the hiding they had received from the fighting buffalo ambush. There were gasps of shock from the gallery and the well of the court. The court-appointed defence solicitor looked open-mouthed at what appeared to be the contents of an eighteenth-century prison ship. Mortimer gave them only a cursory glance and smiled thinly as he recognised the signs of an intensive but effective interrogation. He concentrated on the copy of the *Racing Post* in front of him until the court was called to order by the clerk. He peered over his half-moon spectacles.

'What have you for us this morning, Mr Hannah?' he asked breezily.

'Your worships, a total of thirty-four individuals from the Leeds area, arrested last night following a disturbance at the Stonehouse public house in Handstead. They are charged jointly with affray and individually with other assaults, criminal damage and assault on police.'

'Assaults on police officers?' asked Mortimer loudly

and very theatrically, looking from one of his colleagues to the other to let them know where this lot were destined. 'Assaults on police officers?' he repeated, emphasising his incredulity that anyone would assault a police officer.

'Indeed, sir,' replied the clerk who also knew where things were headed. 'There is an application before the court to remand all thirty-four in custody for a further seven days while police inquiries continue.'

'I'm not at all surprised, Mr Hannah,' said Mortimer. 'Assaulting police officers indeed.'

'Quite, sir,' interjected the clerk, eager to try and establish at least a semblance of impartiality. 'Shall we enter pleas now, sir?'

'Yes, yes, please let's proceed,' agreed Mortimer, eager to hurry proceedings through to lunch so he could get up to the nick bar for a drink with the CID and get the inside story of what had happened at the Stonehouse.

The long process of entering pleas then began which proved difficult as many of the Service Crew, never the sharpest knives in the drawer, had difficulty in speaking a coherent word, such were their injuries. One particularly foul-looking brute resembled a circus exhibit, with an enormous swollen head and lips that looked like a baboon's arse.

'What on earth is he saying?' snapped Colonel Mortimer as Danny Braithwaite tried for the third time to confirm his name and address and deny all the charges. 'Is he foreign, does he need an interpreter? Who's acting for the prisoners?'

The duty defence brief got slowly to his feet and glanced at his unloved and unwanted clients.

'Good morning, sir. Andrew Cannell of Chivers, Palmer and Scott. I appear for the defence this morning and—'

'What is your client saying?' Mortimer interrupted him rudely. 'This court's time is limited enough as it is. What is his name and what is his plea, if it's not asking too much?'

'Your worships, I have had little time to take instructions from any of the defendants. I received copies of their charge sheets only within the last half hour and have spoken to only three of them in the court cells before court. I—'

'Only spoken to three of them?' Mortimer steamed in again. 'Good grief, man, hardly value for money, are you?'

In the dock, even the densest of the Crew could see they were only ever going to get banged up and began to get restless.

'Who is this one?' continued Mortimer, gesturing contemptuously at Braithwaite as he might at a turd on a new carpet. 'What is his plea?'

The defence brief gathered his papers and hurried

over to the edge of the dock where he fanned the charge sheets out until Braithwaite indicated his, which ran to two pages.

'How do you want to plead?'

Braithwaite's slurred reply was unintelligible.

'Guilty?'

Braithwaite shook his throbbing, space-hopper-sized head as vigorously as he could.

'Not guilty?'

He nodded slowly and nearly fainted from the pain.

'Your worships,' announced Cannell, 'Daniel David Braithwaite of number twelve, Saltwood Road, Leeds, pleads not guilty to all the charges.'

The whole process of confirming the rabble's names and addresses and entering pleas took just over an hour, after which JJ walked nervously to the witness box, armed with the case papers, to present the application to remand all the prisoners. As expected, it was pretty straightforward with Colonel Mortimer guiding him through the process and blasting the defence solicitor every time he got to his feet to make objections or submissions. JJ was in the box for about fifteen minutes, reading from the statement of facts prepared earlier that morning by a frazzled pair of CID officers, and gave a decent performance. He certainly didn't disgrace himself there – he saved that for later.

Number One Court at Handstead Magistrates had

been built in the 1920s when courts were designed to look imposing and magisterial, sending a signal that they stood for something – as opposed to modern courts which were all stark white walls, beige carpet tiles, fluorescent lighting and laminate surfaces that made them look like trendy fast-foot outlets. Number One Court was panelled in oak from floor to ceiling, the panels lovingly polished by the resident cleaners, some of whom remembered the court being built; the floors were magnificent York flagstones, and three superb chandeliers hanging from the vaulted, beamed ceiling provided lighting. The stained-glass windows at the side of the room gave an almost cathedral-like quality to the court. The magistrates sat on a raised dais, so high above the well of the court that many a cop had remarked that Colonel Mortimer particularly reminded them of Zeus on Mount Olympus. The enormous royal coat of arms on the wall behind the magistrates, carved from wood and hand-painted, was the finishing touch that shouted: this is a place of serious business and you scumbags in the dock are fucked.

The one major drawback to the court was the uniform oak panelling. The main door in was only distinguishable from the rest of the wall by a brass ring which served as a handle. Pizza had forgotten to remind JJ that he needed to get his bearings on entering the court and register where the door was.

On being thanked for his hard work and instructed to leave the court by Colonel Mortimer, JJ stepped out of the box on to the flagstones – and froze, suddenly aware that he had no idea when the exit was. He was the sole object of attention in the court as his eyes desperately searched the panelled walls for a way out. With relief he spotted a brass handle on the back wall and strode confidently down the middle of the court towards it, completely missing Pizza's desperate hand gestures. The court inspector just stared quizzically at JJ as he passed and then shook his head and turned back to the pile of papers on his desk. When he reached the door, JJ stopped and turned to face the three magistrates and, as he had been instructed, bowed his head politely before turning again, opening the door and stepping quickly through, shutting the door behind him.

He found himself standing in complete darkness surrounded by what felt and sounded like brooms, mops and buckets. JJ decided to stay in the cupboard, hoping that perhaps no one had noticed.

In the court, Colonel Mortimer sat back in his chair and looked at the ceiling. He puffed out his cheeks and twiddled his thumbs. His colleagues glanced nervously at each other but said nothing. Every eye in the court was trained on the cupboard door from behind which they could hear the occasional clatter of a broom.

Mortimer waited a couple of minutes then sat forward and spoke to his clerk.

'Go and get him out, Mr Hannah,' he said wearily.

JJ wasn't the first and certainly wouldn't be the last cop to walk into the broom cupboard, but he was definitely the first to try and brazen it out by staying in there.

The clerk bustled through the court and opened the cupboard door. JJ was standing just inside, facing out, his case papers under his arm.

'All right?' he said to the clerk with a pleasant smile.

'This way, Constable Jackson,' replied the clerk, and led a red-faced JJ back through the silent court to the proper exit. In the dock Danny Braithwaite got to his feet and managed to shout something. It was unintelligible but clearly it was intended as some sort of insult. Colonel Mortimer was incensed.

'Silence in court, you animal. How dare you?' he bellowed. 'That is clear contempt for this court, fourteen days, take him down, officers.' The gaolers quickly bundled Braithwaite down to the cells.

As Allan pulled furiously at himself, his desk phone rang, startling him out of his all-consuming problem-solving. Composing himself briefly, he answered in his usual pompous style, 'Building Operations Manager.'

On the other end of the phone, Pete Stephenson rolled his eyes to the ceiling.

'Get your arse up here, Allan,' he growled. 'I need a word with you about one of your staff.'

'Which one, Pete?'

The noise at the other end was the sound of Stephenson grinding his teeth and popping blood vessels in his forehead. He loathed Allan and went apoplectic whenever he used his first name in such a familiar fashion.

'Little Harry,' he barked.

'What's he done?'

'You may have noticed the canteen's out of bread this morning. Little Harry's scared the shit out of the delivery guy who won't deliver here anymore – just get your fucking arse up here now,' snapped Stephenson and slammed the phone down to avoid further conversation with the odious Allan.

Little Harry, as Stephenson had called him, was better known to the troops at Handstead as Harry the Dwarf and they loved him. He wasn't actually a dwarf, but he was definitely on the short side and a deaf mute to boot. He had been employed as a cleaner at the nick since the early 1960s and had become part of the invisible mechanism that ran it. He did anything and everything happily, always acknowledging his instructions with incomprehensible grunts, but never refusing. The cops, as usual, took advantage of his disabilities but Harry gave as good as he got. They would switch his hoover off at the wall which would take a while to register with him; he would approach officers in the canteen, indicating with hand movements that there was a phone call for them, and follow it up with a roar and obscene hand gesture as the cop held the dead phone to his ear. But to a man and woman, they loved him, always greeting him with a gentle whack around the head or tap on the shoulder, and they especially liked the hours he kept. He generally arrived at the nick at around 4 a.m., which was the cue for the front office PC to go and get his head down for a couple of hours, leaving Harry perched on the stool behind the counter, wearing a tunic usually five or six sizes too big. Early-morning callers would be greeted by this strange-looking little cop who roared at them, and this had proved too much for the middle-aged bakery delivery man who now refused to set foot in the madhouse. Harry lived every day as though it was his last and had they but known his background, the Handstead cops would have wrapped him in cotton wool.

He was a Polish Jew, born in 1941 in Warsaw, two minutes older than his identical twin brother. He never knew his real name, Harry being the name given to him by the British soldier who had found him hours from death under a pile of bodies in Bergen-Belsen concentration camp in April 1945. The soldier had also recovered Harry's twin but what little Harry knew of his past did not include his brother. The sketchy records he had managed to find confirmed that he had been found on 15 April 1945, that he had received treatment for TB and then had moved from one displaced persons camp to another, one foster home to another, until the age of twenty when he had been taken under the wing of an order of nuns who made it their life's work to offer people like Harry a future. It was they who had persuaded Handstead District Council to give a job to the pint-sized deaf mute – all legacies of his appalling experiences in the camp – and the staff at Handstead nick had become his surrogate family. But of his real family he knew nothing, not even their surname. They were not even faded memories for him. And of the kindly British soldier who had saved him Harry also knew nothing. He supposed he may have been amongst the first Royal Artillery soldiers who had arrived at the camp that day, but he had not heard from him since he had carried him ashore at Harwich in 1946.

Despite all the odds stacked against him, Harry was determined to enjoy the remarkable chance he had been given. He was a particular favourite with D Group, the Brothers, Psycho and Pizza particularly, and would always be invited along to drink with the group. Indeed, he was an integral part of their drinking frenzies and was due to meet up with them after early turn next week.

Allan climbed up from the basement and trudged up

to the first floor where he knocked on Stephenson's closed door.

'Come in,' shouted Stephenson who was still twitching with irritation.

As Allan stepped into his office, Stephenson got to his feet and advanced swiftly towards him, brushing past him to slam the door shut.

'So, Pete, what's the—' Allan's words were choked off as he suddenly found himself in an agonising neck lock. Stephenson had grabbed him from behind and now got hold of his bulbous nose and twisted it brutally from side to side. Allan's eyes began to bulge and he screamed like a mating fox.

'Don't ever call me Pete, you little fat twat,' said Stephenson calmly. 'It's Mr Stephenson, or Chief Inspector Stephenson, or Sir, or Boss, or Guv, but you never call me Pete, understood?'

'Yes, yes,' gasped Allan.

Stephenson released him from the vice-like grip and pushed him roughly away.

'What was that all about?' Allan asked, rubbing his throbbing nose, tears streaming down his face.

'I can't make it any plainer – don't you ever call me Pete again.'

'I thought you didn't mind. I am part of the management team in the station, after all.'

Stephenson's brow shot up. 'Part of the management

team? Are you fuck part of the management team. There's me and Mr Harrison and that's it. We don't ask you anything, we don't tell you anything, we don't want anything to do with you. You're the fucking building manager, nothing more, despite what you like to call yourself. Who the fuck authorised you to call yourself Senior Building Operations Manager anyway?' Stephenson stared hard at Allan, waiting for a reply, deciding that he had a face he could happily punch all day.

'Well, it was something agreed with the previous senior managers here,' blustered Allan eventually.

'Is that right? Well, it's fucking unagreed as of now. You're a building manager in my nick, so go and get that ridiculous sign off your door and give it to me. And who authorised this association of toilet cleaners you've created for yourself?'

Allan continued to rub his aching nose and didn't reply so Stephenson continued, 'I'm going to make some inquiries at Headquarters about this little gang of yours, Allan. It all sounds very suspicious to me, very underhand, and if I find out it's all your own idea, I'm going to chin you, understood?'

Allan nodded meekly and turned to leave before Stephenson remembered why he'd called him up.

'Tell that little monkey Harry that if I hear about him dressing up as a cop again and frightening the locals, I'm going to hang him from the mirror in my car, OK?'

Allan nodded again and left quickly. His bubble had been well and truly burst within the last twenty-four hours, first by Ozdemir and now by that big ugly jock, Stephenson. How much worse could things get? he wondered to himself. Still, once he'd got the information Ozdemir wanted, that'd be one less problem to worry about and he was sure he could outlast Stephenson at Handstead, as long as he could avoid the threatened physical attack.

Two floors above him, Stephenson began to concentrate on the Force planning around the Jubilee events due to take place in the town in two weeks' time. As part of a national chain of bonfires, a huge fire was to be lit in Grosvenor Park and its construction was already well under way, supervised by the local Round Table. To his dismay, he saw that the Licensing Authority had granted in excess of two dozen late-night licences to public houses and organised street parties. He was worried they would have a bloodbath on their hands. When he checked the duty rosters for Jubilee night and discovered that D Group were scheduled to work a night duty on a cancelled rest day, he became convinced of it. It was unusual for one relief to have so many delinquents on it at the same time, but it happened occasionally, and D Group was way ahead in the complaints league. Superintendent Grainger from

Complaints and Discipline regularly sent in details of complaints against Handstead officers, and D Group officers – Psycho in particular – featured prominently. That said, they were just what Handstead needed, happy to fight fire with fire and occasionally pour some petrol on the red-hot embers.

Sighing deeply, Stephenson began to draw up his own plans and strategy for Jubilee night, and they most definitely did not include the ridiculous Inspector Hilary Bott's brainwave of sweets for the barbarians.

# Chapter Thirteen

The group had had two days off after a heavy seven night duties and were now back for seven early turns. By 5.50 a.m. they were all gathered in the muster room, yawning and chatting quietly amongst themselves, or in Piggy and Ally's case arguing. They all looked shattered and baggy-eyed. Two days' leave after a long set of nights was simply not enough to recharge the batteries and get body clocks readjusted to the nearest thing to a normal life. The options after the last night shift were either to stay up all day like a zombie and go to bed early that evening, or catch a couple of hours and hopefully sleep that night. But neither really worked and for cops like Psycho who relied on whisky and huge hits of Night Nurse to sleep during the day while on night shift, the two days off afterwards were an unpleasant twilight zone spent wandering about his untidy flat not really sure what day of the week it was.

Over a period of time, cops working the three core shifts could expect to develop stomach ulcers and serious sleep disorders that took years off their life expectancy. It was a well-documented fact that a lot of cops didn't get to draw their pensions for long as they failed to adjust and deal with normal daily routines. They were used to travelling around and shopping at odd times of the day; suddenly having to cram everything into a short weekend or sit in queues of traffic to get anywhere proved a huge shock to the system and often proved fatal.

Early turn was probably the closest they came to a 'normal' day at work, especially in the summer, though an early shift in the middle of a long winter could test the strongest will when it came to leaving a warm bed at some ungodly hour.

Now, in early June, coming to work was almost pleasant. It was light when they got up, light when they got home, and their social lives improved as a consequence. Few were inclined to do more than work and sleep during the winter, but now plans were being made to get on the piss at the end of today's shift and visit a pub in town where Psycho had got friendly with one of the barmaids.

'She said her boss will probably lay on some chips for

us,' he boasted, 'seeing as we'll spend a few bob in there.'

'Who's coming?' asked Pizza.

'Us lot of course, don't know about Andy Collins and I'm sure Mr Greaves won't come, couple of the boys off A Group and I've invited Anne Butler.'

'Fucking hell, Psycho,' exclaimed Ally, 'when are you going to give up? She's not interested in you, she's all loved up with that bloke over at Chipstead.'

'She might have been,' smirked Psycho, 'but I hear things aren't going too well and when I phoned her, she said she'd think about it. Praise the fucking Lord, my luck might be changing.'

'Don't go getting your hopes up, mate, we don't want you getting all punchy and unpleasant when she doesn't show up. My money's on you boning this brassy barmaid you've chatted up. What's she like anyway?'

'Big old thing, huge hooters. You might be right, but we'll see.'

'Has Harry been invited?' asked Pizza.

'Of course, wouldn't be the same without him.'

Pizza and JJ were sitting together just in front of the Brothers, writing up their pocket books in preparation for another day at the sharp end, while Ally shouted at Piggy about his curry breath and Malcy read the paper. They looked up as the door to the muster room opened and Sergeant Andy Collins walked in with a huge pile of paperwork under one arm and the large, burgundy-coloured leather-bound General Occurrence Book in his free hand.

'Morning, boys,' he boomed cheerfully, casting his eyes over them and clocking the weariness etched into their pale faces. 'Good couple of days off, I hope?'

'Pretty good, Sarge,' lied Psycho from the front row. 'We've got a drink arranged for when we go off watch. You fancy it?'

Collins did fancy a drink after work but at the back of his mind a little voice of reason started wittering at him: are you fucking mad, a drink with this lot? You get to draw your pension in five years as long as you're not locked up somewhere. Go home, go home.

'Just a quick one maybe,' replied Collins, leafing through the paperwork. 'Where we going?'

'Got an in at the Partridge.'

'The Partridge on Oakwood Road?'

'Yeah, you know it?'

'Christ, yes, used to be a proper police boozer. CID from here used it all the time. Got a big brassy barmaid not averse to sucking on a cop's ham harpoon.'

'Praise the Lord,' shouted Psycho, turning to the others who were laughing loudly. 'Going to be a quality night out one way or the other.'

'Listen up, boys,' called Collins. 'Plenty of paperwork here for you all so come and grab what's yours when we finish. Psycho, you've got another visit from your old mate Mr Grainger at two o'clock. Don't forget, will you?'

The group began to hoot and catcall Psycho who got to his feet and mock bowed to them with a broad smile on his face. Grainger/Psycho encounters were well known and they all looked forward to hearing about them. If the local bookies were prepared to take the bet, they'd have been down there like a shot to put a few quid on the mad monster.

'Not a lot happened since we finished, lads,' continued Collins, leafing through the Occurrence Book, looking for something to keep them happy and in the right frame of mind. 'A few in for shoplifting yesterday, two for a nasty GBH at the Pineapple last night. Not a lot really. This is a nice one, though,' he announced as he read on. 'Late turn Two One came across a car on fire yesterday afternoon on the Great North Road. The vehicle was a hire car from Heathrow Airport and the driver was an elderly female American tourist from Dallas, Texas. She picked the car up the day after she flew in and was planning to drive north to Scotland and visit family along the way. She told Mick Simpson in Two One that she'd had nothing but problems with the vehicle since she left London, the engine screaming at speed and having to fill up with petrol eight times. She was seriously pissed off and unimpressed with British cars until Mick pointed out that she'd driven the best part of two hundred miles on the motorway in second gear which was why the fucking thing was on fire.'

The group fell about laughing.

'Seems she'd never seen a manual gearbox before so she'd banged it into second at Heathrow and thrashed the bollocks off it up the motorway. Only the Yanks,' he laughed.

When his muster was over and the troops were ambling up the corridor to get their radios and keys from the Blister in the front office, Collins went in search of Inspector Greaves. He had seen him arrive for work earlier wearing a Second World War pilot's leather helmet and goggles and needed to make sure he was put somewhere safe for the day before the bosses saw him. Collins was amazingly loyal to his deranged inspector, constantly covering for him and refusing to hear a word said against him. 'There but for the grace of God,' was the only opinion he ever offered on him, which Psycho, for one, heartily agreed with.

In the front office the group waited to get their kit while the Blister was busy dealing with a caller to the desk.

'Yes?' she asked rudely, her red moon face set in a scowl and her huge breasts resting on the glass counter top as she slid the partition aside.

Ntende Adebayo looked fearfully at the fat perspiring

policewoman and wondered if he was doing the right thing. The lorry driver who had just dropped him off – after a lengthy journey up from the docks at Grimsby hidden in a crate – had assured him that this was the right course of action.

'I have lost my passport please,' he stammered.

'Lost your passport, have you?' said the Blister, raising her eyebrows knowingly. 'Don't you worry, you've come to the right place.' She reached under the counter for the buzzer controlling the doors from the front office into the nick and held it. 'Through the doors, sir, turn right and then first left. Lost passports are all dealt with there.'

Gratefully, Adebayo pushed the door open, turned right and then first left through the door into the cell area.

Sergeant Jones looked up from his desk where he was busy writing in his first visits of the day to his overnight prisoners. He frowned.

'What the fuck do you want?'

'I have lost my passport please,' said Adebayo, now deeply unsure of where he was. He could see the barred gates and the full custody chalkboard and hear the echoing shouts from the cells.

'Lost passport? Oh, I see,' said Jones, before the door opened again and Pizza and JJ walked in.

'One for JJ, Sarge,' said Pizza, guiding JJ forward. 'Nick him as an illegal immigrant, JJ.'

Ntende Adebayo was booked in and banged up within ten minutes and on returning to the cell area, JJ noticed that Jones had already put him on to the custody board. His name and offence were clear enough, but the disposal column contained only a chalk drawing of a plane.

'What's that all about?' he asked Pizza as they left to write up their notes.

'The big silver bird that's going to take him home,' replied Pizza, patting his protégé on the shoulder.

It was a quiet morning by Handstead standards. In common with the rest of the country, the town seemed to be waiting for the Jubilee celebrations in a couple of weeks, everything was on hold. The summer weather was fresh and warm and the cops were out and about in shirt sleeves. The locals were enjoying the weather as well, and by lunchtime the few green spaces in the town centre were filled with office workers eating al fresco. Psycho and Malcy were keeping an eye on things, particularly the young office girls who were spreading themselves out on the grass in various stages of undress. Psycho and Malcy had decided to undertake foot patrols around the town when time permitted and were having a quick stroll around Church Green before they closed for refreshments at the nick, when Psycho suddenly grabbed Malcy's arm.

'Oh my sweet Lord, look at that,' he hissed quietly, indicating a group of laughing girls sitting on the grass bank below the old church. 'The one on the far right's gone commando.'

Malcy didn't reply but stopped in his tracks and tried to see what Psycho had spotted without showing out – which wasn't going to be easy.

'I saw her fangita,' promised Psycho.

'I can't see anything,' complained Malcy.

'Angle's all wrong, we need to sit down,' said Psycho, dropping to the grass and trying to appear inconspicuous. Malcy did likewise and the two perverts began to shuffle about for a better view.

'Nothing,' said Malcy bitterly.

'Definitely commando, saw the beauty clear as day,' said Psycho dreamily. He lay on his side, head on his hand, peering up the bank towards the group of girls. Malcy followed suit and passers-by were treated to the extraordinary sight of two coppers in full uniform stretched out on the grass apparently sunbathing.

'Bingo, there she is,' announced Psycho from his prone position, leering broadly as the light breeze ruffled the girl's short summer dress.

'You beauty,' said Malcy as he glimpsed it as well, but too loudly – the girl looked up and saw the two prostrate, grinning coppers twenty feet from her on the grass and very obviously looking up her kilt.

'Fuck, she's spotted us,' whispered Psycho. 'Quick, get going, Malcy,' as the girl got to her feet and told her friends what was going on. The entire group rose and began to shout insults as Psycho and Malcy beat a hasty retreat to their car.

Summer had definitely arrived.

The canteen at Handstead was packed, mostly with desk warriors and paper shufflers, but half of the early turn group had managed to find a table. Psycho and Malcy were telling the Brothers about their spot at the church when H suddenly looked up, wide-eyed.

'What the fuck is he doing here?' he said.

The others turned to look and were astonished to see the hated Superintendent Grainger walking into the canteen. He was accompanied by Inspector Bott, whose wittering he was ignoring, and Detective Inspector Chislehurst, who looked absolutely terrified about stepping into the lion's den.

'He's early to serve papers on me,' said Psycho. 'Got a fucking nerve using our canteen. Thought this canteen was for coppers,' he said loudly as the trio passed their table, 'not cop catchers.'

Chislehurst glanced fearfully at him but Grainger ignored the comment and Bott was too busy talking to hear anything.

'Fucking nerve,' agreed Jim.

'Actually, this is just what I need.' Psycho smiled mysteriously. 'I've been waiting for an opportunity to use these.' He reached into a trouser pocket and dropped three dried, husky seeds on to the table.

'What are they?' asked H.

'Jamaal seeds, fried and dried.'

'Jamaal seeds?'

'Yep, guaranteed to make the world drop out of your arse.'

'What you going to do?'

'If I can get them into Grainger's food, he won't know what's hit him.'

'What, poison him?'

'No, not poison him,' scoffed Psycho unconvincingly, 'just help him get rid of some of that shit he's full of.'

The others looked sceptical.

'Psycho, you can't just poison him. He's a twat all right, but poisoning him?' said H.

'He'll be fine, just a touch of the runs for a day or two,' said Psycho dismissively and got up to put his plan into operation.

Inspector Bott had telephoned Grainger herself when she heard he was due to visit, and invited him and Chislehurst to have lunch with her in the officers' mess at Handstead before they saw Psycho. Grainger had accepted the invitation only because he was aware that

Chief Daniells rated her and he would take any opportunity to ingratiate himself with him. It would give him the opportunity to casually remark to the Chief next time he deliberately bumped into him at Headquarters that he'd recently had lunch with one of his favourites.

Like most stations with canteens around the country, Handstead had an officers' mess which was for the exclusive use of inspectors and above. The Handstead senior officers' mess, on the same floor as the canteen but on the other side of the stairwell, had a long rosewood dining table that seated twelve and four battered old sofas dotted around the far end of the room facing an ancient black and white television. A couple of mildewed prints of old Handstead and a portrait of the Queen on a horse were the only decoration on the whitewashed walls. The majority of the shift inspectors chose to eat with their groups, but Hilary Bott saw the officers' mess as clear confirmation of her exalted status and used it all the time.

She examined the menu Sellotaped to the canteen wall and then turned to her nervous guests.

'Not a great choice I'm afraid, sir,' she simpered. 'I'd recommend the lasagne to be on the safe side.'

'That's fine, two lasagne will be fine,' said Grainger tersely, keen to be on his way. 'Where's the mess?'

'Just through the doors,' replied Bott, indicating with her hand.

'See you in there,' said Grainger, hurrying away with his bag carrier who was simmering with resentment that he had not even been asked if he wanted lasagne.

Bott went into the kitchen and placed their order with big 'Sweaty' Sylvie McGraw, the canteen lunch chef and late turn short order cook. She was an uncouth Geordie from the same town as Jim, who dripped sweat from her reddened jowls as she worked in the steaming kitchens with a cigarette clamped between her teeth. Bott was appalled to find her up to her elbows in a bowl of God only knew what, sweat dripping off her hairy chin into the mixture and a large pencil of ash threatening to join it.

'Three lasagne for the officers' mess please, Sylvie,' she said, praying the mixture had nothing to do with her order.

Sylvie looked towards her, screwing her eyes up against the cigarette smoke.

'H'way, pet, nay worries, be about five minutes, OK?' she said, her cigarette bouncing up and down as she spoke, dislodging the ash which disappeared into the bowl.

'Thank you, Sylvie. Put them on my tab, will you, please?' continued Bott. 'Should you be smoking while you're preparing food? It isn't very hygienic, is it?'

Sylvie's response was lost in the heavy coughing fit that enveloped her, the cigarette butt joining the ash in the bowl as it flew out of her mouth. She coughed herself blue in the face, her eyes streaming, before huckling up a large greenback which she spat into the sink behind her.

'What's that, pet?' gasped Sylvie eventually, but Bott was close to being physically sick and left without pursuing the matter.

Wiping her mouth on the back of her tattooed arm, Sylvie called Bott's order to her staff and thrust her nicotine-stained hands back into the bowl of contaminated batter.

Five minutes later, one of the kitchen staff put the three meals on a large double-handled tray which she placed on the preparation table behind Sylvie. She had stubbed out another cigarette on the greasy floor and was about to carry the tray to the officers' mess when Psycho bowled into the kitchen.

'Hello, darling,' he breezed, 'how you doing?'

'Great, pet, great. You?'

'Bearing up, Sylvie, you know how it is. That tray for the officers' mess?'

'Aye, pet, it is, I need to take it through.'

'Sylvie, you'd better wash your hands before you go in, you know what Bott's like.'

'Aye, you're right, lad,' she agreed and wobbled over to the sink, running the taps hard to flush away her earlier greenback which had stuck around the plug. As she scrubbed her hands, behind her back Psycho quickly opened the pepper mill, dropped three dry jamaal seeds in and then screwed it shut tight.

'There you go, Sylvie,' said Psycho, politely holding the kitchen door open for her. 'Done something nice for them?'

'Lasagne, darling, all three of them,' advised Sylvie, though none of the three plates looked the same.

'Great, hope they enjoy it,' said Psycho and returned to the table where the others waited. He was grinning like a wanking Jap.

'Well?' asked Jim.

'In the pepper mill,' replied Psycho, rubbing his hands together. 'By the time Grainger gets to see me, he should be well gone.'

In the officers' mess, Grainger, Bott and Chislehurst stared at the unpleasant offering dumped in front of them by the fat smelly woman who was scratching her ample arse as she left. Grainger reached immediately for the pepper mill and ground away for at least a minute until the entire blob of whatever it was had been covered in a layer of pepper. Bott followed suit, but Chislehurst took a suspicious sniff at the meal and decided to give it a miss.

'Not hungry, Paul? Almost edible if you put some pepper on it,' said Grainger with his mouth full.

'I'll give it a miss if it's all the same to you,' he said sullenly. 'I can't stand lasagne anyway.'

'Oh dear, you should have said. Can I get you anything else?' said Bott, forking another large slice of lasagne into her mouth.

'I'll be fine, I'll eat later.'

'Suit yourself. We're seeing that bastard Pearce in forty minutes – you might feel better with a meal inside you,' suggested Grainger.

'I'll be fine, don't worry,' insisted Chislehurst, folding his arms and sitting back in his chair.

Twenty minutes later, Grainger declined the offer of a chocolate mousse for dessert and clutched at his aching stomach. A bead of sweat rolled down his forehead and he puffed out his cheeks in discomfort as he stifled a belch.

'Enjoy your lunch, sir?' asked Bott who was also feeling a little windy.

'Eaten too much, I reckon,' he replied, the first stomach cramp shooting across his midriff. 'Either that or I've got food poisoning.'

'I'm not feeling all that well either,' said Bott, suddenly clutching at her stomach. 'Not well at all.'

'We need to get ready,' said Grainger, getting to his feet and grimacing as the cramps worsened. He groaned and leant forward slightly.

'You OK, sir?' asked Chislehurst.

'Fine. Let's get on. We're using your office, I believe,' he said to Bott.

'Yes of course,' she replied, regretting the offer as she desperately needed to get to the toilet and didn't fancy having to use the general ladies' toilets, preferring her own, private facilities.

Bang on two o'clock, Psycho knocked on the door to Bott's office, which was opened by Chislehurst. He gave Psycho a beaming smile.

'Good afternoon, Constable Pearce, do come in.' He stood aside to let Psycho in.

Psycho gave him a wink as he passed him, causing Chislehurst's heart to miss a beat. Maybe he was on side after all, he thought to himself.

Psycho took the chair opposite Grainger and was delighted to see that he had his head down, his deathly white face bathed in sweat and his teeth clenched.

'Everything all right, Mr Grainger?' he inquired pleasantly.

'Never mind me, Pearce,' he growled, looking up at him.

Psycho could see the distress in his face and he smiled. Got you, he thought.

'You wanted to speak to me about something?' he said.

Chislehurst took his place alongside Grainger and

opened the folder in front of him. The gurgling from Grainger's stomach was audible to all of them. Grainger leant forward, clutching his stomach, and groaned.

'You OK?' asked Chislehurst.

'Let's get on with this,' snapped Grainger. 'Give me the file.'

Chislehurst pushed the file along the desk to him and placed his chin delicately on the points of his fingers.

'Right,' said Grainger, trying to focus on the documents in front of him, sweat dripping off his nose and on to the papers. He groaned again and then loudly, involuntarily, passed wind. Chislehurst looked at him aghast.

'Oh, that's fucking charming, isn't it?' protested Psycho. 'Calls me in for an interview and starts dropping his guts. Not what I expected, Mr Chislehurst, not what I expected at all.'

Chislehurst mumbled something and continued to stare at his boss.

'Are you all right?' he asked again.

The rumbling from Grainger's stomach was getting louder and the gases were threatening to escape from both ends. His wispy hair was plastered to his head and he was starting to pant as the cramps worsened.

'Let's get on,' he said shakily through gritted teeth. 'I've called you in today, Pearce, in connection with a complaint made against you by Mrs Agnes Myers who has alleged you indecently assaulted her in the Discount Supermarket in Bells Lane. We're here to serve a Regulation Nine notice on you and get a first-account explanation from you.' Then he passed wind again.

'Fucking hell, Mr Chislehurst, what's this all about?' asked Psycho, holding his arms aloft.

Chislehurst was becoming uncomfortable with Psycho's repeated requests to explain Grainger's problems. It was a deliberate tactic to isolate Grainger who was clearly in difficulties anyway.

'What have you got to say about the allegation?' Chislehurst blustered, avoiding the question.

Psycho sighed deeply. 'Yes, I remember the old girl very well, bless her.'

'Bless her?' You remember her?' groaned Grainger who had been expecting total denial of the entire incident. Surely he wasn't going to admit everything? Momentarily he forgot the pain he was in.

'Of course I do. Dear old thing's only knee high to a grasshopper, so I was giving her a hand to get things off some of the higher shelves.'

'Including bread?'

'Including bread,' agreed Psycho. 'Funny thing that. She asked me to get a loaf off the top shelf, Mr Grainger, and when I got it down, I thought of you. But then I looked at it again and realised it said thick cut.'

There was a pause as Grainger and Chislehurst

243

digested this and then Chislehurst put his head back and howled with laughter until he thought he'd be sick. Grainger slumped forward on to the desk, his wet forehead smudging the ink on the documents, groaning loudly as he was racked with stomach cramps.

'Fuck off, Pearce,' he moaned as yet another interview with Psycho ended in abject failure and he escaped his clutches again.

As Psycho closed the office door behind him, the sound of Chislehurst weeping with laughter was still audible along the corridor.

'How'd it go?' asked Malcy when Psycho bowled in.

'Four nil,' smiled Psycho, holding up four fingers.

'Quality. Come on, big man, we've got a bit of time to kill before we go off watch.'

Hilary Bott wandered around the nick in growing discomfort as her dose of jamaal, smaller than Grainger's, gradually took hold and got worse. As her stomach cramps began to seize her, she hurried back to her office in the hope that the interview was over and she could use her own toilet. The stench as she opened the door was dreadful, causing her to gag and beat a hasty retreat to the ladies' on the second floor. Needs must.

Grainger had rushed into the ensuite toilet as soon as Psycho had left, and he sat there in agony until his body had cleared itself of the toxic jamaal seeds. At one stage he genuinely feared that he was passing internal organs. He didn't dare leave the nick for nearly an hour. Chislehurst had abandoned him to his suffering – the stink in the office had become unbearable – and made his own way back to Headquarters to let his uncle know that Grainger had failed miserably, again, to rid the Force of the monster Sean Pearce.

Grainger eventually shuffled painfully out of the rear doors into the yard where his car was parked. He was taking tiny steps as though his shoelaces were tied together, such was the agony from his ring of fire. His underpants were stuffed with wet toilet paper to alleviate the pain and he felt as if he'd been raped up the arse by a horse. No doubt, he fumed, that little twat Chislehurst would recognise the feeling. He had assumed, quite correctly, that Chislehurst would take the opportunity to report back to the Deputy Chief Constable and he decided to go straight home and avoid the snake pit at Headquarters. At least the stomach cramps had diminished and as soon as he was fit enough, he planned to send a letter of complaint to Pete Stephenson about the standard of catering at Handstead. The canteen had shut after the lunch session and the spiked pepper mill now sat in one of the cupboards waiting to inflict damage on other unsuspecting victims.

# Chapter Fourteen

By six o'clock the group were well pissed in the bar on the top floor of the nick. Although they had plenty of time, they had as usual bolted as much down their necks as they could as quickly as possible. The two women behind the jump were well versed in dealing with heavy drinking sessions such as this and had lined up pints on the jump ready to go. The older of the two women smiled as she looked at her younger colleague who was swapping coarse insults with one of the cops. She could remember her friend's first day at the nick and how appalled she had been at the behaviour she had witnessed, but as she had predicted, the younger woman had quickly grown to really like the majority of the cops who drank up there. They were some of the funniest men she had ever met, with razor-sharp wit and endless supplies of stories that were true, in all likelihood. On the other side of the coin they also talked about things that made her blood run cold, things they had seen and done, but she liked them a lot. Some more than others. In the year that she had been working there, she had shagged two of the single officers who lived in the police hostel, and had also proved willing to offer up a blow job on occasions when she was in a really good mood.

The officer she was currently swapping insults with was Psycho who had heard of her benevolent nature and was determined to take advantage of it. Despite his quite startling brutal physical appearance, he had a definite presence about him, something that many women found attractive. Clearly she did as well, as twenty minutes later she had been persuaded to join Psycho in the darkened ladies' toilets on the deserted second floor and was on her haunches in the end cubicle of three, playing with Psycho's blue-veined bowel trowel as he relaxed on the pan. She was working hard and Psycho could feel the telltale tingling in his old chap when to their horror the main door to the toilets burst open and someone came running in. Psycho quickly lifted the barmaid on to his lap, clamped a large hand over her mouth and hissed, 'Quiet,' into her ear.

Sweaty Sylvie McGraw dashed into the cubicle two down from Psycho and slammed the door shut. By the most wonderful irony, she had made herself a bacon and tomato sandwich half an hour earlier and given it a good blast from the spiked pepper mill, which had been put away in a cupboard when the canteen closed after the lunch session. Now the filthy old crone who had made a career out of poisoning generations of Handstead coppers had fallen foul of an altogether more dangerous poisoner, who was himself about to suffer the consequences of his actions. Sylvie had the screaming pukkalucks and Psycho sat listening in abject horror as she let loose a flock of starlings into the pan, accompanied by loud, choice Geordie phrases.

'Hadaway and shite, you bastard,' she shouted as her arse began to drink water from the pan. 'Fucking hell, man.'

The sounds and smells of her distress soon began to fill the room and Psycho and the barmaid buried their noses in his fresh shirt to counter the attack. Soon their eyes were watering and the girl began to gag but, worse, Psycho could feel his pride and joy begin to wilt under the onslaught. For the first time in his life, Psycho lost wood, though under the circumstances no one would have held it against him.

Sylvie emptied her bowels for a good twenty minutes, each deposit sounding like someone drowning puppies. At last, completely drained and feeling quite weak, she flushed a good half dozen times before leaving –

significantly, without washing her hands. Psycho vowed he'd never eat a crumb from her kitchen again and waited quietly until he was sure the old witch had gone back upstairs. He took a look at the barmaid who was still curled up in a ball on his lap.

'Fucking hell, that was something to tell the grandchildren about,' he said quietly.

'God, that was gross,' replied the girl, getting off him and straightening her shirt. 'What a monster.'

'Listen,' said Psycho, 'fancy finishing what you started?'

'What, here? After that?'

'Well, I'm game if you are,' he replied, determined to keep up his record of success with women. She didn't look too keen but Psycho took her small hand and placed it on his cock which began to harden instantly. Ten minutes later she had achieved lift-off and resembled a plasterer's radio as she took both barrels in the face. When she returned to the bar and began to clear away some of the empties, her older colleague eyed her damp hair suspiciously but said nothing. After all, people in glass houses don't throw stones.

'Right, drink up, boys, we're off to the Partridge,' shouted Psycho who was feeling very pleased with himself. Tanks emptied and the prospect of his true, unrequited love turning up at the pub, Grainger poisoned – God was definitely in his heaven. Andy

Collins had stayed longer than he had intended but the move to the Partridge was a no-no. He might be recognised by the brassy barmaid, for a start, and Mrs Collins expected him home for a parent/teacher meeting and it just wasn't worth the weeks of unpleasantness if he missed it.

'Got to go, boys,' he said, draining his glass and popping it into the large plastic basket the barmaid was carrying. 'Behave yourselves and don't get nicked.'

Shouting their farewells, the group began to leave, Harry the Dwarf who was as drunk as a skunk riding on Jim's shoulders.

As the loud echoing voices departed from the nick and a semblance of normality returned, Rod Allan came quietly up the stairs from the basement and stood briefly in the stairwell, peering up into the dark void. The noise from the bar was barely audible and through the double doors that led into the main corridor he could hear muffled voices from the front office and cell area and see a caller to the front office being dealt with by the office PC. The nick was apparently nearly empty and so he decided to check out the first floor where the CID lived. He trotted silently up the stairs and pushed through the double fire doors on to the corridor, which was in darkness. Directly in front of him was the door to DCI Harrison's office which was closed as usual, but no telltale light shone from underneath. Allan walked slowly down the corridor. The CID office to his right was in darkness and empty, as was the DI's office further up on the left and Chief Inspector Stephenson's office. Beyond that were only property stores but he checked them anyway and found them all locked. The corridor was completely empty and at his mercy.

He returned to Harrison's office and tried the door. As he had anticipated, it was locked. He reached into his pocket and drew out the master key he had brought with him, quickly opened the door and stepped into Harrison's office. He shut the door quietly and stood for a moment with his back against it, breathing deeply, heart thumping. The room smelt of stale whisky and was fairly well illuminated by the evening light from the window that looked out on to Bolton Road East, but he would need the desk lamp to search the office properly. He pressed the button on the base of the lamp to switch it on and cast his nervous eyes around the room.

Where would the information he wanted be? The glass-fronted cabinets appeared to contain only legal documents, but a cupboard at the other side of the room was piled with brown manila folders. He started there, carefully flicking through the pile. They were all cases awaiting hearing or trial. Once, as he leafed through, he thought he heard footsteps at the door and his heart leapt into his mouth, but it was a noise out on the street and he continued even faster. No joy there, so he turned his attention to Harrison's desk. It had two large wire trays on either side, each piled with paper and other coloured files and he sat in Harrison's chair to go through them. Again, lots of interesting stuff, but no sign of anything to do with Brian Jones, whoever he was.

The desk had a section of three drawers to the right which Allan tried next. They were locked shut. He began to panic about how he was going to get them open without damaging them when he noticed the key in the lock. A turn to the right and the drawers slid open easily. In the top drawer he found what he was looking for immediately. He flicked through a blue A4 hardback notebook and as he did so an envelope fell out. It was the envelope that DC John Benson had taken from Brian Jones's flat in Handstead the day he packed Jones off to London, giving the address where his old prison companion lived. The name and address on the envelope didn't mean anything to Allan but the writing in the notebook where the envelope had been concealed certainly did. There it was. Brian Jones's name, an address in Lennox Road, London, a Met DI's name and phone number. This had to be it.

Allan rummaged through the top drawer for a piece

of paper and a pencil and quickly jotted down everything written on the two pages. He slipped the piece of paper into his trouser pocket, replaced the notebook, locked the drawers and switched off the desk lamp. He remained seated for a few seconds as he listened intently and allowed his eyes to adjust to the semi-darkness. The only sound was the traffic outside and his thumping heart. He was nearly there; just get out and downstairs and you're home free, he told himself.

He crept back to the door and put his ear to it – silence – then opened it quietly, stepping out backwards and pulling the door silently behind him with both hands. As the door shut, he felt a stunning blow to the back of his head that propelled him into the office he'd just left, the door banging against the far wall. He crashed into the low coffee table and against a chair before ending up on his back, his feet towards the open door.

'There you are, Bob, I told you I heard something in here. Rats my arse,' said DC John Benson, walking in and hitting the wall light switch. He and DC Bob Clarke stood staring at Rod Allan who looked back at them, wide-eyed and petrified.

'No, I was right, John,' said Clarke. 'That's the biggest rat I've ever known.' He looked menacingly at the trembling building manager. 'What the fuck are you doing sneaking about the boss's office in the dark?'

'I was just checking all the bulbs on this floor,' managed Allan hopefully. 'No need to hit me, was there?' He rubbed the back of his head ruefully and gave them a cheesy grin. 'No harm done,' he said benevolently, getting unsteadily to his feet. 'Don't worry, I won't be making a fuss about this, boys, you weren't to know it was only me.'

'Nothing wrong with his bulb,' said Benson, flicking the light off and on several times.

'I know that now,' replied Allan as if he was talking to an idiot. 'I didn't know until I checked it.'

'You didn't need to go into his office and shut the door to check it,' persisted Benson. 'Look, you can do it from here,' and he flicked the light off and on again.

Allan licked his lips and his mean little eyes darted between the two large detectives who blocked his exit.

'I wasn't in his office,' insisted Allan. 'Excuse me, I've got to get on.' He tried to push past them but Benson laid a large hand on his heaving chest.

'Your old ticker's a bit agitated, Rod,' he remarked. 'You a bit nervous about something? You got something you need to tell us?'

Benson and Clarke were skilled interviewers as

well as torturers and recognised the body language they were now witnessing, the evasiveness and lack of eye contact.

'He's well at it, John,' observed Clarke quietly. 'What you been doing in here, you little twat?'

'I told you, checking the bulbs. Can I go now please?'

The detectives ignored him.

'Where's the boss, Bob?' asked Benson.

'He was upstairs in the bar half an hour ago. I'll go and check.'

Allan's heart froze. If Harrison was still in the nick, he was going to have his work cut out to get out of this mess.

'Why don't you sit down, Rod, while we wait,' said Benson, pointing to the chair he had crashed into. 'And keep your hands where I can see them.'

'Hands, why?'

'Just keep your fucking hands where I can see them, Rod, else I'll nail them to the wall to keep them in view, OK?'

Allan slumped forlornly into the chair and sat chewing his bottom lip nervously, occasionally glancing up at the huge detective who was leaning against the door frame picking his fingernails.

'You're in the shit, Rod,' said Benson quietly, smiling at him. 'You know it and so do I.'

'I don't think so,' replied Allan weakly. 'I was just doing my job and suddenly I'm public enemy number one. This is ridiculous.'

'You're at it, Rod,' said Benson dismissively.

They waited in silence for a couple of minutes until they could hear voices approaching from the stairwell, the corridor door burst open and then DCI Harrison hurried into the office and stopped. His face was flushed, partly because of the drink he'd consumed but mostly with anger. He stared at Allan.

'What the fuck are you doing in my office?' he finally demanded.

'I told these two, checking your bulbs.'

'There's nothing wrong with the bulbs.'

'I know that now, but I had to check.'

'How'd you get in?'

'I've got a master key.'

'Show me.'

Wearily, Allan handed him the key. It had a plastic tag on it and was clearly marked 'DCI's office'. 'Can I go now? I've got the rest of the station to do.'

'No you can't,' said Harrison aggressively. 'Turn your pockets out on the table.'

'I certainly will not,' stammered Allan nervously. 'You've absolutely no right to do this to me, I've done nothing wrong. This is outrageous.'

'Search him, boys,' commanded Harrison, stepping

aside to let the two grinning detectives get at the quaking Allan.

He was hauled to his feet by John Benson and, protesting vainly, pushed face first against the wall with his hands pinioned above his head. Clarke patted him down roughly and pulled his pockets out. The piece of paper fluttered to the floor and was picked up by Clarke, who unfolded it and read it. The colour drained from his face and he turned and handed it to Harrison. Harrison read it, his florid face expressionless. Benson had released Allan's hands and he turned to face the detectives, rubbing at his wrists. With one swift movement, Harrison lunged towards him and punched him hard in the side of the jaw, sending him crashing back against the wall. He slumped to the floor unconscious.

'Nice shot, boss,' remarked Benson, looking down at the prostrate building manager. 'What did you find?'

Harrison handed the paper to him and Benson's jaw dropped.

'Fucking hell,' he said slowly. 'What's he doing with this?'

He handed the paper back to Harrison who walked round to his desk and sat down in his chair. He rubbed his top lip thoughtfully for a second or two before opening his bottom drawer and pulling out his ever present bottle of Bushmills and three glasses.

'We'll nick him as soon as he comes round, boss,' said Clarke.

Harrison motioned to the two detectives to sit down and poured three large shots.

'Think this through, boys,' he said as he pushed their glasses towards them on the desk. 'There's only one person who'd want that information, isn't there?'

'Ozdemir,' they replied in unison, sipping their drinks.

'Exactly, but what I need to know is how that oily little bastard got into Allan and what the arrangement is. We could use this little set-up very nicely to our advantage.'

'Go on,' said Clarke.

'First, I need to confirm it was going to Ozdemir, although I can't believe it could be anyone else. Then I want to know what he's got on Allan to make him try and get the information, and I want to know what the arrangements are for getting it to Ozdemir. We get all that and Ozdemir's arse is mine – we set him up again.'

'Shouldn't be too hard,' said Benson, glancing at Allan who was beginning to stir. 'Can't see that fat bastard holding out on us, can you?'

'No way, he's fucked. Captured with his fingers in the till. He'll give us everything, don't you worry, and then we start pulling the strings.'

They toasted each other in anticipation as they waited for Allan to come round, and a few minutes later he sat in an armchair rubbing his jaw and looking mournfully up at the three detectives who were standing in front of him, grinning broadly.

'You're well fucked, Allan,' began Harrison. 'I should have you nicked for what you've just done.'

Allan hung his head but said nothing. Even his rat-like instinct for survival was struggling to see a way out of this.

'Tell me,' continued Harrison quietly, 'who asked you to get this information for them?'

'A bloke I met the other day, don't know his name,' replied Allan sullenly.

'A bloke, someone you've never met before, asked you to do him a big favour and screw my office to get a specific piece of information and big-hearted Rod Allan just did it because he's that sort of bloke?' asked Harrison.

Allan still refused to see sense and stayed quiet. Harrison sighed deeply.

'Allan, it's entirely up to you what happens now. You be a bit sensible and tell me what's going on and I'll do what I can to make things easier, even make them go away perhaps. The alternative is you get nicked, publicly humiliated, convicted in court, which will be well covered by the newspapers, I promise you, and the chances of you ever getting another job are zero. It's completely up to you, we're not even going to give you another slap.'

The phrase 'make them go away perhaps' was what Allan was seeking and he responded immediately.

'I'm being blackmailed,' he said loudly, looking up at Harrison. He glanced at Benson and Clarke who had thin smiles on their faces.

'What is it, Allan? Little boys or something? Always thought you had the air of a kiddie fiddler about you.'

'No, no, not boys,' shouted Allan. 'I got some grief in a brothel.'

'A brothel, not little boys?' Harrison sounded surprised.

'I was with a couple of toms. They were filming me, the bastards.'

'Who was?'

'I don't know their names, foreign blokes.'

'What's the deal with them? What pressure did they put on you then? It's not the end of the world, shagging a couple of prostitutes.'

'They threatened to send copies of their film to everyone at the nick and my wife.'

'In exchange for what?'

'Their boss said you were keeping him from a friend of his. Said if I found out where you were keeping him, he'd lose the film.'

'This friend of mine – Brian Jones, you mean?'

'Yeah.'

'And what's the name of this man who asked you to get Brian's address?'

'I don't know, but he's definitely the boss. The others were all bowing and scraping to him.'

'So describe him.'

'I don't know. Foreign, black hair, flash suit, just some flash foreign bastard.'

'What did the others call him?'

'Never heard them use a name.'

'What's the arrangement for getting this information to him?'

'I've got until tomorrow to get it to him.'

'Where?'

'Back at the brothel, by tomorrow.'

'Where's the brothel?'

'Birchwood Avenue, above the bookies.'

'Hmm. You're really in the shit, aren't you? That said, I can see a way out of this for you, Allan, but can I trust you, can I really trust you?'

'I'll do anything you want,' pleaded Allan who could finally see some light at the end of his very long, dark tunnel. 'What do you want me to do?'

Harrison sucked thoughtfully on his teeth and went back to his chair, slumped back into it and gazed at him.

'Tell you what, Allan,' he said finally, 'you can take that piece of paper over to your friend tomorrow.'

'Take it to him?' queried Allan.

'Yeah, you can take it to him, but the last thing you want to do is tell him that any of this happened, understood? You tell him that and you'll end up in small pieces, trust me. You just tell him you got the information, no trouble at all, and leave things to us. You breathe a word of this to him and try and make some sort of deal, you're off to prison and I'll make sure you go in with the nonces and arse-punchers. We clear on this?'

'Yeah, of course. Thanks, Mr Harrison, thanks very much, I won't let you down, I promise,' gushed Allan, getting to his feet.

'Best you don't,' snapped Harrison. 'What time are you due to drop it off?'

'Lunchtime, one o'clock.'

'You let me know when you're leaving and these boys will watch your back. Don't think about going early, you just book in with me and these guys will tag along.'

'I understand, I'll ring when I'm about to leave.'

'You'll need this,' said Harrison, throwing the piece of paper on to the floor in front of the desk. Allan scuttled about to pick it up.

'I won't let you down, I promise,' he said earnestly. 'Can I go now?'

'Go on, fuck off,' said Harrison dismissively. Clarke and Benson stood aside as Allan hurried nervously between them and left the office, shutting the door behind him.

Harrison took another swig from his glass before he spoke.

'Do we know anything about the brothel?'

'Run by the Ozdemir family, but didn't know that Sercan was directly involved,' said Clarke.

'Chances are he's not,' replied Harrison. 'I'll bet the family know fuck all about his extra-curricular activities there. Not their style at all, blackmail. Honest to goodness sex and that's that as far as I know. I reckon young Sercan is branching out again, silly bastard.'

'What now, boss?' asked Benson.

'First up, I need Phil Eldrett, and quickly. Find him for me, will you? Get him to come in if he's working or give me a ring. Got a job for him that's right up his street.'

Phil Eldrett was a 28-year-old uniformed PC with a military background. A veteran of two tours in Ulster, he had served with 14 Intelligence Company, 'The Det', in the province, and spent much of it rummaging about and watching people in the bandit country of South Armagh as part of a team working closely with the Special Air Service and the Royal Ulster Constabulary's own surveillance units of the Special Branch. When his wife put pressure on him to lead a more normal life and stop blacking up his face to go to work, he had bought himself out and joined the police where he soon established himself as a watcher of extreme skill, gaining the nickname 'The Shadow', but he always refused to leave his uniform role, which he loved. His wife had welcomed a degree of normality to their lives but was still not that happy; she had heard one of her children tell a friend at the school gates that her daddy was one of the Black and White Minstrels.

Such was Eldrett's expertise, he spent very little time doing any uniform work, and was regularly deployed around the county on any number of surveillance jobs. Using his contacts within the armed forces, he continued to attend courses designed for the military operating in trouble spots and, if anything, had become even more proficient since leaving the army. He was a highly competent car thief and housebreaker, and had he been that way inclined he could have enjoyed a life of some luxury as a burglar. He could disable alarms, silence dogs and make himself disappear into the environment wherever he found himself. He was the best, and generally he worked for DCI Harrison who guarded him and kept him close, only letting him go to neighbouring divisions or forces as a huge favour. He would do almost anything to get close to his target, but nothing had yet beaten the fifteen hours he had spent in a water butt under a window listening to a career criminal discuss his next job. He had resembled a prune on legs when he returned to the nick, but the job had been done. Eldrett was gold dust and just what Harrison needed to nail the lid on Sercan Ozdemir's coffin.

'He's working late turn tonight, boss,' reported Benson, putting his head round the door. 'Bob's gone out to get him off his beat, should be here in a few moments.'

'Thanks, John. Just let his group guv'nor know, will you? Don't want to fuck things up with him.'

'Already done,' assured Benson, who was well aware that Harrison needed to keep the uniforms sweet if he wanted to continue to use Eldrett as often as he did.

'What, again?' the late turn duty inspector had protested. 'Fuck me, I haven't seen him for months, can't actually remember when it was. You do know he's one of mine, don't you?'

'I know, guv, I know,' Benson had replied sympathetically, 'but Mr Harrison's got something lined up which he really needs Phil for, sorry. Shouldn't be away too long, I reckon.'

'Right, heard that last time and didn't see him again for ages. Go on, go and get him, and get him back to us in one piece, OK?'

'Will do, boss,' said Benson cheerfully before giving Clarke the thumbs-up to go and fetch Eldrett.

'Ever heard of Sercan Ozdemir, Phil?' asked Harrison half an hour later as he showed Phil Eldrett to the armchair. 'Drink?'

'Not for me, boss. Ozdemir? Runs a haulage business on the edge of town, right?'

'That's the man.' Harrison poured himself another Bushmills. 'Not just a haulage business he's running, though.'

'That right? Didn't know that.'

Harrison slumped into his chair. 'Yeah, he's a bad lad, is Mr Ozdemir. He was behind the Tamworth gun shop robbery that we interrupted last year. It was part of an operation to finance and supply bigger and better jobs.'

'Really?'

'Oh yeah,' said Harrison, leaning forward to look at Eldrett across his desk. 'Bigger and better but we set his plans back a bit. There's some unfinished business still bubbling away from the Tamworth job, which is where you come in. I can't tell you everything, but within the next twenty-four, forty-eight hours, Ozdemir will be going after an informant of mine who gave up the Tamworth team. I need you to keep an eye on things.'

'Ozdemir himself?'

'Unlikely, probably get a team together to deal with him, but I need to know when that team's on the move.'

'OK. What do I need to be doing?'

'You know where Ozdemir's haulage yard is?'

'Never been there but I've a rough idea where it is.'

'It's where he does all his business, where everything comes to and goes out. He never does anything from home in case his other half starts getting nosy and asking questions. The team he puts together will start and finish at the haulage yard and I need to know when they leave.'

'Fine, when do I get started?'

'Ozdemir won't know until tomorrow afternoon where my informant is. Chances are, his team will be up and running that evening so I'm going to need you plotted up by tomorrow lunchtime at the latest. Sorry, but I can't be more precise.'

'No worries. I can go and have a look at the area tonight and again when it gets light tomorrow. I'll be in place soon as I can. I take it I'll need a radio if you want a quick heads up?'

'Definitely, but not on the main channel just in case he's got people monitoring. John and Bob will sort out a back-to-back set for you.'

'Where will you be?'

'Here in the office. I'll be staying here until this comes off which I don't think's going to be long.'

'OK, I'll go and get changed and have a punt round,' said Eldrett. 'I'll use my old van but probably won't have any transport on the night, so I'll need to be dropped off, OK?'

'Good lad, Phil,' said Harrison, getting to his feet and clasping Eldrett's hand in his bear-like paw. 'Have a discreet look and let me know if you can get hidden up. I'll be here, OK?'

'See you later, boss.' Eldrett smiled as he hurried away to get out of the uniform he loved, to go and do something he had been born to do.

# Chapter Fifteen

At the Partridge pub the raucous behaviour of the large group at the back of the bar was starting to piss off the other customers. It wasn't so much the noise or huge waits at the bar as the loud group attempted to drink it dry, but the flying arrival of Harry the Dwarf in the middle of other gatherings, invariably causing drinks to scatter all over the place. He would be collected by a couple of the noisy group with muttered apologies and taken back to the melee, only to reappear shortly afterwards, to loud cheers and shouts.

D Group were indulging in their favourite drinking game in which Harry was a more than willing participant – dwarf throwing. The group had split into pairs and were launching Harry across the bar area on the count of three, with one of the group marking Harry's landing area with a piece of chalk borrowed from the dartboard. Several throws had gone badly awry, with little Harry crashing on to a table where an elderly couple were having dinner and once over the bar itself into the brassy barmaid. The elderly diners had complained bitterly as Harry was recovered from the woman's lap, only to be treated to one of his more aggressive roars and his usual obscene hand gesture using his two thumbs and forefingers. It was not unusual for little Harry to arrive for work after a drink with D Group covered in cuts and bruises after an evening spent flying through crowded pubs. His colleagues and even his boss, Rod Allan, all assumed the tough little bugger was a drunken scrapper, little suspecting that he was in fact a willing human tenpin bowling ball.

So far, the Brothers, with their usual coordination and teamwork, held the furthest throw of twenty-two feet, unsteadily paced out by Psycho who had assumed the mantle of Dwarf-Throwing Adjudicator. His own feeble team mate, Piggy, had let him down badly by mistiming their own count and letting go too early of the arm and leg he was holding, which had led to Harry flying over the bar. Eventually, the brassy barmaid pleaded with Psycho to put the dwarf away, with the promise of a free round and chips.

And then, wonder of wonders, Anne Butler walked into the pub. Her arrival caught the attention of a couple of young bucks at the bar who exchanged knowing glances and were about to make a move on her when a bellow of 'Praise the fucking Lord' from amongst the noisy crowd made them freeze in their tracks. It was fortunate that they did, as a large, unshaven beast with untamed black hair barged his way out of the crowd and approached Anne with a broad smile.

'You came then,' he cried joyfully, 'you came.'

'I said I would, but I can't be late, Andy's picking me up at ten thirty.'

'Who's Andy?' asked Psycho sourly, his smile fading.

'My boyfriend, of course.'

'I heard you'd split up.'

'Well, we haven't, just a silly tiff, that's all. You shouldn't listen to idle gossip, Sean.'

'Ah well, you're here now, that's what's important. Come and join the others,' said Psycho who had no intention of giving up just yet. He stood back to admire her slim legs and pert bottom encased in tight denim jeans and caught a glimpse of her superb breasts in a lacy bra as he leered down the pale yellow silk blouse she was wearing. Her long blonde hair was tied back in a simple ponytail, and her face was tanned and devoid of any make-up. As she passed Psycho, she looked up at him with large doe-like blue eyes. He thought his heart was about to burst. His initial desire to simply fuck her brains out was being replaced by something completely different. He had feelings for her that were new territory for him and he was finding it difficult to cope.

He glanced at the two would-be suitors at the bar who were again staring at Anne and gave them a murderous glare. The message was clear: Anne was with the group and outsiders were not welcome. This was the way of every police drink when WPCs attended. Usually shunned or the object of every wind-up imaginable at work, when they were out with the groups, they were off limits to the public. Any unwary or brave outsider who decided to hit on one of their girls could be guaranteed the company of several of the usually drunk male officers who would make their options clear to them: she's with us, fuck off or you'll be swallowing your teeth.

The group made space for Anne around the three tables they had pulled together and invited her to join the whip for ten pounds which was put into the empty pint pot in the middle. Soon she was totally integrated into the drunken mayhem. For a devout member of the Christian Police Association, Anne could put her drinks away with the best of them. After half a dozen triple Malibu and Cokes, she had become as loud as any of them and to Psycho's undisguised delight she had a nice range of dirty jokes. He had forced JJ out of his position and now sat alongside her, their legs seemingly welded together – he could feel her body warmth through her jeans. He was starting to stare and she soon noticed.

'You're very quiet, Sean,' she yelled drunkenly into his face. He scarcely heard the words, so intent was he on watching those perfect, naturally red, full lips form his name and then something else. She was the only person in his world who called him Sean.

'What's that?' he eventually shouted back above the din.

'I said you're very quiet. What's up?'

'Me, nothing, why?'

'You pining after someone?'

He wished he could tell her, but bellowing his undying devotion for her would probably not be a good idea.

'Course not,' he laughed.

'Not pining for that fat lump on this group?'

'What, Belinda Wheeler?'

'Yeah. What's that name you all call her?'

He laughed again. 'The Blood Blister.'

She put her head back and laughed, showing him her wonderful straight, white teeth and he yearned to clamp his mouth to hers and kiss the air out of her lungs.

'The Blood Blister, yes,' she hooted. 'What a sight that is. I've seen her in the showers, you know.'

'Oh God,' gasped Psycho, afraid for a moment that she was about to reveal that she was a rabid rug muncher.

'Yeah, awful,' she reminisced. 'Her fanny looked like a pit pony's mane.'

'Jesus.'

'Do you know the difference between the Blister's box and a cricket ball?' she continued loudly.

'Go on.'

'At a push, I could eat a cricket ball,' she shrieked and Psycho knew he'd fallen in love with her.

The others had been listening intently – including Sergeant Mick Jones, who had initially been furious to hear more disparaging remarks made about his secret shag buddy – and they all roared with laughter. References to the Blister's unfortunate physical appearance continued for another five minutes, culminating in a round of 'impossibly horrible scenarios for a million quid'.

Anne took the lead. 'OK, a million quid to go down on the Blister after little Harry's emptied his tanks into her,' she shouted so loudly that customers at the far end of the pub stopped to listen.

There was general hysteria and moaning and groaning at the dreadful prospect, other than from Mick Jones who in his drunken stupor was pondering the possibility that he may have done exactly that for fuck all.

'OK, OK, I've got one,' interrupted JJ. 'A million quid to give your dad one up the arse as he looks over his shoulder pleading, "No, son, please, no." He roared with manic laughter and then stopped as he became aware of the deathly silence. All that was missing was the low tolling of a church bell and a ball of tumbleweed passing in front of him on the wind.

'You fucking sex case,' snarled H, breaking the silence. 'What the fuck's the matter with you? Stupid boy, shut the fuck up and drink your lemonade.'

JJ was crestfallen; he'd undone all the good work of previous weeks and slid all the way down the longest snake, past all the ladders he'd climbed in the most difficult game of snakes and ladders in the world. Fitting in would take time and a little more than a good display at a pub fight. He sat back and sulked into his lager as the noise levels rose again and his faux pas was gradually forgotten. Certainly, no one would remember it the following day.

'More drink,' bellowed Anne, puncturing the unpleasant lull in proceedings and reaching for the whip pot which was in need of replenishing. 'Get them in, JJ.'

Happy to be able to do something, anything, to ingratiate himself again, Jackson did as he had been bidden and very soon proceedings were back to their usual intensity.

As she sat alongside Psycho with her head resting on his shoulder, gulping her rocket-fuelled drinks, Anne had an idea.

'That whip of ours doesn't look safe in that glass,' she slurred.

'It's OK, we always keep it in a glass,' he replied, looking lovingly down at her, only just resisting the urge to kiss the top of her head.

'Anyone could help themselves,' she continued as she struggled to focus on the glass, and oblivious of the fact that any potential thief would need to walk into a lion's den to pinch the money. 'Give it to me and I'll look after it.'

'OK,' said Psycho, puzzled but willing to indulge her every whim. He leant forward and grabbed the whip glass and handed it to her. She took it and held it close to her eyes as she tried to see what was left in it. Unable to see clearly, she shook it. It was largely full of coins and she smiled inanely as she listened to the clinking and held the glass to her ear.

'I'll keep this safe,' she giggled. 'Anyone needs a drink, I'll have the money tucked away,' and with that she emptied the coins down the front of her gaping blouse and into her bra cups, gasping quietly as the cold coins touched her breasts. Psycho stared at her cleavage open-mouthed.

'Outstanding,' he eventually offered, before reaching for his pint, necking the remaining three-quarters and wiping his mouth with the back of his hand.

'I'm as dry as a witch's tit,' he burped happily.

'Well, you know where the money is,' said Anne dreamily.

'Praise the Lord,' said Psycho quietly, before he reached into her blouse and rummaged about in her bra until he retrieved a handful of coins. The others had been watching and also began to pour their drinks down their throats.

'Same again for me,' said Piggy, getting to his feet and shuffling along the side of the table towards Anne and Psycho, his eyes fixed on her blouse.

'I'll take care of allocating funds,' said Psycho threateningly, fixing Piggy with a look that left him in no doubt at all that if he planned to stick one of his grubby paws into Anne's cleavage, it would be his last act on earth.

Soon, Psycho was regularly but gently reaching into Anne's bra for money as the rest of the hugely envious group went for it, all harbouring the forlorn hope that eventually they might be allowed to get their own cash out. Anne sat with her head on Psycho's shoulder, giggling madly and gasping as his hand went into her bra, before she eventually fell asleep, dribbling.

'She's well out of it,' said Malcy, rubbing his hands together and winking at his mate. 'Come on, Psycho, out of the way, I'm thirsty.'

'You lay a finger on her, you heathen bastard, and I'll

break your arm,' replied Psycho simply. 'Anyone wants a drink, I'll get the cash. No one touches her, OK?'

It was the end of the debate and rather took the wind out of the sails of the party.

A little after half past ten, the doors to the pub opened and a tall young man walked into the bar and looked around. He was wearing a blue Ben Sherman short-sleeved shirt, Farrah slacks with a pair of green flash tennis shoes, and his hair cut short and tight. Everything about him screamed 'off duty cop just out of training school'. He looked around and then walked towards the large, loud group. He stopped alongside them and waited for someone to say something. H eventually obliged, glancing up at the stranger with watery, bloodshot eyes.

'You want something?'

'You D Group out of Handstead?' asked the stranger nervously but with a clearly detectable hint of irritation.

'What if we are?' said Jim, getting to his feet.

'I'm looking for Anne Butler,' said Andy Rafferty. 'I told her I'd pick her up at ten thirty.'

'What's she to you?' slurred H with some difficulty, the brief question taking longer than usual using numb lips and a pickled brain.

'I'm her boyfriend and she's on a driving course in the morning. I need to get her home.'

'She's fine, we'll get her home in time,' said Psycho from the far end of the table.

Rafferty looked over at him and noticed Anne for the first time, apparently asleep and almost completely enveloped by this enormous, ugly bear of a man. He gulped before speaking.

'I need to get her home. Is she OK? What's happened?'

'She's having a great time,' said Psycho, holding her closer until her ribs creaked and she stirred. She could hear the conversation but her eyes appeared to be welded shut. She peered towards her boyfriend through puffy slits.

'That you, Andy? What time is it?' she shouted, unable to control her volume.

Andy Rafferty gritted his teeth and glared at Psycho. Despite his anger he knew he'd be no match for the drunken monster and certainly stood no chance against the whole group who now positively radiated menace. The stranger was spoiling their party and threatening to take away *their* woman. Anne settled the stand-off by forcing Psycho's arm off her shoulder and getting unsteadily to her feet. She swayed like a tree in a high wind.

'You're not going, are you?' asked a clearly devastated Psycho, looking up at her from the bench seat.

'Driving course,' she babbled, trying frantically to see

which one of the blurred shapes was her pain-in-the-arse boyfriend.

'We're all early turn,' pleaded Psycho. 'Don't go yet.'

'Early turn,' she repeated like an automaton before she began to push her way through the forest of legs and bags to leave. 'Early turn.'

Andy Rafferty was incandescent with rage as he watched Anne stagger through the group who were mostly too pissed to get out of her way, causing her to trip and fall on to a couple of laps where she shrieked loudly at their loud cheers.

'Come on,' he hissed as she cleared the group and turned to say goodnight to them all. 'Look at the fucking state of you.' She didn't hear him, but waved at the group who were staring sullenly at her, Psycho looking as though he was about to explode.

'Driving course,' she explained slowly. 'Bye.'

Rafferty grabbed her wrist and pulled her towards him roughly.

'Come on,' he hissed again, his pale face contorted with rage and jealousy. He began to drag her towards the door.

'You keep your fucking hands to yourself, son,' bellowed Psycho, getting to his feet and pointing a menacing finger at Rafferty. 'You touch her and I'll snap your fucking back.'

Rafferty wisely dropped Anne's wrist and guided

her towards the door, where she stopped to wave and shout goodnight to the rest of the bar before he bundled her out into the car park with a fixed grin on his face.

Psycho stood at the window watching Rafferty load Anne on to the back seat of his Datsun Cherry; he didn't return to his seat until the tail lights of the car disappeared from view. Then he sat quietly, staring at the table. The others looked at him.

'You OK, Psycho?' asked Malcy, sliding alongside him and lighting up a cigarette.

'Hope she's OK,' replied the morose monster without lifting his eyes.

'She's probably going to get nicked turning up for a driving course in that state.'

'I meant that little cunt of a boyfriend,' said Psycho. 'Don't like him at all, he had a nasty look in his eye, like he enjoys slapping women about.'

Malcy looked briefly at his mate and then patted him on the shoulder. 'Psycho, he wouldn't dare. She's going to be OK.'

'Fucking hope so,' said Psycho eventually before turning to look at Malcy. 'You know what, Malcy, you're not a bad lad despite what you get up to.'

'What you on about?'

'You know, you and shagging Mongs. Despite all that, you're still a good lad.'

'Oh, the nickname,' sighed Malcy, stubbing out his cigarette and sitting back on the seat. 'Malcy the Mong Fucker,' he said quietly and sipped from his pint.

'Yeah, great name. You've never explained it.'

'Not a lot of point, is there? No doubt you've heard the usual version of events.'

'Usual version?' said Psycho. 'We heard you were captured boning some retard in a hospital over at Kray Hill somewhere. Rather than go public with it, the hospital agreed to keep quiet on condition you got moved here. That's what we heard.'

Malcy sighed again and lit himself another cigarette.

'That's all bollocks,' he said, blowing a jet of smoke towards the ceiling. 'The retard, as you put it, was my fiancée.'

Psycho frowned and pulled away from Malcy to look at him.

'Urgh, that's horrible,' he said, pulling a face. 'You got engaged to her as well? That's what you had to do to get a shag out of her?'

'Fucking hell, no,' said Malcy wearily. 'She wasn't always like that.'

'What you on about?'

Malcy paused. He had never discussed what had happened with anyone but tonight with the maudlin Psycho alongside him, it suddenly seemed right to tell someone how his life had been blown to pieces.

'Her name's Karen, she used to be an air stewardess,' he said quietly.

Psycho moved closer again.

'I met her at a party four years ago, we had a house together, we got engaged and we used to have holidays all round the world through the airline. We used to go scuba diving together and have diving holidays somewhere nice, twice a year.'

'Diving holidays? Was she crumpet?'

'Stunning.' Malcy smiled, rolling away the past few unhappy years. 'Very like Anne actually. You know, when Anne walked in tonight, I thought for a moment it was Karen.'

'I saw you staring. I just assumed, well, you know,' said Psycho awkwardly.

'I know everyone assumes they know.'

'What happened, for fuck's sake?'

'We were on a diving holiday in Egypt, year before last. The day before we were due to come home, we hired some mopeds to do a bit of sightseeing. She got taken out, head on, by some local in his van. Didn't kill her but broke her back and severed her spinal cord. She's paralysed from the waist down.'

'Oh no,' was all Psycho could manage.

'Yeah, Karen's the retard you all know about,' said Malcy bitterly.

'Why the fuck didn't you say anything?'

'I did initially. Obviously the guys at West Darrick knew Karen and what had happened, but when it all kicked off at the hospital and I got moved, the rumours just got worse and worse. There was fuck all I could do about it. You know I was suspended for a while.'

'Suspended? What the fuck for?' said Psycho loudly.

'Bringing the Force into disrepute,' replied Malcy sadly, shaking his head.

'What happened at the hospital?'

'Karen was in hospital in Egypt at first, then we got her brought back to the UK. She was down in Birmingham for a while, which was awful, she was so far away. But then we got her up to the Falconer Hospital at Kray Hill which specialises in treating spinal injuries.'

'So what happened there?'

'It was difficult. Karen was in despair that I didn't want her anymore, that I was going to leave her because she wasn't the same person anymore. She couldn't see that I probably loved her even more because of what had happened. I couldn't believe I'd been so lucky that she'd survived the crash. Does that make sense? She was always going on that I didn't find her attractive or sexy anymore, always worrying that I would be going after other women for sex.'

'Sex?'

'Yeah, well, she has no feeling at all below her waist. All that's gone for her. To look at her, you wouldn't know she'd had the accident, but all the feeling has gone, physically.'

'Jesus.'

'I kept telling her that would never happen. I'm not interested in anyone else but that's hard to believe, I guess, when you're flat out paralysed on a bed.'

'Will she ever get better?'

'No, not until there's some major breakthrough in treating spinal injuries. No, that's it for Karen for the rest of her life.'

'And yours?'

'And mine,' agreed Malcy, stubbing out his cigarette and gazing into the distance. 'Anyway, I went to visit her every day, all day on my days off, and I was there one evening and she was very down and tearful. She was crying about our sex life, that I didn't want her anymore because she couldn't feel anything. She was in a single bedroom and she pleaded with me to make love to her, just to see if she could feel anything, you know, some kind of miracle.'

'And did you?'

'Yes. It was awful. She was crying because she couldn't feel anything, I was crying because she was crying. Jesus, it was terrible and then this cunt of a ward sister came in.'

'What happened?'

'She went berserk, shouting and screaming, had me

removed by security. Karen was screaming and crying and they threw me out of the hospital. Then they made a complaint and I was suspended before that bastard Grainger sent me to Handstead.'

'Grainger,' growled Psycho, 'that gelding.'

'The rumours started while I was suspended. Trouble was, no one knew what had really happened and Grainger never bothered to quash them when he had the chance. So, here I am now, Malcy the Mong Fucker.'

'Fucking hell, Malcy, you poor bastard.' Psycho stared long and hard at him, swaying slightly as he concentrated. 'Listen, Malcy, you want me to say something to the boys? Put an end to all this bollocks?'

'Forget it, Psycho, it's far too late for that now. I'm saddled with it, I'll just get on with it.'

He was right. Malcy was the victim of a common occurrence within the police service which was notorious for rumour and speculation becoming accepted fact, with officers' reputations besmirched for the rest of their careers. The last thing any of those unfortunate enough to fall foul of the practice did was try and defend themselves. There would be absolutely no point as in most cops' eyes a denial was the obvious response of a guilty person.

'Too true, too true, Malcy,' mused Psycho into his glass. 'One unfortunate, drunken mistake with a farmyard animal and I've never heard the fucking end of it.'

Malcy stared at him and focused slowly, then realised that he was joking and roared with laughter with him, forgetting for a moment his beautiful crippled girlfriend. At least, he hoped Psycho was joking.

As Psycho and Malcy staggered out of the Partridge twenty minutes later in search of their cars, shouting their goodbyes to each other, Andy Rafferty dumped the unconscious, snoring Anne on the large double bed in their small rented terrace house in the south of the town. He was drenched in sweat, having manhandled her out of the car as she began projectile vomiting and then carried her upstairs in a fireman's lift. He looked angrily at her as he got his breath back and was on the verge of leaving her to get on with it when it occurred to him that this was as good an opportunity as she had given him lately to get his leg over. Things hadn't been great between them for the last month, they were arguing constantly, and their previously frantic sex life had dwindled away to a big, fat zero. Now she was going to get large portions, he smiled to himself, beginning to unbutton her blouse which was covered in large stains where she had spilt some of her drinks. Then he went spastic as he unclipped her bra and dozens of coins and two banknotes spilt from the cups and she giggled drunkenly in her stupor. He packed a bag and was gone within the hour.

It was significant that Psycho had not been offered a lift home with anyone, or a bed for the night. Certainly not by Piggy, who had done it once and regretted it ever since. After a huge drink two years ago, Piggy had very foolishly offered Psycho a bed, rather than let him drive home totally wankered. Ever the gentleman, Psycho had accepted on condition that he did not have to shag Piggy's dreadful wife, and allowed him to drive him to his police house where Mrs Piggy had been instructed to relocate their six-year-old son to the spare room so Psycho could have the boy's bed. Psycho had snuggled down under Master Piggy's Magic Roundabout duvet and gone into a deep, drunken sleep, snoring like an old door in a heavy wind, rendering sleep for the Piggy family virtually impossible. In the small hours, he had suffered a bad coughing fit, so bad that he had shit the bed before going back to sleep. In the morning, he staggered downstairs for breakfast, ate everything, and then left without mentioning the mess all over Dylan and friends. It was so typical of Psycho – he didn't want any fuss, he was always thinking of others. He drove home in his Cortina with the lights off. This was not a drunken oversight on his part; his logic was that the hated traffic cops who regularly went after drunk

Handstead officers wouldn't see him until it was too late, especially if he kept to the unlit B roads. He had caused dozens of accidents driving home like this in the past and on two occasions lost the road himself and ended up in fields from where he had had no alternative but to walk home.

This time he made it home in one piece and parked his Cortina, as he often did after a drink, almost inside the bus shelter outside his block of flats. He lurched into his ground-floor flat to grab a couple of hours' sleep, dreaming drunkenly of the ravishing Anne, her blonde hair blowing in the wind, waving at him from the basket of a hot-air balloon that floated just a few feet out of his reach. As he lay on his grubby, unmade bed, his legs were twitching as he tried to jump higher and he made urgent grabbing motions with his hands as he tried to catch the basket. Eventually he woke, drenched in sweat, sitting bolt upright with his pillow stuck to his back, shouting her name. Psycho was in love.

As Psycho pined for the apparently out-of-reach Anne, Phil Eldrett lay behind a thick privet hedge across the road from the darkened Ozdemir haulage premises. He had driven past the place a couple of times in the space of half an hour without slowing and eventually parked up in a secluded farm track just over a mile away and made his way across the fields using the skills he had picked up on his Covert Rural Observation Posts course, courtesy of his old mates at Hereford. He was dressed head to toe in ancient camouflage kit that he had brought out of the army with him, his head covered by a black woollen ski mask which rolled up to form a cap, and his face streaked with black greasepaint. He had crept like a silent shadow through a small wood and then along the edge of a huge wheat field towards the distant lights of the road on which stood the Ozdemir premises, before he slid into the welcoming, concealing depths of the hedge and began mentally to record everything he could see from his position.

The building was a low, modern, two-storey brick construction with a wide car park in front of the reception area, and over to the right was a huge, razor-wired compound guarded by massive steel bar gates, behind which he could see some of the Ozdemir haulage fleet. The building was in complete darkness, the countryside still and quiet apart from the bark of a faraway fox and the hoot of an owl in the wood behind. Then, as Eldrett whispered quietly to himself, describing what he could see, a cigarette glowed in the window to the far right of the top floor. Eldrett tensed – the building was not as empty as he had hoped, dashing his plans to break in and have a quick look around. It would have been a doddle, as the building appeared to be without a burglar alarm. He remained motionless for another half hour with his ski mask pulled fully over his face, his breathing slow and controlled, watching. The cigarette glowed briefly a second time and then faded. He had seen enough for now and began to carefully extract himself from the hedge, crawling slowly backwards, like a retreating snake, and then back along the edge of the field on his stomach until he was sure that none of the residual light from the street lamps would catch him. He returned to his battered old van the way he had come and took a circuitous route back to Handstead nick.

In the darkened office on the top floor, Sercan Ozdemir stood naked on the expensively carpeted floor and drew heavily on the Turkish cigarette he was smoking before stubbing it out in an ashtray on his desk. Blowing the cloud of smoke towards the window, he gazed out at the quiet, dark countryside and smiled happily to himself. Things were coming together nicely, he told himself. The idiot Rod Allan was due in tomorrow with the whereabouts of Brian Jones and Ozdemir was quietly confident he would come up with the goods – he would if he knew what was good for him, anyway.

Ozdemir turned and smiled down at his secretary, the stunning Carmen who had modelled lingerie in her teens before the crime family had brought her into the fold. She lay naked on a wide sheepskin rug, her coffee-coloured skin shimmering in the dark. She was holding out a fluted champagne glass for him.

'You want some more?' she asked, arching her thin dark eyebrows and grinning.

'Champagne, or you?'

'Both sound good.'

Ozdemir laughed and dropped to his knees in front of her, gently pulling her legs apart and putting his lips against her swollen, moist vagina. She gasped as his tongue began to flick between the lips. She dropped the glass on to the carpet, the expensive champagne soaking quickly into the deep pile, and arched her slim hips to meet his mouth. Ozdemir was celebrating early, unaware that outside in the dark, deep wood was someone planning to stick a large nail in his Jap's eye.

# Chapter Sixteen

'Look at this twat,' observed H, staring at the tatty brown Range Rover twenty yards ahead of Yankee One on the Handstead Road. 'All over the fucking place at twenty-five miles an hour.'

Despite the skinful they had drunk the night before and their hangovers, the Brothers were still out there looking for it. Looking for anything. Most of the rest of the group were parked up, quietly trying to recover, but over the years the Brothers had worked together they had found that the best cure for a hangover was a bit of graft. That, and the time-honoured three pints of water and two paracetamol before they had collapsed into their respective beds.

'Still pissed from last night maybe,' offered Jim, picking up the handset and checking the registration number with the PNC operator on Channel Two.

'Current keeper out at Angotts Mead, no current excise licence though,' he said as he replaced the handset.

'Let's give him a pull then,' answered H, and Jim twisted the blue lights knob and gave the twin air horns a single blast to alert the driver of the Range Rover that they wanted words with him.

Spitting his large spliff on to the rubbish-strewn floor, Guy Mitcheson glanced in his rear-view mirror and felt his stomach leap into his throat. Just what he didn't need right now, especially with the interior of the car shrouded in a thick cloud of pungent cannabis smoke and covered in torn Rizla packets. The two, pale-faced, emotionless cops in the car behind stared at him, daring him to make a run for it, but he decided to try and talk his way out of this mess. He pulled over and quickly wound down both front windows to try and get rid of as much smoke as he could and watched nervously as the Brothers approached his car from either side, adjusting their caps low over their dead eyes. Jim went to the driver's side. Standing a couple of feet away to give himself time to react if need be, he looked into the vehicle.

'Fuck me,' he said. 'What you been smoking in there, pal? Smells like a wet bonfire.'

'Couple of roll-ups, officer, that's all. Is there a problem?'

Jim clocked the bloodshot eyes, dilated pupils, flushed cheeks and slightly slurred speech. Coupled with the overwhelming smell of some quality Lebanese gold, this equalled a prisoner.

'Smells like weed to me. This your motor?'

'Certainly, officer, all bought and paid for,' said Mitcheson chummily.

'But not taxed,' offered H who had walked over from the other side of the car.

'Not taxed?'

'Your excise licence is six months out of date, mate. You got insurance for this pile of shit?'

'Certainly,' lied Mitcheson.

'I doubt it, but we'll give you a producer for all your documents anyway. Come on, out you get.'

Sighing heavily at the indignity he was suffering at the hands of these two ignorant peasants, Mitcheson got out of the Range Rover and stood unsteadily in front of the Brothers. H leant in behind him and picked up the still smouldering spliff from the driver's floor mat.

'Some spliff,' he remarked, sniffing at the joint. 'Paki black?'

'Gold,' replied Mitcheson in a resigned tone. 'Look, officers, can we sort this out, off the record, just between us?'

'Off the fucking record?' scoffed Jim. 'You offering us a bribe or something?'

'Of course not,' said Mitcheson quickly. 'Perish the thought. I just hoped we might be able to come to some sort of mutual arrangement, that's all.'

'You've got fuck all of any interest to us, pal,' said Jim, spinning Mitcheson round, face against the car, and snapping on handcuffs. 'You're nicked on suspicion of driving under the influence of drink or drugs. Don't say anything else unless you want to make a complete cunt of yourself.'

Mitcheson closed his eyes and rested his head against the side of his car in despair as the handcuffs were ratcheted hard, but he kept quiet. Jim marched him back to Yankee One and pushed him firmly into the back seat while H had a quick search of the Range Rover for any further evidence of drugs use. He got his stick out to move the rubbish around – the vehicle resembled a skip on wheels. It was full of crap. Newspapers, empty glass and plastic bottles, tins, fish and chip wrappers, Chinese food cartons, a half-eaten takeaway curry, discarded clothes and two pairs of mouldy shoes minus their soles.

'What a shit pit,' he muttered to himself, and he was about to step out of it and rejoin Jim when he spotted a small piece of paper which had been deliberately placed on the instrument panel. He picked it up, read it with a puzzled look on his face and then folded it in half and slipped it into his trouser pocket. H strolled over to

Yankee One and got back into the driver's seat, adjusting the rear-view mirror to get a better look at their sullen prisoner in the back.

'What's your game then?' he asked.

'My game? What are you talking about?' replied Mitcheson irritably. This was just what he didn't need at the outset of his career as a major, global drug manufacturer, but he was happy there was nothing in the car to alert the Brothers. He'd put his hands up to driving under the influence and whatever else they came up with, but he was satisfied they would find nothing else.

'Your job, what do you do?'

'I'm unemployed.'

'A sponger, you mean? You sound like an educated man, how come you're not working?' said H, starting up Yankee One but still looking at him in the mirror.

'Never had to, not interested. Look, can we get on with this?'

'Rich sponger,' said H to Jim, who nodded in grim agreement.

They did a U turn and headed back towards Handstead.

Two hours later, after he had been released on bail pending analysis of a blood sample he had given to a police doctor, H pulled out the piece of paper he had recovered from the Range Rover.

'What do you make of that?' he asked Jim, pushing it across the desk in the report writing room where they were finishing off their paperwork.

'Fuck knows. Where did you find it?'

'Amongst all that shit in his car. Never heard of it before. Let someone know, d'you think?'

'Like who?'

'I don't know. CID maybe?'

'Could do, I suppose. It don't look like much but it wouldn't hurt to run it past someone, I guess.'

After finishing their report, they made their way up to the first floor in search of a friendly CID face – which would be a feat in itself.

DCI Dan Harrison glanced up as they passed his office – the door was open to get a breeze through the stuffy room. He had spent the previous night in the office, having waited for Eldrett to return from his first reconnaissance of Ozdemir's haulage yard before polishing off what remained of his bottle of Bushmills. A fitful night's sleep in one of the uncomfortable armchairs had left him feeling jaded and crumpled but it had been preferable to returning to his empty, silent bedsit. The loss of his marriage, home and children to his career had been a high price to pay, but it had been an almost conscious decision. He lived, breathed and now slept Handstead nick. He had a lot of time for the Brothers – he'd love to have got them out of their blue suits and on to his team – and he called out to them.

'All right, boys? What you up to? Locked any up today?'

They paused and stood in the doorway.

'Got one locked up earlier for a bit of gear,' said H.

'What did he have? Come in, come in,' motioned Harrison, getting to his feet.

'Off his face on some Lebanese gold in his motor,' said Jim.

'Bailed out, I take it. Nothing else?'

H was about to reply no when he remembered why they had come up to the first floor.

'Probably nothing, boss,' he said, rooting about in his pocket until he located the piece of paper. 'I found this in his motor. Never heard of it before. Mean anything to you?'

Harrison read the paper and shook his head. 'Nothing, but I know a man who might know it. Hang on, I'll give him a call now.'

He returned to his desk, consulted his Force internal telephone directory and dialled a number at Head-quarters. He waited briefly before he was answered.

'Morning. DCI Dan Harrison at Handstead. I need to speak to DI Rick Moulder on the Drugs Squad ... OK, thanks.'

As he waited he looked up at the Brothers and smiled.

'Hello, Rick, how's tricks?' he said after a short wait. 'Same old shit here, you know Handstead. Listen, mate, couple of my quality uniform guys found something in a motor this morning that interested them. You ever heard of ergotamine tartrate?'

As he listened his mouth opened slightly and he stared at the Brothers. They glanced at each other – had they stumbled on to something?

'Call you back, Rick, we may need your help with this,' said Harrison abruptly, replacing the phone and getting to his feet again. He walked slowly round his desk and stood in front of the Brothers with a grim smile on his face. 'Guys, ergotamine tartrate is a precursor chemical used in the production of LSD. Best you tell me everything you can about the bloke you nicked.'

Rod Allan was starting to get anxious. Harrison's phone was permanently engaged and it was getting very close to the time he was due back at the brothel with his information. What the fuck was he doing? He didn't relish knocking on his door and risk another crack round the head, so he replaced the receiver and waited, unconsciously pulling, as always, at his limp dick.

He finally got through, five minutes before his one o'clock appointment.

'Mr Harrison,' he began reverently, mindful of the

concise instructions he had received the night before, 'it's Rod Allan. I'm leaving now.'

'You got what you need?' asked Harrison brusquely.

'Yes. Are DCs Clarke and Benson ready?'

'I'll get them now. You wait until they tell you they're ready to follow you off, understood?'

'OK.'

'The guy's going to ask you lots of questions about where you found it and whether you had any problems so you better have your wits about you, Allan. You give him any cause to suspect you're setting him up, you won't get out of there alive even with my blokes outside. You clear?'

'Perfectly. I'll wait in the front office for them, all right?'

Harrison didn't reply but slammed the phone down and strode quickly out of his office, down the corridor and into the main CID office. Clarke and Benson were standing by the open windows at the far side of the office looking out on to the back yard, smoking and chatting quietly.

'Bob, John,' he called from the door, 'he's waiting to go.'

They acknowledged the command with nods of their heads, grabbed their jackets from the backs of their chairs and hurried out after Harrison who stood waiting for them in the corridor.

'Just make sure he gets in there safely, boys,' he said. 'I'm not too bothered if he never gets out, but that piece of paper's got to go in, understand?'

'Got it, boss,' replied Benson as he held open the fire door on to the stairwell for Clarke to pass ahead of him. 'We'll hang around for a bit to see what happens.'

'Don't show out, for fuck's sake.'

'We won't, don't worry. See you later.'

Harrison watched the two detectives trot down the stairs from behind the wired glass panels before going back into his office and shutting the door behind him. He went back to his desk and opened his bottom drawer before swearing quietly.

'Bollocks.' His Bushmills was finished and he could murder a couple of fingers right now. He glanced at his watch. He reckoned he could get to the off-licence and be back before Benson and Clarke returned, so he took his jacket off the wire hanger on the back of the door and headed down the stairs.

Bolton Road East was full of lunchtime pedestrians who made the task of following Allan even easier for the two detectives. Working on opposite pavements to each other, they tailed him the four hundred yards to Birchwood Avenue and watched from a safe distance as he glanced nervously behind him before disappearing into the gloomy doorway and out of sight.

Kazim Dimiz also watched him enter the premises, albeit through still puffy and swollen eyes courtesy of his encounter with the Alligator and Jim. He was focused on Allan and completely failed to clock Benson and Clarke leave the nick separately. Once Allan was inside the brothel, he disappeared into the café opposite the parade of shops and passed within six feet of John Benson walking the other way without giving him so much as a glance.

Upstairs in the brothel, Allan was greeted by Marge as a long-lost brother. He grimaced and flinched as she pushed her stubbly lips to his face and breathed what smelt like fox shit all over him. As he gagged involuntarily and wiped his mouth with the back of his hand, one of the goons who had filmed him appeared from further along the corridor.

'You have it?' he asked simply, his face expressionless.

'Yes.'

'You come,' said the goon, turning on his heel and leading Allan along the corridor and back to the small room where he had been so utterly humiliated and broken two days earlier. Thirty seconds later, he found himself standing in front of Sercan Ozdemir like a small boy caught shoplifting. Ozdemir smiled broadly at him. He was enjoying life again. His plans to become a huge drugs manufacturer were all advancing, he'd boned his beautiful secretary all night, and now he confidently expected Rod Allan to make his day even better.

'Have you got something for me?' he asked pleasantly, holding out a manicured hand, his tailored suit jacket sleeve riding up to give Allan a glimpse of his gold Breitling wristwatch.

Allan didn't reply, simply pulled his booty out of his trouser pocket and handed it to him. Ozdemir glanced at it and smiled. He laughed softly.

'London? He really did pull out all the stops, didn't he?' he said quietly. Then he fixed Allan with his piercing eyes. 'Where was this information, my dear friend?'

'In a file in Mr Harrison's office.'

'Not locked away?'

'The office was locked but the file was in an unlocked drawer in his desk.'

'How did you get in?'

'I've got a master key for every lock in the station.'

'Very handy, I'm sure. And nobody saw you, you had no problems?'

'No, I got it late last night. The place was deserted.'

'Why are you sweating, Mr Allan?' demanded Ozdemir suddenly. 'Are you nervous? Have you forgotten to tell me something?'

Allan could feel the sweat running down the small of his back and beads forming in his eyebrows. He forced himself to look Ozdemir in the eye.

'Of course I'm nervous, I'm in the shit, aren't I?' he replied as firmly as he could, swallowing hard and clenching and opening his fists.

'Yes, you are,' said Ozdemir more genially, 'but if this information proves correct, perhaps we can talk about where our business arrangement goes from here.'

'But you said once I'd delivered, we were done,' protested Allan.

'Once we've confirmed it and I've been reunited with my old business acquaintance,' said Ozdemir as if he hadn't heard, 'we'll talk again. In the meantime, you keep your head down and behave. I might have need of your services again.'

'Hold on,' said Allan, raising his voice slightly. 'We never agreed anything like that. You said I get the information, job done.'

'Did I? I think not, Mr Allan. Perhaps I didn't make myself clear. This is just part of the deal we have. If I need something from Handstead police station in the future, I'll be coming to you for it. Otherwise your limp penis gets wide viewing. Do you understand?'

Allan hung his head and stayed quiet. His world was in absolute tatters, all hope torn from his grasp by the unscrupulous Ozdemir who intended to keep him on the team for the foreseeable future.

'You do understand then, good. You can fuck

off now, Mr Allan. I'll be in touch,' said Ozdemir, dismissing him from the small, hot room with an imperious wave of the hand and turning his back on him.

As Allan stepped out into the bright sunshine, he stumbled slightly. He had a thousand-yard stare and saw nothing, certainly not Benson and Clarke who smiled across the road at each other and made tracks back to the nick.

Harrison was back in his office and enjoying a large drink by the time Clarke and Benson knocked on the door and walked in on his shout.

'Everything OK?' he asked, producing two glasses for them from his bottom drawer and pouring them a drink.

'In and out, no problems, boss,' replied Benson, raising his glass in silent salute.

'Was he followed?'

'Oh yeah. One of Ozdemir's boys was up his arse from the moment he left the nick. Funny thing, he looked like he'd had a right good hiding from somewhere, face all over the place. Maybe he had a run-in with Ozdemir.'

'Maybe, who knows?' mused Harrison, settling back into his chair. 'Sure he didn't spot you?'

'Not a chance,' said Clarke. 'He was only interested

in Allan, making sure he made the appointment, I reckon.'

'Yeah, I'm sure you're right. Well done, boys. I'll give my mate at the Yard a ring this afternoon and get hold of Phil Eldrett as well. I reckon they'll be off down to London to get young Brian tonight.'

'Tonight, you reckon?'

'He won't want to hang around, not now he's got an address. He won't want to risk him moving on and having to start looking for him all over again. No, my money's on a team going south tonight. I'll let Phil sleep on a little longer and then give him a call, give him plenty of time to get himself plotted up.'

'What's the plan, boss?'

'Simple really. Phil keeps an eye on Ozdemir's place and gives us the heads up when the team leaves. He'll be on a back-to-back channel so I'm going to need you two nearby, OK?'

'Yeah, no problems.'

'Once we know they're on their way, I'll give the Met the heads up and they'll deal with them down there.'

'What's your bet on their plan?'

'They'll want to bring him back here. Ozdemir will want to bleed him for everything before they top him. They won't do it down there, no way. They'll bring him back to Handstead.'

The three detectives toasted each other and sat

sipping their drinks in silence as they considered what lay ahead, both for themselves and for Brian Jones. They felt no loyalty to him at all, regarding him merely as the means by which they would hopefully bring about another catastrophe for Sercan Ozdemir.

The Brothers left the nick in high spirits after their lengthy conversation with DCI Harrison. He was sure they had stumbled on to something significant and as they drove slowly out of the razor-wired yard, the station collator was busy drawing up a detailed profile of Guy Mitcheson. The Brothers reckoned they had earned a break and decided to make their way up to Handstead Crematorium to have a cup of tea with one of their sinister contacts, 'Smoking Joe' Davies, the manager.

The recovery of the piece of paper with the name of an obscure chemical ingredient on it was a joint success. The fact that Jim had been nowhere near when H had found it was insignificant. It was a find attributable to the Brothers. They took the plaudits and the criticism as a joint enterprise; there was never any question that one was more successful or guilty than the other. They were a solid team and whatever came their way was accepted equally.

As they arrived at the rear of the crematorium, it was apparent that Smoking Joe had clients in. The car park at the front was full of sombre, quiet groups of people standing around watching an expensive, wreath-covered coffin pass between them and enter the chapel.

'Good timing,' remarked Jim. 'Smoking will have the kettle on soon round the back. Come on, H.'

They hurried through an open fire door and into a small office where Smoking Joe Davies was on the phone. He looked up as they entered, smiled and waved a hand in greeting and carried on talking.

'Yeah, yeah, no problem. Got a few due this next couple of days. Yeah, all expensive. I'll give you a ring,' he said and put the phone down. He got to his feet and shook hands with the Brothers.

'All right, boys?' he asked. 'Cup of tea?'

'Murder one,' replied H, peering out of the office to the working area of the crematorium where two of Joe's staff stood shirtless, bathed in sweat alongside a huge furnace. The furnace was just a short distance away from a conveyor belt which stood on sturdy steel legs and led away to some heavy velvet curtains, beyond which was the chapel from where H could hear the singing of a hymn. The conveyor belt had a clever hinge device which allowed the end of the belt to be swung left towards the furnace and along a set of small runners into the furnace itself. Standing on its end by the side of the furnace was a simple pine coffin with its lid nearby. H frowned but said nothing before stepping back into the

311

office and motioning to Jim with a nod of his head to come and have a look.

Smoking Joe joined them and soon the heavy curtains parted, the organ music got louder before they closed again, and the expensive mahogany coffin they had seen brought into the chapel rumbled into view.

'Bet that cost a few bob,' remarked H, looking at Smoking.

'Fucking right it did. Be a proper shame to burn it, wouldn't it?' laughed Smoking, showing them his spookily white teeth which looked a bit pointed. The Brothers shook their heads and sipped from the mugs of tea he had given them. The two furnace men sprang the conveyor belt hinge and guided the coffin towards the furnace doors. Then they brought it to a halt and turned to look at Joe. He nodded at them. One of them prised the lid off the coffin while the other positioned the plain pine one on the floor alongside the belt. Both then lifted the mahogany coffin off the belt with enormous difficulty and banged it none too gently on to the floor.

'Keep it down, for fuck's sake,' hissed Joe who had taken the precaution of turning up the piped organ music anyway. The furnace men reached down and opened the mahogany coffin and quickly lifted the corpse of a frail old lady dressed in a brown tweed shirt and jacket, her hair perfectly coiffured and made up to the nines, and transferred it to the plain pine coffin. A quiet electric nail gun was then used to nail down the lid, the coffin placed on the conveyor belt and dispatched through the furnace doors. The mahogany coffin then disappeared into the darkness with the two furnace men.

Smoking Joe and the Brothers returned to his office.

'What's your mark-up on that transaction?' asked Jim.

'Pretty good. The mahogany coffin probably set the family back a couple of hundred quid, the pine one cost me twenty. Not bad work if you can get it. That one's been through here at least three times that I know of. I sell it back to the undertakers for a hundred and twenty a time, they sell it for another two hundred. I sell it back for another hundred and twenty. Works very well.'

'You're an evil, evil old man, Joe,' said H, finishing his tea, 'which is probably why we like you. Come on, Jim, we've still got time to lock up some villains, but if we don't find any we can always come back for old Joe here.'

The colour drained from Smoking Joe's face until he saw the Brothers do something they rarely did – smile broadly – before they said their farewells and left.

D Group were all in bed early that evening, to make up for the heavy night before, by the time Phil Eldrett settled himself in the privet hedge opposite Ozdemir's yard. He had been dropped off on the far side of the wood by Benson and Clarke who had then parked themselves up in a layby about half a mile away from the observation post. Eldrett sat amongst some deep ferns on the fringes of the wood, waiting for the last of the light to fade. As the birdsong was replaced by the calls of night animals, a light breeze moved the fern leaves against his face. He breathed in deeply, enjoying the smell of the countryside, and turned his face towards the blood-red sun as it dipped below the distant Pennines and the lengthening shadows began to slip a cloak over everything. The evening sky was clear, other than some high wisps, still tinged orange by the sun. Eldrett recalled similar evenings long ago in Armagh's bandit country and the same knot of tension and apprehension he had felt then was back, deep in his bowels. He wasn't concerned about it then and he wasn't now – he knew he worked best when he felt that fear, his senses honed to razor sharpness, reactions like lightning. As a dark blue, velvet night settled over the scene, he reached into his combat jacket and pulled out the heavy black plastic radio set and switched it on.

'Getting into position now,' he transmitted quietly. 'Be ready in about five minutes.'

In their car in the layby, Clarke and Benson looked at each other with a smile, before Clarke acknowledged the call with a simple, 'Received.'

Moving like one of the shadows around him, Eldrett crept along the edge of the field, stopping occasionally to listen, and then slid silently into the deep leafy hedge opposite the yard. He was delighted to see lights on in an upstairs room of the building and briefly a man standing looking out of the open window, framed by the light behind him.

'Life on the premises,' whispered Eldrett into his radio. 'Male in an upstairs room, lights on,' then he switched off to prevent any accidental transmissions or giveaway static.

In the large open-plan office on the fourth floor at New Scotland Yard, DI Paul Johnson sat on the edge of a battered old wooden table and looked at eight of his detectives, all part of A Team. None of them looked best pleased at being pulled in at fairly short notice on a rare rest day, but knowing Johnson as they did, they were all pretty sure that whatever the reason, it wouldn't be petty. He didn't disappoint them.

'Sorry to bring you in on your rest day, boys,' he began, 'but there've been some developments in a job up north that I've been involved in and it's pretty certain it's all going to kick off down here tonight.'

He had their full attention now.

'You've all been keeping tabs on a little toerag for me at Lennox Gardens for the last few months.'

There were murmurs and nods.

'Well, that little toerag is a quality snout for a mate of mine up north. About a year ago, he put a team of blaggers away to my mate and they all got wasted on the job. He was the sole survivor and they got him south the same day.'

'That the one where they walked into an ambush at a gun shop?' asked one of the DCs.

'That's the one – three killed in the shop but the getaway driver had it away and was never nicked. That's the toerag. The dead blaggers all worked for a major-league Turkish crime boss who's been looking for our man ever since. I got a call at home this afternoon from my mate telling me that the Turk got his hands on the Lennox Gardens address at lunchtime today. All the clever money is on a very nasty little team coming into the smoke tonight to take him back.'

'Won't they just top him down here?' said another DC.

'No, they're pretty certain he'll be taken back up north, tortured to get everything out of him and then murdered up there.'

The group of detectives began to fidget and chatter.

'Listen up, fellas,' interrupted Johnson. 'We'll get a couple of hours' notice that they're on their way so we can relax for a while, but I want to get shooters issued now so we can move at a moment's notice. Once you're tooled up, I'll see you downstairs in the Tank for a couple of pints.'

'What's the plan, guv?' asked DS Tom Moffat from the back of the room.

'We'll plot up on the flat early and make sure he's in, then keep a two-man team on the place. When they turn up, we let them grab him and leave. The rest of us will be around Seven Sisters and Holloway Road and that's where we take them out.'

'Take them out? I thought he was going to be taken back,' said Moffat.

'Too risky. They might have to top him in the car on the way and my mate's happy for us to take them out down here and get his snout back alive. We'll let them get on to the Holloway Road and the first red light they get we'll ram and slam them.'

There were cheers and claps of joy at the announcement. This was going to be a blinding extra night duty after all.

'OK, OK,' shouted Johnson. 'Who's got a pink ticket?'

A pink ticket was the small laminated piece of card issued to officers authorised to carry and use firearms in the Met and had to be produced to the firearms issuing officer before a gun could be handed over. To Johnson's dismay, only three hands went up.

'Three? Why the fuck haven't the rest of you got

tickets?' demanded Johnson. In his eyes, a Flying Squad officer without a pink ticket was as much use as men's tits.

There was a painful silence before the excuses began. Ticket expired, failed the re-qualification shoot but scheduled to do it again next week, not had time to rebook, and so on.

'All right, all right. Fuck me. Just get your fucking tickets sorted and up to date or your days on this squad are numbered,' he threatened. 'OK, we'll try another route,' he continued with a deep sigh. 'Who's been in the army?'

Another three hands went up. Including himself, he could get seven guns on to the streets of north London. The odds were looking much better.

'That'll do,' he declared. 'You three can have shooters as well as I won't put anything in the Occurrence Book unless we shoot somebody. Right then, get your guns and ammo and then down to the Tank.'

Chatting and laughing loudly, the team wandered into Johnson's partitioned office at the end of the room and the six gunslingers were issued with Model 10 .38 Smith and Wesson handguns and a box of ammunition each. The issue of three guns was recorded by Johnson in the Firearms Register on production of a pink ticket, but the three rogue guns would only be recorded if the wheels came off. The men tucked the guns into their belts and pulled their suit and leather jackets closed, then went downstairs to the Tank, leaving Johnson with his paperwork, waiting for a call from Handstead. With luck, fuck all would happen and his boys could spend the night on the piss, courtesy of the Commissioner.

# Chapter Seventeen

There were two men in the office on the top floor of Ozdemir's premises. Ozdemir and Guy Mitcheson were discussing the first deliveries required to get their production line up and running. Two of Ozdemir's fleet of trucks were currently on the west coast of Ireland waiting to collect the first shipment which had been smuggled into the port of Foynes on a small merchant ship that had left San Francisco ten days earlier. He expected the lorries to be making their way back to England within forty-eight hours; Mitcheson should get ready to start cooking or whatever it was he needed to do to produce the LSD.

'Two days, you reckon?'

'Should be,' said Ozdemir. 'Getting the drums into the lorries at Foynes won't be a problem, there's no customs post there and we're well known at Rosslare. It's all marked up as agricultural feed even if anyone bothers to look at the cargo manifest. Then it's only a couple of hours from Pembroke to your farm. I'll get a phone call when the trucks leave on the ferry from Rosslare so you'll get a call well in advance of arrival.'

'Excellent. I'm all set up and ready to go,' said Mitcheson happily, his first million virtually banked.

Needless to say he had not mentioned his encounter with the Brothers to his new, violent business partner and was a little shaken when Ozdemir suddenly asked, 'Everything OK with your arrangements? Anything I need to know about?' It was only Ozdemir checking and double-checking, dotting the i's and crossing the t's, but it threw Mitcheson.

'What do you mean?' He gulped nervously.

'I didn't mean anything specifically,' he replied, eyeing him suspiciously. 'Why are you so jumpy?'

Mitcheson recovered well and laughed. 'Just what you said, I thought maybe you'd heard something, that our enterprise had got to the ears of the wrong people or something.'

'No, nothing like that, just checking to make sure you're keeping your side of the deal.'

'No concerns on that score, I assure you, Mr Ozdemir. As soon as I get the precursor chemicals, I'm up and running, and production of at least ninety-nine per cent pure LSD will be about two weeks' work.'

'Good. You better be on your way, I've got some business associates due here in a while and I don't want them to start asking questions about you.'

They shook hands and Mitcheson was shown down the fire escape at the back of the building by the delightful Carmen. A motion-activated security light in the rear yard came on as he walked to his tatty Range Rover parked alongside a liveried Ozdemir haulage lorry. Carmen activated the automatic gates and he drove quickly out of the yard and on to the quiet road.

Eldrett saw the security light in the yard come on and as the Range Rover appeared briefly illuminated under a street light he noted its registration number in a small notebook, writing by the red glow of his miniature torch. Then he sat and waited for the main event.

Only three miles apart from each other, the two main players in this particular drama sat quietly in their respective offices drinking alone and thinking. Ozdemir had dismissed Carmen for the evening once Mitcheson had gone and she had screeched away from the yard in her Triumph Spitfire in high dudgeon. Despite her obvious attractions, the less she knew about his business the better, considered Ozdemir. He poured himself a small glass of raki which he topped up with water from the carafe on his desk and stood at his lit window, looking out at the dark wood in the distance. Sometimes he got urges to go home to his roots in the bustling port city of Antalya, but he had hated the dirt and noise and humidity there and had grown to love the lush, damp greenness of his adopted country. And as a high-ranking member of the Ozdemir crime family, life was pretty good for him as well. He was financially secure for the rest of his life and wanted for nothing, but that inherent streak of rebellious independence remained his weak point.

Harrison swilled a mouthful of Bushmills around and sat back in his chair, facing the open window that looked out on to Bolton Road East. He had turned the lights off in the hope that he might catch a brief catnap before Eldrett made contact, but his mind was racing and he was literally twitching with anticipation. He hardly had a pot to piss in, he lived in a rented one-bedroom studio flat, owned two suits and an elderly Datsun, and paid his ex-wife substantial sums in maintenance for two daughters he hadn't seen in years. Yet he, too, was happy with his lot. He adored doing what he did, especially something as devious as this latest operation. He knew he was bending the rules but he salved his conscience with the thought that he had never fitted up anyone who didn't deserve to be fitted up. And besides, he wasn't actually trying to fit Ozdemir up at all, he was merely encouraging him to commit a crime that he would have committed eventually anyway, and setting the parameters and the timing of the offence to ensure a satisfactory result. 'That's how it should be,' said Harrison quietly to himself and closed his eyes.

Benson and Clarke had run out of small talk and Clarke now had the driver's seat fully reclined for a snooze. Benson leant against the bonnet of their unmarked Morris Marina, smoking and gazing up at the spectacular, star-filled night sky. The peace and tranquillity of the night were in sharp contrast to what he and Clarke were now party to, and hardbitten though he was, Benson could appreciate it. He turned to look at his partner of the last two years; his mouth had dropped open and his head lolled to one side, he was clearly dropping into a deep sleep.

As Benson lit another cigarette, he glanced at his watch in the flare of his lighter. It was ten thirty; they had been parked up for an hour and a half and not seen a single vehicle along their isolated layby in that time. He turned to look in the direction of the wood about half a mile away, beyond which Eldrett lay in his hedge – watching, watching, and waiting. Without disturbing his mate, Benson began to walk slowly along the layby, listening to the silence which was only occasionally broken by sounds of the countryside at night. He was intrigued by them. Born and bred on a council estate in

Manchester, the countryside was as alien to him as it was to the scumbags of Handstead, but unlike them he was not afraid of it. Rather, he saw the darkness, the absence of any artificial light, as a friendly cloak, something he could happily live with. Once this is all over, he resolved, I'm going to come out here with the missus and kids and explore.

His ruminations were disturbed by the back-to-back radio in his trouser pocket suddenly bursting into life.

'Stand by, vehicle on to the forecourt,' he heard Eldrett hiss urgently. He could hear the tension in his voice and ran back to the CID vehicle, banging on the bonnet to rouse Clarke.

'What's up?' complained the bleary-eyed detective, smacking his dry lips together.

'Phil's got a car on the forecourt, this could be the off,' said Benson excitedly, dumping his huge frame into his seat, causing the car to rock like a boat in a heavy swell.

'Four males out of the car and into the main front door,' said Eldrett quietly into his radio. 'It's a black Mercedes, can't see the index yet.'

Clarke and Benson looked at each other but said nothing. It was looking promising.

Thirty seconds later Eldrett saw shadows moving in the lit office and it was obvious that the four visitors had joined the man he had seen earlier. He couldn't see any of them but the flitting shadows were all the confirmation he needed. He saw the man again in the lit window, his back to it, clearly making an important point to his visitors with urgent hand movements. Then he walked back into the room and just the shadows showed themselves to Eldrett. Five minutes later he saw four figures leave the darkened main door and walk back towards the Mercedes. He could make out their low voices but not what they were saying. They all got back into the car and were briefly illuminated by the interior courtesy lights but they were too far away to get any meaningful description. Then the front courtesy light came on again, and Eldrett could see the front seat passenger closely examining something on his lap, and the driver leaning over towards him, also looking at it. Then the light went out, Eldrett heard the engine start and the headlights lit up the front of the building.

'Stand by, vehicle on the move. Four up, black Mercedes back on to the main road; wait one, wait one; got it – index is Tango Oscar Tango, nine, nine, six, Hotel,' said Eldrett quickly, 'heading south towards the motorway,' and he repeated the registration number.

In their layby, Clarke and Benson exchanged triumphant smiles before Clarke started up the Marina and headed back towards Handstead. Eldrett would remain in his hide for at least another hour in case there were further callers.

Just outside town, Clarke pulled over alongside a lonely telephone box which, unlike most in the town itself, had not been vandalised and was still lit, standing out in the dark like a welcome lighthouse at sea. Benson hurried into the box and telephoned Harrison's office, waking him from a restless sleep. He passed on the details of what Eldrett had seen.

From his hedge, Eldrett saw the light in the office go out and he concentrated his attention on the front door to the building, expecting to see someone leave. Instead, a few seconds later, he saw a brief flicker of light from within the office and then the telltale glow of a cigarette. The man was back at the window, watching nothing again. There was no way Eldrett would be going anywhere until he was sure the building was empty so he settled deeper into the hedge, pulled his balaclava down fully and made himself comfortable.

# Chapter Eighteen

'They're on the move,' called DI Johnson to his team who were gathered at the bar in the Tank situated in the basement at New Scotland Yard. 'They just left, four-handed, in a black Merc, Tango Oscar Tango, nine, nine, six, Hotel. Two and a half, three hours' maximum travelling time. Tom, you and Danny go and find out if shit-for-brains is home and then set yourselves up and keep an eye on the place, OK?'

The group of detectives rapidly finished their drinks and began to hurry out to the underground garages to get their vehicles ready.

'Knock him up if you have to, Tom,' advised Johnson as he walked out with Moffat. 'It won't be unusual for the Old Bill to be knocking on doors in Lennox Gardens. Tell him a neighbour's place got screwed or something.'

'No problem, guv,' replied Moffat, belching loudly and wiping his mouth on the back of his hand. 'If he's not in, we'll find him in one of the boozers nearby, I'm sure.'

'Good lad. Keep in touch, all right? I'll be out with the others around the Holloway Road area. Once they've grabbed him, just get in behind and keep us informed, OK?'

'Got you,' said Moffat, opening the fire doors to the garages and waving his governor goodbye.

Johnson returned to his office, switched off the flickering single fluorescent ceiling strobe light and put on his desk lamp before picking up the phone and dialling.

'Dan, it's Paul,' he said after a short pause. 'We're out and about and waiting for them. You got anyone up their arse on the way down?'

'No, sorry, mate, don't have the resources. Just letting them run, I'm afraid,' replied Dan Harrison up in Handstead. 'Don't worry, they'll be there, I promise.'

'Looking forward to it. Tooled up, d'you reckon?'

'Can't believe they won't be. All your boys going to be carrying?'

'Oh yeah, we'll have seven shooters on the ground. Should be sufficient, I reckon.'

'Don't doubt it for a moment, pal, and of course you'll have the element of surprise.'

'Got to get on, Dan,' said Johnson, getting to his feet. 'I'll give you a bell when it's gone off.'

'Good luck, Paul,' replied Harrison. He replaced his phone and leant back in his chair with a broad grin on his face. He doubted very much that Ozdemir himself would be amongst the passengers in the Mercedes now sweeping swiftly south along the motorway towards London, but what he wouldn't have given to be a fly on the wall when it became apparent that he'd been turned over again. He chuckled to himself and opened his bottom drawer to retrieve his new bottle of Bushmills which was already half drunk. Or, as Harrison the eternal optimist would have it, still half full.

Shortly after two thirty in the morning, a befuddled and aggressive Brian Jones rolled on to his side on the mattress he was lying on as he became aware of repeated knocking on the flat's front door. He had staggered back a little after eleven after another day on the piss along the Seven Sisters and Holloway Roads, and as usual his head was thumping. It was what he had done pretty much every day since he had fled south after the massacre at the Tamworth gun shop and now that his former cellmate was once again spending some quality time courtesy of Her Majesty's prison service, he lived alone in the squalid flat on the third floor of Barbers House on the Six Acres estate. The place was filthy, his descent into physical and moral ruin epitomised by the mattress he was lying on in the kitchen. The flat had a bedroom with a rickety old bed in it, but Jones had hauled the mattress into the kitchen where he could collapse more easily on to it after a day's drinking. The mattress was covered in sweat and vomit stains and the underneath showed recent evidence of a loss of bladder control.

Jones had become a mess over the last year, constantly fearful of a visit from the vengeful Sercan Ozdemir, friendless, unemployable and now resembling a rough sleeper. His always long hair now reached his hips and was unwashed for months at a time, and his sallow face was almost hidden from view by a thick, filthy, unkempt beard. He lived and slept in his clothes which had become almost a second skin, his trainers would probably need surgery to remove them, and he stank. He smelt like the hunted animal he had become.

He ignored the knocking, but it continued unabated. 'If it's those fucking coppers back again . . .' he muttered to himself as he heaved himself up off his rancid mattress. His head swam and he felt sick. He glanced at the kitchen sink which was awash with the vomit he had deposited earlier and dozens of empty beer cans and cigarette butts and began to retch as he caught a whiff of the full evidence of his spiral into oblivion.

'Fucking coppers,' he slurred as he staggered slowly

along the hallway, intent on giving the coppers a mouthful of abuse. What the fuck would they want again? They'd already pissed him off asking fucking stupid questions about some burglary and disturbing him – he was going to give them some serious grief this time.

'What the fuck do you—' He vaguely made out some large men in the hallway before his lights went out.

The large goon who had felled Jones with a baseball bat over the top of the head motioned for the others to come into the flat and he shut the door behind them. One of the group knelt alongside Jones to check for signs of life. His scalp had split from the single blow and blood was coursing through his long hair and already beginning to pool under his head.

'He'll live,' said the slugger, looking dispassionately down at the deeply unconscious Jones. 'Strap his head up and then bind him.'

Two minutes later, with a filthy shirt they had found in the bedroom wrapped over his head, and his ankles and wrists bound tightly with packing tape, Brian Jones was ready for his journey back to Handstead and a fearful torturing at the hands of Sercan Ozdemir.

'His mouth,' commanded the Turkish Babe Ruth, pointing at Jones.

The heavy with the tape knelt back down beside

Jones and quickly wrapped the packing tape twice round his head, covering his mouth.

'OK, we can go. Bring him out and wait by the main doors. I'll just check everything's OK outside.'

Fifty yards away, DS Tom Moffatt and DC Eamon Howley sat in their darkened Cortina which was parked up outside an adjacent block of flats.

'One of them is out of the front door, just checking the coast is clear,' transmitted Howley quietly. 'Stand by.'

The large Turk stepped out of the main door to the flats and walked forward a few paces, looking left and right and then up at the flats above him for signs of life. Lennox Road was as quiet as the grave and he turned back to the doors, indicating with a nod of his head and an urgent wave of his hand that the coast was clear.

'They're out, three of them carrying a body,' said Howley.

The two Flying Squad detectives sat quietly and watched as the boot of the Mercedes was opened and Brian Jones was dumped unceremoniously inside and the lid closed quietly. The four Turks hurried to get in and seconds later the headlights came on and the car turned back into Lennox Road then towards Durham Road. Moffatt and Howley ducked down out of sight as the Mercedes travelled left to right across the front of them, then Howley again transmitted.

'They're out of Lennox Road, left, left into Durham Road towards Seven Sisters.'

Paul Johnson spoke for the first time since his observation team had announced the arrival of the hoodlums from Handstead.

'Same plan as before, lads. Central Two, you stay with them. Everyone else hang back.'

Moffatt and Howley kept back about sixty yards and saw the Mercedes slow and then make a right turn on to Seven Sisters Road.

'They're right, right, into Seven Sisters Road towards Holloway Road,' announced Howley. 'Not hurrying it, nice and steady.'

'Keep well back, Central Two,' cautioned Johnson. 'Everything's arranged to take them out in Holloway Road. Central Five, stand by, they're not far away.'

Another voice acknowledged the Mercedes' progress and Howley continued his brief commentary.

'Just crossing the Hornsey Road junction, we can see the lights at Holloway Road on red. Keeping well back.'

The traffic lights he was referring to changed as the Mercedes approached them and it made a right turn unhindered by any oncoming traffic.

'They're right, right into Holloway Road, northbound,' said Howley.

'Central Five, stand by,' said DI Paul Johnson tersely from his vehicle parked in Tufnell Park Road. 'Central Two, I need you to call the traffic lights for me. First red light they catch, we need to know. Central Five, start rolling south slowly. Keep talking, Central Two.'

In the Mercedes, the four Turks were chatting quietly, congratulating themselves on a nice slick operation that Mr Ozdemir was going to be very pleased with and discussing what a shithole London was. They were laughing loudly as their vehicle slowed to a halt at the red light controlling the junction with Tavistock Terrace. Even at that hour of the morning there was still plenty of vehicle and pedestrian traffic along Holloway Road, lined as it was with numerous fast food shops and nightclubs. The Turks were people-watching and passing comment on the nocturnal life on Holloway Road.

'Look at the state of that old whore,' laughed one of the rear-seat passengers, leading to a loud exchange of insulting observations from all four occupants. They were unwinding, the tension of their mission evaporating as they began to head home with their reluctant parcel in the boot. Once they got him back, they expected to be busy bleeding Jones, literally, for all the information Sercan Ozdemir suspected he still held in his alcohol-ravaged brain.

*

'Go, go, go, Central Five,' yelled Johnson as Howley gave the urgent update.

The driver of the Mercedes turned back to face forward after a joke with one of his passengers, and his brow furrowed immediately.

'What the fuck . . . ?' he said out loud as he clocked the tatty white Transit van, travelling in the opposite direction, suddenly veer across the carriageway and begin to come directly at the Mercedes at ever increasing speed.

The three passengers heard his shout and also looked ahead at the headlights coming towards them. They all froze, mouths open in shock, until a split second later Central Five, a salvage vehicle with the front of the engine panel reinforced with blocks of pig iron for just such an occasion, rammed the Mercedes at sixty-five miles an hour. Such was the impact that the front-seat passenger was slammed into the dashboard, fracturing his skull, while the two rear passengers hit the backs of the seats in front of them with enough force to stun them. Only the driver who had put on his seatbelt remained relatively unscathed, though he, too, was temporarily stunned. The front of the Mercedes crumpled like a Venetian fan and the windscreen disintegrated, showering the occupants with small pieces of razor-sharp glass that cut their faces. The driver recovered first, shaking his spinning head to see the vehicle that had rammed them stop a few feet ahead of them. He saw the driver and a passenger begin to leave the Transit which had steam hissing from its broken radiator and he automatically reached into his jacket pocket to get his handgun.

The two Central Five crew members saw the telltale movement. DCs Barry James and Colin McRae were both carrying their model 10 Smith and Wessons and James shouted the warning as they quickly lined up on the driver.

'Armed police, arsehole, get your hands up,' he screamed.

The instruction was ignored. The driver continued into his pocket and was withdrawing his weapon when the two Flying Squad officers opened up on him from a distance of four feet. Five of the .38 rounds fired at him struck him in the chest, a sixth going through his throat and windpipe and then through the back of the seat and into the top of the head of the Turk sitting behind, who was still leaning stunned against the seat in front of him. Both died instantly in the car. The other rear-seat passenger sat back frozen in shock, while the Turk in the front seat slipped into a coma from the fracture to his skull.

'Shots fired,' shouted Howley from Central Two twenty yards away, 'shots fired, bandits down.'

'Fuck,' growled Johnson in his car. 'Who's in Central Five?' he asked his driver.

'Barry and Colin.'

'Thank fuck for that,' exclaimed Johnson. 'They've both got tickets. Come on, let's get down there.'

Johnson arrived on scene in a couple of minutes, just as James and McRae were handcuffing the one uninjured Turk, face down, on the pavement.

'You all right, lads?' Johnson asked, walking over to them.

'Fine thanks, boss. The arsehole in the front went for his jacket so we took him out.'

'You find his shooter yet?'

'Haven't looked. Do us a favour, will you?'

'Sure, don't worry, he'll have something he shouldn't if he hasn't got a gun.' Johnson smiled.

He peered into the interior of the Mercedes and grimaced. The front-seat passenger was slumped against his door, blood seeping from his ears, dark rings forming under his eyes as he slipped away. The driver was sitting well back in his seat, his mouth and eyes open and the wounds to his throat and chest still smoking slightly. The back of his seat was splattered with pieces of bloody cartilage and sinew from his neck, and the spray from the exit wound reached the back window. The front of his shirt was black with blood, which was forming a lake on the leather seat between his legs. By his side, alongside the handbrake, was the long-barrelled Magnum that he'd been so desperate to draw. The rear-seat passenger behind him had collapsed in a ball behind the driver's seat, the hole in the top of his head weeping slowly and occasionally bubbling. The vehicle stank of the blood and the urine and faeces the corpses were also releasing.

'What a fucking mess,' observed Johnson.

'Any sign of a shooter?' asked McRae.

'Big one, looks like a Magnum, down by the handbrake. 'Don't worry, boys, it's a clean shoot. You called anyone yet?'

'Not yet, just wanted to get this one bagged and tagged.'

'Done the boot yet?'

'Forgot about him. Do it for us, will you?'

Johnson retrieved the keys from the ignition and Johnson opened the boot of the Mercedes. The terrified Brian Jones stared up at him with saucer-sized eyes. He had come to in the boot just before Central Five had rammed them and then heard the fusillade of gunshots that followed, one round penetrating into the boot, past his head and out through the rear number plate. Now he was convinced it was his turn and he was desperately shaking his head, pleading for his life with his eyes and making little squeaking noises.

'Relax, son,' said Johnson, reaching down and with

considerable difficulty ripping the packing tape painfully away from Jones's face and mouth. 'Mr Harrison sent us to take care of you; you've been rescued by the Sweeney, my old mate.'

Gasping in fright and pulling in as much fresh air as he could, Jones slumped back into the cluttered boot.

'You fucking bastards,' he managed between pants.

'What an ungrateful prick,' said Johnson in disgust. 'Go fuck yourself,' and he slammed the lid shut again. The sound of approaching sirens drowned out Jones's muffled insults.

Soon the scene was crawling with other Met officers with jobs to do as they investigated the shooting and it was just after five before Johnson got back to his office at the Yard and telephoned Harrison.

'How'd it go?' asked Dan Harrison, sitting up in his chair. 'I was expecting to hear from you a while ago.'

'One of them tried to play silly buggers, pulled a shooter on my guys. Two dead, one critical and the fourth unhurt.'

'Fucking hell. All your guys OK?'

'Not a scratch, thanks.'

'What about Jones?'

'Fit and well and as obnoxious as ever. When I got him out of the boot all the ungrateful bastard did was bad-mouth the Old Bill. Shame he didn't catch one.'

Harrison laughed. 'Yeah, he's lovely, isn't he? Where have you got him now?'

'I've stuck him in the cells at Islington for the time being to keep him safe. Don't suppose he'll be too happy about it but I need him alive for the trial.'

'He'll be the original reluctant witness, Paul, but you could always threaten to bring him back to Handstead. Should concentrate his mind on where his best interests lie.'

'May have to, I reckon. Listen, mate, I've got a shed load of writing to get done before I get away. Anything else you need from me?'

'Just one more thing, Paul,' said Harrison. After a few more seconds' chat, he replaced the phone, puffed out his cheeks and relaxed back into his chair. The first part of his plan had worked out very nicely. The Met had done all his dirty work for him and his grip on Ozdemir's balls was tighter than ever.

The first copper-coloured strands of light were beginning to show on the horizon beyond the hedge where Eldrett had remained all night. There had been no further visits to the yard but he had seen the telltale glow of cigarettes being smoked in the darkened office throughout his vigil.

Sercan Ozdemir had chain-smoked his way through the long night, and as time wore on and there was still no contact from his team of thugs despatched to London, he began to panic. Worse, there was no way to make contact with them and no one else he could trust to go and try and find out. He would have to wait it out but he needed to freshen up so he decided to head home for a quick shower before returning. Why haven't they phoned if they're having problems? What the hell's going on? he asked himself as he locked the main front doors behind him and hurried out to his own Mercedes parked opposite the doors.

'Thank fuck for that,' murmured Eldrett from deep within the hedge as he watched him start up his car and drive quickly away. Once silence had returned to the area, and all Eldrett could hear was the early-morning dawn chorus, he slid out of the hedge and gingerly stood upright. He had remained prone and motionless for over six hours. He rotated his hips and massaged his numbed limbs before he began to limp back along the hedgerow towards the wood.

'Last one's out and away, I'm coming back,' he transmitted wearily as he entered the cool wood.

Clarke and Benson had returned to their lonely layby after they telephoned DCI Harrison and had remained there, taking turns to monitor the back-to-back radio while the other tried to get comfortable and snooze.

Clarke fired up the Marina and he and Benson stretched out the long night from their stiff backs as they waited for the extraordinary Phil Eldrett to return. He didn't keep them waiting long, choosing to jog through the woods to get his circulation back to normal. Checking the road was clear, as it had been all night, Eldrett crossed quickly to the layby and jumped into the rear of the car.

'Morning, fellas. Good night?' he asked cheerily.

'Not bad, Phil. Much going on out there?' asked Benson.

'Very quiet. The last guy was there all bloody night but no visitors after the Merc left.'

Benson let the comment go without reply.

Eldrett continued to chat as he gazed out of the window at the fields they passed on the way back to Handstead.

'He had a visitor when I first got there, though. Bloke in a grotty Range Rover.'

'Get the number?' asked Benson.

'In my book,' he replied, patting the breast pocket of his camouflage jacket.

'Boss will be interested. He wants to see you quickly before you go off anyway, all right?'

'Yeah, no problems. I'll need a while to wind down any way. Might even have a glass of that stuff he keeps in his bottom drawer if he offers me one. Any news about where the Merc went, what happened or anything?'

'Not a word.' said Clarke. 'Maybe Harrison will have some news when we get in.'

Twenty minutes later the two detectives and Eldrett sat in DCI Harrison's office sipping an early-morning glass of Bushmills. Harrison looked tired and worn out after the long, restless night he'd endured in his ropey old chair, but his mood belied his physical appearance.

'Well done, Phil, fucking good job,' he enthused as he slumped back into the uncomfortable chair and raised his glass in salute. 'We've had a fantastic result, by the way.'

'Go on, boss, what's happened?' pressed Benson, leaning forward in his chair.

'The team you saw leave Ozdemir's yard turned up at the flat in London about half two this morning. They snatched him and stuck him in the boot and the Flying Squad took them out just round the corner.'

'Took them out?'

'In every sense of the phrase. One of the Turks went for a gun so they topped him and one in the back. Another one's seriously ill with a fractured skull, not expected to live apparently, and the fourth is locked up unscathed and at the tender mercies of the Flying Squad. Poor bastard.'

'Result,' boomed Benson, beaming at Clarke and Eldrett. 'What about that little shit Jones?'

'He's fine apart from a crease down the middle of his

345

head where the Turks floored him with a baseball bat. The Squad have got him locked up somewhere for his own safety. What a result.'

'Can Ozdemir know any of this yet?'

'Not a chance, not even the media in London knows about it yet and his team didn't make any phone calls before they were ambushed. He'll be shitting himself worrying about where they are and what's happened. I'm expecting a delivery later this morning so I can go and break the news to him myself.'

'Delivery?'

'It'll be a nice little touch, John,' said Harrison with a sly grin, tapping the side of his nose with his forefinger, 'a nice little touch. Anyway, Phil, what sort of a night did you have lying in cow shit or whatever?' he asked with a friendly laugh.

'A quiet one, boss. Nothing happened after the Merc left but the one guy stayed all night. Didn't leave until half an hour ago.'

'Driving a black Merc?'

'Yeah.'

'That'll have been Ozdemir. Obviously waiting for his team to get back with Jones. Oh, fucking beautiful, he'll be crapping himself.'

'Tell him about the caller earlier, Phil,' said Benson.

'Earlier caller?' queried Harrison, peering over the top of his crystal tumbler.

'Yeah. When I first got plotted up he had someone in the office with him. I saw him leave in a crappy old brown Range Rover.'

Harrison sprang to his feet, his sudden movement startling the others.

'Range Rover?'

'Yes, real piece of junk.'

'Did you get the index number?' asked Harrison urgently.

'Of course,' replied Eldrett, putting his glass on the low coffee table and fishing around in his jacket pockets until he found his notebook. He leafed slowly through the pages, watched intently by the three detectives in silence, until he found the page he was looking for.

'Here we are, twenty-two fifteen, brown Range Rover, index Lima Mike Juliet, seven, nine, two, Delta, leaves yard. Solo male driver – not a great description, I'm afraid, but I think I'd know him again.' He looked up at Harrison expectantly and was surprised to see him slumped back in his chair, looking up at the ceiling.

'Sweet Jesus,' he said quietly.

'Everything all right, boss?' asked Eldrett, looking worried.

'Oh yes, Phil, everything's fine, couldn't be better really. I know that motor, that's all. Holy shit, this is just eighteen carat.' He paused, deep in thought, undisturbed by his guests who let him ponder in peace. After a few minutes he got back to his feet and walked round his desk to stand in front of Eldrett.

'I can't tell you everything right now, Phil, but you've just slotted in a huge piece of a very nasty jigsaw. Get yourself off home to bed, get some kip and then be back here, say nine tonight? I've got another job right up your street, OK?'

'Fine, suits me,' said Eldrett, getting to his feet. 'Give me a clue – what do I need to bring along?'

'Rural location out at Angotts Mead; you'll be watching a very remote farmhouse. I doubt you'll be able to have any comms at all and I've no idea how long you'll need to be there. But you'll know when you've seen enough, I'm sure. Just watch, listen, record and, if you get a chance, have a look round. This is so important, I can't tell you. Jesus, what a piece of luck. Go on, Phil, get yourself to bed. I'll see you tonight.'

Harrison shook Eldrett's hand warmly, as did Clarke and Benson. Once he had left, Harrison sat in his chair again and gazed into his glass. He was silent until Clarke spoke.

'What's going on, boss?' he asked quietly.

'Ozdemir's financing an LSD factory out at Angotts Mead,' he said simply, looking up at them with the biggest smile either of them had ever seen.

# Chapter Nineteen

Harrison's delivery from New Scotland Yard arrived just after 11 a.m. It had left the Yard in the despatch box of a Met motorcyclist who had travelled north into Leicestershire where it had been handed to a local motorcycle cop who had then carried on north into Manchester. There a Greater Manchester Police traffic car had met their colleague, relieved him of the package and brought it direct to Handstead. Harrison received a call from the front office PC to say it had arrived and he hurried down to collect it. He glanced at it with a satisfied smile, rolled it into a tube and then went out to the rear yard to get his car.

Twenty minutes later he strode into the offices of Ozdemir Haulage Company, ignoring the calls of the two girls on the reception desk, trotted up the carpeted stairs and into Ozdemir's offices without knocking.

Carmen got to her feet as he entered, but he held up his hand to silence her.

'Not now, darling. I just know he'll want to see me,' he said cheerfully and pushed open the door to Ozdemir's private office. He was pleased to see that Ozdemir was on the phone and looking worried. Unfortunately he was speaking Turkish and Harrison couldn't understand a word he was saying, but the tone of his voice and the frown on his face told him that he was very, very worried.

'You look a bit down in the dumps, Sercan,' he said, dropping into the plush leather sofa. 'Business bad?'

Ozdemir rang a finger round his collar and licked his lips nervously as he stared at a man he was beginning to develop a deep personal hatred for. He swallowed hard, replaced the phone and poured himself a glass of water before replying.

'My business is fine, Mr Harrison,' he said slowly. 'Why are you here? I didn't invite you so I assume you have a warrant or some other kind of court order?'

'Good heavens no, nothing like that, Sercan. But I have got something for you to read. Cast your eyes over that.' He tossed the rolled-up newspaper he was carrying on to Ozdemir's desk.

With a deep, feigned sigh of indifference, Ozdemir

opened the first morning edition of the *London Evening Standard*. His face remained frozen like a mask but Harrison saw the colour drain away and his eyes dart frantically across the text. 'Sweeney in Holloway Road Gun Battle – 3 dead' screamed the banner headline. The crime reporter responsible for the story had possession of few of the facts but a discreet briefing from DI Paul Johnson had given him enough to scoop both the local and national media by at least six hours. 'Three Turkish hoodlums die in clash with elite Flying Squad,' continued the blatant piece of Yard propaganda. 'No police hurt. Yard chiefs praise officers' bravery under fire.' Harrison watched intently as Ozdemir read silently and then put the paper down on his desk.

'Well done the Yard,' he finally said awkwardly. 'They must be feeling very pleased with themselves.'

'Oh, I bet they are, Sercan, I bet they are. And so am I. I know that team left here last night and I know what they were doing down there for you.'

'Doing for me? What are you talking about?'

Harrison laughed and got to his feet. He had deliberately not mentioned that Jones had been recovered and was back in hiding, preferring to keep Ozdemir dancing.

'I'll be back to talk about this again soon, Sercan. You keep the paper, the *Standard* has an excellent crossword,

I'm told.' With that he turned on his heel and was gone as quickly as he had arrived, leaving Ozdemir trembling like a leaf behind his desk.

It took him nearly ten minutes to recover his composure and begin to try and think things through rationally. If Harrison could prove he had sent the team, he'd be wearing a pair of handcuffs now. Clearly, the sole survivor of the Mercedes was not saying anything and any other evidence, whatever it may be, would be very weak. What was Harrison after? What had happened to Jones? Was it money? He'd never mentioned cash. A piece of the action maybe? Unlikely, but maybe some kind of business arrangement. How had the Sweeney managed to get wind of the job? Who knew it was coming off? Only a few trusted confidants and three of them were now apparently lying in a morgue in Enfield Hospital. And Rod Allan. That fat, treacherous bastard, it had to be him, but Ozdemir was sure he'd have spotted something in Allan's behaviour that would have alerted him. Was Harrison involved? He had to be, but how? His head was spinning, wild theories threatening to take over his brain, and he needed fresh air. What he needed after the fresh air was someone to get hold of Rod Allan and find out what he knew but he was getting to the stage where he could no longer trust anyone.

\*

352

On his triumphant return to his office, the exhausted Harrison, who had now worked nearly three days without going home, telephoned his mate at the Drugs Squad.

'Morning, Rick. About the LSD inquiry I've got on the go, I reckon I've identified the money behind the operation.'

'Anyone we know?'

'Doubt it, local Turkish scumbag, part of the Ozdemir family.'

'The Ozdemirs? Yeah, we know of them but drugs isn't part of their portfolio as far as we know. You sure?'

'Pretty sure. Our guy is looking to go freelance. Tried it last year robbing the gun shop out at Tamworth. We reckoned it was part of a bigger plan to go large in the drugs trade but we got into his team and took them out in the shop.'

'Yeah, remember it well, Dan,' laughed DI Rick Moulder at the other end of the phone. 'What's his connection to the LSD operation?'

'He got a visit last night from the chemist, the guy whose car we found the note in.'

'Very interesting, looks good. What are you going to do next?'

'I'm putting twenty-four-hour surveillance on the chemist's farm out at Angotts Mead. Be really useful to know what we might expect to see, Rick.'

'We talking about a major production job here?'

'Probably.'

'He's not going to need significant quantities of the precursor material so don't expect to see lorry loads of stuff turning up.'

'Great, so what are we talking about?' asked Harrison.

'Very roughly, and assuming the Turk's got someone producing it who knows what he's doing, five kilos of ergotamine tartrate could produce one kilo of pure crystalline LSD, which probably equates to something like fifteen to twenty million doses.'

Harrison whistled quietly and did some quiet calculations on his desk blotter.

'Fifty pence a dose – Jesus, ten million quid? That's can't be right, Rick. Ten million?'

'It's why people are prepared to take the risk of getting locked up, Dan. It's not hard to produce it, it's easy to smuggle, it's cheap and the market is enormous. Your man's overheads won't be huge; most of the money is pure profit.'

'Jesus,' said Harrison again.

'Listen, Dan, sounds like your man is still in either initial or early stages of production but you need to keep close tabs on him or we'll have a massive problem. I can let you have six guys to come over and give you a hand.'

'Thanks, Rick, I'm sure I'm going to need them, but right now I'm just going to keep an eye on where I think the lab is. The guy I've got watching is the dog's bollocks. I reckon we'll know soon enough.'

'Who's your guy?'

'Phil Eldrett, you know him, the ex-army guy who did that job for you over at Ashington eight, nine months ago?'

Moulder remembered him well. 'Oh yeah, quality. What do they call him, the Shadow or something?'

'Something like that, but whatever they call him, he's the business and I'd stake my ex-wife's beautiful three-bedroomed detached house on him getting what we need.'

Moulder laughed. 'OK, Dan. Listen, soon as you've got what you need to make a move on the place, give me a ring, OK? I'll give you as much help as I can. You told Headquarters about this yet?'

'Have I fuck,' said Harrison. 'Not even told that idiot Findlay at Division yet. I don't plan on this being common knowledge until a couple of hours before we put the door in. Fewer people that know the better, especially at Headquarters. Christ, most of them can't even hold their own water.'

Harrison was right to be cautious about who knew of the potential LSD lab. The fewer senior officers who knew, the better. Especially a knob like the divisional commander, Chief Superintendent Philip 'The Fist' Findlay. He was a massively overpromoted dullard who owed his rank to his membership of the all-powerful Freemasons. His operational experience could have been listed on the back of a postage stamp – with space to spare. He had previous for flapping his gums about ongoing operations to investigative journalists over boozy Masonic dinners, twice leading to complete compromise of the jobs in question. While he fondly believed that his nickname, 'The Fist', was something to do with him being a tough, respected leader, it was in fact a name that had followed him into the police service from the navy: the Electric Throbbing Sailor's Fist. Whenever he was discussed he was always, but always, referred to as 'that wanker Findlay'.

'Keep in touch, Dan,' said DI Rick Moulder before they hung up.

Harrison and Moulder had been DCs together years ago, trusted each other implicitly and had some serious mileage under their respective belts when it came to getting a conviction at court one way or another. Harrison was absolutely confident that his mate wouldn't breathe a word about his potential problem until he told him to. And that wouldn't be until the last moment when it would be far too late for anyone to say, 'Hold on, just wait a minute, let's look at the implications of this, shall we?'

Operational detectives like Harrison and Moulder did their reflecting and pondering on their feet and quick-time, as a job developed, rarely going upstairs for advice and guidance. They had trusted their instincts and gut feelings throughout their careers and to date they had been generally right. Sure, things had not always gone exactly to plan, but the bottom line was that there was no substitute for a 'copper's nose': the ability to know instinctively that something was wrong or out of place, the experience to detect the guilty reaction to your mere presence or the physical signs that someone was lying. Harrison had made quite a name for himself two years ago when he had produced a short paper, accompanied by a film, about an investigation he had run into a series of thefts from vulnerable old people in a home. His premise was that the guilty and the innocent answer the same simple questions in different ways. And his film appeared to prove it. He had narrowed his list of suspects down to eight members of staff at the home, two cleaners and six nursing staff, all of whom would have had the opportunity to commit the thefts. Then he prepared a list of carefully thought out questions which each of his suspects was asked, without any changes or additions – exactly the same. Unknown to any of them, their interviews were filmed and the camera concentrated on their faces. Harrison had presented his findings to a collection of senior detectives and the Deputy Chief Constable (Crime) in a conference room at Headquarters. First, he had handed them all a piece of paper and a pencil.

'I'm going to show you the eight interviews we conducted,' he said. 'What I want you to do is score the responses you hear and the reactions you see to the same questions. The scale is one to ten, with one being very honest and ten dishonest. Any questions?'

There were none; most of them had no interest in what Harrison had to say, regarding him as little more than a hooligan from Handstead, but Chief Daniells had expressed some interest in his theory, so here they were, watching Harrison's slightly out of focus film of the staff being asked: have you stolen any property from any of the patients here? Do you know of any of your colleagues who have stolen from them? What do you think about people who steal from vulnerable old people? What would you do if you saw one of your colleagues stealing from them? And so on. The film lasted half an hour, after which Harrison switched on the lights and stood in front of his audience. They were glancing at each other's scores and frowning. He walked to a large whiteboard which was covered with a sheet of paper. He pulled it away to reveal the names of his eight suspects, and proceeded to fill in the scores his audience had given them. He also asked questions about the reasoning behind their scores.

When Harrison had recorded all their scores, he did some quick calculations and then stood back to let them see the results. Of the eight potential suspects, two had significantly higher scores than the others – two of the ward nurses.

'Those two nurses shared a flat together,' he told them. 'We executed a search warrant there and recovered most of the missing jewellery. The cash was gone, needless to say.'

He saw a few mouths drop open and glances exchanged but nothing was said.

'Nurse A was a junkie, stealing to support her habit. Her flatmate, Nurse B, knew she was doing it but said nothing. Both their answers to the questions we set them gave them away. To the question, "What do you think about people who steal from vulnerable old people?" Nurse B replied that it could be that the thief had problems of her own. She didn't condemn them like the matron did. You picked that up, sir,' he said to the Deputy Chief Constable. 'In fact, you all did.'

He continued to analyse the answers.

'To the question, "Do you know of any of your colleagues who have stolen from them?" Nurse B replied, "It depends what you mean by stealing. They may give it back, perhaps they've put it somewhere safe" – she knew her flatmate was stealing to support her habit and hoped she might be able to get her back on the straight and narrow. Nurse A was aggressive and uncooperative but scored better than her colleague who knew what she was up to, but they both scored worse than the others. Nurse B put her colleague away with her prevarication and excuses for her.' He paused and looked at his audience expectantly.

'Who have you run this past, DCI Harrison?' asked the Detective Chief Superintendent (Operations) tersely; he was furious he had not been consulted and felt he had been made to look foolish in front of the DCC.

'No one, sir, it was just an experiment to test a theory I had.' Harrison could see where this was going.

'Unauthorised, unsupervised and unscientific,' snapped the DCS. 'Where's the research behind it?'

'You've just seen the research, sir. You heard the answers and saw the body language. I'd like to conduct the same process on some other inquiries we've got going on.'

'Forget it,' said the DCC, getting to his feet and dropping his score sheet on to his chair. 'You've overstepped the mark, Mr Harrison, with this mumbo-jumbo, quasi-psychological analysis. Forget it, won't work,' and he strode out of the room, followed by the DCS who glared at Harrison. Some of the other senior detectives present, however, took a more enlightened view of what they had seen, and resolved to give the theory a run in their own divisions, albeit without any official sanction. It was an example of Harrison's ability to read people and make rational judgements about what they said and did, but it had no future in a police service managed by men with closed minds and huge egos.

# Chapter Twenty

Jubilee night in Handstead differed from every other town in the country in that the fires had been alight for days beforehand, as usual. While most towns set out to celebrate the Jubilee with one vast bonfire as part of a chain across the entire country, abandoned stolen cars had been alight in Handstead for most of the week, well ahead of the main event planned for Grosvenor Park. There, the local Round Table had painstakingly built a huge bonfire from wooden pallets collected from local businesses and thwarted three attempts by the local yobs to set it alight early. A guard of members had been placed around the bonfire twenty-four hours a day in the week leading up to the night itself. The ceremonial lighting was planned for ten o'clock when it was anticipated that a few locals would trudge through the dog shit to the bonfire site, watch the huge fire and then depart for one of the dozens of licensed or unlicensed street parties. It promised to be a long night for the local police who planned to be out on the streets in force, including all of D Group who had had a rest day cancelled to take part in the expected mayhem.

Nearly thirty officers were crammed into the muster room at Handstead nick for the eight o'clock muster, which was to be taken by Sergeant Andy Collins, the senior sergeant on duty. Inspector Jeff Greaves was the designated night duty inspector but Collins had hidden him away in front of the television in the officers' mess – he had intercepted him arriving for work dressed to play tennis. Collins had taken the precaution of locking him in in case the crazy bastard tried to come out on the ground to join in the celebrations.

There was a tangible air of expectancy, the tension was almost a living entity you could touch, the raised voices and laughter disguising the anxiety all the cops present felt deep in their guts.

'Heads up, ladies and gentlemen,' shouted Collins above the din. 'Let's make this brief and get out there. Right, it's here, Jubilee night, and you people are the difference between keeping a lid on things and complete bedlam. Last count, we've got sixteen licensed street parties, but unfortunately we've heard about another twelve unlicensed events. If we know about twelve, you can stake your life on plenty more that we don't know about. Bottom line is, we could be very, very busy. We won't be closing for any breaks back here, take your refreshments out on the ground. All prisoners are to be brought back here until we're full and then we'll be going to Alpha Tango. We've got two sergeants in the cells tonight to process bodies quickly, then you get out again and write up your notes in your vehicles. People, keep your wits about you because this is just another opportunity for the scumbags to put one over on you. This could get very nasty so don't switch off. All D Group officers, you'll be crewing the night duty vehicles, all A and C Group officers, you'll be crewing the three mobile public order vehicles. Runners and riders are on the board behind me so check before you leave which one you're on. Traffic have supplied drivers for the night so all you've got to do is police the town. I'll be out and about in Bravo Two all night so just give me a shout if you need anything. Anyone got any questions?'

There were none and the officers began to crowd round the board at the back of the room to find their designated vans and the D Group team wandered up to the front office to collect the keys for the beat vehicles.

The late turn crews were already in and reported a surprisingly quiet day. Then they disappeared upstairs to the bar before they worked through until 2 a.m.

'Quiet?' said H quizzically to Jim. 'What's going on?'

'Saving it up for us, mate,' replied Jim as they waited

in the queue to be issued with their personal radios and car keys by the Blister.

'Lull before the storm,' agreed Psycho, standing behind the Brothers. 'Going to go tits up later, I can feel it in my water.' He had a huge grin on his face, clearly relishing the prospect.

Fifteen minutes later, Yankee One eased out into the early-evening traffic on Bolton Road East, which was heavier than usual. It was a beautiful, warm summer night – perfect fighting weather, the cops called it. None of them saw the good side of a dry, balmy night shift.

'Plenty about,' remarked H from the operator's seat after he had booked them on with the main Force control room. 'Fancy a punt round to see what's what?'

'Yeah, good idea. We'll have a look at the rats' nest first, shall we?' replied Jim, doing a right into Liverpool Road and heading for the Park Royal estate.

The reception they got there was quite unlike anything they had encountered before. Instead of the normal loud abuse and occasional missile-throwing from large groups of bored locals, their slow drive past instead generated wolf whistles and two girls flashed their tits at them outside the Park Royal pub. Mostly they were ignored by the ever increasing number of people on foot, all heading in the same direction.

'What the fuck is going on?' said H quietly, staring out of his window as the young girls in the group of youths they were passing waved and shouted greetings to them.

'Only one way to find out,' said Jim firmly, stopping Yankee One alongside the group. 'All right, girls, having a good night?' he called, leaning across H.

The group crowded around H's window, noisy but good-natured, even the males.

'Come on, boys, we're off to a party. Give us a lift,' said the girl closest to the window, resting her huge breasts on the window edge.

'No room for all of you,' laughed Jim. 'Besides, the back seat's covered in vomit from a drunk they nicked earlier,' he lied.

'We don't mind,' she said, probably quite truthfully. 'Come on, give us a lift and you can have a feel of my tits.' Her friends were roaring with laughter, and encouraged by them she began to wobble her breasts in H's face.

'Come on, Jim, time we weren't here,' he managed to shout from deep within her cleavage which reeked of cheap perfume and drink – though he had to admit they were a particularly firm set of bangers.

Jim was still enjoying himself. 'Where you all off to?'

'Street party in Finch Rise,' shouted one of the boys in the group. 'You coming?'

'Love to, pal, but we're working right now. Maybe catch up with you later.'

'You make sure you do,' said the girl, releasing H's head from her breasts. 'Always fancied shagging a copper. Will you wear your hat for me?' He surfaced red-faced and panting like a long-distance runner.

Her equally drunk friends pulled her away and Jim eased Yankee One away from the kerb. They continued their slow progress through the crowds of drunken pedestrians, all of whom seemed pleased to see them.

'This is crazy,' said H again. 'Have they put something in the tap water? No one's throwing things at us or giving us any verbal. What the fuck is going on?'

'Who cares, H, enjoy it while it lasts. Just pray they stay in this mood because if it changes, we are in deep, deep shit,' said Jim, braking hard to avoid two young men pushing two girls along in the middle of the road in a shopping trolley.

'Don't get many of those to the pound,' he called out to the two lads. 'Buy one get one free, was it?'

His remark was greeted with laughter and the offers of a good drink.

'You're right, this is crazy,' he remarked to H.

Something had happened to the town, almost overnight. Maybe it was a one-night wonder, but for a brief period Handstead was like most towns across the country on Jubilee night. Virtually without exception, people went out to enjoy themselves and have a good time, but not at others' expense. Over the next six hours, there was no crime of any description reported or found by police. Nothing. There were no pub fights, or domestic disputes, or stabbings or street robberies; no criminal damage, no public order offences, just lots and lots of amicable drunkenness.

So quiet was it that by 11 p.m., Greasy's burger van was doing a roaring trade, exclusively with bewildered cops. Fortunately for them, there was no sign of the infamous Claws who had recently been sectioned again by his desperate parents, but Greasy himself was starting to seriously miss him. The bored cops were eating him out of house and home and taking full advantage of the freebie arrangement, which of course they would never have done with Claws involved in the catering arrangements.

'Cheers, Greasy,' said Sergeant Collins with his mouth full as he ploughed into his third cheeseburger with onions and ketchup oozing from the sides. 'Keep them coming. Looks like it's going to be a long, quiet night.'

'Fucking great,' muttered Greasy to himself as he opened another large box of burgers on the grimy floor of his van. He hadn't taken a penny all night and had nearly exhausted the supplies he had brought out with him two hours earlier. Worse, coppers he didn't recognise, probably from surrounding divisions, were turning up to join in the feeding of the five thousand.

Collins stood chatting in a small group of D Group officers who were discussing the extraordinary state of affairs currently enveloping the town.

'Listen, guys, this is a one-off, but under the circumstances I'm sure no one's going to mind if you put in the odd appearance at a street party. Just keep an ear on your radios and make sure any calls get answered, OK?'

There was a chorus of approval from his troops who had all been considering such a move but his semi-official sanction was what they needed. Such was their respect for Collins that none of them would have considered going to a street party in case they incurred his disapproval had he found them. They were devoted to him; they knew he fought their corner and shouldered much of the crap that flowed downstairs from senior officers who knew little of the environment they policed. They worked in the U bend of life, and Collins was the sturdy plug in the sink of dirty water above them.

'Cheers, Sarge, God bless you,' shouted Psycho as he hurried back to his beat vehicle with Malcy. They'd spotted a belter of a party on the Crabtree Avenue estate, with more than its fair share of drunken young girls on the site, and despite his stirrings of love for Anne Butler, Psycho was determined to see what might be on offer.

Pizza and JJ also returned to their vehicle.

'What d'you fancy doing, JJ? Want to try some street parties?'

'Wouldn't mind. You OK with it?'

'Yeah, come on. Won't hurt to have a quick look but you need a prisoner tonight, OK?'

'OK, great,' said JJ cheerfully. 'Where we going then?'

'I don't know, we'll find one. Plenty to choose from,' said Pizza, driving their vehicle off the hotel forecourt and back down the dual carriageway, past the pulsating Stonehouse pub which looked as if it was about to burst at the seams.

'Wouldn't be surprised if we're back there later,' he remarked quietly and JJ nodded his head and smiled contentedly.

An hour later, every night duty unit in Handstead, with the sole exception of the Brothers in Yankee One, was indulging itself in the orgy of bonhomie and peace to all men. It was not, however, something that interested the Brothers, beyond passing the time of day with anyone prepared to be civil to them. Besides, they reasoned that a night like this was a great night to be out committing crime – like a cold, snowy night in the winter when Handstead villains bargained on the Old Bill being tucked away in their warm nick. The Brothers were determined that Andy Collins and D Group didn't get caught with their trousers down.

At street parties all over town, D Group were welcomed with open arms, plied with drink and mobbed by women who suddenly all wanted to wear a policeman's hat. As they happily obliged, some of them began to question the ethos by which they policed Horse's Arse. The equation had always been so simple. Handstead locals were all scumbags, ergo they were policed accordingly, with little sympathy or compassion. But there it was – the stark contradiction to that commonly held view. They weren't all scumbags by any stretch of the imagination. The siege mentality that pervaded all policing in Handstead suddenly seemed totally inappropriate and even Psycho found himself questioning everything he had grown to believe in as he poured another bottle of beer down his neck and cuddled the attractive brunette by his side. Yes, there were some truly horrible people operating in the town, particularly on the Park Royal estate, but surely they were a small minority compared to what he could see here. These people were no different to him and Malcy, he mused, making the best of what life had dealt them, inherently decent and mostly law-abiding. Wherever they currently were, all the members of D Group were quietly reassessing Horse's Arse, its inhabitants and their own prejudices. The bullet-proof bubble they operated from within during their working days was dissolving before their eyes as the monsters of Handstead revealed themselves to walk on two legs just like the cops. For many of the cops, it was light on the road to Damascus stuff.

But the Brothers abstained from the celebrations and went looking for a prisoner, their blinkered intolerance and bigotry towards the criminal classes undiminished. They didn't have to wait long to restore the status quo as they understood it. Twenty minutes later as they cruised the Park Royal estate, willing something awful to happen and put things back the way they should be, they spotted a lone drunk urinating against a bus shelter, one arm supporting him as he swayed unsteadily. Draped around his shoulders was an enormous Union Jack flag which, judging from both its size and the ropes hanging from it, had recently been removed from a public building somewhere.

'Thank fuck,' breathed Jim, smiling at H who also looked relieved and stopped Yankee One alongside the youth. The Brothers left the vehicle and approached the drunk who was pissing like a horse into the bus shelter, head down and eyes closed. They stopped a safe distance from him and waited for him to finish, in case he turned suddenly and hosed them down.

'Where'd you get the flag, son?' asked Jim as the youth pushed himself away from the shelter and tried to zip himself up. He turned to look at the speaker with eyes that barely opened.

'Huh?' he eventually slurred, swaying like a tree in a gale.

'The flag, mate, where'd you get it?' repeated Jim, stepping closer now that the man's cock was safely back in his jeans.

'Fuck off,' mumbled the drunk, turning to walk away.

'Thank you, Lord,' called Jim, walking after him and grabbing him by the shoulder. 'Restores my faith in humankind, does this. Where'd you get the fucking flag?' he bellowed at the drunk who now appeared to be asleep on his feet.

'Go fuck yourself,' he eventually said slowly.

Jim and H smiled at each other – order and sanity had been restored. It had only been a temporary hiccup, caused by God only knew what, but things were once again as they understood they should be.

'You're nicked, son,' said Jim, grabbing one of his wrists and quickly twisting his arm across the small of his back. 'Theft and treason.'

'Treason?' asked H as he helped Jim snap his handcuffs on to the now motionless drunk.

'Wearing the national flag like that, H, that's treason in my book,' answered Jim as they marched the youth back to Yankee One and threw him face down on to the back seat.

Normally, they would have called up the Dirty Van,

driven tonight by Piggy, to collect a drunk prisoner, but they were aware that the rest of the group had gone on the piss and they had no wish to interrupt any of them. Not even Piggy. Thirty seconds later, they bitterly regretted the decision as the drunk momentarily recovered consciousness to vomit all over the rear seat and into the footwells. He seemed to spew for hours, hacking and honking as his entire evening's drinking session gushed into the interior of Yankee One. Forced to drive back to Handstead with every window open and hanging out of the vehicle gulping in fresh air, the Brothers, although furious, saw it simply as confirmation that the residents of Handstead were the scum of the earth.

Psycho had unglued the very willing and available young brunette from his lap and gone in search of Malcy whom he had last seen over an hour ago. Even in his nine parts pissed state he knew they should never have got themselves separated. With a sigh of relief he quickly found him helping at the barbecue outside the huge marquee.

'Come on, Malcy, we've been here fucking hours,' he slurred into his ear. 'I'm off my fucking face, need a coffee.'

'Give me the keys, Psycho,' said Malcy, peeling his pinny off and giving the young blonde it belonged to a big kiss. 'I'll drive.'

'Will you fuck drive,' replied Psycho belligerently. 'No way I'm letting some sweaty drive me about. I'm only a little bit off my face anyway.'

'Psycho, you're fucking hammered. Give me the keys,' pleaded Malcy, holding out his hand.

'Bollocks, where's the car anyway?'

'Fucking hell,' muttered Malcy shaking his head and leading the leaden-footed Psycho away from the street party like a gassed First World War soldier, and back to Finch Rise where they had left their beat vehicle. Psycho was stopping to shake hands and exchange kisses en route and the short walk took twice as long as it should have, especially as the monster in uniform was as drunk as a skunk. For him to get himself into such a state was a rare but not unknown event. He had the capacity of a petrol tanker, but every now and then he reached his limit which was roughly three times what a normal adult male could consume. He was there again, only three weeks after he had careered into the rear yard in his Ford Cortina at six fifteen one evening, the vehicle on four flat tyres, wrecked when he had kerbed it at speed, and himself virtually incoherent.

'Sorry I'm late, overslept,' he had shouted as he barged into the nick. A sympathetic sergeant had pulled him into an office to point out that he was in fact twelve hours early for his early turn shift the following morning and then made arrangements for him to get his head down in the single men's section house.

Psycho was drinking heavily all the time now as he struggled to come to terms with the feelings he was harbouring for Anne Butler, still unsure how he could win her affections. All his advice was coming from a bottle and it was starting to show.

'Give me the fucking keys,' insisted Malcy again as Psycho stumbled against the car and began to try and get the key into the lock. After several attempts he opened up and slumped behind the steering wheel, breathing heavily, eyes closed.

'You're wasted, you cunt,' hissed Malcy, getting in and slamming the door.

'Am I fuck, I'm fine,' slurred Psycho, trying to get the key into the vehicle's ignition.

Eventually he succeeded and fired up the beat vehicle, crunched it into first gear and lurched away from the kerb.

'Lights,' screamed Malcy, swiftly buckling his seatbelt and then gripping the sides of his seat until his knuckles showed white.

'Don't need lights,' scoffed Psycho who regularly drove home after late turn like this. 'They can't see me if I don't have any lights on' – the 'they' being the hated traffic police who spent an inordinate amount of their time trying to bag pissed Handstead cops.

'Lights,' screamed Malcy again as the unlit vehicle surged forward and on to a lit traffic island. The tyres on the offside of the vehicle hit the raised island hard and burst on impact as the wheels buckled; the lit bollard disappeared over the roof of the car.

Psycho braked with a skid and looked puzzled.

'What was that?' he asked Malcy.

'You fucking twat,' screamed Malcy. 'You've hit that fucking island and wrecked the motor. You fucking twat,' he repeated furiously. 'You fucking dangerous, mad, selfish twat. Get out of the car – now.'

Their car had rolled to a standstill by the kerb and Malcy got out and ran back to the wrecked traffic island. The bollard itself lay a few yards further back in the road. He retrieved it and brought it back to the beat vehicle, throwing it on to the back seat.

'You arsehole, you're going to kill someone one of these days,' he said bitterly as he looked at the two wrecked wheels and the scratches across the bonnet and roof of the car. The box and blue light had been bashed sideways by the bollard and he was able to reposition it, but there was fuck all he could do about the rest of the damage. 'Look at the fucking state of the motor,' he shouted, then glanced around. Luckily, despite the large number of people in the area, nobody appeared to have noticed that a police car being driven without lights had destroyed a traffic bollard.

He looked into the vehicle at Psycho.

'I said, you've wrecked the fucking car,' he hissed. 'What the fuck are we going to do now?'

But Psycho was fast asleep, snoring loudly as he dreamt of the ice maiden, Anne Butler, who told the dirtiest jokes he had ever heard a woman tell and who had won his black heart.

'Oh great,' exclaimed Malcy, looking desperately around him at the passers-by who still appeared not to have noticed the damaged police car – it was almost as though they were invisible to them. He considered his options which were few and not particularly good. Finally, he picked up the main set radio and got talk-through with the Brothers in Yankee One.

'Can you rendezvous with me in Finch Rise, Hotel Alpha? Need your advise on something.'

'Yes, yes, five minutes,' replied H. He looked at Jim and in unison they said, 'Psycho.'

They had spent the last half hour hosing out the rear of the vehicle and scrubbing at the seat and carpets with industrial-strength disinfectant normally used to clean the drunk cells. Despite their efforts, the appalling smell still lingered over the sweet, cloying perfume of the disinfectant, and all the windows were staying down for the rest of the night.

Yankee One pulled up quietly behind Two Two and the Brothers wandered over to inspect the damage to the vehicle. They looked at the wrecked traffic island and then at the drooling Psycho behind the wheel of the car.

'What happened?' asked Jim quietly.

'Drunken bastard just ploughed through the island, no fucking lights on, absolutely off his face,' said Malcy, looking more and more worried.

'What the hell was he doing driving in that state, Malcy? Why didn't you get the keys off him?'

'Get the keys off him, are you fucking joking?' said Malcy desperately, spreading his arms wide. 'I suppose I could have had a huge battle with him but what would the outcome of that have been? Jesus, I asked him to hand them over but he wasn't having any of it. Look at the motor, what the fuck are we going to do? He's going to get nicked if we can't get this sorted out.'

Jim squatted down by the wrecked front wheel and shook his head ruefully.

'Job for Paddy, I reckon, H,' he announced, looking up at his partner who was running a finger along the scratched bonnet and roof.

'Yeah, reckon you're right. You hang on here, I'll go and get him,' replied H. 'Give us the keys.'

Jim tossed the keys to Yankee One over to H and he departed, leaving Jim and Malcy prodding the totally unconscious Psycho.

'Who's Paddy?' asked Malcy. 'How's he going to help?'

'We use him a lot,' said Jim. 'Keeps us all out of the shit from time to time. Don't worry, Malcy, if anyone can, Paddy can.'

The saviour Paddy was a sixty-year-old car mechanic, originally from the West Coast of Ireland but long settled in Handstead with his large family. He owned a dilapidated car workshop in a small garage complex just off the motorway. Over the years he had built up a thriving business with the local cops, repairing and maintaining their vehicles, not just their personal ones but most importantly their job vehicles, whose small dents and scratches would otherwise lead to onerous report-writing and possibly suspension from driving duties. He was used to being pulled out of his bed at ungodly hours of the night and working through the small hours knocking out dents and filling holes. He had progressed from small body jobs to replacing whole body panels, though liveried panel jobs were still beyond him. Officers at Handstead were still exploring ways to lay hands on the Force livery to equip Paddy for every conceivable job. He had saved countless officers from difficult questions but the practice was known about at the Headquarters garage. It wasn't unique to Handstead; every nick around the county had a similar arrangement with a quiet, back-street garage somewhere to get them out of the shit. Headquarters garage staff regularly came across repair work and replacements that were months, sometimes years old, that had not been done by them and of which of course there was absolutely no record. Numerous inquiries had been carried out all over the county, but no one had ever been captured. It was a practice that would endure as long as coppers drove cars in their job.

H was back with Paddy in about fifteen minutes. The old man shuffled over to the police vehicle wearing a pale blue pair of pyjama bottoms and a tatty brown sweater. He had clearly been roused from a deep sleep; his snowy white hair was sticking up and his bristly face was lined and crumpled. Rubbing his eyes, he wandered over to where Jim and Malcy were standing by the open driver's door.

'Morning, boys,' he said croakily. 'Problems with a couple of wheels, is that right? Oh Jesus, not this big fucker again,' he exclaimed, sighting Psycho for the first time.

'A regular of yours?' asked Jim.

'Virtually rebuilt that heap of a Cortina of his,' confirmed Paddy, kneeling painfully alongside the wheels to get a closer look, his knees popping and cracking like pistol shots. 'The wheels have had it and the tyres are torn to pieces,' he announced. 'Brought a couple with me. Give me a hand, will you?'

The three officers hauled Psycho out of the driver's seat of Two Two and manhandled his huge dead weight on to the back seat where he continued to snore peacefully. Paddy quickly raised the offside of the car on the hydraulic jack he had also brought along and they soon had the damaged wheels off. H and Jim retrieved the replacements from the boot of Yankee One and rolled them alongside Two Two.

'Jesus, Paddy, they're like racing slicks, not a bit of tread on them,' exclaimed Jim.

'It's all I had, boys. Better than nothing I reckon,' gasped the old man as he positioned the spokes on the front wheel. 'It'll get the car back to the nick, if nothing else.'

'Did you bring any touch-up paint?' asked Jim.

'I've got it,' said H, reaching into his pocket for what looked like a large pot of nail varnish and shaking it vigorously, the ball bearing inside clicking loudly as it mixed the paint. 'Should be a good match.' He began to apply the paint along the gouges in the bonnet and roof of Two Two. Five minutes later, as Paddy banged on the hubcaps, the vehicle looked as good as new – certainly under the sodium street lights.

'Right, job done. Thanks, Paddy,' said H. 'We'll get you home. Malcy, get Psycho back to the nick and park up at the back of the garages, give him a couple of hours to sober up. We'll get him up just before knocking-off time. He'll be round to settle up with you tomorrow, Paddy, I guarantee you.'

'I won't hold my breath,' replied the old man mournfully as they rolled the buckled wheels back to Yankee One and chucked them in the boot. 'He still owes me for all the work on his own car.'

'You'll be paid, Paddy, trust me,' said Jim firmly, slamming the boot shut. 'Come on, we'll drop these wheels at your lock-up and get you home. Malcy, we'll catch up with you later, OK?'

'Cheers, boys, thanks for everything,' called Malcy from the driver's seat of Two Two. 'Thanks, Paddy, see you again no doubt.'

'No doubt,' agreed Paddy, yawning loudly and getting into the back of Yankee One which still stank of the drunk. 'Jesus, what happened in here?' he asked, settling on to the waterproof sheet the Brothers had spread over the still damp seat.

'One of Handstead's finest, I'm afraid,' replied Jim, looking at Paddy in the rear-view mirror. 'Thanks again, mate. Happy Jubilee night.'

'You can poke your fucking Jubilee,' said Paddy, 'until such time as the Six Counties are restored to us, you thieving bastards.'

# Chapter Twenty-One

As Jubilee night wore on and the fireworks began to streak into the clear night sky above Handstead, five miles away in the silent fields around Dark Water Farm in Angotts Mead, Phil Eldrett settled down alongside an ancient oak for the long haul. He deliberately avoided turning to watch the pyrotechnics and spoil his night vision and pulled his ski mask on to concentrate his sight on what was in front of him just over two hundred yards away.

Dark Water Farm consisted of a single two-storey farmhouse, probably once whitewashed but now covered in green mould and brown stains from where the blocked gutters poured filthy rainwater down the side of the building. The metal casement windows were rotten and covered in decades of grime and the track to the farm from the isolated road was rutted and potholed with deep puddles along its length. The area to the front of the house was in a similar state of disrepair, with the undergrowth threatening to envelop the farm. To the side of the house stood an ancient cowshed, long devoid of any cattle, with a corrugated roof that in large parts was missing and warped wooden doors that could not be shut properly. The barn was totally empty of any farm equipment and stank of damp and years of neglect, its sole use being to house Mitcheson's ancient Range Rover.

The entire farm exuded decay; it was the perfect place to lose yourself, which was why Guy Mitcheson loved it. He did nothing to it and lived in squalid drug-induced chaos inside, gradually abandoning each room as it became too unpleasant, even for him, to live in. One room, however, had received considerable attention from him recently. What had formerly been a kitchen and dining room looking out over a lawn down to an orchard and open fields beyond that had been converted into a laboratory. It was curtainless, like every other room in the house, but the windows were shrouded by thick ivy that had spread up the wall like a giant dark green hand, threatening to pull the entire structure down into the earth. The first cash injection into the enterprise by Sercan Ozdemir had been spent with a bent lab technician at Mitcheson's old university, who knocked out medical equipment and supplies, and

Mitcheson had completed his construction of the laboratory in a little under a week.

The only piece of furniture in the room, an ancient old six-seater table, had been pushed against the wall next to the similarly old stone sink, and on the table now stood his pride and joy, the source of his future wealth and prosperity. A dull copper-bottomed kettle pan on low feet, encrusted with calcium build-up, stood on the far left. It was about six inches deep and ten inches in diameter, with five concentric copper rings on top, and sitting above the rings was a round-bottomed Pyrex flask secured in the cork jaws of a crocodile grip attached to a metal laboratory stand. The flask, angled slightly off the vertical, had a clear glass tube running off it from the Pyrex adapter in the top. The tube was about two and a half feet long, supported along its length by crocodile grips from lab stands, and its interior was made up of another coiled glass tube. At the far end of the tube was a spigot from which a rubber tube ran to one of the rusty taps above the sink, to provide the cooling source. The glass tube ran downwards to a further laboratory stand where it connected loosely into the neck of a two-pint conical flask, packed with cotton wool to allow for any pressure build-up.

The kettle pan was secondhand but all the glassware was brand new – Mitcheson was determined to produce as pure a product as was possible. Littered around the table were an assortment of Pyrex flasks and beakers, a white pestle and mortar, and underneath were five two-gallon bottles of distilled water, which he had made on his own equipment to ensure purity. He was ready to go; all he needed was the precursor which Ozdemir had assured him was on the way.

As Mitcheson admired his handiwork and ran his fingers lovingly over its cold glass body in the dull light of the single bulb hanging from the ceiling rose, Phil Eldrett settled himself against the oak and ignored Jubilee night over in Handstead, which was getting louder by the moment. In the quiet hours before something happened, he often found himself drifting back to his former life, but more and more lately he found himself dwelling on the impact his job had on his family. He was no longer risking his life as he had in the bandit country of South Armagh but he was still spending extended periods away from his wife and children, with little or no contact while he was away. The initial euphoria his wife had felt when he had left the army and joined the police gradually evaporated as his surveillance skills had begun to be utilised more and more. All her plans for a settled family life, albeit one built around shift work, faded as he spent less and less time in uniform and disappeared for days at a stretch in his old army camouflage kit.

He had tried to talk to her about what he was doing

– none of it was as sensitive as what he had undertaken in the forces – but the light had gone out for her and as a couple they had begun to drift apart. They remained devoted to their two young sons, but the spark that had bound them together during his long tours of Ulster had gone. While both recognised it, neither could summon the courage to grasp the nettle and do what they both knew had to be done. Their physical relationship, once all-consuming and white-hot, had dwindled with time and he now slept in the spare bedroom, ostensibly so as not to wake her with his late departures and early returns but in reality because she no longer had any desire to be near him. A relationship between her and a man at her work, still not sexual, was developing beyond long discussions about her unhappiness and hopes for the future towards something that she had vowed she would never do – sacrifice her marriage. She harboured no ill will towards her husband and often longed for the time when he would wrap his arms round her and bite her earlobes without saying a word – but those days were gone for ever now and she kept him at arm's length.

Eldrett felt the hurt of her rejection but knew deep down that there would be no return to the way things had been. He had clocked the change in her as her relationship with the work colleague developed and knew that their marriage was beyond repair. The worry and regret chewed away in his stomach every waking hour as he spent long observations thinking about her and what he had lost. He had considered packing his surveillance role in and trying to be just a uniform cop, but she had politely told him there was no need, she had grown used to the way things had become – she was fine. 'Yeah, fine with him waiting in the wings,' Eldrett muttered bitterly to himself as he looked around at the dark countryside. He often talked to himself in the small hours, discussing his predicament, solutions and possible outcomes, what he was going to say to her when he got home, how he would confront her with his suspicions, but he never did; all his resolve and bitterness drained away when he saw the woman he still loved.

He was deep in sombre thought when he spotted headlights coming slowly down the winding lane away to his left. The road was elevated at that point and the vehicle nearly a mile away, giving him time to drop on to his front by the tree and watch as the lights approached. Occasionally the headlights disappeared from view as the bends and dips in the road came into play, but the vehicle was still coming in his direction, very slowly. Clearly the driver didn't know the road and was not comfortable driving in the countryside in the dark. Once, Eldrett saw the vehicle come to a complete standstill at the entrance to a field before it continued forward again at the same snail's pace.

Soon the vehicle came to a slow stop at the entrance to the rutted track leading up to Dark Water Farm. There was no sign to tell visitors they had reached their destination, but the driver was clearly looking for a landmark or signal of some sort. Eldrett saw the driver get out of the car, a big saloon of some sort, and walk to the bottom of the drive and peer up towards the farm. He walked a short distance up the drive and then stopped when he saw the building which was obscured from the road. He jogged back to his idling car. He had slightly passed the entrance, so he reversed and then drove slowly up the ruined drive, the headlights bouncing wildly. The car drew up outside the darkened farmhouse, the headlights went out and Eldrett saw the interior light in the car come on and the driver leaning into the passenger footwell to retrieve something. Then the light went out and the driver got out of the car and stood looking at the house. The only light was the frozen blue moonlight but it was clear enough for Eldrett to see that the man was carrying a light-coloured holdall in his left hand. He still seemed unsure of where he was. Then he strode to the front door and knocked loudly on it twice and stood back.

After a brief pause, Eldrett saw the window above the door glow with a dull light as a door somewhere at the back of the house was opened, followed by a muffled conversation between the waiting driver and someone inside. Then the door opened slightly and the weak light cut across the doorstep and into the driveway like a pale lance. Eldrett could make out a figure in the dimly lit doorway, heard a brief exchange of words, and saw the driver hand the holdall to the figure at the door. The door shut immediately and the driver hurried back to his vehicle, reversed slowly and with difficulty in the cramped, overgrown space at the front of the house, and then bounced slowly back down the driveway, the headlights illuminating the top of the tree under which Eldrett lay prone, holding his breath and praying things were starting to happen early.

He watched as the red rear lights of the saloon disappeared into the darkness and waited as total silence settled over the countryside. There was not a sound; no foxes barking or owls calling, just absolute quiet. The farmhouse appeared to be in total darkness again and Eldrett decided he would go and have a closer look at the as yet unknown rear of the premises, where the sole occupant had clearly come from. He would give it another hour to make sure everything was clear. He glanced at his watch and his masked face was briefly illuminated by the glow from the dial as he accidentally hit the light button. He cursed his carelessness. Mistakes like that could have had fatal consequences in his former life. He was getting sloppy, maybe it was time to call it a day; after all, he had other priorities right now. It was

1 a.m. and he resolved to have a proper mooch about in around an hour.

In the event, his plans changed within half an hour. He was again deep in his glum thoughts when headlights appeared from the same direction as before. These were moving more quickly and Eldrett decided that he needed to be closer if this was another caller to the isolated farm. Leaving his cover, he ran quickly along the hedge line, across the road and up the rutted driveway, looking constantly for a place to drop. Quietly he crossed to the front of the house and to his right saw an overgrown ditch directly in front of the door about twenty feet away. He dropped to the ground and rolled under the vegetation hanging above the ditch and into about a foot of water that stank of rotting vegetation. As he did so, the driveway and house were lit up by bouncing headlights.

Crouched down in the ditch, he saw a black Mercedes car pull into the driveway and stop. The headlights were switched off but the engine remained running as the rear passenger door opened and a man got out and approached the peeling front door to the farmhouse. The door was opened before he reached it and the stream of weak light from inside briefly illuminated the visitor before he stepped inside and the door shut. Eldrett began to move, inch by slow inch, through the mud and water to get a sight of the vehicle's registration, never taking his eyes off the driver of the Mercedes who had lit a cigarette and was blowing his smoke out of the fully open window. He could hear music playing inside the car; music that sounded foreign, and he was confident that only movement would give him away. So, like a shadow, he slid along the ditch until he could see the number plate, lit up by a full summer moon. You beauty, he said silently to himself and began to repeat the number constantly until he had a chance to write it into his notebook.

He dropped back down below the rim of the ditch and was reaching into his jacket to get his notebook when he heard the car door open and footsteps crunching on stones and splashing through small puddles, approaching his ditch. He froze, thumping heart in his mouth, and began to breathe through gritted teeth as he tried to stay calm. He was sure that only the whites of his eyes would be visible, so he screwed his eyes tight and concentrated on not looking up. The footsteps advanced slowly to the edge of the ditch and a cigarette bounced off the foliage above him and into the water, hissing as it went out, followed by the sound of a zip being unfastened. A stream of urine splashed against the leaves and began to spray over his head and shoulders as the car driver relieved himself copiously into the undergrowth, sighing in satisfaction as he did so.

Eldrett remained motionless until the flow ebbed to dribs and drabs and a final jet, and he heard the zip go up and the footsteps retreat. As the car door banged shut he began to repeat the car registration number to himself again and slowly raised his eyes above the top of the ditch. As he did so, the door to the house opened once more and the visitor stepped out, talking quietly to the person in the hallway, and then shook hands with them. As he turned away to get back into the Mercedes, he was momentarily perfectly lit in the weak light from inside and Eldrett nodded his head grimly. I'll know you again, arsehole, and your pissbag of a driver. He dropped down out of sight into the filth and piss as the Mercedes was manoeuvred out of the driveway and back down towards the main road.

As the engine sound faded away and silence again enveloped the farmhouse, Eldrett began to plan a full reconnaissance of the property. Clearly, there were no dogs to contend with and there appeared to be only the one occupant – the risks were minimal. Before he did anything else, he quickly noted the registration number and time of the visit, along with descriptions of the driver and passenger of the Mercedes, in his dog-eared notebook by the red light of his small torch. He waited briefly, listening intently and watching the house for movement behind the grubby windows that stared back at him like sightless eyes. Everything was still and quiet.

Satisfied that he was safe, Eldrett slid out of the ditch on his belly like an eel, got to his haunches and, still crouched low, hurried quietly to the barn doors which were moving slightly in the light breeze. He slipped into the huge building and immediately recognised Mitcheson's Range Rover. He checked the time on his watch, which he covered with a hand this time before illuminating it, then he left the barn and made his way to the side of the house. He walked slowly towards the rear, brushing overhanging branches gently aside, until he came to the overgrown rear garden. Light illuminated the far side of the garden. He peered round the corner of the building and saw that the light was coming from a downstairs room at the far end. The window itself appeared to be virtually covered in ivy but the light escaping through it indicated it should be possible to see inside the room. Dropping to his belly, he crawled along the rear of the house over broken glass and rusty tins and years of unraked dead leaves before he reached the lit window. Standing slowly, he eased his head gingerly to the side of a large ivy branch and glanced in.

'Holy shit', he said to himself. He stood back against the wall and looked up at the millions of stars above him set in a purple night sky. Holy shit. He had never seen a homemade laboratory before but a degree in chemistry wasn't needed to recognise one.

Mitcheson had been kneeling in front of his

apparatus checking the contents of the holdall as Eldrett had peeped round the edge of the window. He recognised Mitcheson from his visit to Ozdemir's haulage yard and realised he had hit the jackpot this time. It was time to go. What had begun as a job with the potential to run for weeks had been resolved in a matter of hours. It was unique in his lengthy experience but not undeserved.

Quickly getting his exhilaration under control, Eldrett retraced his steps and made his way swiftly and silently back to the quiet country road. There he sat on the grass verge and updated his notebook by the light of his torch before beginning the mile walk to the isolated phone box he had identified earlier as his sole means of communication with DCI Harrison.

# Chapter Twenty-Two

Twenty-four hours later, D Group were back on duty, another leave day cancelled and glowering at DCI Harrison who stood at the front of the packed muster room. They had worked an 8 p.m.–8 a.m. night duty for Jubilee night and before they had gone home they had been told they were required in again for a 2 a.m. briefing the following morning. Their body clocks were all over the place and they had been told nothing about the job behind the briefing at such an ungodly hour. That said, the presence of two units of the Patrol Group and a DI, DS and five DCs from the Drugs Squad gave them at least an indication that it wasn't going to be a load of bollocks. DCI Harrison positioned himself in front of the large whiteboard on legs which had a cloth draped over it and called the noisy throng to order.

'For those of you who don't know me, I'm DCI Harrison. That ugly bastard at the back in the brown leather jacket is DI Rick Moulder from the Drugs Squad. He's my deputy on this operation. OK, this is where we're at, guys, so listen up. Yesterday morning a surveillance officer positively identified a property out at Angotts Mead as an LSD laboratory.'

There was an audible murmur from the assembled cops and Harrison allowed the murmuring to drift until there was silence again.

'We don't think it's up and running yet and we propose to shut it down now before it produces anything. The laboratory is in a room at the back of the property, on the ground floor. There appears to be little or no security on the premises, no dogs and, as far as we can tell, only our illicit chemist. The place has been under surveillance all day and night and I heard from our guy ten minutes ago that the chemist is in and on his own. We're going through the front door and the rear windows at 3 a.m. Local uniform and CID officers will go through the front. Patrol Group, I want you through the back windows to secure the lab and the chemist who we think probably kips somewhere downstairs. I've got the warrant issued under the Misuse of Drugs Act,' he said, holding it up in the air.

'The chemist's name is Guy Mitcheson,' he continued. 'He was nicked two weeks ago, driving under the influence of drugs, by Constables Walsh and Stewart. We don't have a photo of him, but Stewart and Walsh can ID him, right, boys?'

The Brothers, sitting two rows back, were beaming with pride and nodded their heads.

'Quality bit of routine police work,' continued Harrison, massaging their egos even more, 'and coupled with other information that came our way, we've found the lab. Our surveillance lad has actually seen the equipment set up and we believe precursor chemicals were delivered to the premises last night. This is where we're going shortly.' He threw back the cover on the whiteboard, revealing a large-scale Ordnance Survey map and a black and white surveillance photograph of the farmhouse taken that afternoon by a Drugs Squad surveillance team.

'Dark Water Farm, Angotts Mead,' said Harrison. 'The only approach to it is along this road, and this unmade track from the road. One way in, and one way out. The house can't be seen from the road and we don't believe the road can be seen from the house. We'll park our vehicles way back here, with roadblocks put in here and here to protect our backs,' he said, pointing to positions on the map. 'Access to the rear is easy down the side past this large barn. The room we're really interested in has a light on currently so you Patrol Group boys won't have any problems finding it. If the light's not on, it's the ground-floor room furthest to your left as you approach the rear from the barn. Got that?'

The Patrol Group officers nodded vigorously and smiled expectantly at each other.

'Bang on three a.m. I'm going to give a single blast on my superb original silver-plated police-issue whistle,' he said, holding it up for them all to see. 'No fucking about or any pleases or thank yous, put the doors and windows in, secure the place, secure the chemist, put a cordon round the building then Rick and his team will come in to identify what we've got and start bagging it up. Any questions?'

There were a few logistical queries about transport from some of the supervisors present, but other than that they were ready to go. There was an explosion of noise from the cops as the tension generated by Harrison's concise words disappeared like a balloon bursting.

'Fucking hell, H,' said Jim to H as they walked out to the yard to jump on board their allocated carrier. 'All this from that little bit of paper? What a result.'

H smiled at his mate. 'The harder you work, Jim, the luckier you get,' he said, quoting the mantra the pair swore by.

By 2.50 a.m. they were all in place, the narrow country road blocked for a hundred yards with both marked and unmarked police vehicles. Either end of the road were two traffic units who were sulking because they'd not been allowed to put their blue lights on and generally light the countryside up as they put in the roadblocks. The Patrol Group, all wearing their NATO helmets and fireproof overalls, had crept to the rear of the premises and twelve of them now lay prone under the window of the kichen which was still lit, waiting for Harrison's whistle. At the front of the farmhouse, H and Jim had been granted the privilege of putting the front door in and waited eagerly for the go.

'You've earned it, boys,' whispered Harrison, patting each of them on the shoulder. 'On my call, OK?'

They nodded and took up position near the flimsy front door, ready to demonstrate the practice Jim had brought back with him from his tours of Ulster with the Parachute Regiment and readily embraced by his partner, H. The farmhouse was still, dark and quiet, but the Patrol Group officers had glimpsed someone moving around the lit ground-floor room. They all waited and held their breath.

'We're early, but what the fuck,' hissed Harrison, glancing at his watch by the light of his Zippo lighter. 'In you go, boys,' and he put his whistle to his lips.

In the laboratory, Guy Mitcheson was looking closely at the encrusted copper kettle pan, wondering whether he should clean it properly before starting the production process, when he heard the loud whistle and for reasons he could never really explain, he looked the other way. The whistle definitely came from the front of the farmhouse yet something made him look towards the windows of the kitchen. The ivy tendrils were moving in the light breeze, but it wasn't that; he was aware of large dark shapes moving in slow motion towards the windows, and then they exploded.

He screamed in terror as he was showered with glass and pieces of the window frames and large chunks of ivy as two Patrol Group officers hurled their burly frames straight through the ancient windows. As they landed in a cloud of debris, the other officers began to vault through the gaping holes, shouting at the tops of their voices, totally disorientating Mitcheson who pissed himself with fright. As the windows went in, he was vaguely aware of a huge crack from the front of the building as H, supported by Jim holding him, kicked the front door off its hinges on to the floor. Within a matter of seconds, Mitcheson had been bundled to the floor by two of the back-up Patrol Group officers, his face forced into some of the broken glass on the filthy wooden floorboards, and the room was swarming with noisy coppers. From his position on the floor he could hear the whoops of delight as the cops realised the enormity of what they had found, and then a pair of well-polished ankle-length round-toed Chukka boots stopped a couple of inches from his trembling face.

'Guy Mitcheson, I'm arresting you on suspicion of conspiracy to manufacture an illegal Class A drug, namely LSD,' said DCI Dan Harrison cheerfully. 'You don't have to say anything, but I'm sure you'll appreciate that in your current situation it's going to be in your best interests to tell me all about it.'

Mitcheson closed his eyes and began to sob as the Patrol Group officers ratcheted a pair of cuffs tightly on to his wrists behind his back and hauled him to his feet to face his nemesis.

'You silly twat,' said Harrison softly, his face totally emotionless. He gently patted Mitcheson's cheek. 'You've been led right up the garden path, son. All this is going to be down to just you; you're looking at twenty years, my old pal. How old are you? Thirty-two is it? Fuck me, you'll be an incontinent, middle-aged old man by the time you see the outside of a cell. What say we go back to the station for a long chat? I reckon you've got lots to tell me.'

Mitcheson nodded meekly, totally broken and bewildered by what had happened, but he remained silent. Not because he wanted to but because he was incapable of speech. Urine ran down his legs on to his shoes and Harrison glanced down at the pool forming at his feet and the stain at his groin. He smiled benevolently.

'You haven't got a fucking clue, have you? Get him back to the nick, boys, get him a change of clothing and I'll have a chat with him later.'

Mitcheson was lifted off the ground by his upper arms by the two Patrol Group officers and taken out of the shattered front door to be deposited unceremoniously in the back of one of the Patrol Group vans parked in the blocked road. Once he was gone, DI Rick Moulder and his team joined Harrison.

'Fuck me, Dan,' whistled Moulder, looking closely at the equipment on the table while one of his boys opened the holdall he had pulled from underneath, 'this would have been the billy bollocks if it ever got going. Jesus, look at it, he's got the lot. What's in the bag, John?'

The DC began to empty the bag on to the floor and soon eight waxed paper bags stood lined up on the table.

'Ergotamine tartrate,' said Moulder, leaning down to examine the printed lettering on one of the bags, 'one of the precursors for LSD production, all the way from the good old US of A. Manufactured in Chicago.' He stepped back and smiled at Harrison.

'Smuggled in, you think?' asked Harrison.

'Very likely. Not readily available here yet. Your other man got the means to bring it in, you reckon?'

'Oh yeah, no doubt. I reckon me and Mr Mitcheson

need a long chat. You and your boys all right getting this lot dismantled and evidenced?'

'Leave it with us. We'll have a good look round as well, make sure there's nothing else stashed away. You get back and sweat the chemist.'

Harrison turned to face the cops milling about in the kitchen and shouted to make himself heard.

'Guys, listen up. We've had a fucking great result here. DI Moulder and his team are going to dismantle what we've found and get it back to the nick. I'm going to need one unit of the Patrol Group to help them search this shithole but the rest of you can get yourselves back to the nick. We'll have a wash-up there and you can get started on your statements. No one goes home until they've made a statement that I've seen, OK?'

There was a chorus of understanding and the room began to clear. The sergeant running the Patrol Group unit designated to remain behind to help with the searches was taken to one side by DI Moulder and soon a quiet, businesslike atmosphere had replaced the madness. Satisfied that his scene was secure and under control, Dan Harrison returned to Handstead, exhausted but buzzing with the excitement of it all, quietly thinking through his next move to slaughter Sercan Ozdemir.

No one went home that day. Mitcheson was interviewed relentlessly by Harrison and his best detectives, while the uniforms wrote and rewrote their statements until Harrison was satisfied that he had a watertight job. All the writing was completed by lunchtime, Mitcheson spilt his guts and Harrison had the bar opened to celebrate their extraordinary success. He was sure that he and his team, CID and uniform alike, had busted the biggest potential LSD source seen in the United Kingdom to date. The only downside, of course, came from Headquarters who had been told absolutely fuck all about the job. An irate Chief Superintendent Findlay at Division was on the phone to Harrison shortly after 9 a.m. to find out if there was any truth in the stories he had heard on the car radio on the way into work, and by 9.15 a.m. the Detective Chief Superintendent (Crime) was screaming abuse at him.

'Why the fuck wasn't I kept informed of what you had going on?' he raged from his desk on the tenth floor at Headquarters.

'Didn't have time, boss,' lied Harrison calmly. 'We had to move quickly and what I needed was action, not theory,' he finished crushingly.

'You get an interim report on my desk today, Mr Harrison,' snapped the DCS, 'and it better add up, because if I find out you've done your own thing, I'm going to chop your head off.'

'Of course you will, sir,' said Harrison in the same calm tone. 'The media might find it a little strange, though, don't you think? Us fighting about who knew what about an illicit LSD laboratory?'

'What do you mean, the media?' snapped the DCS.

'TV, radio, the newspapers – they're all over the story, boss. All they've got to say is good things, but you play it your way if you want. Have a day off, why don't you?'

'What do you mean?'

'Don't be a cunt all your life,' said Harrison and hung up. He raised his glass of Bushmills to Rick Moulder who was smiling like the Cheshire Cat.

By four o'clock in the afternoon, the bar was packed. The jump was six deep, the air a filthy fug of cigarette smoke, the noise almost intolerable unless you were one of the pissed mob. Sitting resolutely at the bar was one of the local neighbourhood officers, PC Paul Rice. He had refused to make way for the thirsty hordes and remained where he was, puffing away at his filthy pipe. He was close to retirement, had done little of any consequence in his career and rode a bicycle around his designated beat on the Horsefield estate. He was not a popular officer at the nick, not least because of his views on the new generation of police officers but mostly because of his repulsive, homemade jumpers, one of which he was sporting this afternoon. His jumpers were all made from dog hair, which his similarly scabby wife would spin into yarn after he had groomed their four Alsatians. He was a notorious miser, but his dog-hair jumpers were the single most obnoxious thing about him – that and his pipe, which he filled with homemade tobacco which smelt like dog shit. He remained at his seat at the bar, puffing huge clouds of noxious fumes to the ceiling, berating the younger officers waiting to get a drink for not knowing their arses from a hole in the ground when it came to real police work.

'I'm going to chin that old bastard in a minute,' growled Malcy to Psycho as they necked another pint. 'What the fuck is he like?'

'Don't need to chin him, Malcy,' said Psycho, winking at him, 'this'll do the trick.' He opened the palm of his hand down by his side to reveal two squares of blotter paper he had removed from Mitcheson's laboratory.

'What the fuck's that?' asked Malcy, staring closely.

'Fuck knows, but I found them in the lab. Whatever they are, good chance that one of them in his pipe will keep the old cunt quiet for a while.'

Malcy stared at Psycho who was fast becoming a sort of Dr Crippen character.

'Are you serious?' he asked eventually.

'He's a pain in the arse,' answered Psycho dismissively. 'He's well overdue. Wait till he's gone to the bog and I'll pop one in his filthy pipe.'

As he spoke, Rice got to his feet, dropped his pipe into the ashtray nearest to him and announced, 'You young buggers know fuck all, you don't know your arses from holes in the ground,' and lurched off towards the gents' on the landing.

'I thank you,' said Psycho in the style of Arthur Askey and he wandered over to the abandoned pipe. Using one of the many matches Rice had deposited during the afternoon, he pushed the still smouldering wad of dog shit to one side, squeezed in one of the LSD blotters and then carefully covered it again.

He and Malcy stood watching quietly as Rice returned shortly afterwards, still moaning about young officers today. His pipe had gone out so he picked it up in his filthy nicotine-stained fingers, fired up another match and began to puff away again, clearing a small gap around him as the fug hit the ceiling and began to drift down again.

'This could be fucking priceless,' whispered Psycho as Rice began to circle his head and stare long and hard at the ceiling, blinking wildly.

'You all right, Paul?' bellowed Psycho above the din. 'You had too much?'

'The ceiling's melting,' replied Rice dreamily. 'It's melting.'

'Oh fuck,' said Psycho, getting back into the melee with Malcy.

Thirty seconds later there was a loud cry from the bar and everyone turned to see Rice standing on his bar stool, arms outstretched, his eyes spinning like Catherine wheels.

'Ladies and gentlemen,' he shouted, 'I'm pleased to announce the creation of the Handstead Hang Gliding Club – I love you all.'

Watched in stunned silence, the smelly old geriatric jumped off his stool and then ran through the throng towards the open windows at the far side of the room. Too late, the other drinkers realised where he was going; in a flash Rice had dived through the open window on the third floor of the nick. After a momentary pause there was a mad rush to the windows on that side of the room to see where he'd gone. In fact, he'd ended up on the flat roof just below the second floor, about a ten-foot drop, and was writhing about on the asphalt and gravel with a broken ankle. A rescue attempt was quickly mounted from the second floor, during which Rice's spiked pipe was quietly retrieved by Psycho, dipped into Rice's unfinished pint and hidden away in his trouser pocket.

Revelries were resumed as though nothing had happened.

'Where's the boss?' asked John Benson as he handed another glass of Scotch to Bob Clarke.

'Fucked off earlier, said he had something to do.'

'Where's he gone, did he say? He should be here, this is all down to him.'

'Said he had to see someone in Manchester,' said Clarke shrugging his shoulders. 'Fuck knows, you know what he's like, scheming old bastard. A toast,' he announced loudly, holding his glass aloft, 'to the boss,' and all those not engaged in recovering Rice joined him.

# Chapter Twenty-Three

Shortly after 8 a.m. the following morning, Sercan Ozdemir strode into the reception area of his business premises and stopped dead in his tracks with a puzzled frown on his brow. Neither of the receptionists he expected to see were there and he glanced at his watch to check the time. He walked back out to the car park and clocked only his secretary Carmen's vehicle and his own Mercedes – clearly the lazy bitches were late, he fumed, he'd have to have words. Obviously Carmen had opened the premises on her arrival. Still, it would give him an opportunity to make things up to her in his office since they would be all alone for a while.

He jogged up the carpeted stairs and burst into the reception area where Carmen usually sat with a huge smile.

'Morning . . .' He trailed off. She wasn't there, though her handbag was by the chair and a fresh cup of coffee sat steaming, untouched, by her phone. His office door was shut. He frowned, suspecting that Carmen was spinning his desk in his absence. He tiptoed across the expensive carpet and put his ear to the door. He could hear nothing, so he quietly turned the handle and burst in dramatically. As he took a pace into the room he felt a hand on the back of his shoulder blades propelling him further in and his heart stopped as he registered the scene in front of him.

Swallowing hard, his throat tightening with fear, he gazed at his Uncle Karim Ozdemir sitting behind his desk, picking his fingernails with an ornate letter opener. On the carpeted floor in front of the desk lay Carmen, bound hand and foot, tape across her mouth, her eyes bulging with fear, tears streaming down her red face as she looked imploringly at him. Alongside her was one of his goons, Kazim Diniz, similarly bound and gagged but with a look of total resignation on his face. He glanced up at Sercan where he stood shaking in front of the desk and then looked down into the shag pile. Glancing behind him towards the door, Sercan saw the man who had pushed him into the room, and another similarly unsmiling goon who moved purposefully in front of the door. The message was very clear. Swallowing even harder, Sercan turned to face his uncle who had not yet even acknowledged his entry into the room.

'Uncle Karim,' he croaked uncertainly. 'I wasn't expecting you.'

The old man looked at him for the first time and fixed him with steely blue eyes that flashed with anger. His dark hair was swept back behind his ears, and his hooked Roman nose set on his dark, leathery face gave him the sinister appearance of a hungry vulture. Not for nothing was he the undisputed godfather of the UK branch of the crime family. He oozed threat and danger.

'I know you weren't, Sercan,' he replied quietly. 'I sent the receptionists home, they have no part in this, but these two?' He shrugged as he indicated Carmen and Kazim on the floor.

'Part in what, Uncle?' asked Sercan, wide-eyed with fear.

Uncle Karim, his father-in-law and crime boss, laughed softly and tossed the letter opener on to the desk.

'I think you've got a lot to tell me, haven't you, Sercan? I had a visit from an acquaintance of yours yesterday who filled me in on your extra-curricular activities. Activities that I and the family knew nothing about, Sercan. You have humiliated us all and threatened our business interests.'

'An acquaintance of mine?' stammered Sercan, his left leg starting to shake uncontrollably.

'Knows you very well. Gave me some very interesting information about you. Can you guess what?'

'I don't know what you mean, Uncle. What have I done? I've always been loyal to the family and done the best for us, I don't know what you mean,' he pleaded.

'Don't lie to me, Sercan, or there's little I can do to help you. Mr Harrison gave me chapter and verse on your operations over the last year or so.'

The name Harrison punched Sercan between the eyes and he staggered slightly, the colour draining from his face completely until it resembled parchment, his terrified eyes the size of dinner plates.

'No,' he gasped, wringing his hands together. 'No.'

'Everything, Sercan, absolutely everything. The raid on the gun shop last year, three hooligans shot dead. The team you sent to London to get an informant of his a couple of days ago – three of our own dead. And now an LSD factory. Are you mad, Sercan? Do you realise what you have done?' asked his uncle bitterly.

'Please, Uncle Karim, I didn't mean to compromise the family, I swear it. Please, Uncle,' he begged, tears welling up in his eyes.

'You've exposed the family to the police, Sercan, something that has never been a problem before. Harrison is a dangerous man, prepared to break lots of

418

rules to get to our family, and you opened the door for him. You fool,' he screamed.

'Uncle, I'm sorry,' cried Sercan, all his composure deserting him. 'Please, I'm so sorry.'

'And you've insulted me personally, Sercan,' hissed the menacing old man.

'You, how?'

'This little whore tells me you and her are lovers,' he said, pointing a bony finger at the trembling, sobbing Carmen. 'You cheat on my daughter with this painted slut and spit in my face, Sercan.'

'Uncle, it was nothing, just the once, and I've regretted it ever since. How can I make this all up to you? I'm so sorry, I don't know what I was thinking.'

'You can't, Sercan, it's all over. You're a liability to the family and to your wife and children. They will grieve for you for a while but children are resilient, they will forget you in time, as we all will.'

'Grieve for me?' gasped Sercan, dropping to his knees. 'Uncle, you can't be serious.'

'Act like a man, Sercan,' said his uncle, walking to his side and placing a claw-like hand on his shoulder. 'Be strong in your final moments, make your peace with our God; act like a man.'

'No, Uncle, please,' cried Sercan, breaking down completely and throwing himself face down on the carpet.

With a nod of his head, Karim called his two minders forward who quickly bound Sercan's wrists behind his back and pressed packing tape over his mouth. Sercan's struggles were half-hearted and easily subdued.

'Behave, Sercan,' commanded his uncle. 'You understand how the family does its business. We cut out the weeds that choke growth, you know that. Aunt Selina is expecting us, we shouldn't keep her waiting.'

At the mention of the pig-loving Aunt Selina, Sercan panicked and began to struggle violently. The family intended to dispose of him as he had disposed of Travers and Briggs after the botched robbery at the Tamworth gun shop. His struggles were terminated by a crack over the head with a small wooden truncheon carried by one of the minders and ten minutes later Sercan found himself wedged between the two large men in the back of his uncle's Mercedes as it sped down the motorway. His uncle noticed him coming round from the front passenger seat and turned to speak to him.

'Dimiz and the whore are in the vehicle behind us, Sercan. You will all meet your maker together. Behave yourself and make your peace while you have time.' Then he turned away from him.

Sercan Ozdemir closed his eyes and took a deep breath and sat back as best as he could between the two minders. His heart was pumping and he was terrified of what awaited him but he was helpless. All he could do was die bravely as he was torn to pieces and eaten alive by the evil Aunt Selina's ferocious boars.

The two Mercedes exited the motorway and turned on to the quiet B road that led to her farm and Sercan began to pray quietly as he sought peace and forgiveness from his God.

In his office at Handstead police station, DCI Harrison glanced at his watch. He was sure that Uncle Karim would act swiftly to deal with his errant nephew and son-in-law and decided to ring the haulage yard. He had the number to hand and rang it, listening for five minutes as it went unanswered.

'Hmm, sounds like they're all out,' he said to himself before he settled back in his chair and sipped from his glass.

Christmas Day 1977. If coppers had to work on Christmas Day, late turn was the shift most of them would opt for. That way, the officers with families got to see the kids opening their presents and then had an excuse to avoid the relatives and in-laws by having to go to work. And the double-time pay came in very handy. D Group had pulled late turn on both Christmas and Boxing Day, and as was the accepted practice, they had all brought in food and drink to pass the shift. No one was expected to go out on patrol but one pair would always be nominated as the crew to deal with any calls that might come in. The Brothers had volunteered to cover calls on Christmas Day, but were aghast when the Blister telephoned them in the canteen just after five o'clock.

'Got a sudden death at the flats above the Hawkstead Parade,' she announced.

'Fucking hell,' moaned H. 'Stiffs on Christmas Day, not very Christian, is it?'

He and Jim grabbed their gear, loaded up Yankee One and fifteen minutes later arrived outside the shops. As they pulled up, a fat man in an ill-fitting tracksuit got out of the car in front of them and stood rubbing his hands in the cold breeze.

'You took your fucking time,' he whined. 'I phoned ages ago.'

'Merry Christmas to you too,' snapped Jim. 'Don't suppose the body's in any kind of rush.'

'Yeah, well, I am. Got the whole family round and now this old bastard ups and dies on me.'

'How inconsiderate of him,' mocked H as they followed the fat man up some stairs at the side of a pawn shop.

At the top of the stairs was an open door and the fat man stood to one side to allow the Brothers to pass him and enter. The room was tiny, clean and freezing cold.

At the far end, under a window that looked out over the abandoned petrochemical factory, was a single bed and lying on it was a very obviously dead old man.

'Who is he?' asked H.

'Bob Anderson,' replied the fat man from the door, keen to get on his way and wishing he'd not phoned until after the holiday. Wouldn't have made any difference, after all.

'Been a tenant long?'

'Over twenty years.'

'What were you doing here on Christmas Day?' queried Jim.

'He's missed his rent this week, thought I'd drop by to give him a reminder, that's all. Lucky I did.'

'You horrible fat fucker,' snarled Jim, advancing on the over-weight landlord. 'And there was me thinking you'd popped round to give him a card. Go on, fuck off. We need anything else from you, we'll be in touch.'

The landlord looked daggers at them but, relieved not to be delayed any further, he kept his mouth shut and lumbered away down the dark narrow stairs and back to his family.

The Brothers stood and looked down at the late unmourned Bob Anderson.

'Poor old bugger,' said H quietly. 'Fancy dying in here all on your own.'

Anderson had died peacefully in his sleep lying on his

clean, well-made bed, his carpet slippers placed neatly by the side on the floor. He was wearing a shabby but clean and pressed pair of brown trousers, dark socks that he'd probably darned himself, a worn and frayed open-necked white shirt and a green cardigan with darning on the elbows. His neat white hair was combed and smart and he had obviously shaved shortly before he died.

'Looked after himself, even living in a godforsaken place like this,' observed Jim as he touched Anderson's face. He was stone cold and stiff, his face the colour of marble. 'Been dead a while probably.'

'Fucking hell, Jim, look at this place,' sighed H. 'Not a card or a picture anywhere. Jesus, how depressing. How can you end up like this?'

'Don't go there, H, won't do you any good,' counselled his mate, looking sternly at him. 'There are lots of people like this old boy who just slip through the cracks all their lives, unknown and unloved – don't really exist at all.'

The small room was shabby but neat and tidy. A single-bar electric fire mounted on the wall alongside a coin meter provided the only source of warmth in the room, and a stainless steel sink and drainer under a solitary tap appeared to be the sole items of comfort. Clearly Bob Anderson took all his meals elsewhere, probably the café downstairs in the parade of shops. The small wardrobe on the far wall contained a couple of shirts and a pair of trousers. A pair of clean black leather shoes was on the floor.

The Brothers began to rummage about to see what they could find to tell them something about the late Bob Anderson. Under the bed, Jim found a green cardboard shoebox. He sat down next to the corpse and opened it.

'Got all his personal stuff here, H,' he said as H closed the wardrobe doors. 'Looks like he was ex-mob,' he continued, flicking through an army pay book. 'Lance Corporal Robert George Anderson, 116321408,' he read. 'Sixty-third Anti-Tank Regiment, Royal Artillery. Looks like he served all through the war.'

Anderson's campaign medals were also in the box, carefully wrapped in tissue paper, the medal ribbons still their original vivid colours.

'Any signs of family?' asked H.

'Couple of letters to an address in Glasgow, April nineteen forty-six, both marked "Gone away, return to sender",' said Jim quietly, reading one of the letters. 'Poor sod, looks like his missus bailed out on him after the war and he was trying to get in touch. Wonder if he ever found her.'

'What about those photos?' said H, pointing to a wad of gnarled black and white photographs standing on their edges in the box.

'Look like his old war ones,' said Jim, quickly flicking

through them. 'That's got to be his old platoon,' he said, handing a group photograph to H. It showed a group of young, smiling but hard-faced young men standing in full combat gear.

'Fuck me, he was at Belsen,' said Jim, standing to show H the photograph he was holding.

The photograph showed the young lance corporal smiling grimly at the camera, holding identical twins in his arms. It was impossible to determine the sex of the children but they were probably no more than four or five years old and looked emaciated, the skin on their faces stretched like tracing paper, with black staring eyes, limbs like kindling wood, and wearing filthy smocks. Turning the photograph over, Jim read the faded handwritten note that was barely visible: 'Me and the boys, Bergen-Belsen, April 15th 1945.' He said quietly, 'The boys? Wonder what happened to them?'

'My God,' said H, taking the photograph from Jim and reading it for himself. 'What a life he's had and he ends up in this hole. It isn't right, Jim.'

'Life's a bastard and then you die,' observed Jim, starting to replace the personal effects in the shoebox. 'You want to call this in, get the doctor and undertakers rolling?'

H nodded and left the lonely room to return to Yankee One and spoil some other individual's Christmas Day, leaving Jim sitting next to Anderson.

'Sorry you ended up here on your own, old-timer,' said Jim quietly to the corpse. 'You deserved better.'

An hour and a half later, Bob Anderson had been pronounced dead by a grumpy doctor and removed from his room by two equally pissed-off undertakers.

'Don't suppose it's much of a Christmas for him either, you miserable cunt,' snapped Jim to one of the moaning undertakers as they struggled down the narrow stairs with the body bag. He was carrying a property bag with all Anderson's worldly possessions inside, including the shoebox, and was about to shut the door when he spotted the carpet slippers by the bed.

'What size feet d'you reckon the old boy had?' he asked H who was halfway down the stairs.

'Fuck knows, why?'

'Those slippers of his are almost brand new and my pair are fucked,' he said, looking at H with a mischievous grin.

'Don't you fucking dare,' laughed H. 'Come on, we're missing out on the mince pies.'

Jim shut and locked the door to the soulless, desolate room and drew a line under Bob Anderson's sad life and fruitless search for the two people who had mattered more to him than anybody else.

It was dark and sleeting lightly as the Brothers drove slowly back to Handstead to write up their sudden death

427

report. The roads were deserted and the wheels made a satisfying swishing noise as they headed in. The heater was on, the radio was quiet and they were feeling comfortable and looking forward to joining the others when they spotted a bedraggled man coming out of the railing yard.

'Oh no, not now,' said H loudly. 'Look at this twat.'

The man was struggling to pull a large sack of coal along the pavement behind him. Yankee One pulled up alongside him and H wound down his window. The sleet blew in.

'Hold up, pal. Where'd you get the coal from?'

The man's long hair was plastered to his head, his cheap clothes were soaked and he was shaking with the cold. His face and lips were blue from the chill and the Brothers would hear his teeth chattering.

'I'm sorry, officers, we've got no heating. I'm worried about the baby,' he stammered.

'So you've nicked a bag of coal?' said H, opening his door and getting out to stand next to the shaking man.

'We're so cold, we've got nothing to keep the little one warm,' said the man, looking up at H with red-rimmed watery eyes that spoke volumes.

'Where d'you live?' asked H.

'The flats at Heron Court,' he replied.

The Brothers exchanged knowing glances. The Heron Court flats were little more than slum dwellings, owned by an unscrupulous landlord who was holding out for the long-expected motorway tunnel to pass through his properties and spent nothing on maintaining the flats. They were death traps, cold and leaky and plagued with rats the size of small cats. The unfortunate tenants such as the man they had stopped were all from society's invisible class who lived on the fringes of normal life, neither good nor bad, but just there. And there to be exploited by grasping landlords who charged them extortionate rent to live like animals.

'We'll give you a lift,' said H, opening the rear door. 'Stick the sack in the boot.'

Gratefully the shaking man hauled the sack into the boot and then clambered into the back seat, gasping with delight as the heat hit him.

'Thank you so much,' he said through clattering teeth. 'We're so cold.'

'You better be telling the truth, mate, else you'll be spending the rest of Christmas in the cells,' said H as they did a U turn and headed back the way they'd come.

The flat was appalling. Situated on the ground floor, the shabby door was answered by an unkempt woman who appeared to be wearing every piece of clothing she owned. She was carrying a small baby, similarly smothered, on one arm. The woman and the baby were both shaking with the cold and their lips were almost black.

'Oh no,' she said when she saw the Brothers standing with her husband, her sole source of any respite from poverty apparently now in custody.

'Don't worry, they haven't nicked me yet,' he said. 'They want to have a look round first.'

'Look round at what?' she replied, bemused but standing back to allow her husband to drag the sack of coal in, followed by the two large, unsmiling coppers.

The place was tiny, the walls damp and covered in mildew. A put-up bed was against the far wall, giving just enough space for them all to get into the room, and the child's cot stood against the far wall. Every piece of bedding was cold and damp and the stale air was so damp it quickly became difficult to breathe. An empty fire grate stood on the other side next to a single-ring cooker and a tiny fridge. A single cracked window that looked out over similar slum properties was covered with a heavy blanket nailed to a wooden batten in an effort to keep out the cold and help the family forget where they were. The room was freezing, probably colder than outside; the Brothers' breath formed clouds in front of them. Significantly, the woman and baby's breath created no such clouds, so low had their core body temperatures fallen.

'We ain't nicking him, Jim,' said H quietly as they looked at the abject misery in front of them.

'Give us that sack here, pal,' said Jim, nodding. 'We'll get a fire going for you.'

Ten minutes later, a roaring fire in the grate had begun to warm the room and its occupants.

'Listen, you take care, OK? Look after the nipper, keep him warm,' said H as they took their leave of the destitute family. 'Merry Christmas.'

Just after ten thirty that night, the couple were curled up in their bed, gazing at the flames that cast a wonderful orange glow around their hovel. They were warm for the first time in weeks and their baby was asleep. They had been talking about the two good Samaritans who had briefly entered their lives earlier and then they fell silent, watching the fire. Suddenly they heard a car engine outside and the room was briefly lit up by headlights. The woman hopped out of bed, tip-toed across the cold lino and peered round the blanket over the window.

'Those coppers are back, Alex. Bet they've changed their minds or something.' She hurried back to the warm bed. 'Don't let them knock on the door, they'll wake the baby.'

Fearing the worst, her husband rolled out of bed and threw on the clothes he had been wearing previously which had dried out nicely in front of the fire. He slipped on his shoes and hurried to the door and opened it. There was no sign of anyone. Pulling the door shut, he stepped out, his breath billowing in front of him, and looked left and right, but the police car had gone. Only its exhaust cloud lingered. The sleet had stopped but the ground was starting to freeze and he shivered as a gust of chilly wind caught him. It was bitterly cold. He stepped further out into the dark to see where the coppers had gone and stumbled over two bulging sacks of coal dumped in the middle of the path.

# Foxtrot Oscar

## Charlie Owen

It's 1976 and England is sweating its nuts off.

As an unrelenting heatwave beats down on the nation, the residents of Horse's Arse – aka Handstead New Town, north Manchester – are reaching melting point.

The Park Royal Mafia, having recovered from the loss of its senior members, is under new management and open for the business of mindless violence again. Unfortunately their antics have attracted the attention of a psychotic Turkish gangster, who's decided the Mafia is just what he needs to pull himself to the top of the criminal heap. And wading into the middle of it are The Grim Brothers, Psycho, Pizza, Ally – Horse's Arse's finest and the hardest boiled coppers you'll ever meet.

With this lot hot under the collar it's all going to end in blood, (a lot of) sweat and tears.

Praise for Charlie Owen:

'Charlie Owen is a talent. This is the first book since *Layer Cake* to have an authentic voice that humorously exposes the dark and eccentric world of English street crime' Guy Ritchie

'Rude, crude and grittier than the M8 on an icy day. I doubt there will be a better crime debut this year' *Daily Record*

'Foul-mouthed, scatological and amusing in equal measure' *Guardian*

978 0 7553 3687 6

**headline**

# Horse's Arse

## Charlie Owen

It is the 70s and Horse's Arse is the affectionate name for Handstead new town, a North Manchester overspill and an unholy dump. The police use it as a penal posting – all the bad egg coppers end up there.

Worst amongst the residents of Handstead are the Park Royal Mafia, a gang of violent thugs who terrorise their neighbourhood. They and the officers doomed to serve at Handstead wrestle constantly for dominance.

This is the story of some of those police officers – the Grim Brothers, Psycho, Pizza, Piggy Malone and others, a group of hooligans in uniform and their journey through excess, despair and finally some form of salvation.

'Charlie Owen is a talent. This is the first book since LAYER CAKE to have an authentic voice that humorously exposes the dark and eccentric world of English street crime' Guy Ritchie

'Foul-mouthed, scatological, amusing' *Guardian*

'Rude, crude and grittier than the M8 on an icy day. I doubt there will be a better crime debut this year' *Daily Record*

978 0 7553 3684 5

## headline

DUNCAN CAMPBELL

# The Paradise Trail

Calcutta 1971. A city in black-out as India declares war on Pakistan. Even so, the backpackers who end up in the flea-pit Lux Hotel are determined to have a good time. That is, until two mysterious deaths amongst them change their lives for ever.

Thrown together in the city are Anand, the jazz-loving insomniac hotelier; Gordon, one of the hotel's dope-smoking guests; the philandering journalist Hugh, covering his first war; Britt, a Californian photographer with a jealous boyfriend; and the enigmatic Freddie Braintree, who interprets life through the lyrics of Bob Dylan and the Incredible String Band.

Is it possible that one of them is behind the deaths? And why will it take more than three decades and three continents to find out?

'A hugely enjoyable, ambitious and unusual story, told with wit, humanity and an attractive sympathy for his characters and their flaws' Ronan Bennett

'A marvellous evocation of the glorious madness which was the 70s hippy trail' Felix Dennis

978 0 7553 4247 1

headline
review

# Faces

## Martina Cole

**And the sins of the fathers shall reverberate through the generations**.

When Danny Cadogan's father walks out he leaves his family to face the wrath of the debt collectors. Determined to protect his mum, brother and sister, something changes in fourteen-year-old Danny and, overnight, he becomes set on making his way in a violent and dangerous world.

With childhood friend Michael Miles as the brains behind the operation, he becomes *the* most feared Face in the Smoke. And Danny's ruthlessness doesn't stop on the streets of London. He rules his wife, Mary, and his children with an iron will – and his fists. But if Mary breaks her silence, it could bring down his empire. And for a Face at the top of his game, there's only one way to go. Down. Because, after all, debts *can* be paid – even without money.

Praise for Martina Cole's phenomenal No. 1 bestsellers:

'Reading a Martina Cole novel is a surprisingly physical experience. A few chapters into CLOSE, I had to close the pages and, heart pounding, take a deep breath' *The Times*

'The stuff of legend . . . utterly compelling' *Mirror*

'A blinding good read' Ray Winstone

978 0 7553 4614 1

## headline